The Velvet Curtain

Dedication

To My Husband, Barry

Thank you for your constant encouragement just when I needed it.
Without you, this book would never have been written.

The Velvet Curtain

by

Trudy Harvey Tait

BRITISH ADDRESS
Harvey Christian Publishers UK
P.O. Box 510, Cheadle
Stoke-on-Trent, ST10 2NQ
Tel./Fax (01538) 752291
E-mail: jjcook@mac.com

UNITED STATES ADDRESS
Harvey Christian Publishers, Inc.
3107 Hwy. 321, Hampton, TN 37658
Tel./Fax (423) 768-2297
E-mail: books@harveycp.com
http://www.harveycp.com

Printed in USA

Cover design by Malcolm Farrar

ISBN-10 1-932774-69-6
ISBN-13 978-1-932774-69-6

Printed by
Sabre Printers
Johnson City, TN 37604

Contents

Introduction

For at least twenty-five years, I have intended to write a novel entitled "The Velvet Curtain." Growing up during the Cold War, I heard frequent testimonies of those who had suffered for their faith in Communist lands. I came to realize, however, that true Christians find it tough going to maintain a clear testimony for Christ wherever they might be, and that the West has its subtle counterpart of the Iron Curtain. I wished to write something that would help young people and older ones too, become aware of the dangers of this Velvet Curtain. Now at last, when I have found it possible to fulfill my dream, Communism no longer dominates Eastern Europe as it did when I was first inspired to write this story. But though the Iron Curtain may have indeed fallen, its Western counterpart still makes itself felt in every land where freedom professes to hold sway.

This story is fictional, but my frequent visits to Romania have furnished me with an abundance of material and strongly colored the characters of Esther and her sister, Gabby. On many occasions, I reacted just as Esther did, when I would return to America and find myself confronted with waste and luxury. Some of my readers may wonder why I have never given a clear definition of this Curtain. This is because its definitions are as numerous and as varied as humanity itself.

I am deeply indebted to Beulah Freeman, Margaret Smith, and Jean Ward for their invaluable assistance in proofreading, and to my son and daughter-in-law, Edwin and Jennifer Woodruff Tait, for editing the manuscript and for their timely advice and encouragement. When I shared with them that some of my characters were actually dictating the direction of the story, they assured me that this was quite common to novelists. So if in the near future, there appears a sequel to this book, you will know that Esther, and Ron, and Gabby have insisted that their full story has not quite been told!

I do hope that *The Velvet Curtain* will not only prove to be a captivating and moving story, but that it will inspire all who read it to a closer walk with the Lord Jesus.

Trudy Harvey Tait
Hampton, Tennessee

Chapter One

The Iron Curtain Left Behind

As the plane broke through the heavy curtain of thick, fleecy clouds, Esther gave a gasp of delight. The universe was aglow with rosy light. The sordid world, with its gloomy days and interminable nights, lay far beneath her, out of sight, and for a few hours at least, out of mind. Here one could breathe, could think, could dream.

"Your first trip in the clouds, eh, young lady?" asked a voice at her side.

Esther started. She had forgotten she was not alone in this paradise of light. "Yes, that is, no, not exactly," she stammered. "But it's the first that I can remember. You see, I...."

The girl hesitated. In the world she had left behind, it was too risky to speak too soon or too much to a stranger. And who was he, anyway, this strange little man with the eagle eyes and ready tongue? She was always asking "who?" She simply couldn't help it, couldn't break the habit of a lifetime in a few moments.

The clatter of dishes in the galley behind them indicated that it was nearly time for lunch, and it was not until the last tray had been collected and the shutters drawn in preparation for the movie that conversation was broached once more.

"It's not always smooth flying," commented Esther's companion as the "Fasten Your Seatbelts" sign became illuminated. "You'll find that out sooner or later. But I always enjoy being up in the clouds. It's exhilarating, challenging. Up here, I can breathe more freely, feel more charitable and nearer to God too. In fact," he paused, and Esther glanced at him keenly as he continued, "the world seems so very sordid sometimes; it's good to leave it behind, if only for a few hours or so."

"So you feel like that too?" Esther sounded surprised and seemed to speak in spite of herself.

"Yes, I do, but you, you are too young to experience such things. But I am forgetting," and he glanced at her, not knowing if he should continue or not. "You have just come from Romania, haven't you?"

"Yes, I have." She was really surprised now, for they had just boarded the plane in Paris. "But how on earth could you tell?"

"Well, in the first place, you look like a Romanian." Esther raised her eyebrows. What did this Westerner know about Romanian girls? He seemed to guess her thoughts. "You see," he said softly with just a hint of a sigh in his voice, "my wife was Romanian."

Esther's large, dark eyes were full of sympathy. "He said 'was,'" she thought. "She must be dead, poor man. So he, too, knows all about bereavement. But he is certainly not Romanian; his eyes are so very blue and he speaks such pure English."

"And besides," the man was continuing in a lighter tone, "your accent is Romanian. Oh yes, your English is excellent, but you do have a slight accent, charming actually, and it *is* Romanian. Or am I wrong after all?"

"No," laughed Esther, "you are quite right, at least, almost right. My grandfather was an American, but my grandmother was a Romanian, though she lived many years in the States. Mother was born there and then, when she was about ten years old, the whole family came to live in Romania. Many years later, after his wife passed away, Grandpa actually stayed with us for a while. That's how I learned your language, for my mother wanted my sister and myself to be bilingual. She refused to talk anything but English with us, and, as my father spoke only Romanian, we grew up speaking both languages, at least I did. My sister Gabby didn't seem to take to it the same, and when she was about six or seven, refused to speak it any more. So I guess we're not what you might call pure-bred Romanians though I look like one, evidently."

"You certainly do," was his reply. "And that is meant as a compliment."

"I'm told I am almost the image of my mother at my age," Esther told him rather proudly. "My father was also dark complexioned, but my sister is much more Western looking; she takes her coloring from her American grandfather." Esther stopped. She could not go on. Why had she said all this to a complete stranger? It was not at all like her. It must be the influence of the West working on her already.

She was aware that the man by her side was studying her intently. She, too, had used the past tense so he would know that she was an orphan. Oh well, that was nothing to be ashamed of. And there was something in her companion that inspired trust.

"By the way, young lady, we've not introduced ourselves yet," he said smiling. "I am Hugh Gardner, from Tiny Gap, Tennessee and you are...?"

"Esther Popescu, from Ploiesti, Romania."

"So you have relatives in the States, Esther?" was the next question.

"Yes, my father's older brother and his family live near Indianapolis, and I think there is also one very elderly grand aunt still living, though I'm not exactly sure where, and maybe a few more distant cousins scattered around the country." Esther let out a long sigh as she went on. "I'm really glad to be going to America, but I don't know quite what to expect. It'll be so very different from what I've left behind. And besides," she added rather wistfully, "I'm going to miss my baby sister so much."

"Will she be joining you eventually?"

"Her papers aren't through yet," replied Esther, "but hopefully she'll be in America by next summer after she graduates from high school." She stopped. A vision of two large, expressive grey eyes with more than a hint of green in them, a mop of thick, light brown hair, a very determined chin, and a mouth that changed from laughter to solemnity all in the twinkle of an eye, made her voice quiver slightly as she blinked back a few tears. Then, pulling herself together Esther went on, "I'll miss her this first year in my new home; everything will seem so very different from my old one."

"Very different," agreed Hugh, "though I would think you would be glad to escape the 'Iron Curtain.' From what I have seen, Romania isn't exactly a pleasant place to be in at the moment."

"No," Esther replied, looking out at the billowy clouds. "No, not at all pleasant." She shuddered slightly. Then brightening somewhat she added, "It will be a relief to be able to speak my mind without fearing the consequences."

"I don't know about that," grinned her friend, for he really did seem a friend to the young girl, speeding into the unknown, alone, and just a little afraid, if the truth were told. This somewhat eccentric man beside her seemed to have the ability to reach into her inmost soul and understand her hopes and fears. "You'll find that wherever you are, my dear," he was continuing, "there are consequences to speaking your mind. But I mustn't spoil your dreams of the Land of Liberty. You'll find out all too soon that freedom has its downside, even in America."

"Yes, I suppose so." Esther sounded rather unconvinced. Consequences from speaking one's mind in the USA? They would never amount to much she was sure. How could anyone from the West understand what it was like to live under constant suspicion, to be followed, watched, and spied on? Had this little man by her side ever experienced days of hunger, of pain, of imprisonment even, and all because he had turned his back on bribes and tried to live a consistent Christian life?

Hugh's voice was full of pity as he said softly, "I'm sorry, my dear. My comment must have seemed out of place. I haven't lived in Romania under a Communist regime as you have, though I have visited that wonderful country several times. But maybe it won't hurt you to be just a little prepared, as you step into a new life and escape the grim reality of one 'curtain,' to be on the lookout for another."

Esther started. What could he mean? "Yes, another kind of curtain," he repeated, "not an iron one but," and he paused as if wondering if the girl would think him crazy if he finished his sentence.

"Yes, go on," she encouraged. "What kind?"

"Why, a velvet one," came the odd reply. "The Velvet Curtain! You'll find it anywhere in the West but it especially makes itself felt in America. It seems to me it is just a trifle more enveloping there than anywhere else as you'll find out sooner or later. Meanwhile, enjoy your trip into freedom, for there *is* plenty to enjoy in the Land of the Free and the Home of the Brave," and he rose to stretch his cramped legs a little, sensing, perhaps, that he had said enough.

Esther took off her sweater and folded it into a makeshift pillow. She pulled up the thin airline blanket over her and closed her eyes, but her mind was too active for sleep. The Velvet Curtain! Whatever could that strange man mean? Oh well, she had enough to think about without worrying about more curtains. She was pretty sure that, wherever she went, or whatever she might experience, nothing could be as grim, as awful, as all-pervading, as imprisoning, as that never-to-be forgotten Iron Curtain she had just left behind.

Chapter Two

Traveling into Light

"May I see your passport please?" After what seemed an interminable wait, Esther had at last reached the immigration booth. She had dreaded this moment. Accustomed to unsmiling officials who suspected everyone of some illegal activity or other, she was not prepared for the pleasant voice and kindly eyes of the smartly dressed man who was examining her documents carefully. "So you've come to stay, young lady?" was the next question.

"Yes. I was told to give you this," and she slipped a bulging folder through the opening in the glass window.

"Just step this way a moment, please," and the man led her to an adjoining office. "I'll be back soon," he told her as he took her papers. Half an hour later, a relieved Esther made her way to the baggage claim. It had not been too bad after all. What if she had been turned back? She had heard stories of Romanians who had been refused entry for one reason or another. But she had made it through and here she was at last in the United States of America! Her head swam and she felt faint. It had been a long and tiring journey, preceded by weeks of anxious waiting and negotiating. There had been a few occasions when all hope of her ever leaving Romania had practically evaporated. Now that it was all over, she felt nervously spent and so very alone. She had lost track of Hugh Gardner while going through immigration.

Esther somehow managed to locate her luggage and get safely through customs. Her shabby brown suitcase had attracted little attention. Her heart beat fast. Who would be there to meet her? What would she say? Oh, maybe she should have stayed in Romania. At that moment, all the hardships of the past seemed more bearable than the uncertainty of the future. She did not feel at all prepared to be integrated into this flamboyant new world. Why even the officials chewed gum and joked, and they had actually wished her a good day!

Esther eagerly scanned the crowd awaiting the passengers from Flight 233. She had been told that her uncle would be carrying a small placard on which the words "Esther Popescu" would be written in bold, black letters, but her tired eyes could detect no such sign.

As she paused to get her breath, she heard a familiar voice asking, "Has no one come to meet you yet? I made up my mind not to leave the airport till I'd seen you safely in the hands of your relatives. Maybe you can spare a moment to meet my grandson," and Hugh propelled her to the edge of the crowd and introduced her to a rather stocky young man of average height, with his grandfather's keen, twinkling eyes and a shock of unruly brown hair which reminded her strangely of her faraway sister.

"Pleased to meet you," muttered Esther still in a daze. "Your grandfather has been very kind to me," she added with a smile that lit up her tired face and transformed it.

Aaron Gardner smiled back. "Granddad is always good company and has made many friends on his travels. And he tells me you are from Romania which, in a way, makes us fellow-countrymen."

Esther was about to reply when she caught sight of a tall, well-dressed gentleman in his late forties hurrying towards her. Even if she had not noticed the sign he clutched in one hand, she would have known him anywhere—same eyes, same hair, same mannerisms. Tears came into her eyes as a vision of her father floated momentarily before her. She rushed forward and was soon in her uncle's arms.

"Bine ai venit în America, Estera dragã," he whispered, (Welcome to America, dear Esther) and the Romanian was like music in the girl's ears. But remembering her manners, she turned to Hugh. "This is my Uncle John," she said formally. "Uncle John, this is a kind gentleman I met on the plane, and this is his grandson."

"Thank you very much for keeping an eye on my little niece," said John in perfect English as he shook hands with both men. He spoke with only the merest trace of an accent . "I've been worried about her traveling so far alone."

"It has been my pleasure; she lightened up the long journey quite a bit," Hugh told him. "And, young lady," he turned to Esther, "here is my address and phone no. and don't hesitate to look me up if ever you find yourself in the wilds of Tennessee," and he slipped a folded piece of paper into her hands. "And now we must go. Good bye and God bless," and with a wave of his hand, he was gone, his grandson following as best he could through the jostling crowd.

Esther slipped the paper into her handbag and took her uncle's arm. "Oh Uncle John," she whispered, "I am so very glad to see you. I'm in a dream."

"And so am I," he replied, looking down at her upturned face. "Oh, you're so much like your mother, though you've got your father's determined chin and smile. But come, let's get your luggage into the car and be off. We have a fair drive ahead of us and you must be desperately tired."

"Yes, Uncle, I suppose I am," came the reply. "But I'm so extremely excited I don't feel tired, at least, not yet."

"But you will, all too soon. Jet lag sets in much sooner when you travel west. Yes, they open themselves," and John laughed at his niece's unfeigned amazement as the large glass doors slid open of their own accord. "Here, you sit down and rest yourself while I get the car. I won't be long," and he was off.

Esther edged the luggage cart up to a wooden bench. There were people everywhere even though it must have been well past eight in the evening. It was already dark which made her feel rather strange and alone once more. Her uncle's presence had been comforting and familiar even though she could not remember him at all, for she had been but a baby when he had last visited his native Romania.

So this was America, she thought, as she watched car after car pull up to the curb. Why, how huge they were and how unlike the small, decrepit-looking vehicles that daily limped through the Bucharest streets and which were forever breaking down in the most inconvenient of places. And the people—well-dressed, sophisticated, and self-complacent; even the teenagers seemed so sure of themselves. And they were nearly all laughing and smiling. It was just—so different!

How odd must she look, Esther suddenly wondered—well-worn grey tweed jacket, long black woolen skirt, and shoes that had been resoled several times! She saw a few passersby turn and eye her up and down. She probably looked a fright. What did her uncle really think of her? And what would her aunt and cousins' reaction be? That made her stop in her tracks. Well, where were they anyway? She knew Uncle John had two daughters for she had seen photos of them. She had thought that at least one of them or maybe her aunt would come to meet her. Oh, there was her uncle at last in that large, blue sedan. What a beauty! How would she ever get used to such luxuries?

Soon, however, she had other things to think about. As they wove their way through the lanes of traffic, Esther gasped in astonishment. What a fairyland! Lights, everywhere! Red, orange, green, yellow—car lights, street lights, billboards lit up, gas stations all ablaze, lights streaming out of restaurants, motels, houses—it was all too much. She covered her eyes.

"What's wrong, dear?" her uncle queried gently.

"It's the lights," she muttered. "It's almost too much after years of...." She broke off seemingly unable to finish the sentence.

"Darkness?" came the suggestion.

"Yes, darkness. Even when it's day in our land it still seems dark, especially in the winter. But this is a land of light. Uncle," and she looked up suddenly, "does light go with liberty?"

John's smile was slightly sardonic as he replied, "They are supposed to go together, I believe. Yet it seems that sometimes liberty has its dark side too."

"Its dark side?" This Esther could not understand.

"Oh come now, there will be time enough for philosophizing. Just relax and enjoy yourself. This is America at night. Quite a sight, isn't it?"

"It really is," agreed the girl, and they both lapsed into silence. They had swung onto Interstate 70 and were fast leaving the city behind. "Relax!" she kept telling herself. "There are no potholes to avoid, no horses and carts looming suddenly out of the darkness, or no lookouts with armed guards demanding where you are going and why. And what roads—so straight and smooth!"

"Where exactly do you live, Uncle?" Esther asked, as they sped along.

"About halfway between Indianapolis and Terre Haute," he replied, "in a smallish town called Velours. Nice quiet place. I lived in Indianapolis for years. Just moved out here three years ago. I had the chance to buy a car dealership." He was silent for a few moments until the sign for Velours loomed out of the darkness. "Just another twenty minutes and we'll be there. Ramona will have supper ready. I told her to buy some Kentucky Fried Chicken. She wanted to come to meet you in the worst way, but some extra lecture at college kept her later than usual. She's away all week and usually comes home Friday nights. But she came back specially to see you tonight, so she will have had time to have a warm welcome ready for her long lost cousin."

Esther smiled. "Ramona? But you have two daughters, don't you? And Aunt Mary, where is she?"

For the first time that evening, her uncle's handsome features darkened as he bit his lip and said nothing for some time. Then, remembering his manners, for John Popescu was always polite, he replied slowly, "Yes, I have two daughters, but one of them is not at home at present. She's away with her mother. You'll see them both soon enough."

"I certainly hope so, Uncle," was his niece's response. But she got nothing more from him until he exclaimed as they swung into a driveway and came to a stop outside a large, two-storey house. "Here we are! Home at last! And there is Ramona herself to welcome us!"

Esther glanced at the doorway, and framed in the light streaming out from the hallway behind her, stood a well-built girl of about her own age, with a mass of blonde curls framing her very pretty face. Before Esther could reach the house, her cousin had run to meet them and flung her arms round her.

"Esther, I thought you'd never come," she exclaimed in a very American accent. Esther had been speaking Romanian with her uncle since she arrived and had to switch quickly to her English mode. "I've been at the door a dozen times in the last five minutes," Ramona went on. "Here, come in and let me get a good look at you." And she dragged her cousin into the hallway, chattering incessantly all the while.

"You look quite a lot like Dad and Rachel," remarked Ramona as she held her cousin at arm's length in order to look her over. "Yes, you look more Popescu than I do. I take after my mom, and no one ever guesses that I have any Romanian blood in my veins." There was a slight superiority in the girl's voice and Esther, dazed as she was from the events of the day, did not fail to notice how very Western Ramona looked.

Her feet sank into the thick, green pile of the wall-to-wall carpet as she slipped off her shoes and placed them neatly by the door. Esther wondered privately why her uncle didn't do the same. Then she saw Ramona staring at her. She tried to speak but words refused to come. Where was she really? In a dream world? How could one day's travel have transformed her life so utterly? Twenty-four hours ago she had been in her aunt's tiny apartment in Ploiesti with its threadbare rug and faded curtains, and now here she was in what seemed to her like a veritable palace. She could imagine the scolding Aunt Ana would have given them if they had dared enter her humble little apartment with their shoes on. How on earth did everything stay so clean here, she wondered?

John carried Esther's case up the broad staircase and beckoned her to follow. "We've prepared what we call 'the pink room' for you, Esther," he told her as he opened the door into the most exquisitely decorated bedroom Esther had ever seen. Everything matched—carpet, curtains, comforter. He slid open the closet doors. "There's plenty of space for your things, as you can see," and he smiled down into her tired, dazed eyes. Perhaps, as he spoke, he recollected the small, cramped rooms back in his homeland where you were lucky to get by with less than three or four to a bedroom. And perhaps he also remembered another pair of eyes remarkably like Esther's into which he had gazed long ago. But whatever his thoughts might have been, John simply bent down and kissed his young niece, saying gently, "You are very, very welcome here, my dear. Now there's the bathroom. When you're ready, there's supper waiting downstairs."

Esther opened the bathroom door and gasped. She understood why you might want elegance in a living room, but she had never in all her life imagined such taste and décor in a bathroom. Even the toilet paper was luxury to the weary girl—soft and thick and slightly scented, a pleasant contrast to the coarse grey rolls at home which occasionally took the place of cut-up newspaper when her aunt could afford to buy them. And the soap! Oh it was all just too much, and Esther buried her face in the fluffy, pink towel hung up especially for her, and let out a long sigh. To be surrounded by such soft, pretty things seemed like Heaven.

Ramona had set the table in the dining-room. Tomorrow, she told her cousin laughing, they would go back to roughing it in the kitchen, but tonight was a very special occasion. Esther said little the rest of the evening. The chandelier glittering above her, the sparkling silverware, the rich food, and her cousin's overwhelming hospitality, were almost too much for the weary girl. Her uncle's kind eyes detected her exhaustion. "You need to get to bed; you're utterly worn out," he said kindly, as he saw her toying with her chicken. "Come, let me help you upstairs," he added as he took her arm gently.

Ramona's face fell. "The food is wonderful, but I'm just too tired to eat," apologized Esther as she stooped to give her cousin a goodnight kiss. "But I'll make up for it tomorrow, I promise."

Ramona nodded. "I hope so. But now, get to bed and sleep till lunch if you want."

"Doubt it," put in John. "If I remember correctly, those seven hours difference will have you up at the crack of dawn." He led his niece up the stairs to her bedroom. "Oh Esther," he whispered as he drew the exhausted girl into his arms, "everything must seem so strange and overwhelming for my little niece!"

"Yes," she replied, "very strange! It's a completely different world."

"I know," Uncle John agreed. "I can still remember vividly my first impressions of this great country. And you've gone through a lot these last ten years or so."

Esther's silence seemed to give consent, and looking down into her upturned face he muttered softly, "You know, Esther, you have turned into a very beautiful young lady!"

His niece blushed. She could hardly deny the truth of her uncle's compliment. She was too honest for false modesty. True, there had been quite a few girls equally as good-looking as she among her friends at school and at church. She was not the only one to boast of glossy, black wavy hair, smooth olive skin, and a graceful figure, but as her Uncle had already noted, there was something special in those large, expressive eyes that held you captive while they seemed to search your inner soul.

John Popescu had been immediately struck by those eyes. They had brought back a flood of memories, for he had been deeply in love with Esther's mother those many years ago. But his younger brother had won the day, while he had been left to lick his wounds. Not that the tender, loving creature had meant to wound him, but her words, "We have little in common, John. You are kind and charming, but what would we talk about in the dark, winter evenings?" had stabbed him like a dagger. And she had been all too right. He could never have reached deep into her soul like his brother Andrei could. No wonder he had made her happy in a way he, John, could never have done, but here his niece's words broke into his reverie: "Uncle, when will I get to see Aunt Mary and Rachel? Tomorrow?"

The question was innocently put, but it once more brought a frown to John's handsome face. "Well, you'll probably see Rachel tomorrow, but I'm not sure about your Aunt."

Something in his tone made his niece draw back a little. Her uncle saw it and said more gently, "Don't worry about anything tonight. Just get over your jet lag and then there will be time enough to see everyone. Now, noapte buna, Estera dragã, (good night, Esther dear). Somn u°or." (Sleep well.)

"Noapte buna," was the somewhat subdued reply as she kissed him goodnight.

"Now look what I've gone and done," muttered John as he went back downstairs. "I've troubled the girl on her first night here. Poor thing! Oh well, it couldn't be helped. She'll have to get used to divided homes." He gave such a long sigh as he entered the kitchen that Ramona looked up from the sink where she was rinsing off the dishes before putting them into the dishwasher.

"Tired Dad?" she asked affectionately.

"A little. But Esther has asked several times about your mother and Rachel. It's all very awkward."

His daughter dried her hands and came over to where her father was standing. "Don't worry, Dad. It's not your fault," she reassured him.

John gave a faint smile as he ran his hand through her curls. He was so fond of his pretty daughter. "Glad you don't think so, Ramona. What Esther will think is another matter."

"Oh come, Dad. I'm sure she'll take it all in her stride. She seems pretty level-headed and fond of you already."

"She's just so like her mother." It was out before he could help it.

Ramona looked at him curiously but held her tongue. The clock struck eleven. It was time they were all in bed. She gave her father his usual goodnight kiss and tripped upstairs. She did hope her cousin's coming wouldn't upset things too much. Her dad didn't need that at present.

Meanwhile Esther was getting out her old blue pajamas. They looked so shabby as they lay on the floral comforter. Everything she owned seemed shabby, in fact. She brushed her long hair and knelt down to say her prayers. They would have to be short that night, she was so exhausted, but she did want to thank God for a safe journey. And then she asked Him to bless her newfound family. Something seemed to be wrong somehow. Her uncle was troubled when she mentioned his wife or Rachel. What had happened?

As she nestled down for the night, she was at first scarcely aware of how unusually soft the bed was and how strange it felt not to go to sleep to the screech of brakes, or the querulous voices of their neighbors in the apartment above. What had her uncle said while driving from the airport? Something about liberty having its dark side? And that odd little gentleman's comment on there being a velvet curtain? What did it all mean? What...? But her question trailed off in a long contented sigh as she snuggled deeper into the blankets and the peace of her first night in this wonderful new country enveloped her. She was exceptionally comfy, and ready for a good long night's rest.

Chapter Three

The Price of Freedom

Mary Popescu picked up the receiver reluctantly. Who could it be this time of morning? "Mary?" came the well-known voice.

"Yes," she clipped, "it's me."

"Mary, Esther arrived last night, and she's asking to see you and Rachel." Mary was silent. "Well, what do I say to the girl?" John pressed.

"Say? Why tell her the truth, if that's possible," was the curt reply.

John's voice rose a little. "The truth? Why of course, eventually. But Esther's been through so much, and to land all our problems on her right away would be very unfair."

"Well, what's the alternative? Act a lie to keep her happy for a few days till she learns your slant on the affair from Ramona if not from yourself?"

"Mary!" John was turning reproachful now, a mood his wife just could not stand.

"Look," she spluttered, "it was *you* who invited her over here, wasn't it? I had nothing to do with it. You knew what you were getting her into. I don't want to see her. Why should I? She's no relative to me, is she? Or soon won't be at any rate."

"Is that your final answer, then?" John saw it was no use to pursue the matter further. "I'm to tell Esther that her aunt refuses to see her?"

"Tell her anything you want."

"But what about Rachel? She has a right to see her, hasn't she? She is her cousin after all." John was getting angry in spite of all his attempts to keep his cool.

"Well," and Mary's voice grew colder than ever, "you'll be picking her up tonight as usual, won't you? So she'll see her soon enough."

"You hard-hearted woman," John spluttered.

"I'm what you made me, John. Bye," and down went the receiver.

John put his head in his hands. It had been a long time now since any tender words had passed between them. In fact, it had really been a relief as well as a shock when Mary had packed up and left twelve months before. But all the same, it was very depressing. She could at least be civil to him.

"Dad, what's wrong?" Ramona had just entered the room. Soon her hand was on his shoulder and her cheek pressed his. "Oh, you've been speaking to Mom, right?"

"Right," her father replied tersely.

"And...?"

"She won't see Esther." John's voice was bitter.

"Well, Dad, did you really think she would?" Ramona took a chair next to her father and went on: "Let's face it, why should she bother with Esther? She's never met her, has she? She considers her your niece, not hers. And she doesn't want anything to do with you or your relatives."

"I know all that, Ramona," said her father pettishly, "but what do we say to your cousin? How do we break the news?"

"Just tell her the truth. What else?"

"The truth, the truth, always the truth. But sometimes the truth is harsh and cold. Sometimes it burns, hurts, divides." John's voice rose.

"I know, Dad, I know," soothed Ramona, as if she were talking to a child. "You don't want your little angelic niece to be shocked by all our family scandal. But sooner or later she'll have to face life. Well then, let me tell her if you can't. I'll watch what I say, promise I will. Trust me."

"Trust you?" And John gave his daughter a resounding kiss. "Why of course I trust you. At least I think I do. But look! What's Esther doing out there this time of morning?"

Ramona went to the window and looked out. There was her cousin standing in the middle of the lawn, her face raised towards the sky and her hands outstretched.

"Is she saying her morning prayers, Dad? I hope the neighbors can't see her; she's acting crazy. And she's got on those same old clothes she wore last night. Hasn't she anything else to wear?"

"Probably not, but there's little danger of the neighbors taking much notice of her," returned her father dryly. "Our lawn's immense. That's what the girl is reveling in. You can't understand it, Ramona, but it must seem like paradise to her, all this space I mean."

A few moments later Esther burst into the house and ran up to her uncle, face bathed in tears. "Why, my little niece, crying on your first day in America?" John asked playfully as he gave her a good-morning kiss.

"I'm crying all right, Uncle, but it's for joy. Oh, it's like Heaven here—green as far as the eye can see and space, just sheer space. Though," she added, her face clouding as she spoke, "I suppose there are tears of sadness mixed in. I can't help but think of Gabby and Aunt Ana and all the children in the apartment building where I lived for four years. Everyone's cooped up like chickens in a pen. But here, why Uncle, you must be so very rich to have such a palace as this!"

Her uncle looked at her quizzically. "Rich, Esther? No, I'm not rich. Nor poor either, thank God," he added, patting her dark hair affectionately. "But this is no palace by any shot of the imagination. You'll find nearly all the houses in this subdivision are equally as spacious as ours and some more so. And I could take you to some districts in Indianapolis where some folks have grounds twice as large. You're in America now, you know, where it's every man for himself. If you've a will to work, a bit of ambition and enterprise, you'll go places over here. But come, dry your eyes, and Ramona will get you breakfast. I'm off to work. Now be good both of you while I'm away," he told them with a wink and a smile as he grabbed his brief case and made for the door.

Esther watched through the living room window as he got into his smart, blue saloon, looking very much the successful businessman in his tan shirt and tie, brown tweed sports jacket, and khaki trousers.

"Did you sleep well?" asked Ramona, as she led her cousin into the kitchen.

"Did I ever! But I was awake at dawn just as Uncle John said I'd be," Esther told her as she sat down on one of the tall bar stools. "I've been gazing out the window for hours. It's so peaceful here," and she gave a long, contented sigh.

"Actually, I thought you'd have slept till lunch. You were dead beat last night," Ramona exclaimed. "But then, it's late afternoon in Romania, isn't it? No wonder you couldn't sleep longer. But come on, let's eat, for you must be ravenous. You ate hardly anything last night. But then that's why you're so slim," and the girl rattled on incessantly as she poured the coffee and made the toast. "Now choose one of these cereals," and she pointed to the array of boxes on the countertop.

Esther stared as she read out the labels: "Raisin Bran, Cornflakes, Fruit and Fiber, Honey Clusters. Why, Ramona, I haven't a clue what these are. We eat bread and jam every morning for breakfast back home. And if we're lucky, we might just add some butter or maybe even cheese or salami once a week. I'm not used to having all these choices. Just pick one out for me, will you?"

Ramona laughed. "OK. You can try out a different one each time and then you'll come to know for yourself what you like and don't like," and she poured out a dish of Fruit and Fiber.

Esther sampled one spoonful. "Delicious, Ramona. You really do have variety here."

"Yep. In almost everything."

Esther raised her eyebrows. "You mean you have this kind of variety in everything?"

"Just about. I mean, if you traveled around, you'd find all sorts of people living here from every country imaginable, and in some places, there's a different church on nearly every corner. As for clothes—you name it, you can find it in most of the big stores. And...."

"That's enough, Ramona," Esther interrupted laughing. "You've convinced me."

"You'll see for yourself soon enough," her cousin told her as she buttered her third piece of toast. "But today, you can sleep all you like. My sister Rachel will be here tonight, and we thought you might like a trip to town tomorrow to buy a few things you probably need."

Esther blushed as she looked down at her well-worn grey sweater. "Well, I don't have many clothes suitable, I guess, for America. Most are old," she paused. It had been a sore point with her to come to her affluent relatives dressed like she was. She had lived on hand-me-downs most of her life as did nearly everyone else around her. But here it was different. Yet with not a penny in her purse, how could she remedy the situation?

Ramona seemed to read her thoughts. "We'll soon fit you out. Don't worry if you don't have cash. Dad's very generous; he can afford to be."

"What does he do?" put in Esther. "I really don't know much about you."

"He owns a showroom here in Velours. He's got quite a success story. Came to this country with hardly a cent in his pocket twenty-three years ago, got a job in a GMC dealership in the city and worked his way up from odd job man to top salesman. Then he got the chance to buy up the business in town here. But there's plenty of time for all that family history stuff. At least, I hope so. You are here to stay, aren't you?"

"If you'll have me," was the reply. "I need to talk over the future with your father. But you said Rachel was coming tomorrow. I do want to meet her and Aunt Mary."

Ramona knew the moment had come. She gulped, tossed back her curls, and began: "Esther, my mom and dad are no longer living together."

"Not living together!" her cousin gasped in horror. "You don't mean they're...?" Esther couldn't get the word out.

Ramona came to her rescue. "Divorced? No, they aren't yet. But if things go on as they are now, they soon will be."

Esther's expressive eyes widened in horror then filled with tears. "Oh Ramona, I'm so very sorry. Divorced! But that will be terrible for you all. I mean, it's simply awful!"

"Awful?" repeated her cousin. "Look, Esther, you're in the USA, not Romania. If a couple don't hit it off, then divorce seems better than yelling and squabbling all day long or else giving each other the silent treatment. That's far worse. And I sure know all about that. If you live here, you'll just have to get used to it."

"Get used to it? Why, I don't ever want to get used to it." The usually mild-mannered Esther was heated now. "I suppose, though, that's the price of freedom, isn't it?"

Ramona shrugged. "I've never thought much about it. I just know that I live a pretty comfortable life. But maybe it's only fair that we have to pay a bit for our liberty and for all this—and she waved her well manicured little hand around the kitchen—"dishwasher, microwave, washer and drier, TV in most rooms, music center. And," she added proudly, "one car each, swimming-pool in the back yard, vacations in Florida or even in Hawaii. Now, how's that compared with Romania?"

Esther flushed. "Well, I admit that Romania has nothing like that, not a patch on it, though it's too early for me to make comparisons; I've not even been here twenty-four hours yet. But about Rachel? She doesn't live with you and Uncle? Oh Ramona, how terrible. A divided family!" Esther could go no further. It was just too much for her to take in. Her own family had been so close. They'd known poverty and there had been troubles in plenty. Real tragedy had hit them several times. But divorce? It was seldom heard of among her acquaintances at any rate, and now here it was right in her own family. But Ramona's soothing voice brought her back to earth and to the America she would have to embrace as her home.

"Come, Esther. Don't take it so hard. I sound as if I couldn't care less about all this mess our family's gotten itself into, but I was really devastated when it all started. Then I realized I'd have to put a brave face on it for Dad's sake and for Rachel's; she's nearly three years younger than I am and still at high school. Mom wanted us both to go with her, but I refused. And I'm old enough to decide for myself. I felt Dad needed me more than she did. And anyway, he's a lot easier to live with. But my sister had really no choice as it seemed only fair that one of us would go with Mom. Rachel will be eighteen next year, and then she'll choose for herself. But what about you? I've heard you've had a rough time of it the last few years."

Ramona seemed to be inviting confidences, and though Esther still found it hard to talk about the tragic events of the past few years, she felt instinctively that if she could share them with her cousin, it might help Ramona to face her own problems. So while she sipped her coffee, she slowly began her story: "You're right, Ramona, I suppose I've had trouble enough for my age. Four years ago my father died. He'd been sick for a while, but we didn't think he was that bad. Then we discovered that he had developed tuberculosis and had other complications, and he just seemed to fade away. His two imprisonments had taken their toll, for he never did have a strong constitution."

"Yes, I heard something about his being in prison," interjected her cousin. "He was a poet, wasn't he, and wouldn't write propaganda for the Communists?"

"Yes, he was a poet all right," and Esther's voice swelled with pride. "He could compose verse about nearly anything if he chose. My sister Gabriella takes after him in that."

"Your sister?" exclaimed Ramona. "Oh yes, I remember now hearing you had a younger sister. Have you got a photo of her? But sorry; I interrupted you. Go on, please, but hold on. Eat some of your toast first. Here's some marmalade if you want, or blueberry preserves, or honey."

Her cousin smiled as she spooned the marmalade onto her whole wheat toast. She took a few bites and then continued. "Later, as Dad's faith deepened, he found himself writing mainly religious poetry—hymns, songs, and that sort of thing. In fact, they're sung all over Romania now. Of course, Ceausescu and his men didn't like it. They wanted to control his talent and turn it to their own advantage. First they tried to bribe him to write in their newspapers.

That didn't work. Then they threatened him. They found that didn't do any good either. So they tried to stop him by...." The girl's voice faltered at the bare remembrance of her beloved father's sufferings and she struggled to regain her composure. Just then the phone rang.

"What a nuisance!" Ramona sounded annoyed at the interruption, but Esther was rather glad for the break. She had adored her father, and his death at the relatively young age of forty-three had turned her life inside out and wrung the depths of her loving and sensitive nature. To relive those tragic days was always painful, yet she knew she must eventually share her past with her newfound relatives. But on her first day in America, it seemed just too soon to open her heart to those she scarcely knew.

Ramona had taken the portable phone into the living room but she soon returned. "It's Ron," she explained as she resumed her seat. "I first met him in Dad's office just before the fall semester began. His mom had started to work there part time as receptionist. Well, we got talking that morning, and I fell for Ron at first sight." Ramona's blue eyes sparkled. "And he seemed to like me too. Not that there's anything serious between us. We see each other some at college but not a lot. He's not living at school this semester—he's staying with his mom to be company for her at nights."

"But why live at school in the first place, Ramona? Is the college so far away that you can't go there every day? You all seem to have cars." Esther was puzzled. Back in Romania, most of her friends stayed at home as long as they could. Boarding at university was no joke.

Ramona laughed. "Far? Not really. It's only about forty minutes away. But nearly everyone lives in a dorm or else rents an apartment nearby, at least all my friends do."

"But why?"

"Well, by the time we leave high school, we're all dying to do our own thing for a change—to get away from home and start thinking for ourselves. It's only normal, isn't it?" she asked, noticing the slight frown on her cousin's face. Then she went on without waiting for a reply: "But about Ron. He's going to be a lawyer. Esther, you should see him. He's real cool. He has just one class this morning so he's free after eleven. He's coming over later and taking us both out for a pizza."

Esther's expression made her chuckle. "Cool?" she asked, puzzled.

"Oh, I forgot. You're not used to American slang yet. I mean, he's just a great all-round guy—real smart, awfully handsome, good fun, always has plenty of cash in his pocket. But that's not all," and she threw Esther a triumphant look; "he drives a brand new red sports car, and he's real good at baseball and a fabulous swimmer."

Esther's expression made her stop. "He sounds too good to be true, doesn't he? All the girls are crazy over him. Anyway, if we go out with him, it'll save me cooking lunch. I hate cooking. Dad's at work so he won't miss us, and you'll have a great time."

Esther gave her a doubtful smile. She wasn't sure she liked the sound of this Ron Atwood. Why did she have to meet him so soon? Too much was happening too fast. What she needed was a whole week of adjustment to her new life. Actually a whole year was more like it. And yet she really liked Ramona and knew she was trying to make her feel at home by sharing her friend with her.

"Besides," her cousin added, "you'll still have time for a nap if you like. We won't leave till twelve and it's only nine now."

And so it was settled. How could anyone refuse Ramona anything, Esther wondered as she helped clear away the breakfast dishes? Then, as soon as she could, she made her escape upstairs to finish her devotions. She had not gone far before the words, "I will never leave you nor forsake you," leapt from the page.

"Thank You, Father," she exclaimed, tears filling her eyes. "Thank You. Please be with me in my new home, among my new family. I'm frightened, a bit confused, and oh, so very lonely. It's so comforting to know that You've promised to be with me always. Help me to know how to follow You in this bewildering new world I've been plunged into. I really, really need You, Lord. Do please help me. Amen."

Her eyes closed, and when Ramona entered the room half an hour later to take something she needed from the closet, she was struck by the faint smile on her cousin's lips and the aura of peace that seemed to surround her. This quaint little Romanian was certainly very attractive in her own sort of way and as innocent as any angel.

She stood gazing at her for a moment, wondering what her coming would mean to them all. What would her friends think of her, or what was more important, what would Ron Atwood think of her? And how exactly would America change her? Ramona had no way of knowing. It seemed to her as she softly tiptoed out of the room, that Esther had fallen among them from another planet, and deep inside her, she sensed that, somehow or other, her coming into their family would be momentous for them all.

Chapter Four

Esther Steps out of the Ark

Esther opened her eyes and yawned. She felt so comfortable between her pretty pink sheets that she could have stayed there all day. She was about to turn over for another nap when she caught sight of the clock on the dresser and jumped up with a start. It was past twelve already! She had slept in! Ramona would be waiting, or maybe she had gone out already with her friend. Jet lag was certainly catching up with her and she felt totally unfit for company.

Esther sighed as she slid open the closet door. She had unpacked her few belongings earlier that morning but they didn't take up much space. With only one skirt besides her Sunday one, she didn't have much choice, but at least she had one decent blouse that she could wear. She gazed at Ramona's shorts, tops, and pants. They took up at least half the space and she suspected her cousin had another closet full of clothes in her own room. These Americans were surely extravagant. Why did they need so much, she wondered, as she brushed out her long, thick hair?

A few moments later she made her way down the wide stairway and then stopped abruptly. The kitchen door was open and there was Ramona, sitting at the bar, chatting animatedly to the tall, broad-shouldered young man beside her. He was strikingly handsome, Esther thought, just as her cousin had said, with his close-cropped blond hair, keen grayish blue eyes, and radiant smile. He seemed the ideal match for Ramona who looked absolutely stunning that morning; her tanned skin glowed with health and the deep blue of her sparkling eyes was perfectly matched by her stylish top and the ribbon which held back some of her silky blonde curls, leaving others to cling to her neck and temples in a most alluring manner. How on earth, Esther wondered, could these American young people look so casual in such a studied and sophisticated way? To her bewildered mind, these two young people, not much older than herself, seemed to have already attained a sort of physical perfection which both attracted and frightened her at the same time. They exuded health and wholeness, and made her feel totally flawed.

A sudden discontent with her own appearance swept over Esther. Her skin seemed too sallow, her eyes too large, her figure too thin. She felt a pale, undernourished weakling. She wanted to drop through the floor and deeply regretted having agreed to go with them for lunch.

Tongue-tied, Esther waited nervously for one of them to start the conversation. Her eyes fell on her clumsy walking shoes which had covered so many weary miles back in Romania and which had always seemed so sensible and serviceable. But today they felt like a pair of veritable Judases betraying her origin. Her long, well-worn black skirt was no better. She remembered how happy she had been when her aunt had given it to her for a birthday gift three years previously, apologizing for the fact that it was not new. But now it seemed totally incongruous with her youth and surroundings. The only redeeming feature in her outfit was her gold silk blouse, a parting present from the girls at church. She guessed that they had clubbed together using all their spare cash to purchase it. At least it was new and her one pride and joy. But gold blouse notwithstanding, her intuition told her that, by American standards, she was dressed totally inappropriately for a midday drive to a pizza parlor on a balmy October morning.

Ramona stared at her cousin for a long while, amazed that she could make so much of her old worn-out togs, and Ron couldn't fail to notice that the gold blouse set off the girl's olive skin and dark lustrous eyes to perfection. Like her cousin, she had chosen a bow to match her blouse, only her tresses were long and thick and would have waved nearly down to her waist had they not been tied back. But more striking than the blouse or the bow or even her undoubtedly remarkable eyes was the utter enigma the girl presented as she stood in the kitchen doorway—so old-fashioned and yet so graceful, so simple and yet, as you looked into her eyes, you had a feeling that this young woman was deep, yes very deep.

There was a long, awkward silence then Ron was the first to speak. "Hi, there," he greeted her in typical American fashion. "Why, you must be Esther, Ramona's Romanian cousin. Glad to meet you," and he held out his hand. Ramona studied his face as he spoke but could make nothing of his expression.

"Pleased to meet you too," replied Esther timidly. Then her eyes fell on the giant pizza which her cousin had laid out on the bar. "Oh, I'm so sorry. I've spoiled your plans," she exclaimed. "I just slept and slept and never realized it was so late."

"That's OK, Esther," Ramona reassured her. "We knew you must be absolutely burned out and didn't want to waken you, so we decided to bring the food here instead of going out to eat. Sit down and join us. We've hardly started."

Ron took out a stool and helped her to get seated while Ramona dished out some pizza. "That's quite enough," Esther protested. "Please, I'm not used to eating so much. Half that amount is about all I can cope with."

"That's why you Romanians are so slim. You half starve yourselves," Ramona joshed, but Esther did not laugh. What her cousin had said was all too true. Her aunt's gaunt face and figure rose before her, reminding her of the countless times she had given nearly all that she had in her pantry to her two growing nieces.

There was another awkward silence as Esther bowed her head and silently thanked God for her food, conscious of four curious eyes upon her. Ramona remembered that her cousin had done the same thing before eating the previous evening, but that had been different. For the first time since her arrival, Esther sensed her cousin was not pleased with her and blushed with confusion as she sampled the pizza. But Ron, who thought privately that this young Romanian was very plucky for having the courage of her convictions, turned to her and asked, "Fill us in a little on Romania, please, Esther. I suppose it's a tremendous contrast to what you have seen so far in the States?"

"Yes," the girl replied her face clouding a little. "Romania, at present, is not very bright or prosperous or," and she paused, then added slowly, "happy."

"Ceaucescu's dirty work I suppose," growled Ron. "A totalitarian state, a grasping dictator with an even more grasping wife, right?"

Esther gasped in unfeigned surprise at his knowledge of the situation in her beloved land. The young man grinned. "I read a lot. I try to keep up with political events in the world as much as my studies will allow, so I know just a little about your infamous Ceaucescu and his partner in crime."

"Yes," Esther commented, "Romania is not a typical communist state like Bulgaria or even Czechoslovakia. We are communist in name, though we are distancing ourselves from Russia more and more as time goes on. Our country is really under a dictatorship, governed completely by one man and his family."

"Especially by his wife," Ron added with a grin. "Never forget the women. When they lay their dainty little hands on the reins of power they're more tyrannical then any king or emperor!"

"What can you as a single guy know about women's rule?" taunted Ramona, eager to get the conversation back onto her level.

"More than enough," was the retort. And for half an hour or more, Esther sat in awkward silence as she listened to their banter. Her English was pretty good as Ron had already noted with surprise, but sometimes she felt she lost the gist of the conversation, for she was not up on American slang or colloquialisms. And even when she could follow every word, she found she had little to say about any of the topics under discussion.

Try as she would to concentrate, her mind insisted on wandering. "The price of bread has gone up again this week," she could hear her aunt saying to her best friend when they got together for their weekly chat on a Saturday evening. And she found it hard to forget the tremulous tones of the old lady next door announcing piteously, "My electric was cut off last night, was yours?" In the metro, on the bus, or waiting in the long lines for the allotted ration of milk or meat, the theme was unchanging—keeping alive, staying warm and fed and at least tolerably healthy. Gloomy, yes, but real. It was all about life. But here? The latest movie, what song was topping the charts, the college baseball team, and so it went on. But wait, Esther pulled herself up sharply. What was she thinking of. That was life too, wasn't it?

"You didn't talk much," Ramona commented as they watched Ron's car speed off down the tree-lined avenue. "Did he frighten you that much? Fantastic, isn't he?"

"You both are," was Esther's evasive and rather diplomatic reply. "Remember, Ramona, everything is so new to me. You really can't know what a different world this is from the one I have lived in for nearly twenty years."

"No, I am sure I can't understand," admitted her cousin. "But you'll get used to being here, and to being with cool guys like Ron. Just you wait and see!"

"Used to it?" thought Esther as she made her way upstairs. "Will I really ever get used to it? I wonder!"

Fifteen minutes later, Ramona found herself picking up the phone. "Well, Ron, what do you think of her?"

"Come on, give me a break," said the voice at the other end. "I've only met the girl once. It's too early to judge. She was tired from her long journey and is obviously overwhelmed by everything. Of course, she's definitely not American. And she's terribly serious. I think she only smiled once or twice."

Ramona breathed a sigh of relief. "Yes, and she's so awfully old-fashioned."

"Well," agreed Ron, "she's not exactly dressed like you, Ramona; you could give her a lesson or two on how to be more with it."

Ramona's face was all smiles; she could afford to be generous now. "Just let her give me the chance!" she assured him. "But she's so religious. See what she did before she ate?"

"Yes, and I thought it took real guts for her to do something different from the rest of us," was Ron's answer.

"But she looks so ancient," laughed Ramona.

"Yes, just as if she had stepped out of the ark."

"But she's not really that bad-looking, is she?" Ramona protested.

And now Ron simply could not resist it. "No, not at all bad-looking for a contemporary of Noah," he told Ramona with a chuckle. "I wonder if all the females in his family were aware that gold silk blouses and bows went extremely well with smooth olive skin and long, dark, wavy hair!"

It was good he could not see Ramona's face just then. Why had she ever put it into his head that her cousin might be just the least bit pretty? And it bothered her that, just occasionally, this fabulous friend of hers seemed on a totally different wavelength from herself. Oh well, he was extra bright and she wasn't and that's all there was to it. But maybe, if he was as fond of blondes as most boys seemed to be, that wouldn't matter very much. She certainly hoped not.

"Well," Ron was speaking again, "Esther sure is lucky to have you for a cousin. You'll show her the ropes all right and have her as glamorous as yourself before many weeks are out. Though to tell you the truth, I just can't imagine Esther Popescu transformed into a typical American. I mean, can you visualize her parading around in a mini skirt or skin tight pants? And I can't really imagine her bleaching her hair, or putting on eye makeup or lipstick, can you? But I guess we'll just have to wait and see." And on that rather ambiguous note, Ron said good-bye, leaving Ramona, just as he had intended, none the wiser as to his real opinion of her mysterious cousin.

Ramona saw little of Esther for the remainder of the afternoon. She supposed she was having another long and much needed nap. She was curled up, watching her favorite soap opera when her cousin finally made her appearance. She normally didn't get much chance to watch them when she was away at school.

"Come, sit down Esther, I don't suppose you've looked at much

TV in Romania, at least, not this sort. Now look, isn't she fabulous? Looks a bit like me, right, or rather like the girl I'll be when I've slimmed down a bit?" Esther stared at the young blonde dressed for an evening out in a very revealing gown, accompanied by a young man not unlike Ron Atwood in appearance.

"Yes, she does look somewhat like you, Ramona," she admitted rather reluctantly. Her cousin smiled contentedly. For the next half hour, Esther watched in shocked silence. It seemed everyone was in love with someone else rather than their spouse. No wonder, she thought, that Ramona had seemed to take it in her stride when her parents' marriage had broken up. Then the clock in the hall struck five.

"Can I help you prepare a meal for your dad?" she ventured when she saw her cousin finally switch off the TV.

"Are you kidding?" Ramona seemed genuinely taken aback. "I hardly ever prepare supper for Dad. Of course, I'm usually away during the week anyway so he fends for himself. And at the weekends, we either go out for a meal or he brings something home, or we heat up a TV dinner."

"TV dinner?"

Ramona laughed merrily. "Yep. They're frozen meals that we often eat while watching TV. You've certainly got a lot of learning to do, that's obvious. Here, I'll show you," and she led her cousin to the garage where she opened the door of a large upright freezer and showed Esther neat piles of packaged, pre-prepared meals.

Esther was not impressed but said nothing. Didn't Ramona know how to cook, she wondered? She shook her head in disbelief.

"Oh, come, Esther," Ramona's voice was a bit defensive now. "Remember you're in the USA. There are fabulous restaurants everywhere and so much prepared food in the stores. Reminds me, we need to do a bit of shopping before Dad comes home. And he told me to bring home some Long John Silver's for tonight. I've an hour before he gets back. Come on, let's go."

"Long John Silver's?" queried Esther.

"It's a fast food restaurant," Ramona informed her, laughing, as she hopped into her car and started up the engine.

A few moments later, Esther was trying to keep up with her cousin as she scooted down the aisles of the nearest supermarket. "Let's see: milk, butter, cheese, eggs, cereal, and frozen dinners, oh yes, and the TV guide. Mustn't forget that. That's about it, I think," muttered Ramona as she wheeled her buggy towards the checkout.

But where was Esther? She was nowhere to be seen.

"Lost your friend?" the girl at the cash register asked her. "She's over there. Seems done in. Is she ill or something?"

Ramona paid for her groceries and then found Esther sitting on the bench by the door. "Sorry Ramona," she apologized, looking very white and drawn. "I just couldn't take it any more. I had to sit down."

Ramona looked concerned. "You must be very tired, Esther. Sorry for dragging you here. I thought you might enjoy seeing our store."

Esther smiled weakly. "I'm OK Ramona. It's just I can't seem to take all the variety, all the food—rows upon rows of it. It's too much. I mean, it's overwhelming."

"I suppose so," her cousin replied, trying hard to understand. But when she told her father about it later when they had finished their meal of fish and French fries and when Esther was safely out of earshot, he laid a hand on his daughter's shoulder and said firmly, "Ramona, you'll need a lot of patience with Esther in the coming days. She's been thrown in at the deep end, you know. First, she lands in a house like this, so unlike what she's used to. Then you break the news of our separation and half scandalize her to death; not long after that you introduce her to a guy like Ron, sit her down to watch a soap opera, and then take her to a modern supermarket and all in one day. She's in utter shock. Remember, Romania's at least fifty years behind us in most things. So give her time to get adjusted to life here and let her do it as gradually as possible. Understand?"

Ramona nodded as her father left to pick up Rachel for the weekend. So that explained it. She wasn't sure if Esther had exactly stepped out of the ark as Ron had put it, but she had certainly landed on them from another era. "Fifty years behind?" she repeated to herself as she turned on Jeopardy. She wanted Esther to watch it too but she was up in her room again. How long would it take her cousin to catch up on things, she wondered, that is, if she ever did catch up? And maybe it might be just as well if she didn't, at least not yet. A modern Esther might be a bit too dangerous to have around.

Chapter Five

Esther's Shopping Spree

Esther eyed herself in the full length mirror. It was perfect, so warm and elegant. What more could she want? But the price!

"You do look fabulous in that," commented Ramona. And it was true. The white, faux-fur jacket transformed the simple old-fashioned Romanian girl into an extremely attractive young lady.

Esther ran her hand over the soft fabric and sighed. She had never owned anything like it in her life, but $200 just for this? And she needed so much more than this one jacket. No, she just couldn't buy it, not when she knew that many of her friends would be able to live for five months on that amount. It would be sheer extravagance!

Ramona groaned inwardly as the saleswoman took the jacket from her cousin and hung it back on the rack. Esther glanced at Rachel who, for the first time that tiring afternoon, seemed to be showing some interest in what was going on and flashed her the merest suggestion of a smile as they made their way out of the department store.

When she had met Rachel the evening before, Esther had noticed immediately that her younger cousin possessed none of her sister's glamour or good nature. She resembled her father in coloring, with dark brown hair and eyes not unlike her own. She was slimly built too, like herself. But her features were too angular, her hair too lifeless, and her skin too sallow for beauty, a fact of which the unhappy girl was only too conscious. Spoiled by both mother and father, she had developed into a petulant teenager, whose tantrums were the dread of the entire family. She resented always living in the shadow of her attractive and popular sister. And now her parents' separation and impending divorce had only made her more fretful and impossible to get on with. Her mother could not handle her and always ended up giving her her own way for peace and quietness' sake. Her father truly loved her but was at a complete loss as to how to help his adolescent daughter. Some well-meaning friends said she would grow sweeter and better as she got older but so far, this prophecy had not been fulfilled.

Yet despite all her young cousin's deficiencies, Esther felt strangely drawn to her. Maybe it was the fact that she was neither self-assured nor sophisticated like Ramona or Ron. Here was someone, Esther felt very certain, who was sending out signals that she desperately needed help. What Rachel's real problem was, she had little idea, but she was determined to find out, determined to ignore, if possible, her rudeness and get to know the real person within.

Once outside the store, Ramona turned to her cousin and protested, "You'll have to get used to prices here, Esther."

"But I just can't, Ramona," Esther retorted. "How can I spend $75 on a pair of shoes, or $200 on a winter jacket, when my friends and family in Romania receive $40 or less in monthly wages, much of that going to buy bread to merely survive? And why do I need the latest name brands anyway?"

"But, Esther," Ramona argued, "you've got to look more with it if you want to be accepted."

"Accepted by whom?" Esther wanted to know.

Ramona sighed. She was tired and just a little cross. "I mean, you'll fit into life here so much quicker and easier if you dress like everyone else. That's all."

Esther gave her cousin a significant glance. Ramona squirmed as she went on: "Of course, we love you just as you are but my advice is, don't stand out like a sore thumb or you'll find it tough, at college especially."

"You mean I won't get good grades if I dress differently?" The girl's tone was a little sarcastic. "Do you bribe the professors by wearing certain brands of jeans and shoes? Now in Romania, there's a lot of bribery. It's almost impossible to enter university without resorting to that tactic, but I never thought...."

"Oh Esther," laughed her cousin, amused and mortified at the same time, "of course it isn't like that. We're fair here in America," she went on proudly. "Your grades depend on your brains and how hard you work, nothing more. But I was thinking especially of guys like Ron. If you want a boyfriend, I mean one that's really worth having, then you'll have to be a lot more cool, and more sexy too."

Esther couldn't believe her ears. No one decent even used that word where she had grown up. She glanced at Rachel who was glaring at her sister. Ramona tossed her curls and frowned a little. She thought privately that her cousin was a real prude. She'd have to broaden out a lot if she wanted to survive college. But she only said in a slightly patronizing tone, "I mean, you're really attractive in spite of your clothes, and I'm sure could look really nice if you put a bit of money into what you buy."

Esther was suddenly carried back to her conversation with the strange little man on the plane. "Velvet Curtain," he had said. "It is everywhere in the West, especially in America." Maybe, just maybe, she was beginning to feel its folds closing in around her. So, in this land of freedom, she was not truly free, not, that is, if she wished to really feel at home in this new culture.

Just then Ramona sighted an ice cream parlor. "Just the thing," she exclaimed, keen to get Esther's mind diverted from their recent conversation. "What kind of ice cream do you fancy, Esther?"

Now if the Romanian girl had a liking for anything it was ice cream. Her eyes widened as Ramona pointed out the different flavors. "Vanilla, chocolate, coffee, cherry, strawberry, lime? Take your pick," her cousin told her, "and make it as big as you like. It's my treat."

Stalling for time, Esther turned to her younger cousin. "What are you going to choose, Rachel?"

"Oh, plain vanilla, plain just like me," the girl said with a grating laugh.

"Well, I'd like a mixture if I could," Esther began hesitatingly. "You see, I've never tasted anything but vanilla and then I think it was probably only imitation ice cream."

The lady behind the counter was listening. She glanced rather curiously at the girl at the counter, in her gold blouse and long black skirt. "She's just come from Romania," Ramona hastily explained. "I'm treating her to our best ice cream."

The lady grinned. "Then I'll treat her too. How about a scoop of as many kinds as you like, and all for the price of one?"

"Great," agreed Ramona. "But don't make yourself sick," she warned her cousin as she put down a five dollar bill on the counter. In the end, Esther decided she could only cope with tasting three flavors at once.

The girls carried their ice cream over to a small table where they could see what was going on in the mall outside. Esther took out a snowy white handkerchief and began to wipe her chair. Ramona reddened. "Whatever are you doing that for?" she demanded.

"I always do it," the girl replied, surprised at her cousin's tone.

"Well, I really don't think you need to do it here and if you do, don't make it so obvious and please, use a Kleenex," and Ramona slipped her a tissue while she cast a furtive glance at the lady behind the counter.

Esther sat down embarrassed. "Sorry Ramona, but at home everything's so dirty, we have to do it. At least I do. I am a bit fastidious as Gabby would say, but then I haven't got that many clothes, and we don't have a washing machine either," she added significantly. "You see, we have maybe two or three decent outfits in all. One we keep for Sundays, one or two for shopping like this or for school, and then our really old things for around the house, so we don't want to wash them more than we can help. I guess this has made me extra fussy when it comes to watching out for dirty seats and benches when I'm out somewhere. I keep forgetting that America isn't Romania."

Ramona stared in disbelief and took a large bite of her chocolate sundae. "Forget about it, Esther. It's nothing really." She felt guilty at even noticing her cousin's action and remembered her father's admonition to let her adjust slowly.

The three girls finished their ice cream in silence. Esther stared out the window. People seemed so carefree, she thought, but were they really? Was it all just a show, a façade?

"This is great, Ramona. Thanks so much," she told her cousin, as she plopped the last bit of cone into her mouth. "It's the best ice cream I've ever tasted, only I've eaten far too much."

"It'll fatten you up a bit," grinned her cousin as she rose to go. "Now for business. It's getting late and you haven't really begun to shop yet."

Esther's face clouded. Stores would be closing in an hour or so. It was true, they hadn't much time. She thought again of the beautiful white fur jacket as she put her hand to her ears to block out the music which vibrated through the crowded mall. Then she suddenly remembered the promise she had read the day before. "Yes, God," she whispered inaudibly, "I need You now. I need You to help me find clothes that I can buy with good conscience and soon. I can't keep my cousins waiting much longer and yet You know my money is Your money and I'm not free to squander it. Please, oh please, show me what to do."

Ten minutes later and just when Ramona's exasperation was reaching its limit, Rachel pointed to a large sign, "Closing Down Sale," on the window of a store opposite them. Entering, they discovered that almost everything was drastically reduced, even the best brand names. It did not take Esther long to select a red fleecy jacket for the winter, certainly not as elegant as the white fur but, as Rachel whispered in her ear, it would be just as warm and a lot more practical. Within half an hour, she had chosen several other items which satisfied even Ramona's fastidious taste.

"Why are all the shop assistants smiling at me?" she whispered to Rachel as her purchases were being put into a large plastic bag, "and what do I pay for all these bags they are giving me?"

"Nothing. But it's all a sales gimmick, their smiling so much I mean," muttered Rachel. "They're trained to it. Makes you feel like buying more than if they looked sour like me," and her cousin gave her one of her most sarcastic smiles.

"How cynical she is," thought Esther, but she said nothing. Rachel had not uttered two words for a couple of hours except to grumble at each new store they entered. Yet Esther fancied that her gaze was becoming just a little less hostile as the afternoon wore on.

The one point of controversy, however, was jeans, blue jeans. Esther had never worn them in her life. She did not feel feminine in them, and why she should wear them to go shopping, or to college, she had no conception. And so tight! "Shows off your shape, Esther," Ramona had explained. "And you can afford to, you're so slim!" Esther sensed a tinge of envy in her cousin's voice.

She finally consented to buying two pairs which at least left her some room to breathe and were drastically reduced in price. Ramona was still not content. Her cousin had only spent half her money and had not nearly enough clothes to see her though the coming months.

Esther, however, was thinking of other things besides clothes. Try as she would, she could not refrain from contrasting everything around her with her native town of Ploiesti. She gazed out the window dreamily as they began their homeward journey. The whole landscape seemed to breathe of hope and liberty; there were no towering apartment buildings to disfigure the skyline and choke the very life out of the hundreds of families crowded into their two or three roomed apartments. And there was order and cleanliness everywhere.

It was a thirty minute drive back to Velours, a rather quaint little town of about 20,000 inhabitants. The brightly painted town hall with the American flag proudly waving from a pole just outside the door bore no resemblance to the massive dull, grey building back home which housed the party headquarters and which she had had to pass on her way to school each morning. It had always seemed to stand as a symbol of all that was repressive and repulsive. But here she could see no armed guards to protect any building, public or private. And churches! As Ramona had told her the day before, they seemed to be on nearly every street corner—Baptist, United Methodist, Episcopalian, Pentecostal, and Roman Catholic. Esther pinched herself. Was it all a dream? Had she come to Heaven?

Then, suddenly, as they rounded a bend in the long, tree-lined avenue flanked by beautiful homes with spacious, well-kept yards, she exclaimed excitedly, "There's that garage sale again, Ramona, over there. The yard is full of things and there's a crowd of people gathered."

Ramona gave a long sigh. Earlier that day, they had passed that same garage sale. Her cousin had wanted to know what on earth it was, and had been told that it was where people sold their castoffs and got a chance to empty out their basements and attics. Esther had suggested they stop there and maybe it would save a trip into the city. But Ramona had laughed at her naivety and driven gaily on. She had no intention of allowing a relative of hers to parade round town in what might turn out to be her neighbor's castoffs.

But now, after what had been a very frustrating afternoon, they were returning without much to show for their hours of shopping. Her father would not be pleased. So when Esther laid a hand on her shoulder and pleaded, "Oh, please, let me go. Maybe there'll be something I need there. Please, Ramona, just this once," she very reluctantly pulled into the driveway hoping that none of her friends would see them. Esther, sensing her reluctance, told her to wait in the car and she would go herself.

"I'll go with you," Rachel volunteered most unexpectedly; then embarrassed at her sudden show of generosity, she added patronizingly, "You'll need someone to make sure you don't waste your money on junk."

Esther hid her surprise and smiled her pleasure as they walked up the long drive to the many tables spread with a whole array of electrical gadgets, draperies, bed linen, pictures, toys, and a variety of trinkets and knickknacks. The "extras" of this one household, Esther could not help thinking, would supply the modest needs of more than one Romanian family. But what really caught her eye and made her gasp with delight was a thin rope strung between two trees on which many clothes were hanging, swinging in the light October breeze. And oh joy! There were blouses, and tops, and sweaters, and skirts, and dresses, and pants, and many of them Esther's size!

With Rachel's help, she selected a pile of nearly new garments, a few pair of shoes, a handbag and pocketbook, some scarves, perfume, and a few toiletries, and could not conceal her delight when told that everything came to the grand sum of $50. She loaded them into the trunk in great glee. What a lot she had bought and yet still had $200 in her pocket!

The evening before, her uncle had taken her aside, and slipping five one hundred dollar bills into her hands when no one else was looking, had instructed her to buy whatever she needed. Esther's protests had fallen on deaf ears. No, he had made up his mind to do this, and she would have to agree. Maybe, Esther reasoned, her uncle felt that $500 was a cheap price to pay to see that the little waif and stray from across the water was transformed into a respectable member of the Popescu household, looking as refined and modern as his own daughters. But she had also observed in the two days she had been in his home that her uncle was extremely generous and good-natured and genuinely wanted to do something to make her feel happy and contented in her new environment, and she was sure that he had given largely out of the goodness of his heart.

When they returned to the house, she proudly showed off her bargains. Uncle John bit his lip at first when he realized that most of her purchases were second-hand. But he had to admit, in the end, that she had chosen well, for everything seemed to really suit her and even Ramona had to agree. Certainly there were no shorts, or mini skirts, nothing startling or really eye-catching among her purchases, but Ramona thought privately that after a few months' exposure to American culture that would all change. Just give her time. That's all she needed. And something deep down within her that she could not seem to control suggested that, after all, did she really want Esther to be that accepted, praised, and admired? Did she want her to look as glamorous as herself? No, she really did not, so it was probably best the way it was.

As soon as Esther had put away her clothes, she went back downstairs. Her uncle had gone out and she meant to give him a real surprise when he returned. With Ramona and Rachel's help she soon had a pot of ciorba on the boil.

"What's that delicious odor coming from the kitchen?" John shouted from the door a few hours later.

"Guess, Uncle," Esther told him, laughing.

"It's ciorba, I do declare," he exclaimed as he walked over to the stove. "Real Romanian ciorba."

"Well, not quite," Esther confessed, "but near enough, I hope."

Her uncle washed his hands and sat waiting on his bar stool. He smacked his lips as he took the first bite. He hadn't tasted anything like that for years and years.

Esther went upstairs that night with a light heart. Her uncle had devoured three large bowls of her soup and Rachel and Ramona had each eaten two. And besides, she knew that God had answered her prayer that afternoon. True, some of the clothes she had bought that afternoon were not quite what she was used to, a bit showier, more up-to-date, but all were modest and attractive when all was said and done. And that was the criteria Esther meant to go by in the coming months. She would respect her relatives and their friends and look as decent as possible in this strange new world into which she had dropped as an alien from outer space, as long as she could do so with a good conscience.

She had felt so sure of the existence of that Velvet Curtain that afternoon, but now it did not seem real at all. She felt so free, so happy. Yet she could not help wondering if she had just escaped being imprisoned in its folds, or so it had seemed at any rate. At least she was safe for the time being and the future was in her Father's capable hands. To escape being imprisoned by one Curtain only to be entrapped by another was unthinkable. But she would have to heed Hugh's wise warning and be careful, very careful!

Chapter Six

Esther's First Sunday in America

"What a beautiful baritone voice Uncle John has," Esther commented to herself as she stood beside him in St. Jude's Episcopal Church, situated just a few blocks from her new home. She had been surprised when her uncle had asked if she wanted to attend church that Sunday morning. She had taken it for granted that they would all go as a family and worship God together. Then her uncle explained that he had faithfully attended the Orthodox Church in the heart of Indianapolis when he first came to the States, but after a few years, it just seemed too far to go every Sunday. Esther then remembered her father saying that religion had never been as vital a part of his brother's life as it had his, though John Popescu was considered a highly respectable man, who carefully avoided what he considered the grosser sins of the flesh—drunkenness, adultery, fraud, and such like. And Easter and Christmas always found him seated in his pew at St. Jude's. But for the remainder of the year, he had considered it much more convenient and practical, after a busy week at work, to spend the day relaxing at home with his wife and two young daughters.

John, however, was willing to do almost anything to please Esther and make her feel at home. So ignoring the sighs of one daughter and the scowls of the other, he had insisted that for once they all go to church together. Esther was glad. It would have been devastating to spend a Sunday without going to some form of public worship. She realized later to her relief that St. Jude's was within walking distance and she could go alone by foot in future if it were necessary. She had discovered to her surprise that there were no buses or trams in Velours as there had been in Bucharest or in Ploiesti or in any decent sized town in Romania onto which she could hop whenever she wanted.

There was no doubt about it; the large stately stone building with its well-dressed and fashionable congregation was a world apart from the church which had been her home for four years. If Esther closed her eyes, she could see all the familiar faces—her aunt, pale and wan but neat as a pin in her grey headscarf, white starched blouse, and black woolen skirt which was kept especially for Sundays, and elderly Nina Sandelescu or "Granny" as she was called by everyone, her face as wrinkled as an Egyptian parchment from years of work in the fields, but with a smile as sweet as any angel's. There they all were, five hundred or more of them—men and boys on one side, ladies and girls on the other, row after row of them, crowded eight to ten on a backless bench, caring little that they had scarcely any room to breathe, that the service lasted three hours, or that their church was only four or five rooms knocked into one in what had been an old rambling house situated in the back streets of Ploiesti. Neither August's stifling heat nor January's freezing winds kept even the most aged from their Sunday worship. They were only too thankful to be allowed to exist at all, as was not the case in so many other Communist controlled nations.

No wonder, then, that Esther found this church so different. Here there were no secret police lurking in the wings, listening, spying, and shadowing. Here the preacher might speak his mind without running the risk of imprisonment or other forms of reprisal. Why then, she asked herself, where there was comfort and elegance and, oh bliss, space to stretch and move without sticking an elbow in your neighbor's ribs, why was the large sanctuary only one third full and the majority of the congregation middle-aged or older? Where were all the people on this beautiful, balmy October morning? America was supposed to be a Christian land, was it not?

But though the service seemed so full of enigmas to the young girl and the sermon contained almost everything except the Gospel, there was considerably more Scripture read than in her aunt's church back home. And some of the liturgy reminded her of the old days when she had gone with her parents to the local Orthodox Church in Bucharest; it made her long to feel her mother's arms around her once more and to hear her father singing his favorite hymns in his deep bass. And though it saddened her to see Rachel sitting sullenly in her seat, scowling as she watched the others make their way to the front, Esther liked the way they received the Lord's Supper, kneeling in reverent silence at the altar rail.

As the last hymn was being sung and the benediction said, she wondered what her cousins had really thought of such a service. She glanced first at Ramona, sitting by her father in her plum-colored pant suit with shoes and handbag to match, her face revealing nothing but boredom; it was evident she had tolerated the whole procedure as a sort of necessary evil. Then her eyes fell on Rachel, clad in blue jeans and sneakers, defiance, frustration, and sadness etched on her angular features. Esther wanted to reach out and hug her right there in the church, but she knew that such a gesture would be premature and only do harm. Then she glanced down at her white, frilly blouse, tan skirt, and handbag with shoes to match, all someone's castoffs, as Ramona would say. No longer dressed in her old black skirt and gold blouse, she did not feel as conspicuously alien as she might have done.

Her new outfit, however, did not prevent her receiving some well-bred stares as she made her way to the basement where refreshments were being served. Many wanted to know about Romania and the political situation there. She was a sort of curiosity, she thought, a souvenir from a faraway land. But she was ill at ease. The atmosphere felt more like a social club than a church. Everyone spoke the right thing, was dressed in the right way; she shuddered a little. Yes, she sensed it again—that enveloping, smothering "something." She felt it was virtually impossible to simply be "Esther Popescu from Romania." America was already attempting to pour her into another mold.

At last it was over; Esther couldn't help breathing a sigh of relief as she climbed into her uncle's car, and she was aware that the others were all feeling the same way. A lavish lunch in a nearby restaurant seemed a not surprising finale to the morning's ritual. It seemed that everyone else thought so too, for the place was crowded with what appeared to be church-goers.

"This is a buffet lunch," her uncle told her as the waitress took their order for drinks and pointed them to the food bars in the middle of the room. "There's a salad bar there, and a dessert bar over there," he went on. "But here's the main entrée bar. Let's begin with it if you like."

Esther's face was a picture. Ramona burst out laughing. "She looks as if she hadn't seen so much food in all her life," she remarked thoughtlessly as she rose from her chair. Her father gave her a warning look, but Esther had already heard her comment.

"That's exactly right, Ramona," she said soberly. "I never have and I really don't know if I can cope with it."

Her uncle handed her a plate and said reassuringly, "Just take it easy, Esther. Now, tell me what you would like to sample and I'll put just a little on your plate."

The bewildered girl stared at the meat loaf, fried chicken, barbecued pork, and roast beef. So much meat and all in one meal! Although she had not taken much breakfast that morning, her appetite seemed to have evaporated. Her uncle realized too late that he had made a mistake to bring her to a buffet lunch after only three full days in the country.

By the time all three bars had been visited, Esther thought she had never consumed so much food in her life and she had eaten only a fraction of what her cousin Ramona tucked away. Then she noticed that the table next to theirs had just been vacated. Her glance fell on several plates still half full of meat and vegetables. Her eyes roamed over the restaurant. Wherever she looked, it was the same story. Food everywhere left untouched on plates! Then it hit her. The waste! At the table next to theirs, a boy of about nine years had just taken a bite or two of roast beef and chicken, pushed away his lunch, and then devoured a huge dish of ice cream and a large piece of chocolate cake with amazing rapidity. The chicken breast he had discarded seemed to stare at Esther from the plate, begging to be eaten, to be put to good use. She tugged at her uncle's sleeve and whispered, "What do they do with all the food that's left over?"

John looked surprised. "Do with it?" he repeated. "Why, throw it away, of course. What else? Who could eat it after someone had toyed with it?"

His niece could take it no longer. Visions of thin, wasted children in overcrowded orphanages rose before her eyes. "Excuse me please," she muttered, as she rose hastily and went outside. Her uncle followed in alarm and found her leaning against the wall, sobbing as if her heart would break.

"My dear child, whatever is the matter?" He put his arm round her trembling shoulders for he saw that the tears were pouring down her face and her whole frame was shaking in the vain effort to control her emotions.

"I can't take it, Uncle John," was the piteous reply. "I just can't take it. Here we are, nearly making ourselves sick with all this good food and so many of my friends nearly at starvation point. And all the waste! It boggles my mind. I'm in a sort of shock. And it's not just this. It's everything. I can't take it in. I need to go home, please. Don't worry, this will pass."

It did pass, but not for many hours. All the pent-up emotions of the past days had to find an outlet. Downstairs, Uncle John and Ramona discussed Esther's reaction that noon. "I don't see why she was so upset, Dad," began Ramona. "She must be real hyper."

"Hyper? Is that what you call it?" John's voice was tinged with sarcasm. "I'd call it the sign of an extremely loving and sensitive nature. But then, how can you understand someone who has just left the Iron Curtain and come to a land of plenty, when you've never been outside this country all your life?" Her father spoke heatedly for he was taken back twenty-three years to his arrival in the States. He could remember vividly some of his reactions during those first weeks and months. And he had not begun to experience the trauma this young girl had undergone so recently. Then he had an idea.

"You know, Ramona, I think it would be a healthy experience for all of us, your cousin included, if she were to tell us something about her life during the past ten years or so," he suggested. "You would understand her better and, though it won't be easy for her, it will be a safety valve for her emotions if she can talk about it. I know bits and pieces of her story, but not the details."

"I think you're right, Dad," Ramona replied thoughtfully. "Esther started to tell me the day after she arrived but we were interrupted so she didn't get very far. Let's suggest it when she comes down later."

Esther did not come down until nearly five that afternoon, and when she did, her face showed traces of the storm which had finally passed, leaving a subdued and exhausted girl in its wake. Uncle John waited till she had eaten her sandwich and then plunged in: "Esther, my dear, Ramona and I have just been thinking that we really would like to hear about your life in Romania. After all, it is my native land and a land which I hope my daughters will visit some day. I think it would also do you good to talk about it though I know it won't be easy."

His niece was taken aback and gulped, "I don't know if I can, at least right now. Maybe some day soon." Her uncle smiled sympathetically but made no reply. Then her face brightened as though some happier idea had struck her. "No, Uncle John, you're right," she told him. "I'll do it, but on one condition."

"Make any condition you like," he told her. But he was not prepared for Esther's reply:

"I'll tell you my whole story if you call Rachel down. She's part of the family and should hear it too."

"Rachel?" Her uncle was startled. He had become so accustomed to his younger daughter's moody ways and unsociable moods, that he had never even thought of inviting her to hear Esther's story.

"But I'm not sure she'll come," he protested. "You must have noticed, Esther, that she can be extremely awkward at times and usually if we want her to do something, she will do the exact opposite."

"I've noticed that all right," was the quick reply. "But let me go and ask her. I can at least try."

"Go ahead and good luck. She's in her room." John bit his lip as he watched his niece trip upstairs. He was not hopeful that this Romanian girl could work a miracle with his stubborn daughter. But he little knew Esther's perseverance and power of persuasion, or realized that she often seemed to possess wisdom well beyond her years.

The minutes ticked by. They seemed hours to those waiting in the living room, and then they heard two pairs of feet on the stairs and, to their utter surprise, there was Rachel, somewhat subdued and with downcast eyes as if ashamed to be in their presence.

Her cousin led her into the room and deposited her in a chair. "There, now, I can see you all. And so I'll begin my story. Mind you," Esther warned, "you'll need to have patience for it's rather long and, in places, not too happy, so have your Kleenex ready," and she laughed rather nervously as she curled up in a chair, cleared her throat, and began.

Chapter Seven

Esther's Story

"As far back as I can remember, my sister and I were loved and cherished by two of the best parents in the world. And every day we watched the unfolding of the most beautiful love story you could ever imagine.

"My father, as you already know, Uncle John," and here Esther smiled at her uncle as if his very presence were comforting and brought back sweet memories, "was exceptionally gifted—poetical, musical, sensitive, patriotic, and more than anything else, deeply religious. As the years went by, his religion became such an important part of his life that it affected everything he said and did. God to him was a real Person; he consulted Him about every plan, trusted Him in every sorrow, and thanked Him humbly for every bit of happiness that came his way. It seemed to us children that his joy came from a source deep within him, certainly not from his circumstances. This is what the Communists could not understand. They had rarely come across such a practical type of religion, and Dad's love for God and for those around him, yes, even for his enemies, utterly confounded them.

"At first, it wasn't too bad. He was allowed to do pretty much as he liked as we all were, within certain limits that is, but gradually our president and his wife grew more and more fanatical and tyrannical. Villages were razed to the ground and thousands were moved hastily to poorly built apartment buildings, ten to twelve stories high, in order to fulfill our leaders' vision of a highly industrialized Romania. Of course, all property belonged to the government and nothing was private any more; even our most well guarded secrets seemed open to the prying eyes of the Secret Police and their spies. Neighbors were bribed to spy on neighbors. Electricity was often cut off for hours on end. Food began to be drastically rationed.

"And then churches came under suspicion. The Lord's Army which we belonged to at the time was especially harassed. As Uncle knows, it is an Evangelical Movement which has sprung up within the Romanian Orthodox Church. For months the Communist Party tried to coerce Dad to write political poetry for them. He was spied upon for ten long years and imprisoned twice during that period. Finally, his constitution collapsed under the strain, and we had to watch him slowly waste away. He had not been allowed adequate medical care while in prison, and when he returned home it was too late. The doctors who were available could do nothing more for him; the specialists who might have been of more real help demanded more money than we could afford. So four years ago, my wonderful father peacefully passed into the Presence of the One for Whom he had so faithfully lived and so willingly died."

Here Esther broke down and sobbed unrestrainedly. And each one listening, in their own individual way, was deeply moved. Uncle John blinked back the tears as best he could; Ramona had to use her Kleenex every few minutes, while Rachel's moist eyes and clenched fists revealed the feeling she was trying so hard to hide. At last Esther managed to continue:

"And Mother," she paused and broke down again, looking so pale and worn that Uncle John was on the verge of bidding her stop her story-telling for that night at least but, as if reading his thoughts, she choked back the tears and said reassuringly, "No, Uncle John, it's all right. I have to go on. You need to know and I need to tell it all. And you must be wondering why I began with Dad and not with my mother for, as you will remember, she died six years before he did. But her death was so sudden, so very horrible and unexpected, that I still can't think of it without horror."

Again her uncle would have interrupted but his niece hurried on. "No, let me get it over. I have to talk about it. I've bottled it up for years. You see, she was Dad's true soul-mate. She was beautiful, very beautiful." Esther's voice choked as a vision of her mother rose before her.

"Yes, she was very beautiful," John couldn't help but put in. "Just like you, Esther."

His niece blushed and shook her head. "She was more beautiful than I am, Uncle, and much more gracious, capable, and intelligent. And she backed Dad in all that he did. She was a wonderful mother.

"And then, one weekend about ten and a half years ago, during the first of Dad's imprisonments, my sister Gabriella and I were invited by my aunt in Ploiesti to spend the weekend with her. Mother was alone in our two bedroom apartment on the ninth story when it struck the center of Bucharest, the earthquake I mean, at about ten that Friday evening. It registered 7.4 on the Richter scale. Many had warned the government that the buildings would never stand a severe earthquake, but the selfish bureaucracy was not concerned with the safety of the masses. Mother and quite a few of my school friends were found under the rubble the next morning. In fact, the total death toll was 1500."

Esther paused again to regain her composure. Ramona gasped in horror. Uncle John's face blanched, and Rachel clenched her fists still tighter.

"And," continued Esther, "if we had not accepted my aunt's invitation and we nearly didn't, I would not be here today to tell you this sad story. It was Mother who saved our lives. She persuaded us to go to Ploiesti that weekend. You see, Aunt Ana is mother's adopted sister. My grandparents adopted her after they returned to Romania from the States. She's very different from mother though she's been awfully kind to Gabby and me, but my sister never has gotten on that well with her, and that memorable Friday she made it plain she did not want to stay with her for the weekend. But finally she agreed to go, just to please mother whom she absolutely adored. You see, with Dad in prison, we were each other's security, in a way, and even though I was only nine, Mom often confided her loneliness and heartache to me as if I had been her equal in age and in experience.

"When my aunt broke the news to me that never-to-be-forgotten Saturday morning, I rushed out the door, intending to catch the first train back to Bucharest, but I realized I had no money of my own and turned back in despair. My sister was sleeping so peacefully we hated to disturb her, but when we finally broke the news to her she was utterly inconsolable. I suppose having to take care of her, she's just over two years younger than I am, helped me cope with my own grief. In the end, they never did let us see Mother's body. They said it was mangled beyond recognition.

"You can imagine Dad's grief when he heard the news. Alone in prison, a prematurely old man, he was now facing what remained of his life without his one and only true love. He was released just after Mother's death on compassionate grounds, and he and I would console each other with the reminder that our loved one was in Heaven, in a land far better than Romania, where the Ruler was all Love, where there was no night, or sorrow, or tears. We told each other that we must trust Him, that He knew best, and for some purpose unknown to us mortals, He had chosen to take Mother to Himself when she was just thirty-five years of age. At times, Dad and I were beside ourselves with a weight of sorrow which seemed utterly unbearable. Then, through prayer, it would lift and life would go on once more."

Esther paused again, and it seemed to those watching as though some unseen Presence was with her. John's eyes were transfixed on his niece's face as she continued: "Then Dad was imprisoned again and we had to live with Aunt Ana until he was released about nine months later. We were overjoyed to have him back and be a family again, but his health got steadily worse, and Gabby and I took turns nursing him day and night. In a way, those were very special years though extremely difficult ones. Dad shared many things with us, and I have jotted some of them down. I want to write about his life one day."

Esther's relatives had never heard the full account of her parents' death as she was telling it that Sunday evening. No one stirred a muscle as she went on, her story not quite over: "We lived together in a suburb of Bucharest for several more years until God chose to take Dad, too, to Himself. As for my poor little sister, I'm afraid she has never really gotten over the double tragedy. She's a deep thinker and finds it so hard to reconcile the God she had been taught to consider as a loving Father with the Supreme Being Who had allowed these terrible things to happen to us. My one comfort was that my parents were now together at last, never to part again.

"My aunt took us to live with her permanently and tried to be both mother and father to us, for she had never married. Our grandparents on both sides were dead, so Aunt Ana was the one living relative we had in Romania. We began going to her church in Ploiesti, and because of my language skills, I was often asked to be an interpreter when foreigners visited our church."

Then Esther explained how her mother and grandfather, between them, had insisted that both girls become bilingual. "So," she continued, "I grew up thinking in English as easily, almost, as in Romanian. After Grandfather died, Mother continued to talk English with us, with me especially that is, for Gabby never took to it like I did. She has a stubborn streak and finally Mom gave up trying to force her, though we all suspect she knows a lot more than she lets on.

"I suppose folks talked about my ability as an interpreter in the church and it got to official ears, or, more likely, the secret police had been present when I had been acting as a translator. The next thing I knew, I had an offer, well, it really amounted to a command, from the local Communist Party Headquarters to become one of their official translators after I finished high school. I was approaching graduation at the time. My friends at school, some of them at least, envied me. But my church family knew what it would mean for my faith. I would have to become, to all intents and purposes, a Communist, something I could never do.

"But my dilemma was real. My fate could be similar to my father's if I refused. If that was to be God's will for me, I could and would face it with the same courage he had shown through all sorts of persecution. And," the girl paused and her face darkened as she went on, "there was another reason why I had to leave so suddenly. The son of a high-up Communist official in the city had dogged my steps for nearly a year. In the end, he made my life nearly unbearable." Esther's voice choked. "I just can't say more now. It was too horrible. Maybe some day I'll tell you more about it. All I can say now is that the letter you wrote, Uncle John, inviting me to make my home with you in America, came just in the nick of time. It was my lifesaver. Even after that, it was touch and go at times whether I would receive permission to leave the country. But, my mother having been an American citizen and my being invited by you, meant that the Romanian authorities were under pressure from the American Consulate and could not very well refuse. So here I am, Uncle John, Ramona, and Rachel—Esther Popescu, aged nineteen going on twenty—penniless or almost, but for what I'm worth, I'm at your service and on your hands, for better or for worse."

Esther gulped, leaned back in her chair, and closed her eyes. She had done it. Another hurdle had been crossed. Then she felt two arms embracing her and heard Ramona's voice speaking softly in her ear: "Oh Esther, what you have suffered! It makes our troubles seem nothing at all." And then, wonder of wonders, Rachel came behind her and laid her hand gently on Esther's dark, wavy tresses. "You are our sister now, Esther, our own sister," she murmured, her compassion for once getting the better of her. "And," she added as an afterthought, "when Gabriella comes, she'll be our sister too. You must miss her terribly!"

Esther put one arm round Ramona and the other around Rachel while Uncle John came behind her chair and planted a kiss on her damp forehead. "Yes, my dear child, you are at home now. We will take care of you, protect you, provide for you, and love you." The feeling of guilt he had carried ever since he had heard of his brother's death seemed to evaporate in Esther's presence. He felt she forgave him without realizing it—forgave him for not coming sooner to their rescue.

John had thought of attending his brother's funeral, but he had been afraid that, once in Romania, he would not be allowed to return to the States. So he had salved his conscience with promises that, some day, somehow, he would do something for his orphan nieces. But absorbed in his growing business, the building of a new home, and with a marriage fast going to pieces, he had procrastinated for three long years. Then when Mary had finally left him, he immediately began to reach out to Andrei and Sylvia's girls, and after a few letters had been exchanged, invited them to come and make their home with him. Esther had sometimes wondered why her American relatives had taken so long to contact them. But now that was all in the past. It was good to feel surrounded by family once more and she felt greatly comforted.

Silence reigned for some moments, and it seemed to the others that Esther's presence was uniting them, pulling them back to a focal point, reminding them of all their blessings. They could, at least for that one night, forget their own tragedy as they reached out to the orphan girl in her loneliness and sorrow.

Just then, the clock chimed eight. John started and glanced at Rachel. He had promised to drive her back to her mother's before it got too late as she had to prepare for school in the morning. And he was sadly reminded as he put on his jacket and got out his car keys, that the family which had just informally adopted the Romanian girl as their own was a fragmented one. Had he been really wise to invite his niece into a divided home? Would she be happy with them? Could she be? Or would she one day, when his heart had entwined itself around hers, echo her mother's words, "We have very little in common, you and I. We can never be truly happy together." And would she exit from their lives as quietly and as suddenly as she had entered? Surely history would not repeat itself. Oh God, it surely would not!

It was a question he could not answer, but that night, for the first time in many years, John Popescu knelt by his bed and asked God to let his little niece be happy in his home, far from perfect though that home might be, and, much to his surprise, he went to bed, his heart strangely lightened.

Chapter Eight

Letter to Gabby

"Dear Gabby," Esther began. This was her first letter to her sister. She could only hope that it would get to her safely. She could never be certain. Letters were opened at random and kept back if they contained anything thought to be contrary to Communist propaganda. But if it did arrive safely, she could imagine bright-eyed Gabby grabbing the letter and waving it wildly in the air as she exclaimed in anything but a quiet voice, "A letter from Esther!" She could also hear her aunt expostulating in her low, even tones, "Quietly, Gabby. The whole block doesn't need to hear you." Then her sister would tear open the envelope, forgetting about saving the stamps, flop down in the rickety old green sofa and devour every vestige of news from the West, stopping occasionally to insert her own apt comments, or giving her hearty chuckle as she read something that amused her.

Writing home brought back a flood of memories to the homesick girl. Several large tears trickled onto her notepaper as she continued: "One whole week has passed since I set foot on American soil. It seems like an eternity—so much has been packed into seven short days. I hope it won't be too long before I adapt to the rhythm of my new life. Oh, how I miss you all back home. Sometimes I can hardly stand it. And then again, at other times I feel how wonderful it is to revel in the love of my newfound family and to indulge in the many luxuries all around me, especially Uncle John's library! Oh Gabby, how you would love it!"

Esther paused, pen in hand. Books had always been her family's treasures but her father had been forced to hide some of his Christian classics. All printed material was vetted and heavily censored. The Communist Party did not want the people to know what they were missing in the way of freedom of speech or economical prosperity, and literature was one way to open their eyes. So although she and her sister had read much more than most of their peers, their voracious appetite for books had never been fully satisfied.

During that first week in her new home, Esther had spent long hours in the comfort of her uncle's recliner, getting acquainted with many well-known English and American writers. She thought it wisest not to refer to any of this in her letter so she went on: "I am sitting writing in the den, or family room, the most comfy spot in the whole house in my opinion, though maybe not as elegant as the living room. Just opposite me are the large patio doors which open out onto the back yard. Sometimes I just stand in the middle of the lawn and imagine I'm in paradise. Oh, Gabby, what space! No high fences here."

Esther paused. No, she could not put that last phrase in her letter, so she jumped from her seat and soon returned with her uncle's "wite out." It was so annoying to be restricted in this way, but she would have to go on as best she could. "Just wide open grass and trees. And beyond, there are low, rolling hills. The trees are beginning to change, though I'm told that you have to go into the mountains to really see the colors. And the birds here—they're so colorful, just like the people. Nothing seems dull or drab. Would you believe it, I bought a bright red winter jacket the other day? Can you picture me in red? Ramona says it really suits me." A fleeting vision of herself in the white fur flitted before her eyes. Then she smiled as she remembered the two crisp one hundred dollar bills that lay tucked away in an envelope in her dresser. The clock chiming four reminded her of the chicken soup and dumplings she had promised to make for supper, so she put her pen to paper once more:

"And inside the house, Gabby, there are thick carpets, soft velvety curtains, chairs that open up so that you can sit with your feet up, and, yes, they don't have springs that stick into your bottom or spine."

Esther paused again. That wouldn't do either. She grabbed the bottle of "wite out" and obliterated the last part of her sentence. She shook her head despairingly. What really was safe to write to her sister? The more time she spent in America, the more she realized just what she had left behind. The contrast was so overwhelming at times that she had to block it out of her mind. She wondered how Gabby would cope when she finally made it to freedom. But she must go on. She took up her pen once more and continued:

"Actually I'm sitting right now on what they call a love seat. Strange name, isn't it? It's a sofa just made for two. Then there's a music center right by me here with a bunch of tapes stacked on one side. Some are classical and some are rock. Ramona loves rock music though uncle and Rachel prefer classical. And the color TV in the corner is the largest I have ever seen; there's one in the next room too, a small portable in my bedroom, and I think Ramona has one as well. You should see her flip from one channel to another with her remote control!

"Ramona, by the way, is as pretty as a picture, though she is a bit plump (*you* would probably call her 'fat'), but by American standards she's far from that; she's very shapely really and extremely glamorous when she gets dressed up, with a mass of golden curls and eyes blue as the sky. Movie stars seem to be her role models though, unlike many of them, Ramona's a natural blonde. Blondes seem all the rage here, at least so my cousin tells me. I don't think I'll dye my hair, though. Seems I'm quite a novelty as I am, at least I get a good many stares, though I think it's my clothes that make folks gawk at me like they do. I felt as if I'd stepped right out of the ark when I first arrived.

"But to get back to Ramona; she's awfully good natured, though doesn't know how to cook which quite amazed me at first. And it seems like she's addicted to the TV for she doesn't read much. Sometimes I slip out of the room when she turns on 'Dallas' or other soap operas. She's obsessed with them. And last Saturday night she stayed up to watch a late movie which was decidedly not to my taste. In fact, it quite horrified me the little I saw of it, though uncle seemed quite unconcerned and even watched it himself for a while. I must admit, though, that at times the TV does often draw me like a magnet; it worries me a bit, but watching it does help me understand this culture better, it really does."

Esther stopped again, biting her pen as she remembered hours of Communist propaganda to which they had been subjected for years. The Iron Curtain had certainly kept them from news of the world outside their little land. Now it was different. The whole universe seemed to be opening up to her. She could travel to almost every country on earth without setting foot on a plane or paying a penny for a train ticket. She seldom missed the news hour which was an education in itself. She would listen spellbound to President Reagan's speeches, and had been fascinated by Margaret Thatcher and her harangue against the evils of Communism. But Esther never could understand America's soft spot for Ceausescu. He had evidently hoodwinked the world, or most of it. Sometimes she would rise from her seat and face the newscaster. "It's not only the Soviet Union that you need to fight," she would tell him. "Turn your attention to our pathetic little land. Liberate us. Don't listen to our leader's speeches or his flattering words. He's a hypocrite, a monster, and his wife is ten times worse." Then she would collapse into a chair, chagrined at her outburst but feeling better for having given vent to her emotions.

She had already learned that her uncle and Ramona were decidedly Republican in their views, but that Rachel seemed to be a thorough Democrat by all she could gather from the little her cousin ever spoke about such matters. And though the presidential election was over a year away, candidates were lining up already. Esther was quite a little politician in her own way and entered into debates with great gusto. Her uncle would laugh at her enthusiasm and say she should run for governor.

But she knew she could speak of none of this to her faraway sister. Nor could she tell her how safe she felt in her Uncle's home in Velours and how those awful nightmares had suddenly stopped. In fact she had not even had one since she had left Romania. But then, of course, she wouldn't be dreaming them anymore. There was no one now to stop her in her short walks to the supermarket up the road; no threatening phone calls late at night; no suggestive letters arriving every few weeks. She gave a long drawn out sigh of relief that made Ramona's pet poodle, Toofy, raise her languid eyes to her face and shake her long silky ears before resuming her nap on the sofa. She had been at the vet when Esther had first arrived but that Monday had made her appearance. Esther wasn't used to dogs in the house and it had greatly bothered her when she found out that Toofy devoured more meat in one day than her aunt did in a week. But that was another thing she couldn't share with Gabby in a letter so she began again:

"Then there are the videos—all sorts. I especially like the classics—Dickens, Shakespeare, Hardy, Tolstoy, Dostoevsky—they are all here. But, ironically enough Gabby, it is when I am enjoying myself the most that I feel the loneliest, the most isolated, and the most alien. Maybe I feel guilty that I am indulging myself like this when you all are so very many miles away," and, she added mentally, putting all your energies into merely existing, in keeping enough bread on the table, or paying the light bills. "Or maybe," she went on, "it's the feeling that I am becoming addicted to the 'box.' True, I never let myself look at anything questionable; Ramona thinks me awfully stuffy in my ideas though she is too polite to say so in so many words."

Another pause, for Esther was aware at times of a disquiet within that she was not accustomed to, she called it a "niggling" feeling, trying to make her aware that something indefinable was surrounding her, enveloping her, imprisoning her. She would sometimes remember Hugh's warnings about the Velvet Curtain and would put up a quick prayer to her Father in Heaven to keep her from the dangers and evils that lurked hidden in her new and extremely comfortable life.

It took a long while to finish her letter but at last it was done. Yet she had omitted so much. She dare not write Gabby of her true religious feelings, of how, when Wednesday evening had come and gone and no mention had been made of going to a mid-week Bible Study or prayer-meeting, she had realized how much she missed her church in Ploiesti and the daily Bible reading with her aunt in their little kitchen each morning. Coming from an environment where God was daily consulted about nearly everything, Esther found it strange and rather frightening that His name was rarely if ever mentioned in her new home. She hoped she would not starve to death spiritually for lack of good, healthy meals to feed her desire for God. So faithfully, every morning and evening, she would read and pray and meditate as best she could and she felt that her unseen Companion saw her efforts and would keep alive that spark of desire which sometimes seemed to flicker sadly and threaten to go out. And it worried her somewhat that if she felt like this after only a week in America, what condition would her spiritual life be in after one year!

But Esther was very human, and what nineteen-year-old who had just left the cheerless, stultified atmosphere of Romania as it was in the 1980's would not bask in the comfort of middle class America? Freedom blinded her at times, frightened her often, but always seemed to beckon her to explore life as she had never done before, to enjoy it, to become a new Esther, an enlightened Esther, a liberated Esther.

After only a week in her new home, there was elasticity in her step, a sparkle in her fine dark eyes, and a smile on her lips that made her uncle comment as he sat over his newspaper that Friday evening, "Why, one week in the land of the free has transformed my little niece. If you keep filling out like that, you'll catch up with Ramona. And I wouldn't do that if I were you," and he dodged as a well-aimed cushion flew past his head.

"Dad, how dare you!" his daughter protested. "And anyway, I'm not really fat, you've said that yourself. Besides, Esther will never catch me up. It's not her style. She'll never lose her slim figure. Anyway, once she starts to college, she'll have more exercise, you know. And in the summer there's the pool. She'll look great in a bikini, won't she? She might even make it to the cover of a woman's magazine." Ramona's eyes looked dreamy as if it was herself not Esther that she pictured as a glamorous cover girl.

Esther winced. She had never worn a bikini in all her nineteen years.

"Don't put such ideas into her head, Ramona," her father warned, frowning a little. "And don't flatter her too much. Her humility is one of the best things about her."

His niece shook her head. "You don't know me yet, uncle. I'm awfully vain at times, really I am."

"You have every right to be," said John fondly. "But speaking of college reminds me, we must discuss your future before we go much further. What do you want to do with your life? Become a flight attendant? You'd make a pretty one and see the world into the bargain. Or even better, what about becoming an astronaut? You'd get a chance to see more than just our world. No, I forgot, your line is politics. Sorry, you're not a native born American so there's no chance for President."

"Uncle," put in his niece laughing, "my ambitions are more realistic. I think I'd like to be a translator. My abilities are along the linguistic lines, I think."

John frowned. "A translator of what, pray tell me? And into what? And from what?"

Esther's brow puckered. She had long had ambitions of translating some good Christian books into Romanian so that when freedom came, and she hoped against hope that it would come in the not too distant future, these books would be ready for publication. There was such a dearth of Christian literature in Romania. But, at present, there wasn't much money to be made out of translating this kind of literature, and she desperately wanted to become independent so that she need not live indefinitely on her Uncle's bounty. So she answered slowly, "Eventually I want to translate Christian books into Romanian, but at present maybe I could get a job locally as a translator of some sort or other."

Her uncle looked thoughtful. "You know, Esther, over here, whatever your final goal might be, you have to start with a degree if you want a decent job. I think you've just graduated from high school, right?" His niece nodded. "So first things first. You will need a BA degree, majoring in languages, and then, we'll see."

"But Uncle," the girl reddened. "I need to start making money. I can't...." She was too embarrassed to go further, but her Uncle came to the rescue.

"I know perfectly what you are trying to say, my dear. But you are my adopted daughter now and I am going to treat you as one. So understand my terms: room and board free, a few hours a week to act as companion to an old man when Ramona takes it into her head to gallivant. Then just make a dish of ciorba (special Romanian soup) at least once a week, and sarmale (stuffed cabbage or vine leaves) every month or so, and our bargain will be complete. After Christmas, you'll go with Ramona to Indiana State University. And I think I won't have to pay a cent for your tuition if I've weighed you up correctly. I think you'll get a full scholarship."

"And, Uncle, I'm real good at housecleaning," Esther announced proudly, "at least so Dad would tell me. He said I scared away the dust like nothing he'd ever seen in all his life." She laughed. The others noticed she was laughing more each day.

"We have a cleaning lady coming each week, Esther," John told her, patting her dark hair affectionately. "She hasn't come for two weeks, so you haven't seen her yet. She was away on vacation and now she's down with the flu. But she'll be here next Friday and will really give the whole house a going over. If Jean's nothing else, she is thorough."

Esther was silent. She couldn't understand this. With two daughters, why should there be any need for a cleaning lady? John seemed to read her thoughts. "When Mary left," he said, his face darkening, "we decided to have someone come. Not that Ramona couldn't do it," he explained defensively, "but she's away all week. Rachel likes that sort of thing better than her sister, but I don't want her spending her weekends cleaning out the place."

"But I'm here now, Uncle," Esther reminded him, "and it will be a while before I can start college so I'll have piles of time on my hands."

"Yes," John admitted, "but in January you won't, so it's not worth stopping Jean and then looking for someone else in a few months' time. She's a good sort of gal and we're used to her. If we lost her, there's no telling who we'd get in her place. So let it drop. Don't worry your pretty head about it. Now if you'll cook a bit for us, that'd help a lot. I don't particularly like fast food or TV dinners. And eating out is OK once a week or so but there's nothing beats home cooking."

Esther was delighted though she wondered again how a girl like Ramona could reach the mature age of twenty and not be more practical round the house. She absolutely loved cooking, though, as she remembered with a smile, Gabby wasn't very adept at it and positively hated housework. But her uncle was continuing, "To get back to the subject of college—you'll need to take the SAT first; it's a sort of entrance exam."

"I'll begin studying right away," promised Esther, "but I'll need some coaching. I'm not used to Western type exams though I've heard they're not difficult if you get the hang of them."

"I'd help you if I could," volunteered Ramona who had just returned to the room after one of her long telephone conversations in the kitchen, "but I'm not the brainiest in the family. Rachel might do it if it struck her the right way. She's brilliant."

Esther was not surprised to hear this. She had correctly surmised that her cousin's precocity might lie behind at least some of her problems.

"Ask her if she'll help me, will you Ramona?"

"No, it'd be better if you ask her yourself. I think you'll have a better chance of her agreeing. When I ask her to do something she sees red."

"Sees red?" Esther didn't understand.

"She gets suspicious and upset," Ramona explained. "She thinks there's a trap somewhere. Right now, it doesn't seem she trusts anyone. But she just might do it for you."

Esther lost no time in calling her young cousin and making her request. After a moment's hesitation, Rachel agreed, though in her own unemotional way, and said she would be over the next evening.

"What time is Rachel coming?" queried Ramona.

"Not till seven."

"Good," exclaimed Ramona in a pleased tone. "That means we can go out tomorrow and get back easily by seven. Ron's taking me to the movies after he's dropped you off."

"Go out?" echoed Esther, not paying any attention to the last piece of information given in a rather triumphant tone. "But where?"

"Ron has offered to take us for a run to Pine Mountain State Park. The trees should be beautiful up there. The forecast is for unusually warm and sunny weather for tomorrow. And," she added, "Ron thought it would be a great chance to show you round a bit. So you'd better go with us. And we've invited his cousin to come along too," she put in hastily seeing the surprise on Esther's face. "He's real religious—youth pastor in a big church on the edge of Terre Haute. Thought you would feel more at home with someone like that in the car. We noticed you were a bit uneasy with us heathen the other day."

This was only partly true. It had been Ramona who had insisted on taking someone else with them. Secretly, she had no intention of sharing Ron with another girl more than she could help and thought that maybe some religious fellow might hit it off with her cousin and take her off their hands now and then. Ron said he knew of no one he could invite, and then Ramona reminded him of his cousin, Len Atwood, whom she had never met herself but had heard about him from Ron and others.

Esther could not hide her consternation. "Oh come on, it'll do you good," Ramona assured her, as she saw the hesitation in her cousin's expressive face.

"When you wheedle like that, Ramona, there's no refusing," laughed Esther, though she was secretly dismayed. She'd much rather curl up with a book, or start studying for the SAT, or cook her uncle the favorite Romanian dish that she had promised him, than spend a whole day with strangers, Ramona excepted of course. "But," she added as an afterthought, "Why is Rachel not going? Wouldn't she enjoy it too?"

Ramona pouted. "Rachel? Oh no! If there's a boy anywhere around, she acts like a zombie. She'd never go. And besides, it would crowd you in the back seat."

"I'm used to being crowded," Esther was going to say but something in Ramona's face made her drop the subject. Another time, when she knew both her cousins better, she wouldn't give up so easily. But right now, plans had been made and that was it. Oh well, at least there would be four of them. The young people from the church back in Romania had occasionally gone on group outings. It was unheard of to go out with a boy alone unless you were engaged to him, and an engagement in her culture was practically as binding as marriage itself. Esther had little conception of the American idea of courtship and wasn't exactly sure what Ramona's relationship really was with the handsome Ron Atwood.

Ron, however, had instantly realized Ramona's scheming and resented it. All he had wanted to do was to show the cute little Romanian girl around, and Ramona had gone and made it sound like a double date. "Women!" he told himself as he hung up the phone; "they twist you round their little finger without an effort on their part. Especially that Ramona."

"What's up Ron?" his mother had asked, hearing him muttering. "What pickle have you gotten yourself into now?"

"Nothing at all, Mom," was the reply. "Just taking Ramona and her cousin out for a ride tomorrow. And Ramona has suggested we take Len along."

"Double date, eh?" grinned Mrs. Atwood looking a little relieved. "Well, Len will act the part OK. He's popular enough with the girls even if he is some sort of pastor. By the way, what's this little Romanian like?"

"Can't tell yet," was the somewhat curt reply. "One lunch together with Ramona chattering most of the time doesn't give much chance to get to know someone. I'll probably be able to tell you more this time tomorrow."

"But is she pretty?"

Her son reddened just a little then admitted, "Yes, well, pretty isn't exactly how I'd describe her." For the first time in his life, Ron Atwood was at a loss for words when he tried to depict a girl! His mother saw this and was puzzled. It made her curious. She wanted to meet someone who had bamboozled her resourceful son and she told Ron so.

"I'll maybe come back tomorrow with such horrific tales about this wild gypsy girl that you won't want to go anywhere near her," he told her mischievously.

"A gypsy," gasped his mother. "Oh no, Ron!"

"Yes, a gypsy," teased her son. "Maybe she's a gypsy queen. She's regal enough."

"Regal?" His mother grasped at the word. "So she *is* beautiful?"

"Well, she is attractive in her own way," he admitted, then stopped. He felt himself blushing again much to his chagrin.

"And?"

"Look Mom, why don't you invite her here and see for yourself if you're all that curious."

Diane Atwood caught the roguish look in his eye and shook her head. "The woman that tames you will have to be a queen with a golden scepter, a will of iron, the patience of Job, and the wisdom of Solomon!"

"Such a woman does not exist in my world or in yours either, so I'm safe," retorted her son. "Good night and sweet dreams about wild gypsy queens." And Ron ran up the stairs two at a time, leaving his mother to look fondly after him. Divorced after years of unhappy marriage and with heart problems that could flare up at any time, she had leaned on Ron more and more over the last few years. What would she ever do without him!

Chapter Nine

Pine Mountain

When Esther came downstairs that Saturday morning, Ramona eyed her approvingly. She had put on one of the sweaters she had picked up at the garage sale—white with small roses embroidered all over. Her thick black hair was tied back in a pony tail to keep the wind from whipping it around. Ramona had practically insisted that her cousin put on a pair of jeans as she said it would be much more modest getting in and out of the car, or hiking through the woods, or climbing up the mountain, and Esther had complied. She had bought some culottes and argued that they would do just as well. But the look on Ramona's face made her think twice. She would be the odd one out anyway, Esther reasoned, so why hold out on something so trivial? But part of her rebelled. Why was she not at liberty to dress as she liked? She was in a free country now, wasn't she?

"Anything seems to suit her," Ron thought to himself, as he handed Esther into the back seat a few moments later, "and what a change in one week!" But while his admiring glance brought color into her cheeks, it did nothing to alleviate her uneasiness. It was the first time in her life that she did not feel herself in her clothes. After only ten days in her new home, it seemed that she was fast becoming an American version of the Esther who had plodded the dusty streets of Ploiesti in search of nourishing food for her dying father, or the girl who had to have her shoes mended before going to her graduation ceremony. But, she assured herself, as they sped along to Len's house, inside she was the same old Esther Popescu.

She had little time for further reflection for soon they had drawn up in front of Len's apartment. Esther groaned inwardly as a tall slim, young man emerged from the first doorway and approached Ron's shiny red convertible. His thick wavy chestnut brown hair, rather longer than average, gave him the appearance of an artist or musician.

The young man beamed benignly upon both girls as Ron went through the introductions, and though he said little as he climbed into the back seat beside Esther, his flashing dark eyes spoke volumes and made her feel more uncomfortable than ever. She had never felt truly at ease with most boys, unlike her sister, who seemed at home with anyone and everyone. And here she was, doomed to sit beside a modern and sophisticated young man for what might prove to be hours.

Ramona tried to keep up a running conversation with Ron as he sped along the interstate, but he seemed quieter than usual, though friendly and pleasant as always. His eyes, she noticed to her chagrin, had a tendency to stray to the rear vision mirror. And more than once she saw him smile and nod, not at his cousin Len she felt sure, for his glances in that direction had not been too amiable.

With the convertible top down, it was difficult to communicate with those in the back so Esther was left to Len. He had soon gotten more information out of her than most people managed to extract in a day and he did it so casually she hardly noticed she was giving it. She suspected, though, that he knew far less about Romania than his cousin did, as some of his questions implied. His sidelong glances and his arm stretched casually along the back of her seat made her fidgety and nervous.

"Put on some music, Ron," Ramona suggested. "Something to liven us up a bit." He popped a cassette into the player. It was one he thought she would like. And he was right. She flashed him a broad smile as the music began to play, but glancing in the mirror Ron saw Esther grimace. "Not used to that type of music are you?" He had to shout in order to make her hear.

"No," came the reply.

"You'll get used to it, Esther," Ramona assured her, as she started swinging to the rhythm.

"I doubt whether she'll ever get used to Madonna's lyrics," Ron muttered half to himself, but Ramona heard him and frowned.

"We must remember," shouted Len above the din, "that Esther has never been in the West before. Here, I've something a bit more Christian. Ron, put that in the player, will you?"

Len handed his cousin a tape. Ramona bit her lip as Gospel words began to vibrate through the speakers. Then she smiled. "What's this group called, Len? It's not bad for a Christian rock group."

"Petra," was the answer. "Comes from the word in Greek meaning 'a rock.' Play on words, probably," and Len grinned. But Esther was not smiling. Why Christians had to mix the Gospel with music like this she had no idea. But she said nothing, for she thought Len was trying his best to bring some religion on the scene. Ron, however, could see her expression through the mirror. "This music!" he grumbled. "It's still too loud. We can't talk decently in all this din," and he switched off the cassette player.

"But I like it!" pouted Ramona. Ron ignored her.

"At least play the one side, Ron," Len urged. "The lyrics are great and inspiring."

His cousin complied reluctantly. Ramona turned round and said meaningfully, "Thanks a lot, Len."

"A pleasure to satisfy the wishes of a beautiful young lady," he said with a wink. "And then," he went on, patting Ramona on the shoulder and leaning towards Esther at the same time, "when this one side is over, we'll try to satisfy the wishes of another, if we can, that is," and he flashed the girl beside him one of his most brilliant smiles. "By the way," he added, "what kind of music do you like?"

"Classical and hymns and some folk music," was Esther's prompt response. "We don't hear much contemporary Christian singing, so I'm just not used to it."

"Actually," put in Ron, "I have a lot of classical tapes at home, but most of my friends don't share my taste. Wait a minute, I have something here you might like," and he fumbled in the glove box until he found a Mozart concerto. "We'll put it in when this is finished. I'm sorry I don't have any hymns. I'm afraid they're not in my line. And I've never heard Romanian folk music."

"I was pretty much brought up on classical," Len commented with a smile, "so I'm fond of it too, though I like a change now and then."

They were approaching the hills now, and Esther was captivated by the beauty of the scenery. The wind whipped stray strands of hair over her face, do what she could to restrain them. America was truly a colorful land, she thought, as she breathed in the beauty of the countryside. Len told her she should go into the Appalachians if she really wanted a blaze of color, but, for the time being at any rate, she was perfectly satisfied with the hills of Southern Indiana.

Soon they turned into a side road to the state park and Esther was entranced. When they reached the parking area, they left the car and began to climb the narrow trail that led to the top of Pine Mountain, really only an oversized hill, Ron told them, but worth the climb. The sweet smell of the pine needles reminded her of the Transylvanian Alps. She pictured the little cottage nestled in the mountains where their family would spend the summer holidays when she and her sister were still quite young and before the really hard times had set in. What long and wonderful walks she had taken with her father!

She wondered if he could see her now in her new and strange surroundings.

The path was too narrow for four, so Ramona took Ron's arm, leaving Esther to walk with Len. "Enjoying this, aren't you?" he commented; they had come into a clearing in the trees; she lifted her face to the sky letting the sun kiss her cheeks.

"The scenery and the weather? Oh yes," replied the girl, taking a deep breath. "It's glorious here, and the air is so clear. Romania is terribly polluted, you know."

"This must be a real change for you in every way," commented her companion. "Sometime, I'd love to hear more about life there and," he paused and looked at her meaningfully, "about the Romanian church. You are a Christian, I take it. You certainly look like one."

Esther nodded, not sure if this last statement was meant as a compliment or not. Then dropping back until he was sure they were out of earshot of the young couple in front, Len whispered confidentially in her ear, "I hope you didn't take offence at my insisting that we play that tape for Ramona's sake?"

Esther looked up in surprise. "Offended? Why of course not? Why should I be?"

Her response was so genuine and unaffected that Len was taken aback for a moment. He was used to girls whose words did not often convey what they really felt deep inside, but this Romanian seemed transparent. For once, he was taken off guard and it was some moments before he resumed, "I don't suppose Ramona is a Christian, is she?"

"That's not for me to say, Len," Esther replied slowly, "though I don't see how she can love the Lord Jesus very much when she doesn't talk of Him or want to go to His house. But then, I can't see inside her heart. She's been kind enough to me since I arrived, and seems a really pleasant sort of person."

Len nodded. "Yes, she's quite charming. Would make a wonderful Christian. That's why I'm trying to win her, you see. I can't lose an opportunity like this to witness, not by words so much as by actions—by being friendly and by showing her that I'm human as well as a pastor."

Esther could not hide the wry smile that would come to her lips; Len's dark eyes shot her a meaningful look. "Laughing at me, aren't you?" he asked just a little reproachfully.

Esther blushed before replying, "Not really laughing, but I'm not used to your type of witnessing."

"No, I suppose not," Len was taken aback again. This girl could take the wind out of his sails quicker than anyone he knew. "But remember, you've lived your life in a Communist country where everything is black and white, I suppose. But here, you have to use any means you can to win someone to Christ." Seeing his companion's expression he added hastily, "St. Paul himself advised this, you know."

Esther was saved any further response for the path was steep now and narrower and she was getting out of breath. But at last the summit was reached. Below them a lake glittered like a jewel. Esther dropped Len's arm and sat down on a boulder. Her eyes drunk in the peace of the October morning as she inhaled the pure, clear air. Her sigh of satisfaction made Ron smile. He liked girls who could appreciate more than just clothes and boyfriends.

"Room for one more on your seat, Esther?" Len queried as he sat down beside her, putting his arm around her to prevent her from losing her balance. His cousin frowned as he saw Esther's discomfiture.

"There's an even better lookout over there," Ron remarked after a few moments of silence.

Esther jumped up. "Where?" she asked eagerly, flashing him one of her rare smiles, as he helped her to climb onto a flat rock from which she could get a panoramic view of the valley below.

Ramona took her place beside Len, who told her with a short laugh, "Glad all girls aren't so scared of me. Makes me feel like an ogre."

"Oh, don't judge everyone by what Esther does," Ramona told him archly. "She's not like most girls."

"I should think she isn't!" was the emphatic reply. "But never mind Esther just now. Looks as if she's being well taken care of," and his eyes roamed to where his cousin was standing, pointing out the various landmarks to his companion.

Ramona's eyes followed his and narrowed ominously. "Seems like they're hitting it off," she said dryly. Then she brightened as she glanced at the young man sitting beside her. He was nearly as handsome as Ron Atwood and maybe just a bit more dashing and certainly much more artistic looking! And judging from those eyes of his, she was sure he would prove to be truly romantic, a contrast to his rather down-to-earth cousin.

For the rest of the day it was Ron, not Len, who kept by Esther's side. It seemed as if he had to protect her from his bold cousin, and

Ramona didn't seem to mind at all. It was decided that they would walk down to the lake and go for a row. Both men were experienced oarsmen, but it was Len who was the life and soul of the party. The more he talked and joked with Ramona, the quieter Ron became. He was taking every chance to study the Romanian girl without letting her know it. He marveled that she could so successfully keep his effervescent cousin at arm's length, quite a feat, he thought. He had never met anyone like her. Never!

The next few hours sped by and before they knew it, everyone had worked up a healthy appetite. Ramona and Esther had prepared a picnic lunch which was spread on one of the tables under the trees. Ramona fidgeted uncomfortably, as she saw Esther bow her head and close her eyes. Then she noticed that Len had done the same. "Bother these Christians," she thought. "Why do they have to wear their religion on their sleeve?" It was all over in a moment, however. Soon her cousin was munching away at her ham sandwich.

"This is good," exclaimed Esther, "I've never eaten so much in all my life as during this past week."

"America seems to suit you," Ron told her.

Esther blushed. "It's Ramona and Uncle John. They spoil me, you know."

"I'm sure you probably needed some spoiling."

"I only know I'm thriving on it," was her reply.

"What do you really think of America, Esther, now that you've been here eight or nine whole days?" and Ron looked at her quizzically.

"It's a beautiful country, and even more prosperous than I had imagined," was her prompt response.

"And the people?"

"The people I've met this week are all very pleasant, gracious, and hospitable," and she smiled at Ramona who did not seem particularly happy with the conversation.

"And the culture in general?" Ron wasn't going to let her off that easily.

"Oh come on, Ron, give her another month or two before you ask her to pass judgment on our culture," put in Len, who could never stay long out of any conversation.

"Very well," conceded Ron smiling, "in exactly six weeks' time I shall ask her the same question."

"I suppose after I've been to college I'll be able to answer you better," Esther said thoughtfully.

Ron raised his eyebrows. "What college and when?"

"She's taking the SAT before Christmas and seeing if she can enter Indiana State in January," put in Ramona. "And," she added significantly, "My sister is going to coach her starting tonight. Rachel's awfully clever," Ramona remarked, "though she's not much good in math, but then, probably Esther doesn't need much coaching in math."

Esther's mind had wandered so she did not see the direction the conversation was taking. She had been comparing the two young men sitting opposite her. Then the word "math" made her sit up. Not need coaching in math? They must be joking. So she answered brightly, "Oh but I do! Like Rachel, math is my worst subject."

"Then I'll be glad to help you out," offered Ron. And not giving her a chance to refuse he went on, "I'll come over next Friday evening if you're free and if your gracious hostess does not mind," and he made a mock bow at Ramona.

Ramona could have choked her cousin. She was growing fond of her, yet at that moment she felt she almost hated her. But she swallowed her annoyance and answered politely, "You're always welcome, Ron. You should know that! And after you've done your stint with Esther we can watch a movie together."

"Depends on how late it is when we finish," he replied without enthusiasm. "So now that's settled. We'd better get a move on as I want to take you another way home."

Len had been unusually silent during this conversation. If only he had been a whiz at math like Ron, he would have offered to coach her himself. He eyed the two girls admiringly as they began to clear away the picnic things. What a contrast they made—the glamorous blonde and her sweet, raven-haired little cousin!

He was just about to offer his help when Esther cried out in alarm: "Don't throw it all away, Ramona. Please don't! We can wash those plastic glasses out again and look, we didn't eat all the sandwiches, did we?"

Ramona's pleasant face clouded. "For goodness sake, Esther," she exclaimed crossly, "can't you remember you're in America now? We don't need to watch every cent, so we're not going to wash out those glasses. They're only meant to be used once. But here, take these two sandwiches. I didn't realize you were still hungry."

Esther heard the sarcasm in her cousin's voice and blushed scarlet, but she took the untouched leftovers and wrapped them in a piece of tinfoil still lying on the table. Ramona felt uncomfortable under

Ron's keen gaze and wished her cousin a thousand miles away. She knew she had been insensitive and felt downright humiliated in front of the two young men.

"I'll sit in the back with Len," she told Ron a few moments later. But to her annoyance, he only nodded and smiled as he muttered in a low voice, "Thanks Ramona. That's thoughtful of you. It'll give Esther a better view going home." And she thought he looked mighty pleased with himself and with all the world as he got into the driver's seat and started up the engine.

Esther said little as they sped homewards. She felt very self-conscious and out of place and was only too aware of her role as a stranger in a strange land. Ron did his best to make her feel at ease, pointing out various landmarks as they whizzed by, and flashing her a reassuring smile from time to time. It was not long before she began to relax and enjoy the beautiful fall afternoon. She found herself telling him about the Transylvanian Alps back home where she had spent so many happy hours as a child, about the quaint Moldovan village where her grandmother had lived and the sandy beaches of the Black Sea where they had gone on a school outing.

The air had grown chilly and Ron had put the top down which made conversation easier. Len found Ramona a much more responsive companion than the Romanian girl had been and was soon describing his job as youth pastor in Pine Grove Evangelical Church and his plans to bring in a more contemporary service as soon as he could. Ramona listened intently. It was all new to her, and she liked to have a handsome young man so close and paying her so much attention.

Ron glanced in the rear vision mirror. Ramona seemed very much at home with his cousin. He was glad of that. He had intended that very evening, when they would be alone together, to make it clear to the girl that their friendship had gone about as far as it could go, for he feared she was getting too fond of him and did not want to hurt her unnecessarily. But maybe he wouldn't need to say anything at all. If she and Len took to each other, it might just be all for the best in the long run.

They were back by five and met John Popescu at the door. He was on his way to pick up Rachel before he went out for his usual Saturday night at the Country Club. "Looks like you really enjoyed yourself, Esther," he remarked, as he glanced at his niece's face, tanned by the wind and sun.

"Yes, Uncle. The weather's been superb," she replied. Inwardly she wasn't sure she could use the term "enjoyed." At times she had been extremely uneasy. Len confused her and made her very ill at ease, though she had to admit that he was a real charmer. And she sensed that the day's outing had somehow increased the gap between herself and her cousin.

Ramona invited the two young men in for some refreshments, and as they entered the kitchen, she took Ron aside for a moment and whispered, "Any objection to inviting Len to come to the movies with us?"

Ron stared at her in surprise. It had been so obvious that she had wanted an evening alone with him. But he secretly welcomed this change of direction so said quickly, "Of course not. But what about Esther? We can't leave her out, can we?"

"Oh, Esther!" and Ramona's lip curled a little as she added, "you can ask her, but she won't come. And anyway, Rachel's coming at seven to help her prepare for the SAT."

As they sipped their soda and ate a large dish of ice cream, Ron turned to Len and Esther who were sitting opposite and asked suddenly, "Ramona and I had planned to go to the movies tonight and I would have asked you both to come along and make it a foursome, but I think you have other plans, Esther. Right?"

Esther was never more grateful for a genuine alibi. "Yes, Ron, though thanks anyway. I have already arranged with Rachel to coach me for a few hours tonight."

"But what about you, Len?" Ramona asked. "Can you go with us?"

"Movies are not exactly the best preparation for a Sunday at church for those of us who go," Len replied, looking significantly at Esther as he spoke. "And I had better first ask what kind of a movie it is. Youth pastors don't go to just any movie, you know."

"Oh, it's perfectly harmless. A comedy. Clean, no violence. Just humorous, I promise," assured Ramona laughing.

"Well then, how about striking a bargain? If I go with you tonight, will you both promise to come to church with me tomorrow?"

"I'm game," answered Ramona promptly. Ron had given her a very clear message that day that he was not interested in her romantically, so there was no point insisting on a private evening together. And Len was so lively, so interesting. Why not give church a chance for once?

"Great, Ramona! And you, Ron?" Len asked, not content with gaining in one quarter only.

"No promise, Len. The bargain is between you and Ramona," answered his cousin dryly. "Now, if we're going, we'd better be off."

Esther was astounded. She felt repulsed at the idea of bargaining to get anyone into church. That tactic wouldn't work in Romania, she thought. It would take more than that to lure a young person to risk their reputation by associating with the despised "pocaiti" ("the repentant ones"). But Len was speaking to her now:

"Esther, you'll come with us to church tomorrow, won't you?" he asked, as he made for the door.

"If Uncle doesn't mind, I'll be glad to," answered Esther.

"Good. I'll call for both of you at nine thirty tomorrow morning."

Ramona groaned as she slipped upstairs to change her clothes. "Nine thirty," she muttered to herself. "It'll kill me to get up that early on a Sunday. But a promise is a promise."

Esther thought she had never seen Ramona so attractive as she left with the two cousins for the cinema. Would she have gone if Rachel had not been coming to coach her that evening? She doubted it. She had never gone to the movies in her life and she was not about to start, at least not just like that.

Switching on the lamp by the window, she curled up in her favorite chair and had just picked up her book when she heard Rachel's footsteps in the hallway. She would be glad of company that evening, for she felt rather morbid and very homesick for Gabby and her friends so far away, friends who understood her feelings, her convictions, and her Christian lifestyle. Here it was wonderful in so many ways, luxurious almost, and yet it was all so confusing. There seemed to be so many gray areas now, when all had appeared so clear in Romania, so black and white. What she would give for just a few words of counsel from dear old Granny Sandelescu back home!

Her mind turned to the strange little man she had met on the plane. She was sure he would give her some useful advice, and he had said to get in touch with him if.... She paused; if what? She couldn't remember his exact words and anyway, she was pretty certain it wasn't the time to contact him yet. Maybe some day she would. Maybe some day!

Chapter Ten

Esther's Surprise Performance

"Shhhh! Someone's playing the piano." Ramona paused as she opened the front door. She had invited her companions to step in for a few moments and sample the cake Esther had made the day before.

"Who plays the piano at your house, Ramona?" Len whispered.

"Mom did, but the rest of us are not that musical," she whispered back. "The piano belongs to her, but she hasn't room for it where she's living just now. Must be Esther playing. Wow! I never knew she could play like that."

It was indeed Esther who was seated at the grand piano. She was no concert pianist, but with an excellent musical ear as well as five years of lessons behind her, she could sight read without much difficulty and played with great feeling. She dearly loved music. Her father used to say that she sang like an angel, and during those last months of illness, her singing had often made his pain easier to bear.

Esther had just finished her lesson with Rachel who had proved an apt teacher but who had withdrawn into her shell the minute the lesson was over, leaving her feeling tired and lonely again. Music had always been her solace, so she had seated herself on the stool and softly ran her fingers over the keys. Turning on the light above the piano, she had begun to play various melodies¯ folk tunes, hymn tunes, and improvisations. She became particularly carried away with the melody of one of her favorite Romanian hymns which brought back memories of past days and loved ones now gone to a better Land.

At first she was choked by too many memories to find her voice, but soon the ever present urge to sing overcame her, and she began at first very softly; then as her courage grew, her clear bell-like voicc filled the room. It was a plaintive, haunting tune in a minor key, typically Eastern and full of pathos.

Her listeners were thunderstruck. They could not understand the words, but the melody and the voice which sang it so beautifully captivated them. Tiptoeing to the living-room door they peeped in but were not prepared for the picture before them. The young singer, thinking herself alone, was totally uninhibited, pouring her very life into her song. Her voice rose and fell in the evening air, carrying her listeners into another realm. Just then, the music stopped, and they became aware of what a striking picture the young musician made. Her fine features were accentuated by the soft light from the lamp, and her long dark tresses, usually tied neatly back, were hanging in waves about her shoulders.

Len went to speak, but Ron held a finger to his lips. He was very musical himself and, though hymn-singing was not generally in his line, he had been deeply moved and was capable of appreciating talent when he saw it, and sincerity. And he realized that Esther Popescu possessed both as well as a rare type of beauty which intrigued and captivated him.

With a seminary training in church music, Len also recognized the young girl's talent, and immediately wonderful visions floated before him of a glamorous and popular Christian singer, who would move hundreds to decide for Christ by her talent and her beauty. Of course, this quaint young woman on the piano stool was a far cry from this vision. But give her time and a good teacher! That is where he would come into the picture. What a challenge lay ahead of him and what possibilities!

But Esther was singing again. Ron and Len looked at each other. They had never heard "Amazing Grace" rendered so beautifully. The young singer seemed to mean every word she sang. Beginning softly, it seemed that each stanza melted into the other, creating one long crescendo. But just as she began, "When we've been there ten thousand years," the front door opened once more, this time rather noisily, to admit John Popescu returning from the club.

Esther suddenly stopped playing. Startled, she turned around and caught sight of Ramona and the two young men in the doorway, her uncle standing behind them. Her face flushed a deep crimson and she half rose from her seat, but Len was too quick for her. Stepping swiftly to her side, he laid his hand on her arm. "Fabulous, Esther! Just fabulous!" he told her. "But come, finish the last verse. It's the climax, you know. And then, let's sing it through again together. That's the kind of hymn that needs a choir to really do it justice. I'm sure we all know it."

Esther sat down again and began to sing the stirring words: "When we've been there ten thousand years," but it was not the same. The spell had been broken. She was in the role of a performer now and that was not what she liked. She was glad when she began the first stanza again and heard Len's rich tenor and Ron's deep baritone harmonize with her clear soprano.

Ramona remained silent; she never had felt she could sing well, at least, not like Esther. She could not help but wonder, as she listened, that these three, such worlds apart in nearly every way, were able to unite their voices as one. When it finally came to an end, Ramona urged, "Play that other song, the first song you sang in Romanian, Esther. It's real cool. Dad may know it."

She was rather taken aback by Ramona's unexpected interest in her hymn-playing, but complied without more ado. As the haunting melody of "Numai harul," ("Only Grace") once more filled the house, John Popescu slipped past the young people and took a seat in the shadows. No one stirred when the last notes had died away in the evening air, until Esther suddenly bolted out of the room and made her way upstairs before anyone could stop her; she flung herself on the bed, shaking. Always a very private person, she never ever tried to make a show of her talents. Tonight, she had been caught by surprise and had performed for an audience—a Western audience! It had taken all she had, and she was utterly spent.

It had all been so spontaneous, so unplanned. Then she remembered reading somewhere that God was a God of the haphazard. Maybe He could bless her singing to Ramona and Ron and her uncle just as she had been blessed. She had been unaware that Rachel had also been listening in the adjoining room or she would have prayed for her too.

It was probably fortunate that Esther could not overhear the young men's comments that night as they drove home. "What a stunning performance, Ron!" Len began. "That girl has a fabulous future ahead of her. Why with that voice of hers, plus her beautiful face and gorgeous figure, to say nothing of the novelty of her being a Romanian—she could become a popular Christian singer overnight!"

"I'm not sure of that, Len," was the rejoinder. "You saw how she ran away from us all tonight? She can't bear being in the limelight."

"Too much attention does frighten her," admitted his cousin. "But after all, she's only been nine days in the country. Give her ten months and you won't know her!"

Ron said nothing. He hoped Len wouldn't get a chance to spoil the girl. Her purity and innocence had made even more impression on him than her singing. He certainly wouldn't like her to be spoiled by too much fame.

As the hum of Ron's motor faded into the distance, Ramona shut the door softly. She peeked into the living room, but her father had gone, so she crept upstairs to her bedroom. The evening had gone so differently from what she had planned. She sensed there was to be no future romantic relationship between herself and Ron Atwood. But Len? He was great fun. She liked his religion better than Esther's. He had been the life and soul of everything. No, not really. It had been her shy, old-fashioned cousin who had really stolen the day, in her own innocent little way. What a performance downstairs on the piano! She would give anything for talent like that.

Meanwhile Rachel was trying in vain to get to sleep in the little bedroom adjoining Ramona's. She was in a tumult of emotions. An uncontrollable longing swept over her—a longing for something that would take care of that distressing though often vague sense of nothingness that gnawed at her soul and aggravated her all the more by its sheer intangibility.

While the three girls were struggling with their various emotions upstairs, John Popescu had retreated to his study, and was sitting, head in hands, in his favorite chair. Visions of the past flooded upon him. "Numai Harul" had been his brother's favorite hymn. He could remember him singing it with his young wife in a religious gathering that John had been persuaded to attend much against his will just before he left for America. He distinctly recalled his brother's pleading words: "John, give God your heart; He deserves it." But John had shrugged it off. He had already given someone else his heart and she had handed it back to him, broken, and then turned and given her own to this religious brother of his. No wonder *he,* Andrei, could sing of God's grace. God had given *him* everything. Why shouldn't *he* serve Him?

As he drifted off to sleep that night, the first two lines of "Amazing Grace" rang again and again in his ears. Esther's singing had reminded him forcibly that God's grace was still there, all around him, and had been for all those years, waiting until he, John Popescu, made room for it to enter.

Chapter Eleven

A New Convert!

Sunday dawned—a beautiful Indian summer's day. Drawing back her pink, frilly curtains, Esther gasped with delight. Her room overlooked the garden and beyond, to the distant, rolling hills. If only her parents were here to share her new life she thought wistfully, or Gabriella, or even Aunt Ana. She never had gotten very close to Aunt Ana who always seemed so very different from her mother. But Esther could never forget that her unemotional and very reserved aunt had opened her home to the young orphan girls and shared everything she had with them, from the bread on the table which was often so hard to come by, to the clothes on her back. And now, in her dream of a bedroom, with more than enough food to eat and $200 dollars still in her purse, Esther would have given anything to feel her aunt's peck on her cheek, or hear her shrill voice urging, as they prepared for the three-hour church service, "Do be quick, Gabby. And, Esther, do you need to spend half an hour on your hair? No one will see it under your scarf. It's time to get going, both of you. We'll be late, you know. It's already eight thirty."

Esther knew that, in her heart of hearts, she was lonely, not so much for Romania with its cold and gloomy days and its long, dark nights, but for her friends who thought and talked like she did. This was the first time in her life that she never heard God mentioned from one week to another. She knew, though, that she had so very much to be grateful for—an uncle who loved her, even pampered her, and cousins who had welcomed her with open arms. She was thankful that they lived respectable lives, glad that she never heard cursing or saw her uncle strike his daughters. But there was a gap between herself and her new family which she could not seem to bridge. And the shadow of the impending divorce was never far away. She had still not seen her Aunt Mary even though she asked about her several times.

Just then, her eyes fell on her old black pocketbook she had brought from Romania. That would never do for church, she thought as she flipped open the snap. Begining to transfer the contents to the shiny tan handbag she had purchased at the garage sale, her eye caught sight of a folded piece of paper. She had forgotten where it had come from until she read the following lines written in a nearly illegible scrawl:

"Dear Esther, I so enjoyed talking with you today on the plane. I believe God allowed us to meet. There are no chance happenings with Him, you know. So having met once, we may well meet again, in God's time and in His way. Here's my address and phone no. if ever you feel that the Velvet Curtain is getting too much for you. Always feel free to get in touch with me. I'm available, day or night. Meanwhile, may the God I know you love and trust in be your daily Companion as you enter a totally new world. I will remember you before the Father's throne every day. Yours very sincerely, Hugh Gardner."

Two large teardrops made their way down Esther's cheeks as she folded the note once more and put it safe in one of the tiny zip pockets in her new purse. These words were just what she needed as she faced another day. She wasn't sure if the poignant loneliness she was feeling was part of the influence of this Velvet Curtain or not. She didn't think so. That feeling of suffocation she got now and then—that day she had been shopping, or that first Sunday morning at church, or at the restaurant later, or on her outing to the State Park—did it have something to do with this mysterious Curtain? Well, whatever might lie ahead, it was good to know that there was at least one person in this vast land who could answer an SOS call from a floundering spirit. That thought was very comforting.

She was still thinking about Hugh Gardner's note as she reached into the closet and pulled out a cream two piece suit, one of her garage sale bargains and a bit outmoded, Ramona had told her, though her uncle had declared it suited her to a T. She went to the mirror and gave her thick, glossy locks a vigorous brush, then coiled them on top of her head. She would put up her hair today, she told herself, as she fastened it with her hand-painted clasp from Romania.

Esther gave herself one last, approving glance in the mirror. She looked pretty good, she admitted, for a Romanian refugee that is. Gabby had liked her hair done that way—said it made her look like a queen. She could not help wondering if Ron Atwood would think the same. She couldn't forget his admiring glance as he had helped her into the car the day before. Then she turned away. America certainly hadn't taken care of her pride, or vanity as she preferred to call it. But where did vanity turn to obnoxious pride, she wondered? Hadn't she a right to be vain, sometimes? She couldn't help being glad that she was not plump like Ramona, or awkward like Rachel, or angular like Gabby. She knew, though, that she needed humility badly, if anyone did. She had told God so, many times in her tiny bedroom back in Ploiesti.

Esther was soon brought down to earth when she met Ramona in the kitchen, still half asleep and grumbling at having to get up at the unearthly hour of nine o'clock on a Sunday morning. Her pride wilted as she took in her cousin's immaculate dress—turquoise pant suit with sandals and pocketbook to match, She glanced down at her cream suit, dark brown shoes, and tan handbag. Well, Ramona had tried her best to get her to buy a matching outfit and she had refused. Then she thought of the money still remaining in her wallet. She visualized Gabby in a new winter coat, bright and warm, and pictured Aunt Ana scrunching through the snow on her way to church in shiny, black, leather boots and was comforted.

They had just snatched a cup of coffee and some toast when the doorbell rang. "Why, it's you, Ron! Surprise, surprise!" Ramona exclaimed upon opening the door.

"Yes, I decided I'd better come to keep an eye on you girls," was his reply. "I live so much closer than Len that it made more sense for me to be the one to drive you young ladies to church. And anyway, he has to be there at least half an hour before the service begins."

Ramona said nothing. She wondered what had really made him decide to go to church that morning. Ron's mother had wondered too. Hearing her son in the bathroom at what she deemed an unearthly hour, she had called out sleepily, "Where are you going at this time of morning?"

"To church," was the curt rejoinder.

"Church?" Dianne Atwood sat bolt upright in bed. "Why, whatever for?"

"Len invited Ramona and her cousin to go this morning. I thought I'd better go along and keep an eye on them, Len being Len you know," he told his mother, as he put away his razor and got out his jacket. And not wanting to be quizzed further on a subject he was unsure about himself, he bolted downstairs and was out the door before she could fire another question at him.

Ron had wakened that morning with "Amazing Grace" resounding in his ears. A vision of Esther at the piano had risen before him and Len's words, "Give her ten months and you won't know her," made him feel that he must keep an eye on her. Len had not been too pleased when Ron suggested that he pick up the girls that morning, but he soon saw the wisdom of the suggestion and reluctantly agreed. Ron shook his head as he pulled out of the driveway. He, Ron Atwood, was actually going to church all because of this Romanian girl who had suddenly come on the scene. What had he gotten himself into, he wondered?

But ten minutes later, he threw his misgivings to the wind as he helped the girls into the car. Both of them were extremely attractive. Then Ron frowned as Esther slipped into the back seat as a matter of course; he didn't see why Ramona should monopolize the front. He glanced in the rear vision mirror. What was there about this girl that drew him like a magnet? Her simplicity? Her purity? Her originality? Her vulnerability? Maybe she drew out his pity. No, you really didn't pity a girl like that. Maybe she was just another beautiful young woman providence had thrown in his way. He stole another glance as he swung onto the interstate. This time, Esther caught his eye, blushed, and dropped her gaze. Ron put his foot down on the accelerator and smiled to himself. Maybe Ramona had done him a favor after all by sitting in the front. After all, the rear vision mirror was very necessary to interstate driving.

It was half an hour's ride to the church. Conversation seemed to flag, for Ramona was never bright in the morning and Esther was too nervous to say much. Every fresh experience in this new land seemed to fill her with a dread of the unknown and a longing for the one she had left behind. She scarcely seemed to see the rolling farmland which flanked the interstate on both sides. She was visualizing a typical Sunday morning in faraway Romania—the ride on a crowded tram, people jostling and shoving just to keep their equilibrium, a long trudge up dark and dirty streets, then the greetings all around as hundreds crowded into the three rooms which had been turned into a church. She recalled how the congregation had sounded like one immense choir, as they sang hymn after hymn; a few were actually written by her father and many more by his close friend who, like her dad, had often been beaten and sometimes imprisoned for refusing to use his talent to propagate atheistic ideology. She remembered how, when the singing would finally come to an end, one after another would rise to their feet—doctors, professors, laborers, housewives—all thanking God for His goodness and bounty, people with practically nothing in their cupboards or in their purses, but with plenty in their hearts. But most of all it had been the warmth of love, the interest shown in each other's lives, the drinking in strength from one another's faith that Esther had looked forward to during the long school week when she was often shunned as being one of the "Pocaiti" (Repentant Ones), a nickname given to evangelicals in Romania.

As they turned into the long driveway leading to Pine Grove Evangelical Church, Esther gasped in surprise. She had never seen such a setting for a church! Pine trees flanked the road on both sides, giving, as she supposed, the church its name. The spacious, well-mown lawn reminded her of the parks back home. As they drew nearer, Esther gaped at the mammoth building looming ahead. Its modern architecture reminded her of a huge library, or theatre, or museum rather than a house of worship. She noticed that whole families were making their way up the paved walks, past the well-kept flower beds to the sanctuary, laughing and talking as if they were going to a picnic or ball game. There were carloads of young people, too, quite a contrast from St. Jude's where the majority of the congregation had been over fifty.

It was difficult to find a parking space. "Popular place this," Ron remarked as he pulled to a halt. "They must be doing something right. Maybe it's Len's charm that's the attraction." Ramona laughed as he helped her out of the car. But as he turned to take Esther's arm, he saw her shocked expression. "Only joking of course," he added hastily.

As they approached the church door, Ron caught sight of a tall, well-dressed young man in suit and tie, obviously waiting for them. Len held out his hand. "Welcome to Pine Grove Church, young ladies," he said. "It's a pleasure to have you today, and you too, Ron. By the way, we're in the process of initiating a contemporary service. It begins next week at eight thirty. Should be great. There're so many youngsters here, as you can see. It's only fair we cater to them as well as to the older members." He paused and took the Romanian girl's arm. "By the way," he told the other two, "I just want a word with this young lady before the service starts. You both go on in. Try to get a good seat, as the sanctuary fills up fast." And before she knew what was happening, he had led Esther into a small room which led off the large vestibule.

Ron started to follow them, but Len had closed the door. "Leave them, Ron," Ramona told him flashing him one of her brilliant smiles as she slipped her arm through his. "Maybe they are praying for us to get converted, who knows? Come; let's get a seat. It's getting full already so we'll have to go fairly near the front."

Ron was pretty sure that Len was not having a time of prayer with the young Romanian. He suspected that he was asking her to sing in the service that morning and he was equally sure that Esther was not up to such a challenge. After all, she had not even been two weeks in America yet.

Fuming inwardly, he let Ramona lead him up the aisle until she found three empty places about four rows from the front. Ramona took the seat furthest from the aisle and motioned for Ron to sit next to her, but he had disappeared. She frowned. He had obviously gone in search of Esther. It was very annoying.

A few moments later, Ron found himself knocking on the door of the room his cousin had entered, and pushing it slightly ajar before Len could say, "Come in," he saw his cousin standing behind Esther, whom he had seated in a chair, his hands placed lightly on her shoulders. "It's OK," he was telling her softly as he bent over her. "You'll be fine. You *can* do it. You just need confidence. God has opened the door for you and you must enter. It's providential, can't you see?"

Esther was obviously very uneasy at Len's close proximity. Her face was pale and there were tears in her eyes as she replied, "Well, I just feel it's impossible, Len, but if you insist, then maybe...."

She stopped abruptly as Ron entered the room. "What's all this about?" he demanded angrily.

"It's really none of your business," Len spluttered. "It's between Esther and me."

"Whatever business it is doesn't seem to be suiting the young lady," Ron commented dryly. Esther's face brightened as she rose from her chair, glad to put some distance between herself and the persistent Len.

"Len wants me to sing this morning," she told him. "The soloist has taken ill, and he says I am an answer to their prayers."

"I'm sure you are in more ways than one," growled Ron. "But the question is: do you want to do this or not?"

"Oh no, of course I don't," Esther replied rather piteously. "But maybe it's as Len says—a door God has opened that I must enter, no matter how hard it is."

Her face paled even more and she swayed slightly. Ron took her arm and began to lead her out of the room. "Len," he said over his shoulder, "I think it's you who have opened this door, not God. He seems to me too much of a gentleman, from what I can make out from the Bible, to force this timid girl to do something she can't face. Can't you see that she isn't up to it today?"

But Len would not be put off so easily. "Well, Esther, I realize you've only been here less than two weeks," he told her trying to put on his usual smile but not succeeding very well. "All is so new to you. But please, promise me you'll do it some time soon."

"I promise," said Esther weakly, and then added in a more determined voice, "Give me a month, Len. I'll do it a month from today."

Len brightened and telling them he must let the choir director know that he would sing the special number, he was off. By the time they had joined Ramona, the service was beginning. Ron seated Esther beside her cousin and sat down on the other side of her. Ramona bit her lip but said nothing though she was fuming inwardly. Things never seemed to go as planned since that Romanian girl had come on the scene.

Esther had mixed feelings about the service. Everything was perfectly synchronized, not a word out of place or a hair either, she thought, as she glanced at the well-groomed ladies sitting in the pew in front. She stared at the program in her hand. Yes, it was all going to plan, probably down to the minute. She had to admit the singing was much heartier than at St. Jude's and the anthem sung beautifully by the fifty-voice choir was extremely moving. Len's solo was also a great success. His voice was superb and he sang with feeling. Esther wondered how he could perform so perfectly after his encounter with Ron in the anteroom. And the preaching! That's what she liked best of all. Her heart was drawn out immediately to the portly gentleman with a kindly face and bushy grey eyebrows as he poured out his heart on the text, "If any man thirst, let him come unto me, and drink."

As they sang the closing hymn, "Just as I am," Esther was carried back once again to the crowded little church in the back streets of Ploiesti, surrounded by old grannies in their head squares, nursing mothers, and a host of bright-eyed children who sat as quiet as mice through three hours of church. But they had only sung two verses when Len got up and gave a highly emotional appeal, urging those who were not Christians to give their hearts to the Lord. The organist continued to play softly as several came out to the altar and Len and the elderly preacher were soon kneeling amongst them while many in the congregation were praying in an undertone. Esther had never seen or heard anything like it. She could not conceive how Ron's cousin had suddenly been transformed from a knight gallant into a fiery evangelical, or how he could possibly feel comfortable in using his personal magnetism to charm the congregation into making a decision for Christ. Maybe Ron's remark in the car park had not been so farfetched after all!

She glanced at Ramona who seemed unusually serious and thoughtful as she listened almost spellbound to Len's appeal, a marked contrast to the young man sitting on the other side of her. It was obvious that he was extremely ill at ease. Their eyes met for a moment. Then Ron shook his head as he fidgeted in his seat. Finally the long appeal ended and Len and his co-pastor introduced many of those who had gone to the front as new converts. Each stated simply that they believed the Lord Jesus had saved them that morning.

It was now Esther's turn to become uneasy. This was not what she was used to. It was all too emotional, too sudden, and too forced. And yet the older pastor seemed so genuine. As for Len, well, he was certainly gifted and eloquent and seemed very sincere at that particular moment. But as the service closed and he approached them again, her misgivings increased.

"Well Ron, thanks for bringing these beautiful young ladies to church with you," he exclaimed, beaming on the two girls. Then his face sobered as he bent forward and whispered something in Ramona's ear. She seemed taken by surprise for a moment then nodded and rose from her seat without saying a word.

"Can you hold on for a few moments or go on out to the car and wait for us?" Len asked Ron and Esther as he took Ramona's arm. "I had planned for us all to go out to eat together at my favorite restaurant, but Ramona and I have some serious talking to do first, if you'll excuse us."

Ron had had his fill of Len. He had no idea what was going on other than that it had something to do with religion. As for Ramona, it seemed she was coming under his cousin's hypnotic influence. But he also knew her pretty well, and was not absolutely sure how genuine her motives might be. So he took Esther's arm and replied,

"Tell you what, Len. Seems you think Ramona needs some time with you privately. May take a while. Why don't you take her out to eat, Len, without us being in the way? Give her plenty of time to talk, and I'll take Esther home. OK?"

Len's face brightened. He had felt rather snubbed by Esther's refusal to sing and her obvious gratitude for Ron's intervention in the affair, and felt, too, that if Ramona were a potential convert then it would be better to be alone with her over lunch. So before either of the girls knew what was happening, Len had taken a rather bewildered Ramona through a side door, leaving Ron and Esther to make their way through the crowd who seemed to be waiting to shake hands with the pastor. Many stopped to say a word or two of welcome to them. Eventually it was their turn. "So glad you could come," the preacher said with a warm smile as he held out his hand.

"This is Esther Popescu from Romania," said Ron, "and I'm Ron Atwood, Len's cousin."

"God bless you my dear young lady," the pastor told Esther as he shook her hand warmly. "And may He help you as you begin a brand new life here in our great country." And he looked at Ron as if, perhaps, he were a part of her new life.

"I have only known Esther for a week or so, pastor," Ron explained, reddening, "but Len invited us both to come this morning."

"That's great. So you are Len's cousin? Can't say I see a family likeness, though. He's a good fellow is Len. Full of enthusiasm and life." Others were coming up to greet him so further conversation was impossible. At last they were out in the car park.

"Sorry, Esther," Ron apologized, as they got into the car. "It all happened so suddenly. I didn't quite know what I was saying. But I was so upset with Len for the way he tried to force you to sing that I just couldn't face having a meal with him. And," he added looking at her full in the face, "I didn't think you would want to either."

"No, not really," she admitted. "But Ramona, is she OK?"

Ron laughed. "Don't you worry about your cousin. I know her better than you do. And, Esther, maybe she'll return home a new convert, who knows?"

Esther looked at him in amazement. "Are you really serious, Ron?" she asked. "Ramona isn't that way inclined, is she?"

"Hasn't seemed to be up to this point of time," he admitted, "but Len is so persistent, especially with the ladies. But let's not talk about him. We need to find a good place to eat."

Esther was silent as they sped along the four lane and finally pulled up at a restaurant, a very classy one she was to discover in the coming hour, as they dined in a small alcove festooned with plants. What was happening to her? How much could she cope with all in one day? But Ron was speaking again: "While we wait for the food to be served, I wondered if you would mind telling your story, Esther. I would know better just where you're coming from, and I really need to know that, if I'm to help you cope with American culture."

Esther could not refuse when Ron asked like that, so pushing back a stray lock of dark, wavy hair that tumbled down over her forehead, she began in a low, tremulous voice to tell the story she had told her Uncle and cousins the previous week.

Her faint accent was charming, her companion thought, as he studied Esther's expressive face intently. Sometimes the tears seemed not far away. At others, her whole face was illuminated by a warm smile which transformed her otherwise over-serious countenance and made it strikingly beautiful. Ron could not help comparing her to the girls he knew, girls like Ramona—girls whose lives seemed to be spent in trying to look glamorous and in enjoying themselves. But this young woman sitting opposite in her cream garage sale two piece suit, without makeup or jewelry, was... well, what was she? He really didn't know, not yet. She seemed an utter enigma to him.

Like Esther's uncle and cousins the previous Sunday, Ron was deeply moved as he listened, though he was rather glad when the food was brought in for he felt he could only take her story in small doses. He wasn't used to people talking like that about God. Besides, he felt rather near to tears, something very unusual for him, and it embarrassed him greatly. No wonder this girl found it so hard to fit in to America. She exuded a different type of religion from those around him. Her faith had been through fire; it was real. But as he watched her quietly and unobtrusively bow her head before beginning to eat, he wondered how she would stand another kind of testing. He didn't know how to express it, but if Hugh Gardner had been present he would have been warning them of the Velvet Curtain and its entangling folds.

Esther finished her story as they drove back to Velours that afternoon. Ron was unusually quiet as he handed her out of the car and made his way home. The church service had made little impression on him, but that Romanian girl? Who was she anyway? An angel in disguise? A modern saint? Or just a beautiful foreigner with an indefinable charm who would soon be like everyone else?

Rachel and Esther were having supper that evening when Ramona burst into the kitchen. "Listen, you guys," she began, "I've had a fabulous day. It's been the best Sunday I've spent for a long time!" Her face was flushed, her eyes shining.

"Been on a new date, that's obvious," muttered her sister as she got up from her chair.

Ramona reddened as she replied, "Not exactly, though it's been better than an ordinary date. Ron's cousin is absolutely fantastic. I never knew religion could be so neat. He's explained it all so fabulously. I have told God, with Len's help of course, that I want to be a Christian. So that's it! He told me I should tell someone right away that I have asked Jesus into my heart. Well, I have now, thank goodness. And that's that!" And Ramona gave Esther a triumphant look as she tossed back her blonde curls, kicked off her high heels, and grabbed a glass of Sprite from the fridge.

Rachel was nowhere to be seen when Ramona brought her drink into the den and curled up in the recliner. Esther sat on the sofa opposite and waited to see if Ramona would tell her more. She was astounded, to say the least, half glad, half sorry, she couldn't tell quite why, and all in all, thoroughly confused.

But Ramona seemed to be in great spirits. She talked incessantly of Len and the wonderful meal they had had, the walk by the river, the ride home. Esther let her rattle on and said little. She was very glad Ramona did not ask what she thought of the day's happenings for she could not have given a coherent reply.

Just then, her uncle came into the room. "What's all this about, Ramona?" he asked inquisitively as he flopped into his favorite chair. "Been spending the day with a preacher? That's a change! Thought that would have been more in Esther's line than in yours!"

Ramona laughed. "Can't blame you for thinking that, Dad. But you're wrong. Len's more on my wavelength than Ron at the moment. He's turned serious and quiet. He suits Esther better," and she gave her cousin a meaningful glance which did not escape her father's keen eyes. He raised his eyebrows and said nothing. Ramona continued, "And I've more news for you. This same preacher's gone and converted me. What do you think of that?"

This time, there was a positive frown on John's handsome face. He had known enough of conversions in the past to be very dubious about this one. He remembered when his brother had made a similar announcement and it had, in the end, cost him his life. But what did Ramona know of conversion?

"You don't believe me, Dad, I can see from your face," Ramona told him. "Don't worry. It won't change me much. Seems to me, Len's the same as I am in most things, only he prays and preaches, sings hymns, and talks of God a lot. But he laughs and jokes, flirts with the girls, and goes to movies and is great fun," and she tossed her curls emphatically as she added meaningfully, "so I don't think I'll have to change that much."

"Well, Ramona," her father finally replied, "whatever you do, don't make a mockery out of your religion. It cost my brother his life and though I'm not religious myself, I think it should be taken seriously. It *should* make a difference. If ever I became a real Christian, I know it would change my life!"

"Such as...?" quizzed his daughter, coming and perching on the arm of his chair and stroking his graying hair as she knew he loved her to do.

John reddened, bit his lip, and said nothing. He was not about to share his inner struggles with his daughter when she seemed in a flippant mood. And Esther was there too. How could he tell the girls that he had spent all day in a soul struggle? "Numai Harul" had brought him face to face with many memories; it had presented him once more with the invitation to do just what his daughter had so lightly professed to do—give his life to the Savior. But the years had not made it any easier for him to make this decision. In fact, it seemed doubly difficult now. Life had brought its complications, and to follow Christ would change the whole course of his life. He would have to abandon some cherished plans, plans which seemed to be developing so beautifully and which would yield him so much, or so it seemed.

"Secret, is it?" asked Ramona with a mischievous smile. But her father was not in a playful mood and got up abruptly and left the room. Ramona excused herself soon after, saying she had phone calls to make to her friends. Just then, Rachel came in with a game of Scrabble in her hands. Esther loved the game and for a while forgot more serious things. But later, as she got ready for bed, the events of the day came back to her in full force, setting her mind in a whirl. And she felt that same oppressive something surrounding her. She had scarcely ever felt so confused. In Romania, fear, timidity, and a feeling of total inadequacy had often been her companions, but this type of confusion was new to her for it had to do with what was dearest to her heart—the Christian walk, God's way of salvation, church, and all that went with it. To her the Church of Jesus Christ was a beacon in a world of darkness, a signpost on life's journey, a haven in the storm. The world and all that it entailed lay outside its walls. But here? It seemed that religious enthusiasm, heartrending appeals, striking testimonies—all blended in beautifully with flashy sports cars, glamorous girls and the latest movie in town.

When she knelt to pray, she was still too bewildered to verbalize her petitions or her praise as she usually did. And Esther would have been a great deal more confused if she could have heard Len and Ramona's conversation as they had driven home that night.

"Thanks for a great day, Len," Ramona had told her companion, as they neared her home.

"It's been great to be with you, Ramona," Len told her as he reached out and gave her hand a squeeze. "There will be a lot of rejoicing in Heaven tonight."

Ramona had looked at him curiously. "I just couldn't help myself today, Len," she told him. "You seemed to have something I didn't—something that I thought might be good to have, and you made it all sound so simple and so easy."

Len beamed at her as she went on. "Now my cousin, Esther. She's so terribly serious. No makeup, no movies, and I suppose she has a lot more 'No's' I don't know about yet for she's only been here ten days. Can't say that sort of religion appeals to me."

Len smiled smugly as he replied. "Give her time, Ramona. She's new to everything. And she did seem pretty happy last night as she sang and played."

"Well, yes, I suppose she did." Ramona admitted reluctantly. "It soon disappeared, though, and she made everyone else real glum. You should have seen Dad when he got up this morning. He looked as though he'd been dreaming about funerals. But you're always full of jokes and fun. That's what I like about you."

They had drawn up to the house now and Len had brought the car to a halt. He was not sure if his senior pastor would think Ramona's words the compliment she had obviously meant them to be. "That's just one side of me, Ramona. But anything good I seem to be or have is all of God, you know. And," he added as he turned off the engine, "I do believe it is also God Who has brought us together. I have helped you to believe, and you..." he paused and looked at her with his dark, speaking eyes. He had always had a soft spot for blondes and this one was very alluring.

Ramona's heart beat faster as her eyes met his. This youth pastor was a charmer, there was no doubt about it. She wished Ron Atwood would look at her like that. "I've done nothing, Len. It's all been you," Ramona replied as modestly as she could.

"No it hasn't," he protested. "You have been such an encouragement to me in my ministry. You have strengthened me in my belief that my religion still can appeal to beautiful girls with everything going for them. You have given me just what I needed."

He took her hand and held it. Ramona leaned towards him as he put his arm round her and drew her to him, but it was just for a moment. "I have to watch myself when I'm with you," he said softly as he kissed her lightly on the forehead. "I daren't forget even for a moment that I am a pastor. But," and he gave a long, drawn out sigh as he opened the car door, "I'm human too, you know, and you are very, very attractive."

Yes, it would have confused Esther very much more if she could have witnessed this scene. As it was, she went to bed wondering how someone considered a non-Christian by Len at any rate, could be such a gentleman—considerate, thoughtful, without overstepping the mark—while Len? She stopped. She would not go to bed thinking of Len. She would pray for dear Gabby so very far away, for Rachel, for Ramona, for the aunt she had never seen, and especially for Uncle John, who seemed to understand much more than his daughter did what giving one's heart to Christ really meant. "Oh," thought Esther, "if only he would take that step. How very, very happy I should be." For the first time that evening, her lips relaxed into a smile as she drifted into a deep and dreamless sleep.

Chapter Twelve

More Discoveries

"Uncle John must be very rich," said Esther, half to herself and half to Rachel who was there for the weekend as usual. It was Friday evening once more and Ron Atwood was due any moment to give her a math lesson.

"Dad, rich?" exclaimed her cousin, surprised. "Why, whatever makes you think that, Esther?"

"Well, look at this house. It's simply gorgeous—four bedrooms, lounge, den, dining room, office, kitchen, to say nothing of a full basement, all fitted out, which you don't even use except for storage. There's a color TV in nearly every room, wall to wall carpet, floor to ceiling drapes. And then there's that swimming pool out there," said Esther pointing through the patio doors to the backyard beyond, "and a two car garage for his expensive car and pickup, to say nothing of the Honda he gave Ramona on her 18th birthday. And I've heard that it's not uncommon for you to take off on a holiday to Hawaii or Bermuda or somewhere exotic. And, besides, Uncle gave me $500 just like that when I came two weeks ago."

Rachel eyed her intently. "And you think that everything is paid for, do you?"

Esther's mouth fell open. "Paid for? Why of course. I mean, it's normal to pay for what you possess, isn't it?"

Her cousin shook her head. "Not here in the good old USA. Never heard of monthly payments, mortgages, or credit cards?"

Rachel might as well have been talking Greek for all Esther understood, so her cousin patiently explained how most Americans lived. If their credit was good enough, their wages ample to ensure decent monthly payments, then almost anything could be purchased even if there was not enough in the account to cover everything when you bought it. This meant paying enormous amounts of interest but that's what nearly everyone did. "Of course," the girl added, lowering her voice a little, "I don't know that much about Dad's financial matters. I know he has an excellent job but I also know that everything is by no means paid for. I suppose it will all come out when the divorce is settled," her voice broke a little as she spoke. "Everything will have to be divided equally."

Esther put her hands to her face and shuddered. "Oh Rachel, it's too horrible to speak about. A family should never be divided in this way."

"Don't I know it, Esther!" Rachel sounded bitter now. "But it's all a part of this wonderful 'American Dream,' you know. Though," she muttered almost inaudibly, "I do wish Mom would drop the divorce. I just don't know why she's done this."

Just then the doorbell rang. Rachel ushered Ron Atwood into the kitchen where he found Esther, looking very flushed and not at all like herself. He seated himself beside her as Rachel disappeared into the den. Ramona had gone out with Len to some Christian rock concert and John had said he had business which would keep him late that evening.

Ron found his pupil decidedly more reserved than she had been on the previous Sunday or on their outing to the State Park. But in spite of her reserve, the lesson was a huge success. Esther was quick to learn, especially when she had a teacher as logical and as capable as Ron Atwood. And after an hour or so of concentration, he announced that they had done enough for one evening, and set her some sample exams to be completed by the next week.

"You won't need many lessons if you improve at this rate, Esther," he complimented.

The girl blushed slightly. "You explain everything so clearly," she said simply.

It was Ron's turn to be embarrassed. He had not expected this praise from his shy pupil.

"I'll get you both something to drink," suggested Rachel who had been studying in the adjoining room. "What would you like?"

"Just water for me, please, with plenty of ice. I've given up junk food and soft drinks," explained Ron, and he laughed nervously. He could not explain it, but for the first time in his life, he was self-conscious in the presence of the opposite sex.

"I'll have orange juice, Rachel," Esther told her cousin. "Without ice, please."

"Esther's not used to ice cold drinks," her cousin explained as she handed Ron his water. He smiled. "Guess she's not used to a lot of things," he remarked. "But give her another year and a scorcher of a summer and maybe she'll change her mind."

Esther shook her head. "I don't think so, Ron. We have pretty hot summers in Bucharest, and no air-conditioning either. But we Romanians don't think ice cold drinks are good for the throat."

"Oh, I see."

"You're laughing at me," Esther protested as she caught his amused grin. "I suppose I seem strange to you all here."

"A bit," he admitted, toying with his ice. "But don't change too fast. It's a welcome change to meet someone who is different from the rest of us."

Rachel handed her cousin the orange juice and glanced quickly at Ron as she did so. He really seemed to mean what he said. She was seeing a very different side of the young man whom Ramona had introduced into the family. What was Esther doing to him? She had been thinking about her cousin all week. What made her so different from everyone she had ever met? Was it just that she was a Romanian in an American setting? Rachel thought not. There was something more to it than that.

Esther bent her head over her book. Ron sipped his water and glanced at the girl. She was writing down in her clear, firm hand the questions she was to answer for the following week. He noticed that she seemed even less a part of his world than before—a little sad maybe, for he thought he detected a wistful expression in her eyes that had not been there before.

What Ron could not know was that her recent conversation with Rachel still bothered her. And besides, the confusion she had felt on Sunday had not worn off. If anything, it had grown, as she had tried in vain to get close to Ramona, thinking that surely they would have more in common now that she was, by her own confession, her sister in Christ. Len had come the previous evening to instruct his new convert in the Bible. He had not invited Esther into the room which seemed a bit strange, she thought. She listened to the laughter emanating from the den. She couldn't seem to share their jokes. Maybe it was the culture gap or maybe it was just her personality. She had brushed back a tear as she tried to concentrate on her studies. How she longed for Gabby who always cheered her up with her outlandish statements and weird humor which Esther, for one, could appreciate though many didn't.

All that week, Uncle John had seemed a little more aloof. He was still loving and affectionate, but it was harder to strike up a conversation with him. It seemed as if he viewed her as a sort of alabaster saint whom he greatly respected and almost worshiped, but whom he found hard to approach in everyday living. Esther tried hard to bridge this gulf which seemed to be widening daily but all to no avail.

Of course, she said nothing of all this to Ron that evening, but he had been quick to sense that she needed cheering up. What was wrong with Ramona and her uncle to go off and leave her like that? Well, he would have to do something about it if he possibly could. She couldn't sit and play hymns every evening. He did wish she wouldn't tie her hair back all the time; it made her look more severe. He remembered the picture she had made as she sat at the piano. In fact, that picture had haunted him all week, but she was speaking now.

"And how can I thank you, Ron, for being such a help to me just when I needed it?" asked Esther, "And," she added blushing, "I have meant all week to thank you for what you did last Sunday. You really came to my rescue and I deeply appreciate it. How can I ever repay you?"

"By being more relaxed, Esther, when you're working with me," he said simply, touched by her genuine gratitude.

Esther was taken aback but managed to say with a slight smile, "I'll try to be more relaxed, Ron, but I don't think any of you know how strange I often feel here. It's all so different," she sighed. "I knew it would be when I decided to come here but I thought I'd cope better than I seem to be doing."

Ron's smile faded. In a flash he realized just a little of what this young girl might be feeling. Then he brightened. It would be very rewarding to help her adapt to this new culture, but all he said was, "You know, Esther, you're right. I can't understand fully the culture shock you must still be going through. Putting myself in your place, I don't know how I would act if I suddenly found myself in your country."

Ron Atwood in Romania! The very idea struck Esther so strange that she suddenly laughed outright and, as Ron made his way out to his car, that merry laugh rang in his ears. So she had another side, that mysterious gypsy girl. She wasn't always singing hymns or reading classics. Well, he would look forward to bringing out that other side of Esther Popescu.

By the time Ron reached home, he still had not settled the question as to how he could best help the young Romanian girl. Seeing he was in another world, his mother playfully tweaked his ear as he ate his supper and said, laughing, "Seems your tutoring this young Romanian gypsy girl doesn't suit you, Ron."

"What do you mean?" he fired back.

"Touchy, eh?" his mother queried. "By the way, what has happened to the fair Ramona?"

"Taken to my cousin," he announced with a twinkle in his eyes.

"Len? That won't last. I'm sure she prefers you. She's probably trying to make you jealous."

Ron glanced at his mother as he pushed his plate aside, got up from the table, and threw himself into the nearest chair. The same thought had actually crossed his mind.

"Be careful, Ron. Having two girls on one string is dangerous," said his mother archly.

"You don't understand a bit," he retorted. "It's nothing like that. I've told you a hundred times, Mother, I don't intend to be serious with any girl at present and I'm not. But that doesn't mean I don't like being round them, especially when they're intelligent and attractive and," he paused, "needing help."

"Needing help, eh?" his mother repeated. "Now you must mean the Romanian. What help does she need? I would think she was pretty well set up with a well-to-do uncle who seems to dote on her."

Ron interrupted her. "How do you know all this?" he asked sharply. "And I'm not sure that her uncle is all that wealthy."

His mother colored but replied coolly, "I work for John Popescu, remember, so I probably know more about him than you do."

Ron eyed her for a few moments without speaking then went on slowly, "As I said, Esther needs help and I'm not sure how to give her the help she needs."

"I wouldn't think so," commented his mother wryly. "I've also heard she's very religious." Then she added sarcastically, "Maybe you could start taking her to church regularly."

Ron was silent for a moment. He didn't know how much church he could endure even for Esther's sake. He'd rather take her to concerts now and then, but he certainly didn't intend to get serious with her; that might signal the wrong message. Maybe going to church would be safer. He had toyed with the idea already but was afraid Esther would think him pushy; she knew he really was not that fond of going to church. But it was the only practical way to help her that he knew of.

"You know, I think that'd be a great idea," he told his mother with a smile, "to take Esther to church I mean. Trust you to hit the nail on the head."

Diane Atwood shook her head in exasperation. "It's no good. You're infatuated with this young lady and will find any excuse to be with her."

Ron was angry now. "I'm not infatuated in the slightest. You'll soon know it if ever I am, I'm warning you. I admit I am attracted to the girl, but so I've been to many another good-looking girl. No, it's more than that. But you wouldn't understand." And he made his exit not a little upset. But a few moments later he was on the phone, out of earshot of his interfering mother.

"Hello, Rachel. Can I speak to Esther, please?"

Rachel handed the receiver to her cousin who was still in the kitchen poring over some problems Ron had set for the following week.

"Esther," Ron was saying, "are you going to church this week?"

"Len offered to take both Ramona and me but I haven't given him an answer yet."

Ron cleared his throat before he spoke again. "Well, how about if I took you on Sunday?"

Esther was thunderstruck. She suspected that he would enjoy the experience no more than her uncle would or Rachel.

"That's very kind of you, Ron," she found herself saying when she got her tongue. "But I can't see the point of you going to worship God if you're reluctant and bored to tears."

"Nothing misses you, does it," he said with a short laugh. "Well, do you always enjoy worshiping God, Esther?" The question came out before he could stop it.

Esther hesitated. "I couldn't exactly say I enjoyed going to St. Jude's or that I liked everything in the service at Len's church," was the honest reply. "But I didn't go reluctantly either and found plenty in both services I could appreciate."

Ron was silent. He had not met this kind of churchgoer before and it nonplussed him.

"And, besides," Esther went on, "I don't really go for pleasure. I go because Sunday is God's day. I love God and want to honor Him by going to His house. He commands it in the Bible."

Ron had no reply for such an argument but he would not give up so easily. "I get the impression, Esther, that you are pining a bit for your sister and your friends and I thought that maybe if you went to church it might help you feel less homesick; I know that church has been a part of your life."

Esther was touched by his thoughtfulness, but she was also well aware that she was young and certainly not unattractive which might have at least a little to do with his concern for her loneliness. But Ron was speaking again: "I tell you what, I'm not sure either you or I want to go where Len is going, at least not every week. Let me take you to various churches in the area until you maybe find one in which you feel at home. In fact, I've heard there is a Romanian church in the city. How about us going there Sunday as long as you will interpret for me if it is all in Romanian?"

Esther found herself agreeing. She did not want to go with Len and Ramona but she strongly sensed her need of church and of Christian fellowship. "Ok, I'll go though if you don't mind, I'll ask Rachel to go with us," she told him.

It was good Esther could not see his wry smile as he replied, "Great. Maybe church will do her a bit of good."

Esther put her question to Rachel and got the answer she expected. Even a Romanian church could not tempt her. "No way can I go with you!" she exclaimed emphatically. "I'd make everyone miserable, and besides, I don't feel like acting as your chaperone. Pretty as you are, you're going to have to get used to being alone with boys. Not that I know much about that." Rachel gave a short laugh. Then she added as she walked out of the kitchen, "All I do know is that this won't be the last time Ron Atwood offers to take you somewhere. He'd do almost anything for you."

Esther blushed scarlet. Her cousin was grossly exaggerating, she told herself. But she was in America now, not Romania. She just had to adapt to her new surroundings. One day she would learn to drive, own a car and go where she wanted without having to rely on friends and relatives. Then her mind turned to Ron's shiny, new sports car, his expensive clothes, and the price he had paid for their meal last Sunday. Was he, too, living on credit? She glanced around her bedroom. Was all this luxury unpaid for? It was really none of her business. Yet maybe that's what her uncle had meant when he said that liberty had its dark side, or what Hugh had implied by the Velvet Curtain.

The next morning Esther woke up to hear the rain lashing against the windowpane. "So it does rain here after all," she thought. She glanced at the clock. Saturdays she allowed herself to sleep in a little though her cousins still thought she got up at an unearthly hour.

A few minutes later the doorbell rang. Esther pulled on her dressing gown and ran downstairs. She bumped into her uncle in the hallway. "It's OK, Esther," he told her. "It'll be Jean, the cleaning lady. She comes at eight each Saturday. Wait, though, I'll introduce you. Now, just don't pay any attention to her odd ways. She's a bit off-putting at first but a great worker. And that's what matters."

Esther was glad of the warning. She hadn't been quite sure what "off-putting" meant at first but she soon found out. "Now why don't you sleep in like your cousins do?" the woman had grumbled when she collided with Esther for the third time in an hour. "They know to stay out of my way on a Saturday morning."

Esther reddened. "I suppose I'm not used to watching someone else do the work," she explained apologetically. She had gulped down some coffee and toast and then began to clean up the kitchen. Ramona had left it in a bit of a mess the night before.

Jean's sallow face softened slightly. "Well, you'll have to get used to it. I'm paid to clean here and don't like any help. Now get some more beauty sleep, or watch a soap opera, or phone your boyfriend, I'm sure you have more than one with your great dark eyes and hair like Lady Godiva. But just stay out of my way, whatever you do. Now that's not much to ask, is it?"

Esther stared into Jean's beady grey eyes. She was a mite of a woman, with wispy grey hair and skin that reminded her of Granny Sandelescu back home. But she had none of Granny's warm smile. This woman seemed at war with the world in general and Esther in particular.

"I'll go upstairs, Jean," she assured her trying to smile.

"Good. I'll be up there in a few hours to clean your bedrooms," Jean warned, as she grabbed the mop and stuck it into the bucket with such ferocity that Esther was sprayed with soapsuds.

"Sorry," Jean grunted. "but if you will stand that near when I'm trying to get my work done, you'll have to take the consequences." She paused then turned to face Esther, mop in hand. "You're John's niece, did he say?"

Esther nodded. "Well, you're the image of the woman in that photo he keeps on his dresser. It's just appeared there since his wife left him. She sure is a beauty. No wonder he likes to look at her."

Esther stared at the woman dumbfounded. "I have no idea what or who you're talking about," she told Jean coldly. "Anyway," and Esther flashed Jean a reproving look, "I'm not used to gossip like that, so in future keep your thoughts to yourself, please," and she turned on her heel and left the kitchen.

"Hoity-toity! Needs pulling down a peg or two with her airs and graces," muttered Jean, as she plunged the mop into the bucket once more.

Esther breathed a sigh of relief when, four hours later, the front door closed upon the cleaning lady. She was the first really unpleasant person she had met since her arrival. Her uncle, she told herself as she prepared ciorba for the evening meal, should be more careful whom he allowed to clean his bedroom, he really should!

Chapter Thirteen

Meeting Aunt Mary

"Why won't you see Esther, Mom?" They had been tidying the kitchen after supper, and Rachel had suddenly laid down her dishcloth and turned to face her mother. The question, abruptly put by her usually taciturn daughter, startled Mary Popescu. She was taken off guard, exactly as Rachel had intended she should be. Blushing to the roots of her naturally blonde hair, she stammered, "Well, Rachel, why should I? I mean, I don't know her. She's no blood relative."

Her daughter said nothing at first but looked her mother straight in the eyes. Mary could not meet her searching gaze and turned to put away the supper dishes. "But, Mom, she's been here three weeks nearly, and you have all but refused to meet her. It's really quite rude, isn't it?" The girl paused, letting her words sink in. "And she's not like anyone I've ever met," Rachel went on. "It doesn't seem fair to keep on giving stupid excuses that she sees through right away. But," and the girl's faced reddened. She wasn't used to saying anything nice about anyone and was as surprised as her mother was to hear herself muttering as she lowered her eyes to the ground, "But she's becoming almost the only real friend I have."

Mary could take it no longer. Her composure gave way utterly and, swinging round, she grabbed her daughter by the shoulders and exploded: "That's a nice thing to say to your mother who has borne you, I must say. Who, tell me, feeds you and clothes you? Who puts a roof over your head? Who puts up with your moods every day? See what that 'only real friend' of yours has done already? She's worming her way into even your icy heart. I know them—these nice, pure, beautiful, unusual girls who use their piety to get their own ends," and her voice shook with rage.

Rachel gasped. She rarely saw her mother lose her cool these days. Her haughty reserve became unbearable at times, but now, at least, she had come out of her cocoon, even if it were in anger. Usually quick in repartee, her daughter was speechless.

But Mary, it seemed, had not finished her tirade. "I may not have met this girl, this fabulous cousin of yours, but I can tell you already what she's like—long black wavy hair, clear olive skin, large dark eyes which look right through you, and lips that cry out to be kissed right while they're mouthing religious platitudes and singing sweet hymns—oh yes, she's good looking enough to capture any man's heart and then cast it on the dust heap. I tell you, niece or no niece, I don't want anything to do with her."

"How can you describe her so exactly—her appearance I mean, not her character? You're miles off target there!" and Rachel's eyes flashed dangerously.

"Describe her?" Mary almost shrieked. "I've seen her in my mind's eye for twenty years or more. She haunted me in the night, invaded the privacy of my, I mean, of *our* bedroom. She came between us when we talked together, walked together, made love together. I should think I could describe her!" And, spent from her outburst, the overwrought woman collapsed into the nearest chair and buried her face in the dishtowel she had been holding.

It had been many long months since Rachel had shown affection to anyone, but for the time being at any rate, she forgot her reserve and, sitting down beside her mother, took her hand in hers and stroked it gently. It was still a youthful hand, soft and pliable. They sat in complete silence for a while, the girl's fertile brain trying to figure out what lay behind her mother's strange words. Was she really going off her mind? Had the trauma of separation after so many years of marriage unbalanced her? It certainly could not be Esther who had haunted her very existence for so long and evoked such venom. Who, then, did she mean? Rachel thought hard. It would have to be someone looking like Esther, probably another Romanian. Why, of course! She must be referring to Esther's mother. Yes, that was it. Esther had shown Ramona and herself a picture of her a few days earlier and her sister had exclaimed, "Why Esther, you're the double of your Mom!" Come to think of it, she had noticed that same picture on her father's dresser when she had to hang up his suit which had come from the cleaners. It had only appeared since her mother had left. Obviously she was touching upon some family secret, but she daren't probe any further, at least, not yet.

Then, suddenly, Mary rose abruptly and, without a word, left the kitchen. Going upstairs some minutes later, Rachel heard convulsive sobs coming from her mother's room. She went to enter but the door was locked.

Back in her own room she did some deep thinking. She knew that her father had put up with a lot ever since she could remember and it had steadily gotten worse—temper tantrums then steely silence at times broken only by torrents of complaints and recriminations. But it was not he who had left; it had been her mother who had said she could not stand it any longer. Stand what? John Popescu seemed to be as patient and tolerant a husband as one could wish. And yet? She could see it all now; he never seemed to treat his wife as a real lover would. His attitude was rather one of pampering a spoiled child. Had he never really loved Mary then? Was his heart still wrapped around someone else, Sylvia Popescu for instance?

Rachel slept little that night, her mind full of the tragedy which had wrecked her parent's marriage. Her mother was also doing a lot of thinking. Her daughter's courage in facing her about Esther had both shocked and incensed her. But as the quiet of the night hours gradually washed away her anger, she began to see reason. What a fool she had made of herself! Even if Esther's mother had haunted her life, it had not been the girl's fault. Here she was, a mature woman of forty-five, nursing her grievances, exaggerating them and refusing to make the best of the blessings of two wonderful daughters and a tolerant and indulgent husband if not a truly loving one. If she had not insisted on magnifying John's obsession with his first love, she might even have supplanted it in time and eventually won his affections. A vision of the "might-have-beens" almost drove her mad until she realized that maybe it was not too late to try again. The divorce was not through yet. She could still stop it.

Rachel was not prepared for Mary's calm announcement at breakfast that Esther could come for supper that Friday. Her sad eyes brightened. This was more than she had hoped for. Soon she was on the phone to tell her cousin the good news and then left for school, much happier than she had been for many a day.

Esther had put down the receiver, stunned. What had suddenly changed her aunt's mind? She had so longed to meet her, longed to have some older and more mature woman in her life. She wondered over and over again what her aunt would be like. Ramona warned her not to expect too much from her first meeting. "Mom's changed so much these last years," she told her cousin. "You never feel you are seeing the real person any more. I just can't think what has come over her, though it's been happening a long time, come to think of it."

This news about her aunt was a wonderful start to a new week. And the day before had also been full of surprises—a visit to a Romanian church in Indianapolis and a wonderful meal of ciorba and sarmale with a delightful young couple who had just immigrated to the States. The warm hospitality of their hosts made Esther swell with pride. In fact, everyone had welcomed them so warmly. The Illiescu family had also invited them for lunch. The parents seemed good Christian people and had known her uncle for years. But Claude, their son, acted rather strange somehow. He had asked after Ramona for it seemed they had gone to school together. Esther had mentioned him to her cousin that evening and she had laughed and said he was an odd ball but good at heart.

The best part had been that Ron seemed to really listen intently to the message which she had translated for him, his eyes never leaving her face, and he had even commented on several points the preacher had made. He told her later as they were strolling through the Botanical Gardens which had been only a few blocks from the church, that it had been the best Sunday he had spent for many a long day.

And now, as she tidied away the breakfast dishes and said goodbye to Ramona who was leaving for another week at college, she began to count the days until Friday. When it finally came, however, she found herself unaccountably nervous as she stood outside her aunt's door and rang the bell. Rachel ushered her into the small, simply furnished, two-bedroom apartment which seemed a stark contrast to her uncle's stately tri-level home, and reminded her, if even just a little, of the apartment back in Romania where she had spent her last four years.

Mary had prepared a sumptuous meal for she was a first rate cook. But though she greeted her niece with a kiss, her smile was forced and her voice cold. Back in the kitchen, she clenched her fists and frowned. "Just as I thought," she muttered. "She's the very image of that woman. How will I survive this evening?" But there was no getting out of it now. There was the Romanian girl in her sitting-room, looking very timid and nervous as she tried to make conversation with Rachel while they waited for their supper.

At last all was ready. Taking the seat opposite her aunt, Esther bowed her head as she always did. Rachel glanced at her mother who seemed not to have noticed. Her daughter had half longed for and half dreaded this evening. She knew Mary's unpredictable moods and Esther's sensitive nature, and felt she would be glad when it was all over.

For the first half hour, conversation flagged. It seemed to Mary that it was Sylvia Popescu not her daughter who was sitting at her supper table. "Why have I tortured myself like this?" she asked herself, trying hard to control her feelings and concentrate on the food lying practically untouched on the plate before her.

Meanwhile her niece cast furtive glances at her aunt from under her long lashes. "She must have been a beautiful woman once," Esther thought. "And she still could be if only she could regain her hope in life. She has Ramona's complexion, but those sky blue eyes are glazed and dull. Everything about her speaks of lost hope and purpose." Esther's tender heart overflowed with pity for the woman sitting opposite her. She must try to ignore her aunt's lack of warmth toward her. What did it matter anyway? Here was someone in desperate need of love and that was something that she, penniless Esther Popescu, could give in abundance.

Just then, Mary glanced at her young guest and saw the teardrops glistening in her large, dark eyes. She little realized that they were tears of compassion; she only saw a lonely orphan girl, far from home and greatly in need of mothering. "Tell me a little about Romania, Esther," she found herself saying in a voice very unlike her own.

Esther started. This was unexpected. Then she began, haltingly at first, to speak of Gabby and Aunt Ana and her church in Ploiesti. And then, finding that her Aunt Mary was expecting something more, she slowly and not without a few more tears, told her whole story. Mary listened intently until her niece had finished; then she rose abruptly and began to clear the table. "Thank you, Esther," she muttered as she took the dirty dishes into the kitchen. That was all she could say. Too many emotions were fighting for supremacy but in the end, it was compassion that won and it was a very chastened Aunt Mary who brought in the coffee and cake.

When they had all eaten their fill, Rachel suggested a game of Scrabble which greatly helped to relieve the tension. Both Rachel and Mary were expert players, but it was the older woman who won in the end. "You are really good, Aunt Mary," Esther exclaimed as she helped clear the board. "This is a great game. It really helps my vocabulary."

Her aunt smiled faintly. It was the first time she had done so all evening. "Maybe you can come again some time, Esther, if you like, that is," she stammered, keeping her eyes fixed on the ground.

Esther wanted to hug her aunt, but instead she only said simply, "Yes, I'd like that very much, I really would." She could not realize how much that evening had cost her aunt emotionally, but she rather thought that some milestone had been passed and went home with a light heart.

"Oh Lord," she prayed before jumping in between her soft, pink sheets, "thank you for answering my prayer and helping me to meet my aunt at last. She seems so sad, so hopeless. Please, God, show me how, in some small way, to help her find hope"; she paused as tears filled her eyes. "I mean, please help her to find YOU. Amen."

Meanwhile, Mary Popescu was finding sleep hard to come by. She thought over the events of the past week and especially of her meeting with Esther. Try as she would, she could not block out the vision of those tear-filled eyes gazing mournfully at her. Finally sleep came in the small hours of the morning but not for long. As the clock struck three, she awoke suddenly and found Rachel bending over her.

"Whatever's wrong, Mom?" she was saying. "You must have been dreaming."

"Dreaming?" Mary asked, opening her eyes wide. Then she remembered, and covered her face with her hands. "Yes, I've been dreaming all right, but how did you know? Did I call out?"

"You sure did," her daughter told her as she pulled a blanket around her for the night had turned cold.

Mary's face blanched as she asked falteringly, "What did I say, Rachel?"

Rachel drew a little closer as she replied, "Nothing terrible, Mom, so don't worry. Though you did seem to be very agitated."

"Yes, yes, I know," Mary sounded impatient. "But tell me, what did I actually say?"

"You said, or I think you did, for your speech was a bit slurred, 'Why, God help me. It's not there after all!'"

Mary leaned back against the pillows and let out a long sigh. For the second time that week, Rachel felt for her mother's hand. It was trembling though her voice was calm as she began: "I remember now, Rachel. I remember very well. Oh it was horrible at first, just horrible. Maybe if I tell you, it'll do me good. Get it out of my system. It's still so vivid. I can still see her, standing in front of me."

"Who, Mom?" asked Rachel. "But first, let me come into bed with you, I'm freezing, and then you can tell me it all. There, that's better," and she snuggled under the blankets as her mother began slowly:

"Well, before I went to sleep, I could think of nothing but Esther. I saw her sitting there opposite me, two large teardrops in her great, dark eyes. And I imagined I was taking her in my arms as her mother would have done, she seemed so lonely and in need of comforting." Mary paused. "I was forgetting she was the image of Sylvia. I just saw her as my little orphaned niece who needed love and compassion. Then I drifted off to sleep, or must have, but it seemed as if Esther gradually turned into her mother. I was walking behind her in a meadow. The sky was blue, the sun bright, and there were wild flowers blooming all around us."

Mary started shaking again. Rachel waited, knowing it was so important for her to talk, to get whatever had poisoned her for so long out of her system. Finally, just as the clock struck the half hour, her mother cleared her throat and continued:

"It seemed that when I realized it was Sylvia and not Esther I just lost my cool. All the passion of the years seemed to reach its climax. Standing there in the sunlit meadow, I became convinced that there was a horrible serpent lurking in this woman's heart, ruining the lives of all who touched hers.

"There was a knife lying on the ground just in front of me. I grabbed it and made for Sylvia. She was stooping to pick some of the poppies that grew in profusion all around her. Hearing my footsteps, she turned around suddenly. She looked up at me with those great soulful eyes her daughter has inherited. Two bright teardrops were coursing down her cheeks as her lips parted, and she said in a low voice but quite distinctly, 'It's not there, Mary. It's not there. It's in you instead.'

"But I would not listen. I grabbed her shoulders, and she made no effort to escape my grasp. It seemed that my family's future depended on what I did next."

Rachel felt her mother's hands. They were clammy. She snuggled closer. "It's only a dream, Mom," she whispered. "You don't need to go on if you'd rather not."

"Oh but I must," was the reply. "I wouldn't listen to her, wouldn't believe her. I had to kill that serpent she was hiding. A few moments later when she lay senseless on the ground, I realized, to my utter horror, that she had told the truth, but it was too late. Waves of guilt swept over me. 'Why, God help me,' I cried out, 'it's not there after all.'"

Mary slumped back into the pillows and closed her eyes. Rachel lay still, waiting. The minutes ticked by. The clock in the hallway struck four. Then she knew by her mother's breathing that she had drifted off into a peaceful sleep. She crept back to her own bed, now very wide awake. There had been no need of an explanation of that strange dream. It was all too obvious it had resulted from a desperate inner conflict that had lasted for years. What its final effect would be she did not dare predict.

Her mother slept late that Saturday morning. When she finally awoke well past nine o'clock, she felt very strange. Where had she been all night? Why did she feel strangely light. The sunlight was streaming in the window when she finally made it to the bathroom. Her frown returned when she caught sight of her haggard face in the mirror. Did she really look that old, she wondered? Was that unsmiling, sour-faced woman the one John had lived with for so long? And Rachel and Ramona? Where had her looks gone?

Trembling, she grabbed a bright red sweater from her closet which she had not worn for months and caught herself grinning a little as she combed her thick blonde hair which she had cut very short to save bother. There, that was better already, she thought. She remembered how John had liked it—long and wavy. Maybe she should grow it again.

As they ate their cereal a few moments later, Rachel's quick eyes took in the red sweater. She noticed, too, that the glaze in her mother's eyes seemed to have vanished. And though they ate in silence as they always did, just as if nothing strange had happened that night, Rachel felt, as she packed her weekend bag, that there just might be a thaw setting into the icy regions of her mother's heart. As for her own, it too felt warmer than it had in months, maybe years. Could it be possible that eventually everything would be all right again? That would take a miracle, but since her Romanian cousin had come on the scene, it seemed like the age of miracles had truly begun.

Chapter Fourteen

Put on the Spot!

"My, what good ciorba you make, my dear," John Popescu told his niece as he held out his bowl for a second helping. "It's nearly as good as my mother's was, and that's saying a lot." Esther smiled at him affectionately.

"I've been meaning to tell you, Uncle, that I met the Illiescu family on Sunday. They say they're old friends of yours."

John nodded. "Yes, they left Romania about ten years ago and came to live very near us until I moved here. They're good people. More religious than I am by a long way. We've lost touch with them somewhat though Claude keeps phoning Ramona. Seems he's got some sort of crush on her. But he's not really her type so she keeps him at arm's length."

"He seems a bit unusual, Uncle," Esther remarked as she put her dish in the sink. "Can't put my finger on it, but he's not like his parents."

"Never was. Always was the odd one out though he's the apple of his parents' eye. Only son, you know, and quite spoiled. He seems a bit rebellious at present. By the way," John exclaimed looking at the clock, "Rachel's late this morning. I wonder why Mary's keeping her so long."

"Well, you can blame me, Uncle," said Esther as she placed the ciorba in front of him. "She was entertaining last night."

"Yes, I believe she was," was his rather cool comment. He looked at Esther intently. "And what did you think of your aunt?"

Esther flushed. "I've only met her once but I rather like her, though she seems to be a very sad and disillusioned woman. But she's very good looking. Not a bit like I expected her to be."

"No? Well, if you'd known her once, you'd see how much she's deteriorated. She was a beauty queen when I married her, believe it or not." John's eyes took on a dreamy look. Then his face hardened as he went on, "But she has a tongue like a razor and a heart of stone these days. I don't know how Rachel puts up with it. But then, she's almost as bad herself, though," he conceded, "I must say the child has improved considerably since you came on the scene."

There was no time for further comment, much to Esther's relief, for just then they heard a car in the driveway.

"Just in time for lunch, Rachel," Esther informed her cousin as she burst into the kitchen. The girl didn't seem to hear. She put down her bag and went up to her father. "Dad, Mom is waiting in the car. She wants a word with you."

John Popescu raised his eyebrows. It had been weeks since his wife had asked to speak to him, but he rose without saying a word. A few moments later he returned and resumed his seat. He ate his second bowl of soup in silence. Then he turned to his daughter. "What's come over your mother, Rachel? She wants to have a long talk with me. That's a change, isn't it?"

Rachel nodded but said nothing. John went on: "I'm going over tomorrow. She wants a private talk. By the way, where's Ramona?" he asked, obviously wishing to change the subject.

"Sleeping in as usual, I suppose," Rachel commented.

"Actually, no," Esther put in. "She's gone to some youth conference with Len."

"And they didn't take you with them?" queried her uncle, frowning slightly. "I thought that kind of thing would be more in your line than Ramona's. Oh, I forgot. She's converted now, isn't she?"

"Converted?" snorted Rachel. "She's no more converted than I am. Just got another boyfriend, that's all. Religious one this time, but she doesn't care. Anyone to make up for Ron."

Esther cringed. It was the old Rachel speaking. Her young cousin was changing slowly for the better, but there was a long way to go yet before she would get that bitterness out of her system. And the trouble was that she felt Rachel's words, as usual, had some truth to them.

That evening found Esther having another math lesson. She could take the SAT whenever she wanted, Ron informed her. "I'll find out about it next week," he said as he got up to go. "And, Esther, have you got the application forms yet?"

"Yes," was the reply. "Ramona got them for me. But I'm supposed to have references and high school credits and such like and I don't see, under the circumstances, how I can get them, at least, not in time for January."

"I worked for two semesters in the admissions office," Ron

informed her, "so I know the ropes pretty well. I'll help you work it all out, that is, if you think you need my help."

Esther hesitated. She had thought Ramona would do all this, but her cousin was not as responsible as Ron and didn't really seem to know how best to help her. "I'll be glad of your help," she told him as she smiled one of her rare smiles.

"She's lightening up a bit," Ron thought as he drove home that evening. "She doesn't smile very often but when she does, she's pretty dazzling. Maybe it's good she's so somber, otherwise I just might not be able to cope with it."

The next morning, John Popescu was up bright and early to take his niece to church. Ron had apologized that he would be away that Sunday. He had promised his mother some weeks earlier that he would go with her to Cincinnati to visit her sister. As for Ramona, she was off again with Len to his church in Terre Haute. Rachel was still in bed when they left. "She's in another of her moods," John had commented as they drove the few blocks to St. Jude's. Esther wondered why Americans insisted on going everywhere by car, and then drove to the nearest park or mall to get their weekly exercise.

She had looked forward to this time alone with her uncle but noted that he was unusually quiet as they had lunch together at his favorite restaurant. She had glanced up several times to find his eyes fixed on her face. It was not his usual, affectionate gaze but rather a mournful and even slightly reproachful look, as if he wished something to be other than it was, as if he wished her to be someone else, not his Romanian niece, Esther Popescu. It made her uneasy. "Perhaps," she reasoned, "he is dreading meeting Aunt Mary this afternoon. Or perhaps I remind him of something or someone in his past." And for once in her life she wished, for his sake, that she did not look so startlingly like her beloved mother.

When Ramona returned rather late that evening, Esther sensed that something had happened to dampen her enthusiasm. And she was right. It had been a truly wonderful day—they had eaten a gorgeous lunch together followed by an exciting boat ride on the river and a rather romantic walk through the woods, hand in hand, discussing, of course, God and the Bible as well as a host of other things. Len had persuaded her to stay for the youth service in the evening. She had entered the fellowship hall, flushed with pleasure. Then, during the refreshments following the service, a young girl called Connie had sidled up to Ramona and looking up at her with the innocence of an angel, had begun, "You're new here. One of Len's converts, right?"

Ramona had resented the tone in which this question was put and replied defensively, "Well, you could call me that, I suppose. Len has been very kind to me and helped me a lot during the past few weeks."

"Yes, I am sure he has," replied Connie a bit too sweetly, Ramona thought. "He has helped many girls. He helped me too last year. Got me to come to church, took me out for meals, dinner dates I suppose you might have called them. He was wonderful company. Was even quite romantic at times, up to a point, that is. No, he didn't disgrace himself. After all, he is a pastor isn't he? He never let me forget that. And he did manage to persuade me, for a while that is, that it might just pay to be a Christian."

Ramona looked at the young girl intently. She was about seventeen and very petite—not exactly beautiful but very attractive in her own way and overflowing with life. She had a mop of unruly auburn curls and sparkling hazel eyes. What message was she trying to convey? Ramona was curious, so she asked in spite of herself, "And then?"

"And then?" repeated Connie, with a sigh, "I got very fond of him and I thought that he..." she paused, this time genuinely embarrassed. "But of course I was foolish. I'm only seventeen and Len—why he must be at least twenty-four and a youth pastor into the bargain. And when I realized that several of the girls in the church, all young and very good-looking, were his 'converts' too, I understood."

"But," put in Ramona, her face flushing as she spoke, "you got over it OK, didn't you? I mean, you still come here, don't you?"

"Oh yes," replied Connie slowly. "I come all right, though I don't really know why I do, except that Len seems to have some sort of drawing power even yet. But I'm not sure now about religion or about what's really right and what's wrong. It's all so confusing. Sometimes I feel smothered as if I couldn't breathe. But," she continued more brightly, "it will be different with you. You are fabulous looking; nearly all the boys in the youth group are crazy about you, and besides, you're older. I'm sure it will turn out differently for you." And with that she turned on her heel and left Ramona, plate in hand, staring after her.

Len found his companion unusually silent during their ride home. "Anything wrong, Ramona?" he asked, reaching for her hand as he often did when he was driving. Ramona pulled it away.

"Has young Connie been talking to you?" he asked abruptly. "She causes trouble wherever she goes with her acid tongue. Take no notice of her, please Ramona. She's just a child."

"She's woman enough to have fallen for you," Ramona retorted, tossing her head, "as have half a dozen others of your 'converts.'"

Len looked as if she had stabbed him with a double-bladed knife. "So you think I'm phony then, Ramona?" he asked mournfully. "I couldn't bear you to think that of me, I really couldn't!"

Ramona didn't answer. She didn't really know what to say. "You girls interpret me the wrong way at times," Len went on. He sighed. "I'll just have to put up with being misunderstood, I suppose. But I get some comfort from knowing that if God sees my motives, then that's really all that matters."

Ramona winced. She didn't like this pious jargon. But as she glanced at the young man by her side, he did seem so genuine and those eyes of his were so good at pleading his cause, that she decided to give him the benefit of the doubt, for the time being at any rate, but she would be more wary. So when he handed her out of the car that evening and bent forward and gave her his usual goodnight kiss on her cheek, she dropped her eyes and hurried into the house.

"Wait till I get hold of that Connie," muttered the irate young man to himself as he drove home. "But let's see, what do I really think of Ramona? She is the prettiest girl in the youth group, that's certain. But is she a genuine Christian? I'm not sure. Maybe I should back off a bit and test her out. I'm not ready to settle down yet. And even if I were, I'm not sure I'd choose someone like her for a wife. Now if it were that extraordinary Romanian girl...." Here his thoughts trailed off. Esther was an enigma to him. He wasn't sure how to take her.

Ramona's mood was not improved when her sister met her at the door and informed her that their father had been at his wife's apartment for hours. She wanted to take Rachel home immediately as there was a movie she was dying to see.

"No, Ramona," her sister told her firmly, "I don't want to go home till those two have finished their talking. I've had enough of their arguments over the years to last a lifetime, and I don't want to be involved in another one. Anyway, they need privacy. I think they're up to a real crisis."

"Another one!" groaned Ramona. "I suppose I'll have to take you back at some unearthly hour then," she grumbled. Just then the phone rang. It was her father telling her to bring Rachel before it got too late; he was leaving the apartment but had to go somewhere else. He would be home before midnight. They were not to wait up for him. His voice betrayed nothing, Ramona thought.

Alone in the house, Esther went to the piano and soon found release for at least some of her pent up emotions. Hymn after hymn, some in Romanian, some in English, poured from her lips and the more she sang, the calmer she became. Her heavenly Father had everything in His strong and capable hands so why should she worry?

Ramona was back at last and was watching a late night movie when the phone rang once more. She answered it eagerly. To her surprise it was her mother on the line. "Ramona," the voice quavered, "I told John I would let you know what has happened today. I wasn't ready to speak to you when you brought Rachel home. But I'll have to do it now as your Dad can't face you girls just yet. So don't quiz him if you're still up when he returns." Mary paused, then took a deep breath as she went on: "I have just told him that I am going to phone my lawyer tomorrow and call off the divorce. If there is to be one, it will be your Dad who chooses to go in that direction, not me."

Ramona listened in shocked silence. Her tongue seemed to stick to the roof of her mouth. She waited for her mother to go on. "I had hoped," Mary told her, "vain hope really, that my decision would bring healing to our family, but instead...." She paused to regain composure and then went on. "But instead, it has only complicated matters. Your Dad was not pleased with the news. But at least we've had the first good heart-to-heart talk for years. We know exactly where the other stands. And, what's more, a weight is off my conscience."

Then she told her daughter about Rachel's challenge to her the week before which had resulted in Esther's visit; she also mentioned that she had had a strange dream which had made her think deeply. "Tell Esther the news, will you?" Mary concluded. "At least, tell her as much as you think she needs to know."

"Of course," Ramona assured her, then added, "And Mom, I'm really glad you've tried to make it up with Dad, but I think you've waited a bit too long." Ramona felt bad the moment the words were out. She had not meant to recriminate her mother, especially not at that crucial moment.

There was a long silence before Mary answered slowly, "I know that only too well, Ramona. And I'm dreadfully sorry." Her daughter could hear the sobs on the other end of the line.

"That's all in the past now, Mom," Ramona began

"I can't talk any more now," her mother interrupted, "I really can't. Good Night."

"I must say, Mom seems to have changed a lot in her attitude," Ramona said as she turned to Esther. "She's decided to call off the divorce!"

Esther jumped up from her chair, her eyes shining. "Oh Ramona, how wonderful! Then it'll all be OK again. I mean...." She paused for she saw no corresponding joy reflected in her cousin's face. "I mean, your home will soon be reunited, won't it?"

Ramona looked at her rather strangely. "Needs two to make peace, Esther," she said abruptly. "Now, excuse me, but I want to see the end of this movie."

Esther grew pale. The idea that her uncle might not be pleased with this wonderful news had never entered her head. "I guess this sure puts your Dad on the spot, Ramona," she couldn't help saying as she turned to leave the room.

"Yep, sure does," was all the reply she got.

Esther said no more. It really was none of her business though she did feel part of the family now. If only this home could be re-united, what a miracle that would be!

Chapter Fifteen

Uncle John Decides

Esther saw little of her uncle all week. He saw to it that he was off to work before she came down for breakfast and he came home late every night, very late. Once or twice, when she had stayed up to make his supper, she had smelt alcohol on his breath. He was always kind to her, though, but never keen to be long in her presence. It was all very strange, she thought, and very upsetting.

The first three days of that long and lonely week dragged by. With Ramona at college and Rachel at her mother's, she saw no one but her uncle. Then Wednesday evening Ron Atwood rang to ask if she could be ready to go for an interview the day following at the university and then take the SAT that Saturday. He would take her both times, he said, so she didn't need to worry.

Esther was glad of a diversion. Waiting for her uncle every night and hoping that he might say something that would relieve them all, had been nerve-racking. Ron was shocked to see how pale the girl looked when he picked her up that Thursday morning. He had worried about her being alone so much and thought her family very thoughtless, though he kept this opinion to himself.

Esther's interview went like clockwork. She had already sent in her admission forms which had been reviewed and, to her great relief, some of the usual requirements had been waived. Her high school records were not necessary in her case, they told her. It was obvious she had made a good impression. All that was needed now was to do well in her SAT and then begin to study for the CLEP which would mean, if she reached a certain level in some subjects, that she would not need to take many of the general education classes.

The campus at ISU completely overwhelmed her. There were impressive buildings everywhere—dorms, lecture halls, and administration buildings. There were students everywhere too! There must be thousands living in this mini-city, Esther thought. She studied them when she could. Most reminded her of Ramona and her friends, but some with their long hair and earrings, patched blue jeans and shabby jackets caught her attention. No one would ever go to college dressed like that in Romania, she thought. America was surely a land of extremes.

Ron found time to give her a guided tour of the campus before they had lunch together with Ramona. She brought along her roommate, a tall, thin girl, with straight brown hair, who looked very intellectual. She had taken quite a few classes with Ron and like him, was in her last year though she seemed considerably older than he did. She drew up her chair close to him as they ate their cheeseburgers, looking boldly up into his face as she chattered on about their classes, exams, and coming events at college. But the young man answered in monosyllables and seemed embarrassed and not at all himself, Esther noticed. He ate quickly and then excused himself. Ramona was to take Esther to see her dorm and then bring her to the library where she could wait for her chauffeur. He had two lectures to attend that afternoon.

"What's wrong with Ron Atwood?" Ramona's friend asked as they made their way across campus.

"He's changed lately, Marci," Ramona muttered. "Not a bit like he used to be. Now his cousin, Len. You should see him. He's awfully religious, but great fun to be with."

Esther felt even more uneasy than she had been during lunch when Marci had given her one long stare and then utterly ignored her for the rest of the meal.

"I suppose you'll be rooming with me next semester, Esther?" Ramona asked in a matter-of-fact tone as she ushered her cousin into the small room she shared with Marci.

Esther looked startled. "Why, I don't know, Ramona. I mean, am I expected to stay here all week?" She sounded so mournful that her cousin laughed.

"It's not that bad, Esther. In fact it's fun to be away from home, some of the time at least."

Esther was glad when her tour of Ramona's dorm was over and she was left alone in the library. Room after room of books, all catalogued neatly and standing row after row, seemed to beckon her to delve into their mysteries. She felt almost sick with desire, yet too dazed to know where to begin. She was like a man who had been starved for weeks and was faced with a three-course meal.

As they drove home a few hours later, Esther told Ron how she had felt. He threw her a rather quizzical glance. "I've just never met anyone like you, Esther," he told her. "You seem, well, so naïve in so many ways, and yet so frighteningly complicated at the same time. Are all Romanians enigmas like you?"

Esther laughed. In fact, she had laughed at least six times during the course of that day. Ron knew, for he had counted. "Well, I really don't know," she told him. "I rather think it may be our culture in general not me in particular which is an enigma to you. But Gabby will be here next year. And if you think I am an enigma you'll think she is...." She paused. No words could describe Gabby. None at all.

"I'm sorry Marci acted so rudely," he told her apologetically. "She's extremely bright but very peculiar."

Esther said nothing and he went on, "It won't be long till you're a student here, Esther. It'll be a big change for you, won't it?"

Esther nodded but said nothing. The campus they had just left behind them seemed a world of its own to the young Romanian. Another world to enter! She just couldn't face it, not yet.

"Why Esther, you're nearly crying," Ron said in alarm. "You've been rather silent ever since you went with Ramona to her dorm. What happened?"

"Nothing happened. Only Ramona takes it for granted that I'll room with her next semester. I never realized I would have to live there. Oh Ron, I'm just getting used to America. I'm beginning to feel at home in my uncle's house and now...."

Ron felt he could shake Ramona as he listened. Hadn't she any tact, any sympathy with this cousin of hers? He leant towards Esther and said firmly and without thinking of all that his words might entail, "Don't worry. You won't have to stay there. You're not ready for it yet. I'll take you every day to college. You can tell Ramona that," and he reached out and gave her hand a light squeeze as if to reassure her that he would keep his word.

Esther blushed, and as she looked up at him through her tears, she seemed so vulnerable and so beautiful in her own unique way. He felt like a color-blind driver who was approaching a set of traffic lights. Were the lights he saw ahead of him orange or green? He looked again at the girl beside him and thought he knew. She needed his help desperately and he could do with the company of someone like Esther. One and a half hours a day alone with her for twelve or more weeks would certainly be a challenge, but it might also prove a very valuable education for both of them. After all, his mother had told him just the week before that she would still need him at home for a while to come, especially at nights, so he wouldn't be living in the dorm anyway. And he had already made up his mind that he would help this girl get adjusted to American life. But, he asked himself, would he have been so quick to make the offer if it had been someone like Rachel or Marci? He wasn't sure.

There was silence between them for a while—the one embarrassed, the other confused. Esther quickly realized the implications of Ron's offer. She, who had never been alone with a boy in her life until she had let herself be taken to church by this Ron Atwood, would soon be with him twice a day for weeks on end, and alone! Could she do it? Dare she do it?

Finally Ron cleared his throat and began, "Look Esther, maybe I should make one thing clear before we go on any further." His voice was so very serious that Esther looked up alarmed so he went on quickly. "I mean, I really want to help you. It must be really very frightening for you at times—facing so many changes." He stopped a moment, but her smile made him continue. "Maybe it would help you to know that I've made up my mind not to get serious with any girl at present. And I know you wouldn't want that anyway. So you can trust me, like you would your older brother, for I really do want to be your friend."

Esther stared at him. She hadn't expected such a speech from Ron Atwood. But he seemed dead in earnest, so her face relaxed as she said slowly, "If that's how you feel, Ron, I think it'll be OK."

"Well, we don't need to decide it all just yet," he assured her. "But I'll stand by my word. If you and your uncle think it better that you commute for the first semester then I'll see to it you get to school every day, and on time," he added laughing. "I'm known to be quite punctual so I hope you are too."

"Actually, I'm not," admitted Esther reddening. "It's one of my failings, I'm afraid. Gabby and Aunt Ana were always telling me to hurry up or I'd miss the bus, or train or whatever. So now you know what you're in for."

"Yes, thanks for the warning," and he chuckled. "Tell you the truth, I'm kind of glad to know you're human after all—have faults like the rest of us."

"Faults? I have plenty of faults, Ron. Ask my sister."

"Maybe I'll just do that one day. But come on, what other faults do you have? I'm curious. Are they Romanian faults or American ones?"

"You're laughing at me," Esther protested. "But I think my worst fault is a very universal one, though we Romanians may have more than our fair share of it." She paused and looked so grave that Ron wished he could change the subject, but the girl went on, "I think I should warn you that I'm very vain, Ron. Gabby and Aunt Ana were always telling me that."

"Yes, that is a terrible fault, Esther," Ron told her in an equally serious tone. "I'm not sure I can cope with a vain young woman and a Romanian at that."

The twitch of his lips and the twinkle in his grey eyes gave him away. "You're making fun of me. But it's not funny, you know. God considers pride one of the worst sins—it's more than a fault, really it is."

The young man beside her was now totally bamboozled. Here was an extremely attractive and talented girl actually condemning herself, and genuinely so, for being vain. "You know, Esther, I think there's a difference between vanity and pride," he told her as he swung off the interstate. They would soon be home now.

"Why, you must think like C. S. Lewis, Ron," said Esther in a surprised tone. Lewis had been one of her grandfather's favorite authors and he had brought some of his books with him when he had come to live with his daughter. "He says the very same in *Mere Christianity*. Maybe you've read it?"

Ron shook his head. "No, but great minds must think alike then." He grinned. "I've read his space trilogy and his Narnia series and a few others but not that one, though I've heard about it. I didn't consider myself religious enough to tackle it. But maybe I will, seeing you've brought it up. Well, Lewis was quite a guy, so if he says that, I think you can rest easy. After all Esther, I suppose I'm not the first one to tell you that you have got quite a lot going for you. I mean, is it any wonder you might be just the least bit vain?" Ron had chosen his words carefully but he had made his point.

Esther blushed scarlet. She desperately wanted to change the subject but she made herself say slowly, "Ron, C.S. Lewis is not God, and *Mere Christianity* is not the Bible. And anyway, he didn't say vanity was commendable, only less evil than pride. And I don't think God makes the same distinctions as Lewis does, and I don't think He would excuse me either, like you are doing."

"You don't? I'm not so sure. But here we are in Velours already and nearly at your uncle's door. Thanks for a great day, Esther. And remember, be ready at seven Saturday morning. The exams start at nine."

"I'll remember," she reassured him. "And I'll be on time," she added with a grin. "But thanks so much for your help. I don't know how I can repay you."

"You have already repaid me. Have a good evening," and he was off before she could say anything more.

Esther had plenty to think of as she went upstairs to change her clothes, but her coming exam soon put all other thoughts out of her head. That evening and all the next day she pored over her books. By supper time she was thoroughly sick of study and was glad of her cousins' company. The air was charged as they sat together in the den that night, for no one felt like going to bed. Esther finally went upstairs sensing that her uncle might want to be alone with his daughters when he came home. At last, the girls heard their father turn the key in the door and he entered, his face pale and looking emotionally spent. As he flopped in his usual recliner, they couldn't help but pity him.

"Well," John began, taking a deep breath; "I suppose you've all been waiting to hear what I've decided. I've just been on the phone to your mother. I saw her earlier this week as you know, but promised I'd phone her on Friday, after I'd had more time to reflect on her recent change of attitude. I've told her that I appreciate her admission that she did wrong all these years and that she was sorry. And," he gulped, "I also told her that I had acted the fool. I had not truly loved her but tried to make up for it with gifts—things instead of true, heart affection." He paused. It was not easy to admit to his own girls that he had also been in the wrong. They waited expectantly, though neither of them was very optimistic as to the final outcome of their parents' conversation together.

"Your Mother was in tears," he went on, his voice steadying a little. "Very emotional, quite a change from the icy coldness of at least ten years. But I had to be truthful with her. What love I ever did have has evaporated over the years."

Rachel interrupted him eagerly, "Don't say it's too late to try again, Dad. If you both don't expect too much from each other, you can make it yet. You really can."

Her father shook his head sorrowfully. "No girls, you'll have to accept the bitter fact. The damage has been done. If your mother's change of heart had come years ago, then it could well have been different between us. But years of coldness, of tantrums, of constant complaining have worn grooves in my heart. I have to make a new start in life and so does she. I have given it much thought all this week. Divorce is the only way out. It will be best for both of us. It will set us free to go our own ways in life."

As Rachel sorrowfully made her way to bed that night, the word "free" echoed in her consciousness long after she had switched off the light. "Divorce . . . will set us free," her dad had told them. Rachel frowned into the darkness. Free to do what, she wondered?

Chapter Sixteen

Rachel and Esther

Esther heaved a sigh of relief as she got into the car that Saturday afternoon. Her SAT exam was over and she had coped better than she had expected. Now came the worst part—waiting for the results. And there were still the CLEP exams to face. When they finally made it home, it was nearly three. Esther invited Ron in for some light refreshments. As they entered the kitchen, they nearly collided with Jean who had just finished cleaning for the day. She had phoned the night before to say that she would be running behind schedule that Saturday.

"Well, so you've stolen Ramona's boyfriend, have you?" Jean told Esther, as she eyed them both with grim satisfaction. "Thought you'd do something like that, the moment I set eyes on you."

Esther flushed scarlet. She tried to stay out of Jean's way on a Saturday morning. It seemed that the cleaning lady had taken a definite dislike to the Romanian girl and didn't hesitate to show it.

"I think you've got it all wrong," Ron told the woman coolly. "I wasn't Ramona's boyfriend in the first place. I'm a friend to both Esther and her cousin, nothing more."

Jean gave a shrill laugh. "Oh tell me another, young man. I wasn't born yesterday," and she grabbed her jacket from the back of the chair and stalked past them to the front door.

"Don't pay any attention to her, Esther," he said gently. "It's just her way."

Esther said nothing. Jean was the only person she had met since coming to America whom she found it hard not to dislike. Nothing she could do or say seemed to please her.

Ron didn't stay long, and Esther was still feeling the smart of Jean's sarcasm when Ramona came downstairs and informed her that her uncle was pushing for a divorce despite his wife's seeming change of heart. Although the news really came as no surprise, she felt very depressed the rest of the day. As for Rachel, she had become her old taciturn self once more, refusing to talk to anyone and spending long hours alone in her room.

Then, early the next morning, Ron phoned to say he had come down with the flu. She walked alone to St. Jude's, for her uncle had made no mention of church. He was still in his room when she left the house, very unusual, Esther thought, for her uncle was an early bird, even on Sundays. Ramona was off again with Len, leaving her with her younger cousin who had hardly spoken two words by supper time.

The long day dragged to a close. Ramona came home before supper but seemed unusually quiet and only brightened up when Marci called to take her to a movie. Loneliness swept over Esther in waves as she munched on her ham sandwich. She had little appetite. Then, as she entered the den where Rachel was sitting moping in the twilight, she heard her mutter to herself, "I might have guessed it would end this way. Nothing works out for us anymore. Nothing."

"Nothing?" Esther sounded surprised. "Are you sure, Rachel?" The girl was not used to being contradicted, so she looked up angrily at her cousin.

"I wasn't talking to you, Esther. You weren't supposed to hear me. It's OK for you. You name it—you've got it."

Esther looked at her in astonishment. "Why, what on earth do you mean?"

Rachel waved her aside. "You have everything that counts. I mean, look at you: you're a real beauty. Oh come on now, Esther;" her voice became sarcastic as her cousin began to protest. "Don't give me all that false modesty trash. I've seen you ogling in that mirror. And I've heard all the compliments and I know you've heard them too. Do you think Ron Atwood likes you just because you're so saintly, or because you've got a figure like a model, a complexion like a film star, and eyes and lips that send guys crazy? Then there's that foreign touch, and that helpless air that seems to work like a magnet." Rachel was really upset now and there was no stopping her. "Let me finish the catalog of your plusses before you interrupt. Then you sing like an angel, will probably become a star someday, and as if that weren't enough, you can speak I don't know how many languages."

Esther was getting upset by this time. Then she calmed herself. That's just what the girl opposite her wanted—to make her angry. So she bit her lip, and prayed for patience with her impossible cousin. But Rachel had not finished. "And, more than anything else, you've had a Mom and Dad who loved each other. I bet you've never heard a bad word between them in all your life. My parents knew a lot and spewed them out when they wanted to, both of them, but especially Mom. Oh don't look so shocked. You need to come down to earth a bit. This isn't Heaven you know, and we're not all saints like you."

Rachel paused and glared at her cousin. "And now our home is split. So what have I to fall back on when our luck goes bad? Oh, I know, you'll say God. Well, you can have your God. I don't see Him, feel Him, or believe in Him, and I don't want to either. He's done nothing for our family that I can see or for me personally. Maybe you've been born under a lucky star." Rachel paused for a moment but she still had more to get out of her system. "So even if you lose your family you still have a lot to fall back on. But I've got nothing." Esther went to protest but her cousin waved her aside with her hand. "I know you've lost both your parents Esther, but I think death would be better than all this trouble we're in now." She stopped, rising abruptly and gazing out the patio doors, her back to her cousin so she could not see her face. But more was to come.

Swinging around suddenly, she burst out again. "Then look at me. What do you see? Now be honest. A girl who looks like a scarecrow, with skin like yellow parchment, who hardly ever smiles and frightens away every boy who comes within yards of her. I only know a smattering of Spanish; I sing like a crow and can't play a note on any musical instrument. To make it worse, what I do know just repels everyone near me. I can't swim, or run, or play tennis, or basketball. Everyone else seems to think I'm the proud one, but they're mistaken. I never look in a mirror, never think good of myself. And now my parents are so messed up I can't really rely on them any more. And I don't have any religion or friends to fall back on when trouble hits. So when I stare into the future I see only a black abyss of nothingness. That's all." And Rachel buried her face in her hands, her lank hair covering her tearstained face.

"But Rachel," Esther faltered, "your mother has changed a lot recently, hasn't she? You have that to be grateful for."

The girl lifted her face, eyes blazing. "Oh yes. She's changing slowly, but it's proving too late. Why couldn't she have done this ten years ago? And why couldn't you have come here before?"

"Me?" Esther asked. "What could I have done?"

"Esther, don't you realize that it was your coming on the scene that really made her think?" Rachel paused realizing she had said too much but the fat was in the fire now and she was too miserable to care much what she said or did not say. Nothing could be worse than it was, or so it seemed to her in the mood she was in at that moment.

"Oh, I shouldn't have said that. But it's true. Didn't you know that Dad was in love with your Mom and she turned him down?"

"Yes," Esther replied still mystified. "But that was twenty odd years ago, wasn't it?"

"Yep, sure was, but I've just discovered that Dad never did get your Mom out of his heart. And you're the image of her, aren't you? That's why Mom didn't want to see you. It all came out when I asked her why. She finally saw how selfish she had been, about you and about your mother, too, all these years, and it made her decide to try again with Dad but it's just too late. Too late." And the wail that accompanied these words went straight to her cousin's heart.

But Esther was wise enough to know that what Rachel needed least at that moment was more pity. Flinging caution to the wind, she went over to the distraught girl and grabbed her firmly by the shoulders. Tilting Rachel's chin until her dark eyes met her own, she said firmly, "Listen to me for a moment will you, Rachel Popescu? You've had your say now I'm going to have mine. Stop having a pity party! Start thinking about someone else's pain for a change. That might just do you a world of good!"

Esther paused. Rachel was staring at her in unbelief. Taking advantage of the lull in the storm, she went on rapidly, "And you need to get into your head that you're not the only one in the world who's had problems. Do you know what it is to be stared at whenever you go outside the door just because you're different? That's what I get every time I go to town here, or to college, or even shopping. Have you ever been sick with hunger and cold, day after day? And have you ever been followed home from school every night by someone who is...." Esther shuddered, "an animal or almost, yet has power enough to crush you in his two fingers, so much power that you had to escape to another country? Have you ever wakened up one morning to find your mother's body crushed to pieces and utterly unrecognizable? Or have you watched your Dad slowly waste away, hunted and hounded by his enemies when he hadn't done a thing to deserve it? Death is better than what you're going through, you say? Much you know about death, that's obvious," and Esther almost flung her cousin from her in disgust. She had begun in real compassion for the girl, trying to bring her to her senses, but had lost her cool in the end.

Esther sat down in the chair opposite, utterly spent and very ashamed of herself. But to her surprise, Rachel was looking at her with a new respect. "Whew," she whistled, "I didn't think you could get so mad, Esther." Then her face darkened once more as she went on, "Do you know you even look prettier when you're angry? I'm glad Ron Atwood wasn't here. He'd have fallen down on his knees at your feet and pledged to be your knight for ever."

Her cousin was tempted to smile in spite of herself. Rachel had bared her soul, all unwittingly, to her that evening. Esther said nothing for a while, but when she did speak her voice was full of compassion. "I know you're very angry but please listen to me, just for a moment more." Rachel had pulled out a book from the shelves behind her and was leafing through it, but Esther knew she had her full attention. "I have grown to love both you and Ramona. But you know, Rachel, I'm a lot more like you than you think, so I really understand you better."

Rachel's mouth fell open. No one could understand her. She was too complex, or so she liked to think. But Esther was continuing, "I know you don't believe me. But you know, I've realized lately that I even look like you."

Her cousin's bitter laugh cut through her like a knife. But Esther tried to ignore it and went on, "Yes, even Ramona remarked on it one day. We've the same figure, haven't we, or almost have? Ramona is plump, you know, and fair. She doesn't look a bit like we do. And we've both got very dark hair and brown eyes. And our complexion is not that different either or wouldn't be if you got outside a bit more and took an interest in yourself. Oh I know your hair is straight and mine's wavy, but straight hair's all the rage now, isn't it?"

Here, to her amazement, Rachel burst out crying. "Oh Esther," she sobbed. "You don't know how bad I feel about myself. If I could only believe that what you said was true. But you know it isn't. If I'm so much like you, then why doesn't Ron Atwood look at me as he does you? Or why doesn't Dad fix his eyes on my face like he does on yours?"

Esther was silent a moment. "Come here, Rachel," commanded Esther as she took Rachel's hand and led her into the hallway. Standing behind her she pointed to their images in the full length mirror. "See? We both look very Romanian, don't we? And look! When you smile like you did just then, your whole face lights up. When I first saw your dad at the airport, I recognized him by his smile, it was so like my father's. And you have his smile, and so do I. Now, see how alike we really are?"

Rachel looked up at Esther who was just a little taller than she. Her eyes were glistening with tears as she whispered, "Oh Esther. I'm so miserable. And I'll never really be like you, at least not on the inside. I feel so wicked, so full of hate and jealousy and everything dark, while you...." She broke down and sobbed.

Esther took her in her arms and found no resistance. Stroking her hair she said softly, "Rachel, God has so much in store for you if you would only let Him be your Father and your Friend. And it isn't being like me that matters, really, but being what He made you to be."

Rachel pulled away and ran off to her bedroom. Esther thought she had said enough for one day. But her eyes grew dreamy as she went back to her seat in the den. Looking down the future she could visualize a very different Rachel Popescu—one that would surprise her whole family and herself into the bargain.

Chapter Seventeen

Ramona's Dilemma

Esther woke up Monday morning with a splitting headache and before long, found herself in bed with a raging fever. Her uncle hated to leave her alone all day but there was no alternative. Len had phoned on Friday to remind her she had promised to sing that Sunday but she told him that would be out of the question. She would do it when she was able. A promise was a promise.

Then Tuesday morning, Ramona came back from college feeling very ill, with a fever even higher than Esther's. The rest of the week the two cousins nursed each other as best they could, and by Sunday evening they were well enough to eat the chicken broth and noodles John had prepared for them.

"Well, well, girls," he commented, as he watched them enjoy their first meal in days, "you've had a week of it. Think you're up to talking about birthday parties? The 20th will be here before you know it, Ramona!"

"After last year I'm surprised you even mention birthday parties, Dad," Ramona said with a laugh. For the past few years, her birthday had become quite a social event. She had seized this opportunity of acting as hostess to some of her many friends. But the previous year had been a fiasco. After much wheedling, John had allowed her to serve alcohol much to his regret. Several of the guests had drunk too much; the neighbors had complained of the noise which had continued well past midnight. Ever indulgent, her father had realized, too late, that he had not supervised the affair as he should have done, and so he warned Ramona that, in future, there was to be no liquor if the party were held at his house.

"Well, but you're a Christian now, right? There should be no problem this year." John glanced keenly at his daughter as he spoke. He had been skeptical from the beginning about Ramona's religious conversion and was waiting to see how it would affect her life practically. So far, he had not discerned much difference. True, Len had replaced Ron Atwood as her chief male companion, which he was not sure had been a good switch. And church had certainly been on her Sunday agenda which had meant getting up at a decent time. That had been a plus, he admitted. But his usually amiable daughter didn't seem to be her own bright, cheery self these days. It certainly looked as if religion didn't suit her too well.

Ramona read her father's thoughts and pouted. "Come Dad. Of course we won't have any booze this year. But apart from that, I'm not sure much needs to change."

"But didn't you know that Esther's birthday is just two days after yours? One party for two would be the practical way to do things, wouldn't it?"

"Oh, Uncle John, you don't need to include me. I'm not used to birthday parties," put in Esther.

"Time you got used to them, my dear," John told her, taking her empty bowl. "And of course you are to be included. You are part of our family now. Don't forget that!" Then he turned again to his daughter. "So Ramona, what's it to be and when?"

"Give me time to think a bit, Dad," said Ramona stretching. "I'm not up to scratch yet. I'll have to talk it over with Esther."

They were still discussing the affair when the phone rang. It was Ron, asking how the invalids were getting on. Ramona took the phone into the kitchen. "I'm glad you phoned just now, Ron," she told him as she pulled out the stool for she still felt quite weak. "I really want to pick your brains."

"Fire ahead, then. You know how few I have so they won't take much picking."

Ramona chuckled. She felt easier when Ron was his usual jovial self. He had become too serious of late, Esther's influence probably. "You know it's my birthday in two weeks and I usually throw a party at our house."

It was Ron's turn to laugh. He had only known Ramona since the spring but had heard about her parties. "Well?" he asked as if to say, "What have I to do with your parties?"

"Well, this year," began Ramona, choosing her words carefully, "Esther is here with us." She paused.

"And that means you can't have a party?" Ramona felt he was laughing at her so continued quickly, "No, not exactly. But, it's her birthday on the 22nd."

Ron interrupted her with a whistle, "Whew! That's a puzzler right enough." Then he added more thoughtfully, "I never knew she had a birthday so soon. Is she your age then, Ramona?"

"She's the same age, exactly," she answered. "But the problem is that we're so different in everything, so I don't quite know how one party can suit the both of us. Maybe you've got some good ideas?"

"But you are supposed to be a good Christian now, Ramona, aren't you? I would have thought you two had a lot in common."

Ramona was silent for a moment. She had puzzled over that too. "I guess we haven't, though," she answered slowly. "She has her own type of religion. While I have..." she paused, "Len's type, I suppose."

Ron snorted. "Then ask Len, Ramona. He'll give you the kind of advice you're looking for. You and he are still good friends aren't you?"

"Of course," Ramona assured him, but Ron thought her tone was not very convincing.

Then he said something that really put the cat among the pigeons. "You know, Ramona, come to think of it, I could solve the whole problem by taking your problematic cousin off your hands for the evening. That would make things a lot simpler for you, now wouldn't it?"

"So that's how you treat my parties?" was the girl's tart reply. "I was gong to invite you, of course, but you would prefer an evening out with my beautifully religious cousin?"

"Oh come on Ramona, take a joke, can't you?"

"Oh, joke is it? Didn't sound like it."

"Well, I wasn't really serious, Ramona, though I've sort of gone off parties a bit lately. Getting too old, I suppose," and he gave a short laugh. "I've never been to one of yours so it's nothing personal. But look, why don't you ask my cousin for advice. I'm sure he'll come up with something, and you'll probably want to invite him this year."

Ramona hadn't thought about that and was silent. "By the way, I'd like to talk to Esther a moment, please," Ron told her, and so the conversation ended. Ramona frowned as she handed her cousin the receiver, and fidgeted as she heard Esther agree to have Ron come over the next evening to give her some further guidelines for passing the CLEP.

Ramona had been growing accustomed to turn to Len for comfort, so was soon telling him her dilemma. He immediately suggested that the group "The Jesus Guys" from his church come and entertain them with some Christian rock. And then he said he knew a fellow who was a good violinist who played classical music. That way, both Ramona and Esther would be catered to and everyone would be pleased. But Ramona knew her friends and was not sure they would be satisfied with Christian music even though it was contemporary. Len sensed her hesitation and urged, "Ramona, this is a time you can witness to your friends. It will be a wonderful opportunity."

"Is that all you can think about, Len?" she asked angrily. "I'd like to have a good time at my party and not drag religion into it."

"Ramona," he began, but the girl had bottled up her frustration for two weeks and now it was all coming out.

"Listen, Len," she said, her voice a little calmer. "I've wanted to talk to you for a while now; I've decided that church is just not up my street. I gave it a try, but it's no use."

Len was serious for once. "You've not been the same since that Connie talked to you. What did she say? Please tell me."

Ramona gulped and then blurted it all out: "Well, she told me that she was also one of your girl converts and...."

Len interrupted her. "I can guess exactly what else she said. Connie is a jealous, immature child. She took my attentions more seriously than I intended."

"Well, Len," Ramona sounded cool now, "all I can say is, don't plan on taking me to your church any more. If you want to be my boyfriend, then take me out on a proper date, or whatever. I really like you. You're great company. But I don't like the way you mix religion with dating."

"But how can I be your friend and not mix religion?" he answered in a defensive tone. "A Christian is a Christian, and can't hide his light under a bushel."

Ramona sighed. It was no use arguing with a guy like him. "Well, it's been good knowing you, Len. And you are invited to the party. Good Night."

Esther had not overheard the conversation but could see Ramona was upset. She sensed that her religious phase was coming to an end, but when she heard Len's suggestion for the party she groaned.

"Len's idea is no good, I agree," her cousin told her as she resumed her seat by the window. "My friends would think I had gone crazy and I'd be a hypocrite if I just had Christian songs and classical music. I'm tired of trying to be religious when I'm not that way inside. But we could invite the church group for the first part of the evening. I heard them once and they're pretty good really. Then you could go upstairs later when we had our dancing. Would that work?"

Esther immediately sensed that smothering, choking sensation coming over her. What was she getting into, or rather how could she stay out of it all and be sensitive to her new family's feelings?

"Right now, Ramona, I'm too confused to know what to do," she said aloud, "but I'll give you an answer in a few days." And with that promise, Ramona had to be content.

Chapter Eighteen

The Party

"You're not enjoying this a bit, are you Esther?" Rachel whispered, as they refilled their plates with ham and cheese, peanuts, fruit, ice cream and a slice of cake, bought in honor of the two birthday girls.

"I'm enjoying the food," and Esther smiled as she plopped a plump strawberry in her mouth and took another scoop of ice cream.

"But not the music or the company," put in Rachel as she plugged her ears with her fingers. "Ramona likes it loud and her friends do too, or most of them at any rate. But it's Gospel and all for your benefit so you'd better go in and enjoy it."

"I can't say it's my taste," said Esther with a grimace.

"Nor mine either," commented her cousin grinning, "though it's better than what Ramona usually has at her parties."

"Hi there, Esther," said a voice behind them. Esther looked up to see a tall, pale-faced, lanky fellow standing by her side. She recognized him immediately.

"Why, hello Claude," she exclaimed smiling. "I think we've met before."

Claude said nothing. He was eyeing the Romanian girl from head to toe. Esther looked uncomfortable.

"Had anything to eat? There's still plenty," and she pointed to the loaded table.

Still Claude remained silent. When his parents had told him of Esther's coming, he had immediately conjured up all sorts of ways to help Ramona's poor little cousin adapt to American society—help her learn English, maybe, if ever he got a chance. And it would be a good excuse to see Ramona again at the same time. But when he had met Esther at church that Sunday with the good-looking Ron Atwood and discovered she spoke English a great deal better than he did, he had been greatly taken aback. She didn't seem to need his help very much and his pity had turned to annoyance.

But now, seeing he had been invited to the party, he meant to enjoy himself. But as always, Ramona was keeping him at a distance. He was used to seeing the boys buzzing around her while he admired from afar. He had always adored this blue eyed, flaxen-haired doll ever since that day when, as a child of ten, she had asked him to rescue her precious kitten from the jaws of a vicious, stray dog who had wandered into her back yard. As a reward, he had demanded a kiss from the fair maiden and a friendship of sorts had begun between them. Whenever Ramona had felt lonely, or blue, or had fallen out with her latest boyfriend, Claude had only been a phone call away. Not that he had ever been satisfied with his role as a standby, but it was better than nothing. But now, since the Popescus had moved to Velours, Ramona seemed to be fading out of his life. But he wouldn't give up. He never gave up on anything he really wanted. This blonde little doll was worth waiting for and he sure knew how to wait!

But as he watched Esther talk and laugh with Rachel and noticed her slim figure and smooth skin, her wonderful eyes and glossy raven locks, he temporarily forgot that he preferred blonde hair to black, and blue eyes to brown, or that he usually shied away from anything and everything that reminded him of Romania.

"You look great tonight, Esther," he blurted out suddenly as he helped himself to a third piece of cake. The girl blushed but said quietly, "Thank you, Claude." Her quiet self-control annoyed him. He wanted to upset her equilibrium, make her depend on him somehow, so he added quickly, "You'd look even better, though, if you'd lighten up a bit. You look as if you were still in the backwoods of Moldova or somewhere like that. Get some slacks on; or even better, buy yourself a mini skirt, let down your hair; put some make-up on. That's the way they do it over here, you know," he said, as he sidled up to her.

Esther was so taken aback she stood stock still and stared at him. "Here," and he gave her a wink, "let's undo this bow and let your hair down," and before Esther realized what he was doing, Claude's long, bony fingers had deftly undone her gold ribbon; and loosened her thick, wavy locks until they cascaded in profusion over her shoulders.

Claude surveyed her with a bold, admiring stare. It gave the girl an alluring, gypsy look, he thought to himself. My, but she was as pretty as a picture. Her rosy lips were parted in anger and her dark eyes were flashing dangerously but Claude pretended not to notice. He grabbed her hands and pulled her to him. "Now you need to learn how to dance. Bet you don't know how," he muttered. "And while I'm at it," he added with a laugh, "I'll teach you how to kiss too, if you give me a chance."

"No way!" retorted the furious girl as she pulled one hand free and gave her tormentor a resounding slap on his right cheek. Rachel chuckled quietly at her cousin's spunk, but her smile soon died away as she saw the glitter in Claude's eyes. As Ramona had told her father years before, that Illiescu boy had a crazy streak in him and you'd just better not rouse him too far.

"Please let me go," Esther pleaded as he began pulling her towards the lounge where the floor had already been cleared.

Claude paused for a moment. The girl looked really scared, and he had only wanted a bit of fun. Maybe he had gone too far already. Then he remembered the slap she had just given him and he gritted his teeth. It was her turn to be humiliated

Just then the musicians quickened their beat. The rhythm fired him again. It might be Gospel but it sure sounded like rock to him. Soon he was attempting to make his partner dance to the music, and Esther found herself, much against her will, gyrating foolishly in the middle of her uncle's living-room floor.

Meanwhile, Rachel stood helplessly by. She was no match for the tall and wiry Claude. Then she saw the door open and Ron Atwood's familiar figure enter the crowded room. He had come half an hour late and was looking around for Ramona or Esther.

"Ron, can't you do something?" pleaded Rachel, as she met him at the door. "Claude has made passes at Esther and now he's making her dance and she doesn't want to. He's making a fool of himself and her."

Sure enough. All present had stopped talking and were gawking at the couple struggling mid floor. Ron's quick eye took in the situation in one glance. He strode over to Claude and commanded angrily, "Let the girl go immediately. Can't you see she doesn't want to dance with you? And, anyway, it's not time for dancing yet."

Claude dropped Esther's hand and looked defiantly into Ron Atwood's face. "Why are you interfering? I'm trying to teach her. Romanians are so stuffy when they first come here to the States. She needs to get with it if she wants to succeed here."

"It's her birthday, isn't it," growled the irate Ron. "She should be enjoying herself and it is obvious that this is not one of the things she enjoys. And anyway, this is Christian music. We should be listening, not dancing." And he took Esther's arm and sat her down in an easy chair by the window. All eyes were following them, and Esther was more embarrassed than ever, though extremely grateful to her rescuer.

Ron looked round for Ramona, but she was nowhere to be seen. He learned afterwards that she had slipped into town to buy more soft drinks. "I'm sorry, Esther," he whispered, "I don't know what got into that Claude. But what did happen exactly? He seemed very upset about something."

Esther looked at the floor. "He undid my bow; told me I needed to lighten up a bit and then, he..." she hung her head, "he tried to kiss me so I gave him a good slap in the face. That made him hopping mad so he decided I needed to learn to dance, to humiliate me I suppose."

Ron stared in surprise then grinned to himself. He'd never have thought the meek little angel in front of him was capable of such fire. But he saw that the girl was shaking almost uncontrollably. She was a very shy and private person and it had mortified her to know that everyone present had witnessed her humiliation. The boys in the group were still playing but having all they could do to keep a straight face. She felt all eyes were still on her as Ron talked with her. Her nerves could take it no longer and she muttered, "Excuse me, Ron, but I'm going upstairs for a while," and she jumped from her seat and made a quick exit.

Upstairs, she threw herself on her bed. Why had she agreed to all this? But what else could she have done. Her uncle had laid the law down to Ramona and made her moderate her plans to accommodate, at least somewhat, her conservative cousin. She would have been an utter spoilsport to refuse to come when that group had been invited for her benefit even though Ramona knew she didn't care for their music very much. Where had Ramona been to allow Claude to behave like that?

Soon there was a knock at the door and Ramona burst in. "What, crying? Oh come on Esther. Can't you take a joke?"

"Joke? Is that what you call it?" retorted Esther, as she sat bolt upright on the bed and began to pour out her indignation to her cousin. Ramona hadn't heard it all and her tone softened as she sat down on the bed.

"I'm sorry, Esther. I didn't know he had done all that. I don't know what got into him. But he has his crazy moments and you are very pretty, you know."

"But you're just as pretty," Esther blurted out. "And he never does that to you."

"Oh doesn't he?" Ramona's voice was cool. "Of course he does when he gets a chance and I don't slap him either."

Esther looked at her cousin incredulously. "Now look, Esther. He really meant nothing by it. It was in front of Rachel, wasn't it? Nothing could have come of it. It's a party and he was having some fun, that's all. Maybe he went a bit too far with you seeing you're so new here but you might as well know that there're always kisses to spare at parties. If you'd ignored it or just let him give you one or two, it would have passed over."

Esther's eyes were ablaze now. "I had thought you had better taste than that, Ramona."

Ramona blushed scarlet and tossed back her curls. "I have taste all right, Esther. But the difference between you and me is that I know how to handle the guys and you don't." Her voice took on a patronizing tone. "But you'll learn in time. Claude acts crazy sometimes and he's awfully stubborn, but as I said, I know him and he meant nothing by it. Come on now, don't be a spoilsport. It's your party too, you know."

"I told you at the beginning, I would go upstairs after a bit."

"After a bit? But it's only begun, and it is Christian music you know. And besides there are some of my friends I want you to meet. There'll be no more dancing for a while, promise, not until we put some of the real stuff on."

Esther hesitated. Her anger faded as she realized that she had given in to hurt pride. Promising Ramona she would be down in a few moments, she waited till her cousin left the room and then flopped, sobbing, to her knees.

"Lord," she began. "Please forgive me. You know how I hate being made a spectacle. Please teach me how to behave tonight. I'm your child in a strange, strange land. Help me to forget myself tonight and to think of others. Amen." She got up feeling strengthened. She was tying back her hair again when she had second thoughts. She glanced in the mirror. Maybe she should leave it like it was. It certainly suited her, and it did make her appear less aloof. Maybe that was one thing she could do to lessen the gap between herself and Ramona's friends.

On reaching the foot of the stairs, she found the young people were still gorging themselves with the goodies laid out in profusion on the kitchen counter. The group had taken a break and were joining in the feast.

Ramona was on the lookout for her cousin at the foot of the stairs. Taking her by the hand, she led her over to a group of two boys and two girls, standing, plates in hand, in the far corner of the room.

"I want you to meet my cousin, Esther," said Ramona. "These are guys I've met at college," she explained turning to her cousin. "This is Marci, you've met her already." Marci gave Esther a brief nod but her eyes were cold.

"And this is Mike and Jeff, and that is my best friend Kelly." All three nodded and said a brief "Hi" as they eyed Esther up and down. She knew she stood out from everyone in her two piece cream suit. Most were dressed casually in slacks and sweaters and she was sorely tempted to run upstairs and change. But it was a birthday party and she was used to dressing up for parties, not that she had been to that many in her twenty years.

Esther shifted awkwardly from one foot to another. There was a brief silence and then Ramona turned suddenly as a tall young man joined their party. Putting on a rather forced smile, she exclaimed, "Why Len, you've managed to come after all! Here, meet my friends from college."

Esther was relieved at the interruption, though Len's coming might complicate things, she thought. Ramona had told her she wasn't going to church with him again, but had made him and his group very welcome at her party. In typical Len fashion, he was soon laughing and joking with the rest. Esther managed to slip away into the kitchen at the first opportunity.

"Shy kid," commented Jeff as his eyes followed Esther.

"Great looker, though," added Michael with a laugh. "And what gorgeous hair she's got."

"But she's awfully stuck up," put in Kelly. "She's dressed as if she were going to a wedding and she struts around as if she were the Queen of England."

Ramona shrugged. "She's awfully stubborn beneath her sweet little smile and her long skirts and is terribly religious."

Len was about to make a rather lame excuse for Esther when he heard a deep voice behind him asking, "Who is awfully stubborn beneath her sweet little smile?"

"Hi Ron," Len exclaimed looking just slightly embarrassed.

"Oh it's you," Ramona said sweetly, taking his arm.

"Yes. It's the notorious Ron Atwood," exclaimed Kelly. "He's quite a stranger these days."

"Yeah," drawled Marci. "He spends most of his time going to church now I hear."

"Ron religious?" laughed Mike. "I don't believe it."

Ron ignored their comments and repeated his question, "But who's stuck up and stubborn and walks as if she were the a queen?"

"Oh come on, Ron," Ramona pouted. "You know who I mean."

"Couldn't guess," was the reply.

"No?" commented Ramona sarcastically. Then turning to her friends she added, "Well, *he* wouldn't think Esther stubborn or straight-laced, though he couldn't deny she's religious. Why she's the one who has taken him to church."

"I might let her do the same," grinned Mike. "She's awfully pretty, Ramona. Well, more than pretty. She's a real beauty. Congratulations, Ron. How do you do it?"

Ron gave him an icy stare and folded his arms. "I don't know what you mean, Mike. And let's get things straight, Ramona. *She's* taken *me* nowhere. The girl's having a hard time adjusting to life here and I've just tried to help out a bit. That's all. Nothing romantic or worth gossiping about."

Mike patted his friend on the back and laughed. "Don't be so touchy. But thanks for the info. Seems she's free after all!"

Ramona groaned inwardly and looked at Len who, for once, had seemed nonplussed during this discussion of the Romanian girl. Wanting, as usual, to offend no one, he had thought silence the best tack to take.

Ron turned on his heel and left them as abruptly as he had come. How could he explain his attitude to Esther? They wouldn't understand anyway. And that fool of a cousin of his, that religious prig who should have defended the girl, had been a real coward. He saw the girls in the kitchen and joined them just in time to overhear Esther saying, "It's just no use, Rachel. I feel so out of it. Can't even hold five minute's conversation with anyone!"

"Never mind, Esther," Rachel was saying comfortingly. "I'm never at home with these guys either. I find them just too boring. And by the way, did you know that Ramona was quite mad with Claude for what he did tonight? Look, he's sulking in the corner. She sure knows how to keep him in his place."

"I thought she didn't care much," murmured Esther.

"But she did, Esther. She was quite upset when she came downstairs from talking to you. But look, Ron's looking for you. It is your birthday, you know."

"I know," groaned Esther. "But I can't seem to cope tonight. Do I need to go out there again?"

"Out where?" asked a familiar voice. "Here, let me help tidy up. You shouldn't be doing this, Esther. It's your party too, you know."

"Yes, so it is," put in another voice. "Hello, birthday girl. Many happy returns!" It was the irrepressible Len.

Esther looked at both the young men in silence. She was a coward and she knew it. Her pride had been hurt that evening and she couldn't face the crowd again.

"Our group's playing, Esther. Come on," he urged. "After all, if you weren't here, they wouldn't be either. And, by the by, they want you to sing a number with them."

Esther turned pale. "No," she groaned, "I can't do it, Len. Anyway I don't know their songs. You know that."

"But they know some of yours, don't forget," reminded Len smugly.

Esther shook her head. "Don't force her, Len," Ron said quietly. "She's about had enough, can't you see?"

"Leave her to me this time, will you?" Len told his cousin coolly. There were too many folk around to make a fuss and Ron didn't want to draw attention to the Romanian girl, so he watched his cousin from a distance. He noticed to his relief that Len had placed her in a chair by the window and they were both listening to the music, or so it seemed.

"That's a great number, Esther," Len was saying. "I'm sure even you have to admit the words are great. Hope some of these youngsters are taking it in."

"Some seem to be listening," Esther admitted. She didn't like the music much but she had to admit the words were pretty pointed.

Len looked down at her glossy raven locks. "You know, Esther," he whispered softly, "I'm very glad you've let your hair down a bit. You don't look so holy and untouchable now. You do need to loosen up a bit."

Esther frowned. That's what everyone told her and maybe it was true but why couldn't they let her chose her own time and way to "loosen up" as they called it. She was greatly relieved when the musicians called Len over to discuss what they should sing next. He always made her nervous.

"Enjoying yourself all alone?" She started. There was Mike, standing by her chair. There was something sad in his eyes, Esther noticed, though his lips were smiling as he asked softly, "Do all Romanian girls have hair like you?"

Esther blushed as she tossed back her thick wavy tresses. She dropped her eyes and said nothing. The young man went on, "A little bird has told me you've a great voice. Won't you sing us something when they're through?" And he waved his hand towards the performers. "Something different. I mean, the music's not bad but a bit boring. Sing something Romanian."

Esther stared at him. "I... I don't think I can tonight," she stammered. "And if you think they're boring, I don't know what you'll think of my singing."

Just then Ron appeared on the scene. "Here Ron, see if you can persuade this young lady to sing us a few numbers. Anything, I don't care. Can be religious if she wants. I've heard she has great talent."

Ron hesitated. He had interposed on Esther's behalf several times already—once with Len and once with Claude. Would she expect him to do it again? He looked at the girl; her cheeks were aflame. If she really wanted to be a good example of her Christianity, here was a wonderful opportunity.

"Leave us alone a moment, Mike, please," Ron told his friend quietly. Mike obeyed meekly. "Good luck," he muttered, as he walked away.

Esther looked at Ron in surprise as he sat down beside her and began in a low voice, "Esther, won't you sing tonight? You have such a very wonderful voice as well as a very beautiful face. Mike's not like Len, you know. He's not trying to use you. And I had already meant to ask you the same thing. But I'm not going to force you. I'm just asking. Won't you do it, just this once?"

Esther stared at her companion. Here was her defender joining her persecutors. What could he be thinking? Hadn't she already gone through enough that evening? And maybe Mike would like it, but most of the others wouldn't, she was sure. She could imagine Marci's cold stare and Kelly's amused smile. This wasn't a place to sing hymns or even Romanian folk tunes.

Ron read her mind. "Some of us at least will appreciate your singing," he told her; "your Romanian tunes are so haunting. What about a few folk tunes and then maybe 'Numai Harul?' If Ramona liked it, some of her friends will too. Please, Esther. Just this once. You see, Mike has just...." But Esther had had enough. She was upset with Ron for backing Mike in what she felt was a very unreasonable request. So she rose abruptly, muttering, "I don't want to hear more about Mike. I've had enough. Some birthday party, I must say!" and she stalked off leaving behind an astonished Ron Atwood. His astonishment, however, soon turned to anger. "She didn't even let me explain about Mike," he grumbled to himself. "She's selfish just like every other girl."

Worse, however, than admitting Esther's faults, was his disappointment in the girl. She had suddenly fallen from the pedestal he had put her up on. His pride, too, was hurt. He had thought she would trust him not to ask her to do anything impossible. He had imagined he could persuade her when others had failed. But, she was awfully stubborn after all, just as Ramona had said.

To make it worse, Mike had been watching and now came back over to where he was sitting moping. "Couldn't handle her, could you Ron? Your charm failed for once. Pity, I did want to hear her. But come on, don't let that Romanian girl spoil your fun." The group had sung their last song and were packing up for the evening. Ramona had put on some music she thought more appropriate for a party and the dancing had begun.

Ramona had seen Esther leave the room and noticed that Ron seemed terribly upset. "Why not go upstairs and fetch your girl down, Ron, if you miss her so much," suggested Ramona coyly as she took his arm.

"She'd think that very inappropriate I'm afraid, and anyway, she's not my girl, Ramona," he retorted as he whirled her around the living room floor. Ron was frustrated with Esther, with Ramona, with everyone. But he was not going to further spoil the party so he danced with nearly every girl in the room, stuffed himself with ice cream and joked and joshed in his old carefree way, or so it seemed.

But it was a very disconsolate young man who met his mother's questioning gaze with a shrug as he made his way to bed that evening. His dark mood had not passed when he picked up the phone the next morning and dialed the Popescus' number.

"Is that you, Esther?" he asked, knowing full well that only she would be up at that time of morning.

"Yes," came the quiet reply.

"You still want to go to church this morning?"

"Of course, but do you?"

"No, actually I don't," was the cool rejoinder.

"Very well, then please don't come for me," Esther told him icily.

"That's right. You don't want an unwilling chauffeur, do you?"

"No," replied Esther. "Let's leave it for today."

There was a long pause and then Ron replied. "OK. If that's what you want."

Esther by this time was really annoyed. She was not used to this coolness from the courteous Ron and was nettled to the core. "It is obvious that's what *you* want, Ron. But thanks for the phone call. Bye," and, much to Ron's surprise, she put down the receiver. But her hand trembled as she did so. "There goes another friend," she thought. "Now I've only Rachel and Uncle John left who love me," and she threw herself on her bed weeping. "Give me Romania," she sobbed into the blankets, "with its Secret Police and its food rationing and its grey days and dark nights. This land is a mirage in the desert. It's a farce." Her whole frame shook with emotion. Despair surged over her in waves. She felt she was falling, falling. And then she remembered.

Why, there was someone. There was Hugh Gardner. Where was his note with his phone number? Fumblingly she fished out the folded piece of paper from her handbag and reread his letter. It seemed a bit audacious to phone him like this. He was practically a stranger, but he had said he was praying for her. Well, she would ring right away. Maybe she would catch him before he went to church.

"Is that Mr. Hugh Gardner?" she asked, as a man's voice answered her ring.

"No, but I'll get him right away," came the reply. "Can I tell him who is calling?"

"It's Esther Popescu. He might not remember me. He met me on the plane about six weeks ago."

"That's right. I met you too, briefly," was the response. "I'm his grandson. Just wait; I'll get him immediately."

"Esther?" came Hugh's voice a few moments later.

"Mr. Gardner," she faltered. "I am sorry to disturb you but I really do need to talk to someone."

"Talk on then, my dear," was the kind reply. "That's what I'm here for. Not good for a lot else at my age but I certainly can listen."

Esther smiled in spite of herself and felt better already. Soon she was pouring out her troubles. When she finished at last she heard Hugh's voice saying quietly, "Sounds terrible, Esther. Maybe you should go right back to Romania."

There was a silence at the other end. Although she had just used those very words a few moments earlier, Esther, for some reason or other, was loathe to agree with Hugh's suggestion.

"If your relatives here are so very hard to live with," he went on, "then you would be better with your old friends in Romania."

"Well," stammered Esther, "actually Uncle John really spoils me, and Rachel has greatly changed towards me in the last few weeks. And I really like Aunt Mary though I've only seen her once. And this Ron Atwood has been very kind, that is, until..." and her voice broke again.

"Do you want me to tell you the truth, Esther?" Hugh's voice was very serious. "Tell it like your father would have done?" he added.

Esther broke down at the mention of her father. "Yes, please do," she begged, sobbing.

"Well, then, I think that you acted like a coward last night. You let the Velvet Curtain completely smother your better impulses. Your pride was hurt by that impudent Claude. You should have shown those young people that you were not ashamed of your dress, of your culture, of your upbringing. You so wrapped yourself in your own righteous mantle, that they couldn't reach you. What's more, when that young man asked you to sing, Ron tried to convince you to do it, and you wouldn't even listen to him."

Hugh paused. The girl on the other end was weeping inconsolably but he went on relentlessly: "And really, Esther," his voice was gentle but firm, "when they had tried to accommodate you as best they knew and planned the evening at least partly for your benefit, don't you think that it was thoughtless and even rude to act as you did?"

At first Esther was stunned, even angry at Hugh's unexpected rebuke. She had supposed he would commiserate with her but instead he had inferred that she was selfish, unfeeling, proud, and a coward. But something deep inside told her that he was more right than she liked to admit.

"Well, Mr. Gardner," she stammered, "maybe I did act selfishly last night. And I haven't told you all the good things my family has done for me. Only I'm not used to this kind of life. It's all so new and I don't know when to stick to my convictions and when to give in."

Esther was seriously asking for advice, and Hugh's heart went out to her. "Yes, Esther, you must feel very alone at times, but think on the bright side a moment. It looks like you have already made a break through with your younger cousin and certainly have at least somewhat impressed that young man you call Ron. It also seems as if a milestone has been passed in your aunt's life and that you had some part in it at least. And then even the fact that your Uncle seems a bit uneasy in your presence since you played that night, is proof that God is speaking to him."

Esther brightened. She hadn't thought of things that way. "Yes, I can see that God has been with me since I came here, Mr. Gardner."

"Of course He has, so why not start counting your blessings, Esther, and I'll help you pray that you will find some Christian friends. But meanwhile, don't be rigid when it comes to non-essentials. Adapt to your new family where you can. Remember that they don't profess to be followers of the Lord Jesus and are watching your life. Love is the way, Esther. True love is vibrant, strong, conquering. Admit that you did wrong last night and go on from there. And my prayers are with you. And one more thing. I think your aunt needs you at this time and maybe you need her too."

But there was one more question she had to ask. "Please tell me," she begged, "how can I escape being imprisoned by this Velvet Curtain? Trouble is, I don't even really know for sure what it is. I don't want to have escaped one Curtain only to be entrapped by another."

"No, of course you don't, my dear," was his kindly reply. "But I don't think it would help for me to define it. It really is indefinable. And different people feel its effect in different ways. You obviously have felt it already and will feel it again. The real danger will be when you cease to feel its influence. It's then I shall really worry about you."

"I don't think there's much danger of my not feeling it," Esther told him. "But if I ever get to that place, I shall pray that God will make you aware of my danger in time."

"I pray that too, my dear, and I just know He will answer our prayers. So for now, goodbye and remember, phone me any time."

Esther smiled through her tears. She felt as if a load had lifted as she sank back in her bed. Yes, she would praise God for all He had done. She would trust Him. She would ask for His love to be shown through her life and, first and foremost she would apologize to her family and to Ron. That would be the hardest part.

Then she remembered her mother's advice those many years ago. She had quarreled with her best friend and was very upset. It seemed to her that she had been treated very unfairly and had every reason to be annoyed. "You may have a right to be angry, Esther," her mother had told her gently, "but you have no right to continue to hold a grudge. God is love and He won't live in a heart where bitterness has taken control."

"But Maria was so very unfair to me," Esther had sobbed.

"Weren't the mob and the Sanhedrin and the soldiers all unfair to our Lord Jesus, Esther? And what did He do. He forgave them in the midst of terrible pain and agony. And He was faultless and in no way to blame. But you...."

She hadn't gotten the sentence out before Esther had thrown herself into her mother's arms. Yes, she must apologize to her friend right away for her part. It would be very hard, very, but she must do it. And she had. She remembered as she lay and watched the sunbeams play on the wall opposite, how wonderful it had felt when she had taken the blame that was hers. And now? She had been proud, unbending, and ungrateful, when her uncle and Ramona and Ron had all gone out of their way to try to adapt the party to meet her needs. She would make things right with everyone involved as soon as she possibly could.

She suddenly felt drowsy for she had been awake very early, and sinking between her soft sheets, she was soon in the land of dreams. When Rachel came in half an hour later, she thought how peaceful her cousin looked. "What is her secret?" she wondered. "I'd really like to know."

Esther lost no time in apologizing to Ramona after she returned from St. Jude's that Sunday morning. Her cousin told her not to think any more about it. "Everyone makes mistakes, Esther, even you."

Esther blushed. This constant reference to her perfection piqued her. But she just gave Ramona a hug and went off to find her uncle. He too made light of the whole thing and told her it was not her fault at all. Ramona should have seen to it that that Claude behaved himself.

It was late that afternoon before she had a chance to talk to Rachel. To her surprise, the young girl looked at her gravely and asked, "Do you know what Ron was trying to tell you, Esther?"

"Tell me? What do you mean?"

"I overheard your conversation with Mike and Ron. And when he tried to persuade you to sing, he was doing it because of Mike."

"Whatever do you mean, Rachel? I don't understand at all."

"Well, you remember he began a sentence but you stalked away from him before he could finish it. You see, Mike has just found out he has leukemia and...."

Esther collapsed into the nearest chair. "Why didn't Ron follow me and make me hear that?" she wailed. "Oh Rachel, that makes it worse than ever. So Ron was wanting me to humor his friend, and maybe to..." she couldn't go on. The thought that her singing could have brought comfort and blessing to a young man facing death sent her almost crazy.

Esther ate no supper that night and cried herself to sleep. Ramona got very angry with her sister when she found out what had upset her cousin. Rachel had left in a bad mood without saying goodbye to anyone.

Esther had intended to phone Ron or maybe write him but she just couldn't, not just yet. She didn't know how to phrase her sorrow and shame. Then, two days later, on the morning of her birthday, the door bell rang. When she went to the door, Esther was absolutely shocked to find a beautiful bouquet of red roses put in her hand. As she read the card attached, "Wishing you a very happy birthday, from your friend, Ron," tears filled her eyes. She knew Ramona had received some white carnations from him on her birthday which had been on Sunday, but she had not expected this. She never stopped to compare the two bouquets; she didn't realize that hers had probably cost twice as much as Ramona's and that "red roses" might have some deeper significance than white carnations.

But Esther's surprises were not over for the day. That afternoon, as she opened the door to welcome her uncle on his return from work, he motioned to her to come outside. "Close your eyes, young lady," he said, as he propelled her to the side of the house. "Now open them," he commanded. There, festooned in ribbons, stood a small Toyota Corolla with a large sign on it saying, "Happy Birthday, Esther." It was a few years old, it is true, but shining like new.

Esther gasped. She could not believe her eyes. This—for her? Her uncle gave her a kiss and assured her that it was hers and only hers. He had had no trouble in picking this up at a good bargain, he told her. Now she wouldn't need to rely on troublesome chauffeurs any more, that is, when she passed her test. She forgot all about that terrible party and almost jumped for joy. Overcome by emotion and gratitude, she flung her arms round her uncle's neck. "Thank you,

Uncle John. You're such a dear! Thank you!" she repeated. "I just can't believe it. A car all of my own!" And she lovingly ran her fingers over the hood.

"Drive it, Esther," her uncle commanded, opening the driver's door and motioning her to get behind the wheel. She had already had several lessons from an instructor in town but now she was out on her very first drive in a car which she could call all her own. She had owned so little in her lifetime, she told her uncle, as they slowly made their way up the tree-lined avenue, that she was simply overwhelmed. "How can I ever repay you?" she whispered as they drove back half an hour later.

"Gifts must not be repaid," was the answer, "but you are repaying me in a thousand ways although you don't know it. Just do one thing more, will you?" and he looked questioningly at his niece as they locked up the car for the night.

"What's that, Uncle?" Esther asked a little apprehensively.

"Just keep on loving me whatever I do or say for your uncle is no saint, but a man of flesh and blood and one day he might disappoint his little niece, whose life seems to consist of praying and singing hymns." John spoke lightly but his face had clouded a little as his eyes searched his niece's as if for reassurance of her continued affection.

"Oh Uncle, how can you even ask such a question?" And Esther reached up and gave her uncle another kiss. "I can't promise to agree with everything you may do, but I can promise to keep on loving you, no matter what."

This was so tenderly put that John was almost overcome with emotion. Esther heard a few sniffs and coughs as he disappeared into his study and knew that tears were not very far away. But although she could truly assure this indulgent uncle of hers that her love would be constant, she shuddered a little at the thoughts that would push their way into her mind. What would he do that might bring down her disapproval on his head or, in his eyes at least, even jeopardize her love for him? She could only think of one course of action that might fit that category, a course she certainly hoped he would never ever take, both for his own sake and for the sake of the family that she was coming to love as her very own.

As she prepared for bed that night, an awful thought struck her. What if this car was not paid for? What if by giving it to her he had got himself further into debt? She couldn't stand the thought.

Tiptoeing downstairs she found herself knocking on the study door.

"Come in." Her uncle seemed surprised. "Why Esther my dear, whatever is wrong?"

"Nothing, only... only." She couldn't get it out but she must get it off her chest. "Only I wanted to be sure that you weren't getting into debt by giving me that car, Uncle." Esther looked so young and innocent in her white dressing-gown, her long hair rather disheveled for once and tumbling all over her shoulders, her eyes glistening with tears.

Her uncle came over to her and put his strong arm round her shoulder. "What a worrier you are, Esther! Why should you bother your pretty head about how I got the car? Can't you trust me?" Then his voice grew sharper. "Has Mary been talking to you?"

It was Esther's turn to be surprised. "Talking to me?" she repeated. "I've only met her once and we didn't talk about you at all, Uncle."

John looked relieved. "Listen. I haven't got myself into any trouble through getting you the car, Esther. It's all above board and hasn't hurt me financially. So go back to bed and dream about driving it all over Indiana," and he kissed her lightly on the forehead.

This land of freedom had its drawbacks, Esther thought as she helped herself to a drink of juice. Her uncle's answer had been enigmatical, but she had done her best. It really was not her business to probe further. It was his gift to her and she must accept it on good faith.

Yet, there it was again, that smothering sensation—that curtain—not rigid as in her faraway homeland with its iron clad restrictions and prohibitions, but so soft and velvety that it surrounded you without your knowing it, making you feel you could do anything, go anywhere, be anything, and there would be no reprisals, no repercussions. What had Hugh said that Sunday morning? "The danger is when you don't recognize its presence?" Well, at least, it had not deceived her, not yet at any rate.

Chapter Nineteen

Esther's First Thanksgiving

When Esther finally got up courage to phone Ron Atwood the day before Thanksgiving, she found he had left town. His mother told her he was spending the holiday with his father in Louisville. Diane Atwood was friendly enough, but something in her voice made Esther wish she had written instead of trying to phone.

The next day Esther learned that, in the Popescu residence at least, Thanksgiving meant turkey and stuffing, cranberry sauce and pumpkin pie. It also meant relaxation, and a time when families got together and enjoyed each other.

When she had eaten the last spoonful of dessert, Esther pushed back her chair. She had told her Uncle that she would like to contact her other relative who lived in the States, a ninety-year-old great aunt, a sister of her grandfather, who, she believed, lived somewhere in the mountains and was very eccentric. Uncle John had never met her as she was a great aunt of Esther's on her mother's side.

It was a miracle that Esther managed to find Aunt Lucy's phone number. Fortunately for her, her aunt had not moved over the years and there seemed to be only one "Farthington" listed for Scuby, Tennessee. Esther could hardly believe her ears when after six or seven rings, she heard a lady's voice answering: "This is the Farthington residence. Who's speaking?"

Esther was taken aback. It was the voice of a sixty or seventy year-old not someone already passed her ninetieth birthday.

"Esther Popescu?" the voice was saying. "Let's see—granddaughter of my flyaway brother who decided to take his family to some outlandish country or other. And what can I do for you, young lady?"

"W.e.l.l.," Esther stammered. "I mean, it's Thanksgiving Day today, so I thought it would be nice to get in touch with you."

It sounded so lame, somehow, and evidently Great Aunt Lucy

thought so too. "Thanksgiving? Yes I know it's Thanksgiving. But even so, you must want something or you wouldn't be phoning me. Are you short of money, eh? Or in trouble? Dear me, young girls get into trouble so easily these days."

By this time, Esther did not know whether to laugh or cry. "No, Aunt Lucy. Really, I just wanted to get in touch. After all, I don't have that many relatives over here or anywhere really. I mean, I suppose you know both my parents are dead?"

There was a silence at the other end and then Aunt Lucy spoke again this time in a much softer tone. "So that makes you an orphan. Poor child. This world is no friend to orphans. So what are you doing for a living? How are you surviving?"

"Uncle John, my father's brother, has taken me into his family, so I'm well taken care of."

"Oh! So you do have an uncle in this country. Well then, I don't have to invite you here. But listen young lady, if ever you get kicked out, and you never know, folks are so fickle these days, then remember, you do have a relative here in the wilds of Tennessee. Remember that!"

"Yes, Aunt, I will." Esther was half amused, half annoyed. "But I don't think it's very likely that I'll be visiting you for that reason. Anyway I do wish you a very blessed Thanksgiving."

"Humph," was the rejoinder. "I suppose I'm to say, 'Same to you,' but I won't. How can Thanksgiving be blessed any more? I think the good Lord has forsaken this land so how can He bless anything in it? But thanks for phoning. There's someone at the door so I'll say goodbye. And remember if you get into trouble, I'm here!"

"What was all that about?" laughed her uncle as Esther flopped into the nearest chair. "Sounds a real hard nut to crack."

"A what?" gasped Esther.

"She sounds a bit of a difficult character," interpreted her Uncle chucking her under the chin. "Keep away from her. That's my advice."

"Well, she implied that I must only contact her if I get into trouble or get put out of your house," laughed Esther giving her uncle a kiss. Her uncle pinched her cheek affectionately and then excused himself. He had eaten too much, he told them, and had to sleep it off.

They had arranged to spend the evening at her aunt's. Esther thought the whole setup very tragic and it seemed especially poignant at holiday times. A divided home! Her family had often faced long separations but they had always been one in spirit. Love had been their very food and she had been nourished on it. What could she do to help in this situation? Nothing, at present, except pour out the love of her warm young heart upon those around her, as Hugh Gardner had encouraged her to do. Her uncle felt this outpouring and basked in it. Rachel also sensed something warm enfolding her and it drew her, little by little, out of the cocoon she had woven around herself for so long.

Ramona felt this same influence, but could not open her heart to it. Esther had upset her secure little world. It had been thanks to her that Len had been invited that Saturday to join them on their outing, and she had been almost bribed into going to church with him. It had been thanks to her, or so she liked to think, that Ron Atwood was slipping out of her life. And more than all this put together, it was thanks to Esther Popescu that she was becoming aware that there was something more to life than glamorous clothes and boyfriends and this awareness made her very uneasy.

Aunt Mary, too, felt Esther's love surrounding her that Thanksgiving evening. She had made up her mind to make the girl feel at home and to put aside her grudges and her jealousies. That evening had been the happiest part of that holiday, Esther thought, as she sank into bed late that night. Really, Thanksgiving was all about love, and gratitude, and hope—not only thanking God for the past, but trusting Him for the future. And she had a lot to trust Him about—her future seemed so uncertain, the path ahead so unclear. But He had promised to be a constant Companion and a faithful Guide. What more could she, Esther Lydia Popescu, want?

She was about to turn off the light when she caught sight of the book Rachel had slipped into her hand as she said goodbye that evening. It was a book of American verse, a belated birthday present from her young cousin. Esther noticed a piece of white paper which she thought at first had been merely used as a bookmark. But when she took it out, she found it contained a poem written in Rachel's clear, bold handwriting. The words "My Tunnel Home" immediately caught her attention. Her eyes widened as she began to read the first stanza. Maybe, she figured, it was the poem more than the book Rachel had wanted to give her for her birthday. She read the six stanzas slowly:

"October 30, 1987.

My tunnel home is dark,
The air is thin,
And what is more
I found today
I'm running very short
Of my supply of oxygen.

"I have long ceased to count
The long night-days
Or sightless hours
As they creep past
And as I stumble 'gainst my stony walls,
I know that it's impossible
For me to last.

"If only I could be alone—
Just I and me,
I might survive;
I might preserve my oxygen
And, isolated from the world,
I might be free.

"But there are others here—
Together or apart.
And they, half frenzied,
Stab the darkness with their cries
And thoughtlessly
Stampede upon my heart.

"Sometimes I like to sleepwalk
Inching my way to darkness' end,
Both hands stretched flat on cold, wet stone.

Sometimes I leap forward,
Maddened by hope—
Awake at last!
But then, I can't...
I really can't...!
I'm running out
Of oxygen.

"<u>November 24, 1987</u>

What are those pricks of light?
I see there're two.
They're not the tunnel's end
They're not the sun,
Or moon,
Or stars,
Because they're moving towards me,
Coming mid-tunnel.
Oh, dear God,
What?
Or who?
Why, for Heaven's sake, Esther!
It's... YOU!"

After rereading the poem several times, Esther took a closer look at the dates, eyes dimmed with tears. The first five had been written on the day her uncle had announced he was pursuing a divorce. And the last verse had been written that very Thanksgiving Day.

She repeated the words "coming mid-tunnel" as she turned over to sleep. "Yes, Rachel," she whispered into the shadows, "it's not easy. I don't like the dark. And I certainly don't like tunnels. But I'm coming. I'm coming. Wait for me!"

Chapter Twenty

Esther Keeps Her Promise

Ron drove up the familiar road to his house. He had returned a day earlier than he had intended. If the truth were told, he wanted to make it up with Esther and take her to church the next day. That's why he had made it home by nine. There was still time to phone her.

"How's your Dad?" Diane asked her son, as she poured him a glass of iced tea.

"Great, Mom, really great!" Ron gave his mother a meaningful glance as he continued, "In fact, I've never seen him look so good in years. He's been dry for six months now."

"I've heard that before," Diane remarked skeptically.

"Yep. I know." Ron's tone was sympathetic. He remembered the many times this father of his had disappointed them both. "We can only wait and see," he told her with an encouraging smile. "It's never too late to hope, Mom."

His mother turned away. She didn't want to discuss her ex-husband any more. There were too many hurtful memories involved.

"Here's a letter for you, Ron." Diane went to the drawer and pulled out an envelope written in a hand he did not recognize. "It's probably from your little gypsy queen," she commented dryly.

Ron said nothing as he took the letter and left the kitchen. He didn't want his mother's prying eyes on him as he read it. Upstairs in his bedroom, he slit it open. So it was from Esther! That was unusual. It hadn't seemed likely she would make the first move to re-establish contact with him after their rift just over a week ago. One couldn't call it a quarrel. In fact, he scarcely knew what had happened except that it seemed to him that the girl had fallen from the pedestal on which he had placed her—a shining, beautiful, almost unearthly creature, who could do no wrong. But she had disappointed him, not that he could really blame her after that incident with Claude. But he had thought her made of tougher stuff. And Mike would have so enjoyed hearing her sing. He needed something, poor fellow, to take his mind off the ghastly news he had just received.

Yet during the drive from Louisville, the Romanian girl had been constantly in his thoughts. It had even crossed his mind that the Esther dethroned might be more approachable than his saintly version of her. But he was not prepared for what he read:

"Dear Ron, I need to apologize for my behavior on Saturday night. I have no real excuse though I made plenty that evening. You rescued me from a very awkward situation and I repaid your kindness by refusing to even listen to you when you tried to persuade me to sing. Rachel told me about Mike and I see now why you were eager for me to do what he wanted. I don't suppose I'll have another chance quite like that, but if I do, I'll certainly, with God's help, make the most of it though, unfortunately, opportunities missed are never quite repeated in the same way. So please forgive me for my rudeness. My pride was hurt that evening. I admit that it's not easy to be sometimes stared at as if I were an alien from outer space, though I daresay a lot of that is my own fault. I hope you and Ramona and Uncle will put up with me while I'm learning through my mistakes.

"As I write, I can smell those beautiful red roses you sent for my birthday. They are lasting well. It was good of you to remember me. I don't deserve it. From your friend, Esther Popescu."

Ron shook his head as he refolded the letter. Here he had just admitted that she was human and had faults enough, and then she went and acted like a saint again. Now picture Ramona apologizing like that, or any other girl he knew. He picked up the receiver and was just about to dial Esther's number when someone called him instead. It was Len inviting him to come and hear Esther sing the next day at his church and join them for a meal afterwards. She was being picked up, he said, so Ron didn't need to bring her.

He put down the receiver in disgust. A feeling very much like jealousy began to smolder within him. Esther had refused to trust him that Saturday evening yet she was trusting Len and now it seemed that she didn't need him any more to take her to church. Well, maybe he wouldn't phone or write her just yet. He would write sometime, though. It was only polite.

As Len got ready for church the next morning, his conscience began to trouble him somewhat. It was true that Esther was going to sing in the morning service. But what he had not told Ron was that it had been the pastor who had arranged it with her and that it would be Margaret, his daughter, who would pick her up the next morning.

He had not had any direct contact with the Romanian girl since the party.

That Saturday afternoon, Pastor Cripps had called Esther and invited Ron and herself to have lunch with them after church the next day. Esther had been touched by his kindness but had informed him that Ron was away for a week. "I'll send my daughter to pick you up for church then, if that's all right," he had suggested. "And by the way, I've heard that you have a beautiful voice, Esther. And Len tells me you have already promised to sing in our church, so why not do it tomorrow, if that's not too much to ask?"

Esther had agreed. She knew she would have to keep her promise some time. But when she drove to Terre Haute with Margaret the next morning, she was totally unaware, for Len had not bothered to tell her, of Ron's return, or that a very disgruntled young man was just climbing out of bed at that very moment and thinking wistfully of the Sunday mornings gone by.

Esther found the pastor's daughter to be a rather effervescent but extremely likable young woman who, it seemed, never stopped talking. She was an only child, adored by both parents, and engaged to a young man who was training for the ministry. It seemed that she was a stranger to trouble and worry and lived on the sunny side of life. Esther doubted if she could understand someone like herself, but she sensed that a girl like Margaret would do her good, and maybe inject some optimism into her serious and sometimes rather pessimistic outlook on life.

By the time they pulled into the church car park, Esther felt she had truly gained a friend. She found, however, that it would be Len, and not Margaret as she had hoped, who would be accompanying her that morning.

"So you are keeping your word at last," Len commented with a smile, as they walked into the sanctuary to practice before the service.

"Yes," was the rather abrupt reply. Soon they were going over the two pieces she had sung that Saturday evening in her Uncle's living-room. Esther was amazed that Len could pick up the Romanian melody so quickly, but then remembered that he was a gifted pianist with a good ear for music.

As she sat through the preliminaries, Esther was glad of Margaret's nearness. It comforted her and made her feel less afraid. But soon she heard herself being announced and found herself facing a full auditorium. She had chosen to wear her gold blouse and a black skirt (not of course the same threadbare skirt she had come to America in) and looked truly Romanian as she began to translate the words of "Numai Harul," in a low rather tremulous voice. But as she sang, she gathered courage, and the haunting melody seemed to echo in every corner of the spacious sanctuary.

When she finished, there was a silence that could almost be felt. Then Len began the opening bars of "Amazing Grace," and the audience was electrified as Esther let out all the stops, and lifting her face heavenwards, seemed to forget where she was and who was listening. As the last note died away, there was another telling silence and then the clapping began. It was thunderous. Esther was not accustomed to applause in a church and it totally unnerved her. She quickly slipped out a side door and sat down on a bench in the church courtyard to regain her composure.

In an instant, Margaret was by her side. "Are you all right? Your disappearance frightened me a little. I had to make sure you were OK."

Esther raised a pale face to hers. "Thanks Margaret. Yes, I'm OK. It was all that clapping. It completely overwhelmed me."

"They don't usually clap quite like that," Margaret told her, laying a hand on her friend's shoulder. "But no wonder. Do you know how fabulous you were?"

Esther's face blushed crimson at the praise. But it did sound very pleasant and ample reward for the colossal effort she had just put forth. She soon regained her composure and Margaret led her around the church building so that they could slip in and sit at the back, unobserved. But after the service, Esther found escape was impossible. "Wonderful!" "Terrific!" "Great job!" "We've got to have you again!" "Praise the Lord, what talent!" And so it went on as one after another shook her hand and told what a blessing her singing had been. Esther blushed, looked down, looked up again, muttered something about it being all of the Lord, but still it went on. This was her first encounter with American enthusiasm and it was quite unnerving.

Finally, when only a few stragglers remained, Len Atwood approached her. "What can I say, Esther, that hasn't been said?" he began.

"Nothing more, please, Len, nothing more," Esther pleaded. She felt she could not take one more word of praise especially from Len Atwood.

The young man stopped and looked at her in astonishment. It was unusual for any girl not to want to hear herself praised. "She'll get used to it," he thought; "she'll have to. With that talent and those looks, she'll go places."

By this time, Pastor Cripps had appeared on the scene and had to add his word of appreciation. This time, Esther listened without protest. "Now," put in his wife, coming up from behind and laying a hand on Esther's shoulder, "it's time for lunch. I've invited Len, too; I know from what my husband tells me, that a bachelor really appreciates a wholesome, home-cooked meal now and then. So come along, my dear. You must be ravenous."

Motherly Mrs. Cripps was short and plump, with rosy cheeks and wavy grey hair that framed her round and pleasant face, an older version of her daughter, Esther thought, as she followed her out to the car.

The parsonage was not far away and seemed, to Esther, a smaller replica of her Uncle's home. This rather surprised her, for she was accustomed to pastors eking out an existence, often working on the side to support their families. But this is America, she thought, as she listened to Margaret's explanation of the many pictures hanging on the walls of the living room. There were ornaments everywhere and it seemed that every possible space was taken up with some piece of ornate furniture. And teddy bears! Margaret collected them, she was told.

Accustomed to eating out on a Sunday, Esther was glad for a change. She enjoyed Betty Cripps' home cooking and did justice to it, much to that good lady's delight.

"That's just what I like to see," said her hostess, beaming as she brought in the desert. "A lot of girls your age pick and peck like little birds, afraid to gain half a pound here or a couple of inches there. But I suppose you don't need to worry about that like Margaret and I do," and she winked at her daughter good-naturedly.

Margaret pretended to be offended. "We can't all be like Esther, Mother," she said. "But it takes all sorts to make up the world, you know."

"Yes," added her father, reaching for a cookie. "God delights in variety. Why we all so try to be like one another, I can't say. And," he went on, looking at Len who had been rather silent up to this point, "in the Church of Christ, as members of His Body, it is our privilege to each function in the way He has designed for us."

"That's right," agreed the young man who looked unusually thoughtful and just a little ill at ease. To tell the truth, Esther Popescu puzzled him. He was popular with the young people in the church and it was said that he had a way with them—could handle them as no one else could, but this girl rather bamboozled him. He had intended to praise her performance and then to enroll her in their choir, but she had cut him short and this was not the first time she had done so either. But he was not one to remain for long at a loss for words and soon he turned to Esther, saying seriously, "Ron tells me you have quite a story. Would you share it with us?"

Esther hesitated. She always found it hard to speak of her parents and of their suffering but Margaret's eager, "Oh please do, Esther," made her say, "Why of course. If you like. But it's rather a long one."

"Then let's take our coffee into the living room," suggested Margaret. "We'll be more comfy there."

By focusing on the pastor's kindly face, Esther got the courage to tell her story. She smoothed out her long black skirt, put her hands on her lap, and began in a low, tremulous voice. When she had finished all were silent for a few moments. Then the pastor came over to where she was sitting and placed his hand on her arm. "Thanks Esther," he told her. "That was deeply moving. We need to know how our brothers and sisters in the East are suffering. You must tell this to our church."

"Yes, and to the young people," added Len. "What about this Friday, Esther? Can you come at seven and tell them just what you told us now?"

Esther nodded. "And maybe you could speak next Sunday night," suggested the pastor. "Margaret will bring you," he added, seeing her hesitate. And so it was settled. Then Len had to put in another word before they parted.

"And, Esther, please join our choir, won't you?"

To this, however, Esther would not commit herself so quickly. "I'll pray over it," she told him and with that he had to be satisfied.

That night Esther lay thinking over the day's events. She had come home about four that afternoon to find that she had had three phone calls, Ramona said, from people who had been in church and who had heard her sing. Esther rang them back as they had requested—one was a Baptist lady who had been present that morning and wanted her to sing at their church in two weeks' time. Another was from the leader of the Women's guild who wished to book her for their women's conference in February as the chief singer. And the third was from an elderly lady who simply wanted to say that she had been so blessed by Esther's singing that she had been praising the Lord all afternoon.

Strange land this, thought the young Romanian as she drifted off to sleep. One day she felt as lonely as one of Wordsworth's clouds and the next she was absolutely swamped by appreciation. Why can't Americans do things moderately, she wondered? All this fuss would probably die down in a week or two, and she would go back to solitary days and nights, sitting alone with her books on a Saturday evening in her uncle's recliner. And which was the more dangerous—isolation or popularity? She thought she knew, but time would tell.

Chapter Twenty-One

Esther in Demand

"Something for you, Esther," Ramona announced, as she placed an envelope on the kitchen table before rushing off to spend another week at college.

"My SAT results," exclaimed her cousin, her mouth full of toast and marmalade. They had come sooner than she expected. With trembling hands, she tore open the envelope.

"I can't believe it!" she burst out, after scanning the contents for a few moments. "I just can't believe it!" and she threw her arms round the astonished Ramona, somewhat unused to such outbursts from her rather reserved cousin.

"Just think, I've done well in everything except math and even there I reached the 70th percentile."

"Congratulations, Esther, but I can't think why you're so surprised. You did expect to do well, didn't you? I mean, you're tops at everything, of course! You must know that by now."

Something in Ramona's tone checked Esther's joy. "I don't think of myself as that good, Ramona." She tried to speak calmly. "I know I wouldn't have done nearly so well if it had not been for all the support I have received."

But Ramona had left the kitchen and she found herself talking into thin air. Picking up the receiver, she dialed Ron's number almost automatically. Mrs. Atwood sounded friendly enough, but Esther was pretty sure she heard her shout, "Ron, your gypsy queen is on the phone." Her heart sank. Why had she been so impulsive and phoned right on the spot?

Ron was soon on the line. "That's just great, Esther!" he exclaimed heartily when he heard the news. "You deserve every bit of the success. Congratulations!"

"But I really phoned to thank you, Ron," she put in hastily. "I would probably have flopped in math if you had not come to my rescue."

"I doubt it," he replied. "But at any rate, you did well and that's wonderful. Now, how about a celebration?"

Esther was taken aback. She had not been prepared for this response.

"Oh, come on," he protested, "you're not still thinking about that party, are you? That's all in the past, you know. You apologized, which you didn't really need to do. I was a bit touchy too. So now let's forget it ever happened."

"Thanks," the girl stammered, not knowing what else to say.

"Anyway, you deserve to celebrate. The Messiah is being performed in Indianapolis. Will you let me take you to hear it on Friday?"

"Sorry," stammered Esther. "I've promised to speak to the young people that evening."

"Trust Len!" muttered Ron. "Well, how about Sunday evening?"

"Sorry again, but I promised the pastor to speak at the church that night."

"Wow! Seems like I've been away too long," was the comment. "You have blossomed into a popular young lady in my absence."

Esther laughed. "Not exactly. But it does all seem to have happened at once."

"Well then, how about Saturday?"

There was no reply. Ron let out a long sigh. "I think I can guess what you're thinking. Ask someone to go along with us; ask Rachel. After all, she should celebrate too, for she has a part in your success."

"Thanks a lot," was her grateful response. "It'll do her a world of good. So we'll see you Saturday. At what time?"

"We'll leave at six," he said rather abruptly. He was still frustrated with the girl and with himself too. It was really his fault. He had made it clear that he was not courting her, so why not have a third person with them? Yes, why not, he repeated to himself when Esther had hung up. He threw himself on his bed. He was ashamed of his attitude over the past week, but Len had made him so mad. Oh well, college would begin and then he might just see Esther more than he bargained for. He was certainly not immune to beautiful girls so he knew he was gambling with his emotions. Hers were probably safe enough he reckoned; an angel like Esther Popescu would never fall for such an earthy creature as himself, so if he got hurt it would be his own fault!

Esther was soon on the phone to Rachel. "Need a chaperone again?" her cousin joked.

"Sort of. But we can't celebrate my success without you, Rachel. You spent hours helping me prepare for the exams."

"Well, I'd really like to go. That comes as a surprise, doesn't it? Never expected I'd be so agreeable?" The old bitterness had crept in just a little. "But I just love the Messiah. Thanks a lot for the invitation."

"Glad you'll be going, Rachel." Esther put down the receiver. She had used the word "glad," but was she really? She turned to the pile of text books on the shelf by the window. There was still a lot of reading to do if she were to CLEP out of American history. And there were other subjects, too, to brush up on before January—French, English Literature, Biology—the list went on and on. She had no time to analyze her feelings. Rachel was going and that was it.

Friday soon arrived and with it a spruced up Len Atwood, ready to take her to the youth meeting. He was on his best behavior, obviously determined not to offend this time round. He was more subdued, more reserved, and in fact the perfect gentleman, for the most part that is.

The young people were attentive enough, but the discussion time afterwards kept her on her toes. One young girl in particular threw some rather off-putting questions at her. Didn't she think, the girl asked, that it was exploiting the sufferings of her fellow-countrymen to go around talking about them? And wouldn't some of the Christians back home think that someone like herself was a bit of a coward in running away from the situation? And as for American religion—in what ways was it superior or inferior to Romanian Christianity?

She found that the first two questions were not that difficult to answer after all. Esther knew that her friends back home would not consider her exploiting their situation by sharing it with Christians in America. How could people in the West pray intelligently if they were not aware of conditions in the Romanian Church? And secondly, she was so conscious of the fact that God had miraculously delivered her in the nick of time through her uncle's timely invitation, that she was not afraid of how others might interpret it. But the third question was a poser. She really couldn't answer a question like that, she told them, when she had only been two and a half months in America, though it did seem to be a rule that persecution tended to make a church stronger rather than weaker. With that, she sat down, quite exhausted, only to be asked by Len to sing a few numbers in Romanian to conclude the evening.

Over refreshments, one of the girls, the same Connie who had so upset Ramona that Sunday night and who had been her chief questioner that very evening, sidled up to her. "I'd like to go to Romania," she announced unexpectedly.

Esther eyed her in surprise as the girl pushed back her mass of red-gold hair from her freckled face and turned her sparkling green eyes full on Esther's dark ones. "Yes," she went on, "I'm fed up with playing church, with mouthing hymns and prayers but really using religion as an excuse for finding a decent date, one my parents won't find fault with. Oh of course I go to church twice a week at least, and I usually manage to read a few verses of Scripture each day and say my prayers at night," Connie added, seeing Esther's shocked expression, "but except for not smoking or using drugs or going to wild parties, my life's little different from my friends at school. Come on, Esther, surely there's more to a Christian life than that?"

Esther was speechless. Was this really what Christianity was like here in the free world? If it was, then no wonder Connie wanted an escape. She smiled to herself. Fancy anyone wanting to escape from a free country to one that was held in the grip of the Iron Curtain! Unless...? Maybe it was a case of exchanging one curtain for another. Was that what she had done?

Connie's voice broke into her reverie: "Can't you answer me, Esther?"

Esther shook herself. The girl was waiting for a reply. She felt attracted to this outspoken teenager who reminded her of her tomboy sister. Laying a hand on Connie's shoulder, she answered gently, "I'm sorry. What you said just now carried me back to Romania for a moment or two. But yes, there's certainly a lot more to the Christian life than that. Of course, I've just come to your country so I haven't gotten very involved here yet, but my life certainly doesn't consist of playing church, or flirting and dating, or movies and TV." She hesitated as she pronounced the word TV for she had been watching more the last few weeks, but she was sure she still spent far less time viewing the "box" than the average American.

"Oh but wait till you've been here a year. You'll be spoiled. Everyone is," and Connie darted her a knowing glance. "You're too good-looking not to be spoiled. Look at Len Atwood there—I've never seen him so dressed up for our youth meeting as he is tonight, and on his best behavior too! He's struck on you already, though it's true that he's been struck on nearly every pretty girl who enters these doors." Connie's face flushed and there was an angry light in her eyes as she went on in the same vein: "He tried to convert your cousin Ramona, too, but her conversion only lasted a few weeks; it didn't even last as long as mine did. You're not a bit like her, though. Maybe he's real serious about you. Then I saw that other young man with you at church one Sunday morning, Len's cousin, I think."

Esther blushed but shook her head. "I certainly hope I wont let my new life spoil me, Connie. There *is* the grace of God to keep us steady when we go offline in anything."

"Grace of God!" the girl snorted. "I hear about it all the time. What I would like is to see it lived out in someone—someone young, I mean, not in old folks over forty. Prove it to me, Esther. Prove it, and then I'll believe it," and with that she turned on her heel and marched defiantly out of the room. Esther heard her slam the door behind her. This girl had given her much to think about. Had she inadvertently referred to this same Velvet Curtain that Hugh had warned her about?

"Don't pay any attention to Connie." Esther turned round. Len was at her elbow. "She's a great kid, only a bit spoiled and rebellious at present. Hope she didn't offend you?"

"Oh no, I really do like her, and she's given me a lot to think about," Esther answered, putting down her plate.

At last it was all over and they were speeding homewards. Neither spoke much till they entered Velours city limits. Len slowed down and leaned towards her. "You have a great voice, Esther," he told her softly. "Great talent! Use it for the Lord."

Esther said nothing. "By the way," he continued, clearing his throat a little, "there's a Christian concert tomorrow and I thought you might like to go, though I know it's rather short notice. It would be a pleasure to take you if you're free."

"Sorry, but I'm booked up for Saturday."

Len raised his dark eyebrows. "Booked up? Has my cousin gotten ahead of me for the second time?"

Esther wished she hadn't spoken so suddenly but there was no way out now. "Yes, well, actually both Rachel and I are going with him to hear the Messiah. They both helped me with my SAT and it's a sort of celebration."

"Oh!" was the comment. "Well maybe another time. But," and he lowered his voice considerably, "I suppose you must know that my cousin is not a Christian."

"Not a Christian?" the girl repeated, thoroughly nettled by this time. "Well, I don't know your American definition of a Christian. In Romania it's clear. It costs everything to be one. But here...?" And she paused giving her companion a significant look out of her great dark eyes, a look which made him extremely uncomfortable. "Here it seems that nearly everyone says they're a Christian, from presidents to pop stars."

"You've sure got spunk," Len remarked to himself as he swung up the Popescu driveway but he merely said somewhat condescendingly, or so it seemed to Esther, "Well, I suppose it is rather confusing changing cultures like you have had to do. In time, you'll sort it all out. And," he added patting her hand as he handed her out of the car, "if you need help in doing so, Len Atwood at your service," and he gave her a mock bow.

"Little chance of my needing his services," she muttered to herself as she waved goodbye.

Connie's words rang in her ears as she drifted off to sleep that evening. "I would like to see it lived out in someone young. Prove it to me, Esther. Prove it!" She clenched her fists under the bedclothes and muttered, "With God's help, I'll prove it, Connie, I will."

Chapter Twenty-Two

Margaret's Troubling Question

Christmas came and took Esther completely by surprise. It proved to be totally different from Christmas back home. Here, everyone seemed to believe in Christmas, from the President to the local football team. And there were nativity scenes in the town square, in the mall, and even on the lawn next door! There were cantatas and candlelight carol services in nearly every church in the area. And parties! Almost every girl at college had either been or was going to a Christmas party. And that was not all by any means! There were Christmas plays in the schools, Christmas shows in the city, Christmas sales in the stores, Christmas lights in the streets, and, of course, Christmas trees in the living-room. Then last but not least, there were the Christmas gifts. Everyone bought and everyone gave, not just gifts from the dollar store, but expensive watches, fur jackets, music centers, bicycles, golf clubs—the list could go on and on.

It wasn't that Esther didn't enjoy doing her own Christmas shopping for once in her life, or being the lead soprano in the cantata at church, or going with her family to the midnight Christmas Eve service at St. Jude's, but she had never been able to quite figure out why, here, in America, where even a president was not ashamed to call himself Christian, the Christ of the Nativity seemed to be taken out and aired only on special occasions. For most of the Season, He seemed to be relegated to the role of Spectator instead of the main Actor in the unfolding drama that was called "Christmas."

It must have been a real miracle, Esther thought, that had kept Christmas alive in a land like Romania, where the government pretended to forget that there had ever been such a Person as Jesus Christ and where the only absolutely safe place to give full vent to the joy of the Season was deep within the Christian's heart! And although Christmas gifts might have been homemade and Christmas dinners lacking the turkey and trimmings, Esther and her friends had always been keenly aware that this wonderful Season was really all about Love Incarnate coming down to earth and being reborn in cold, dark, human hearts.

Esther certainly hoped that the Popescu family was not representative of many American homes that Christmas Season. For the sake of the girls, Mary came over for Christmas dinner and was politeness itself. And though Ramona was gayer than normal, and John tried to be his usual, gallant self, it all seemed a futile attempt to camouflage the turmoil which refused to be hidden under tinsel and bright wrapping paper. Only Rachel seemed unafraid to be herself, but her monosyllabic answers did little to promote the spirit of the Season.

Esther wondered how everyone really felt underneath their pretty and expensive clothes. She had to remind herself constantly that this was her first Christmas in a family which didn't profess to be particularly Christian. She suspected that in Pastor Cripps' home, for example, his daughter Margaret would be celebrating the Season quite differently. Waves of homesickness swept over her. How she longed to hear her aunt's shrill soprano, and Gabby's rich alto, as they sat around the fire and sang their favorite carols. She thought nostalgically of those early morning walks through the snow after the New Year's Eve service. Even the consciousness that their every move was being watched by unseen eyes could not spoil their joyous celebrations.

America, though, had its compensations. She had enjoyed watching Dickens' *Christmas Carol* while eating bowls of popcorn and nearly making herself sick on her aunt's homemade candy. She appreciated having hours to read her favorite books, lying on the sofa with Ramona's poodle nestled beside her, her head cushioned on one of her favorite pillows. She would never forget listening to "Silent Night" being wafted over the music center while the lights on the mammoth Christmas tree in the corner twinkled on and off and the angel on the topmost bow seemed to smile reassuringly down upon her. Then, there was the luxury of playing for hours on the grand piano, the excitement of a Scrabble tournament with her Aunt and Rachel, and the pleasure she felt when her friends cast admiring glances at her white fur jacket which she wore to church that Christmas Sunday. It had been her favorite present, a gift from her uncle, who had taken a special photo of her in it and said he would have it enlarged and framed. She remarked to herself, as she ran her hands through its soft pile, that it was almost an exact replica of the jacket she had refused to buy that first Saturday in her new home.

Esther remembered, too, that superb performance of the Messiah. She could never forget that evening. She remembered closing her eyes and imagining herself among the angels. She sensed that Rachel had felt the same way which really impressed Ron who, Esther felt sure, had grossly underestimated her young cousin. All three had agreed that it had been a perfect evening. In fact, it had been her first real night out since she had come to America and she had enjoyed it to the full. But since then, Ron and she had each gone their own ways. He had been occupied with exams before Christmas and now was spending the holidays with his father in Louisville while she seemed to be either cramming for her Clep exams, practicing for the Cantata, or singing in the various churches.

Now both Christmas and New Year had come and gone. Esther had seen more of her uncle than usual, and had found herself often studying his handsome face. An expression here, a twist of the lip there, and she was carried back to the dear old days. How she wished that Uncle John could truly share her faith. Sometimes he would catch her gaze and drop his eyes as if he wished to hide his soul. Sometimes he would start as the phone rang. It was obvious he had some secret he was not sharing with his family.

Esther had talked over her plans for college with him on New Year's Eve. John had smiled a little when he heard of Ron's offer to take her each day so she would not have to stay on campus. "What it is to be young and beautiful!" he had said in a way she didn't quite appreciate, but he had agreed emphatically that she was not ready to live on campus just yet.

Now, registration day had finally arrived. Ramona had told Ron that he didn't need to worry about Esther; she would take care of her. But after Ramona had helped her fill in the forms and decide which subjects she should take, she had rushed off to a lunch date leaving her cousin to navigate as best she could in the dense crowd of students.

Esther was feeling utterly lost in the shuffle, when she heard a voice in her ear. She turned and found Ron Atwood standing at her elbow. "Alone?" he asked, sounding surprised. The girl gave him a warm smile but said nothing.

"Where's Ramona?" he queried. "Surely she hasn't left you all alone in this mob?"

"Well, she's already registered and she did wait a while but had a lunch date with someone so had to leave me."

"Had to?" growled Ron. "Well, I've also registered, not only today but it seems hundreds of times and I know the ropes pretty well. Give me your paper. Thanks! Now I'll be able to tell you where to go. Wow, Esther, you've taken on twenty hours! Can you do it?"

The girl looked puzzled. She had let Ramona do much of her paper work and was quite unaware of what twenty hours meant or involved. It had been a hectic week. She had "Clepped" out of three subjects and planned to "Clep" out of more for the next semester. So when Ron asked her, "Can you do it?" she looked up at him and muttered confusedly, "I don't know, I really don't. Ramona thought I could, and so did my advisor."

"Well, I think you could too, but I also think you shouldn't," he said firmly. "Those courses are pretty intense and with the adjustment culturally, I think fifteen is plenty. Who is your advisor?"

"Professor Tomlinson."

Ron grimaced. "He's a terror for work. It's a wonder he didn't sign you up for thirty hours! But come on, let's have a word with him. He's over there."

"Whatever you say," said the girl submissively, as they pushed their way through the crowd. Dr. Tomlinson looked up from his papers as they approached his desk. It soon became evident to Esther that Ron was a favorite with the professor and although he mumbled under his breath about modern students not being up to much, he agreed that, in her case at least, fifteen hours might be preferable to twenty.

"But why all this interest in this little Romanian, Atwood?" he had asked Ron, peering at him over his thick-rimmed glasses. "Thought you'd given up girls as a hobby."

"Depends on your definition of 'hobby,' Professor," Ron replied good-naturedly.

Dr. Tomlinson gazed at Esther intently for a few moments, then gave a short laugh as he grunted, "Well, looks like you've struck a gold mine here, boy. See that you don't squander your treasure."

"I'll try my best not to, Professor," Ron assured him. Esther thought he acted very unlike himself as they left the auditorium and made their way to the cafeteria. But by the time they had grabbed a tray and joined the long line at the food bar, he had regained his equilibrium. He seemed totally oblivious of the stares of some of his fellow students as they ordered two hamburgers and French fries and found a table that was free and relatively clean at least. Esther glanced at her red fleecy jacket. It was warm and stylish and seemed at least one link to the world around her. But as her eyes fell on Ron's leather jacket which must have cost enough to feed an entire family back home for months, she was reminded of the gulf that separated them.

During the next few weeks, it seemed Ron was always there when she needed him. Everything had been overwhelming to the young girl, fresh from an alien land. Most of the students were friendly enough though she had to get used to being stared at from time to time. But with Ron as an obvious friend, very few of the boys dared approach her. Most lunch hours found them together sharing sandwiches or eating in the cafeteria. Occasionally, Ramona and her roommate would join them, but not often. Esther seemed to make them uneasy, Ron thought.

Sometimes during their drives to and from school, Ron got her to talk of her life back in Romania; sometimes they discussed college, sometimes politics; sometimes they would even get on the subject of religion, though not often. And once he had told Esther about his father and how he had had a drinking problem. His mother finally couldn't take it any more and had divorced him about eight years previously. But now he had joined AA and had been dry for over six months.

Esther passed her driving test at the end of February and mentioned very tentatively to her uncle that she could now drive to college herself.

"Not while I'm around you won't," he had told her emphatically. "You're not up to driving all that way every day. Not yet. Take advantage of your chauffeur while you've got him. You won't have him forever, you know." It was true, for Ron would graduate in May and then planned to go to law school in September.

"Ron," she said one morning as they sped along the interstate, "you know I've passed my driving test now."

"Congratulations!"

Esther shook her head at him. "You know very well what I'm trying to say. I mean I can drive myself around now."

He looked at her quizzically. "Yes, I know," he replied coolly. "What about it?"

He certainly wasn't making it easy for her, Esther thought. She tried again. "Well, Uncle says that he thinks I'm not fit yet to drive so far on my own every day."

"I don't think you are either," Ron said smiling.

"But it means that you will have to keep on taking me." Esther kept her eyes down as she spoke.

"Yes, it does. Does that bother you?" He spoke half jokingly and half in earnest.

Esther blushed. "No," she told him, "I've enjoyed your company, honestly I have. But how will I get the practice if I never drive?"

Ron laughed. "You can practice around town, and if you like, you can drive this chariot to college. I'll be there to watch you, you know."

The girl gasped. "Oh no! Not this car. I mean, if anything happened to it, I'd never forgive myself."

"Well, we could go in your car, then, if you prefer."

Esther looked at him incredulously. "And what will your friends think of that?"

"Couldn't care what they thought. They already think I'm crazy."

"For helping a poor Romanian girl?" she asked him mischievously. She had grown so used to her chauffeur and, for the most part, felt so relaxed in his company that he wondered why he had ever thought her over-serious.

"Probably," he answered with a grin, "though half of them are jealous. By the way, I've noticed lately that you are making a few friends among some of the girls."

It was true. Ron had suggested once, when she complained how they stared at her, that if she wore her blue jeans more often and let her hair down, she might not seem so aloof. "Not that it bothers me what you wear," he had added quickly. "But let's face it, everyone doesn't think like I do around here."

Esther had thought about what he said. She still felt repulsed at the thought of wearing blue jeans, even if hers weren't as tight as Ramona's or Marci's. They just didn't seem ladylike, but she didn't mind letting her hair down at times.

As the months passed by, John Popescu became more and more removed from his family. Evening after evening he would dress himself carefully and leave the house; evening after evening Esther and Ramona would give each other significant glances as he spruced his hair, adjusted his tie, or brushed imaginary lint from his jacket. Surely, the girls reasoned, he was not going to the country club as often as that. And, gradually, as the weeks wore on, their suspicions grew. Ramona became convinced, though she rarely breathed her fears to anyone, that her father had a girlfriend somewhere. Esther, less worldly-wise than her cousin, pushed such thoughts from her mind and attempted to persuade herself that her uncle was tired of female company and chose to spend his evenings with his business friends. Neither of the girls spoke of these nightly excursions to either Rachel or her mother. Why should they trouble them? Maybe this was just a phase and would soon pass.

But pass it did not. Instead, the evening outings were extended to whole weekends at a time. John grew more and more uneasy at home. If it had not been for Ron Atwood and Rachel, and for the demands of school which kept her evenings well occupied, Esther would have been a very lonely young lady. Ramona was away all week at college and out most Friday and Saturday evenings with her friends. When she was home, she would often retreat to her own room with her music, or watch a movie in the den. As the weeks passed, she and her cousin had less in common than ever. This saddened Esther but there seemed to be nothing she could do about it.

Then, one day in the middle of March, Esther was alone as usual when the phone rang. She frowned a little as she heard Len's voice at the other end.

"Esther, I've just had a brainwave and it involves you," he told her. "I think it's really from the Lord, but I can't explain it very well over the phone. Can I come over and talk to you about it?"

Esther hesitated before answering slowly, "Well, drop by in an hour or so, Len, if you like." She knew her uncle would be home by then. "I'm promising nothing, mind. I mean, I'm busy with school at the moment and…."

"That's OK, Esther. I won't force you into anything you don't feel comfortable with." Esther grimaced. She wasn't sure about that. And when he finally arrived and told her that he thought the church should host a special concert in early April in which she would be the star singer, she gasped in dismay.

"There'll be a special love offering for the suffering church in Romania," Len reassured her. "Please think it over, Esther. I think God is in this, really I do."

Esther demurred at first, said she was not professional enough, that she wasn't used to such publicity, but Len swept aside each objection, as she knew he would do. But she had promised the Lord she would never turn down any opportunity to witness, especially since that awful incident at Ramona's party. So she finally gave in and agreed to meet him at the church the next Thursday. She was relieved to discover that Margaret was to be there also; she had agreed to sing several pieces with her.

"Esther," said Margaret suddenly, when Len had given them a fifteen minute break, "which of the two Atwood cousins is your boyfriend?"

Esther nearly let the glass of Sprite she was holding drop onto the tiled floor of the church kitchen. She blushed a deep crimson but remained silent.

Margaret gave her friend a sly wink as she continued, "Oh come on, you must have a preference. From what young Connie tells me, one of them drives you to college every day. As for the other—it strikes me he's using this concert as a pretext of spending as much time as possible with you. Tongues will begin to wag, you know."

Esther dropped her eyes. She was used to Ramona's joshing which always had an edge in it but she knew Margaret was not jealous in the slightest, so she must be really trying to get some message across to her. She looked her friend straight in the eyes.

"You shocked me a bit, Margaret, putting it like that," she told her, "but you've given me something to think about." And she sat down at the table, cupped her chin in her hands, and went on slowly, "I know you won't believe me when I tell you this, but I've never thought of either of them as my boyfriend."

"Oh Esther, don't be so terribly naïve," Margaret expostulated, scarcely believing her ears; "even if a guy out of the goodness of his heart tries to help you adapt to a new culture, he doesn't have to take you out to eat nearly every lunch break or spend hours after school coaching you when I am sure he has homework enough himself. And as for the other one…."

"Look, Margaret," Esther interrupted, her voice rising a little, "I've only been here six months. In the beginning, I had no car,

Uncle was always busy, and Ramona had her own life to live. So Ron drove me a few places to help me out from time to time, but he made it clear that he was trying to help me as a friend, nothing more. And," she paused, not accustomed to talking about such things, "as for Len, I've no idea why you should think there could be anything much between us. I practice with him just to get through this concert which is going to help my people in Romania." Esther threw back her hair which had fallen round her face and said just a little defiantly for her, "So there's no big secret. And you don't need to worry. I'm not about to lose my heart to either of them."

Margaret gave her hand an affectionate pat as she said laughingly, "Oh, you innocent little Romanian girl. I think you're deceiving yourself about one of these gallants at least. Len Atwood has broken more than one heart so he deserves what he gets and shouldn't be taken terribly seriously, but the other...." Margaret's face grew serious. "I wouldn't want him hurt. He seems a very nice young man, Esther, he really does."

"Speaking of me, of course," said a voice behind them. They had not heard Len enter the kitchen. Esther wished the floor would open under her, but Margaret was always equal to any situation and replied quickly, "Of course not, Len. I'm just giving my friend here a little advice from my depth of experience," and her brown eyes twinkled.

"Well, I suppose you were talking of my cousin then. Yes, I'm right; look how Esther's blushing."

"Oh, she blushes easily," Margaret told him. "Come on, we'd better get on with the practice," Margaret announced suddenly, changing the subject. "I have to be home in half an hour."

Margaret winked at Esther as she followed her into the music room. It was only when she had finally gone home leaving Esther to finish a number without her, that Len cleared his throat and began, "I'm sorry I overheard a little of your conversation earlier. But it made me realize that I need to just remind you of something as a brother in the Lord. You are a dear sister in Christ and I know will be such an asset to His church here in Terra Haute." Len took a sidelong glance at his companion who sat, eyes fixed on her lap, waiting for whatever might be coming next. "But," he continued in a low voice, "the devil always has his trap for those whom God intends to use. And I think he has a very subtle one for you."

Esther glanced up at him now. "I don't know what you can mean, Len," she said coldly.

"Now, don't be offended, please don't," and he reached for her hand and gave it a quick squeeze before releasing it again. "It's just that you ought to know that my cousin, as I told you once before, is not a Christian."

"So he's an unbeliever, then?" the girl asked shrewdly.

"Well, depends what you call an unbeliever. He would say he believes in God and in Christ, I suppose, but there is something else that you should know, though really it isn't my place to tell it. But if Ron is a man at all, he will tell you himself before you go any further."

Esther was thoroughly roused now and retorted with a sarcasm rather uncharacteristic of her. "Further? What do you mean? Let me tell you, Len Atwood, that in all the times I have been with your cousin, Christian or not, he has never squeezed my hand like you did just now, not once!"

Len reddened and bit his lip. So this mild meek little angel did have some fire in her after all? To tell the truth, he liked her all the better for it. "Well, I wish Ron could hear your defense. What would I not give to have a beautiful and talented young lady defend me like that! But seriously, Esther, do give this a lot of thought before you get more deeply involved. Besides," he went on, "folks are talking, you know."

Esther said nothing. She reached for her coat, but Len caught her arm. "Promise me you'll pray about what I've said?"

Esther nodded mutely as she dashed out of the church and ran across the car park. She had a lot to think about that night as she brushed her hair and prepared for bed. Was she being a naïve fool after all? Were these two young men taking advantage of her? She was never quite certain about Len or his motives, but Ron had become a real and trusted friend. She had come to look forward to the lunch break, to those hours after school, to their walks around the campus, and especially to their rides together to and from college.

Oh bother, she thought. Why did Margaret have to put such ideas into her head? Well, she wouldn't think about it any more. She and Ron were friends, that was all, and what would college be without him? She had wondered more than once how she would cope when he went off to law school. Well, sufficient unto the day was the evil thereof, the Good Book said. One day at a time was all she needed to worry about, wasn't it?

Chapter Twenty-Three

Esther's First Concert

"And now we present to you, ladies and gentlemen, Esther Popescu from Romania." The audience broke into a thunderous applause. "This evening," Len continued, as he put his arm on the girl's shoulder, "Esther is giving this special concert on behalf of her suffering brothers and sisters in Romania. There will be a love offering at the end of the program which will be sent directly to her church to be used to relieve families where the breadwinner is either imprisoned or incapacitated through other forms of persecution as was this young lady's father. She will tell you her story in the interval. But now, listen to the thrilling voice of Miss Popescu who has already inspired many in this audience to a closer walk with the Lord."

Len Atwood went to the piano leaving Esther in the spotlight. She bowed slightly, and then said in her clear, silvery voice what a privilege it was to be there that evening and to sing about the Lord Jesus. She asked her hearers to forget the singer and let the Holy Spirit use the words to bless and inspire every heart present.

It is doubtful if Esther would have agreed to be the star singer in this concert if face after face, pale, pinched, and worn had not risen up before her beckoning her to do her best to relieve their pain, their hunger, their suffering. Although she had agreed initially, there were many times during the weeks of practice when she shrank from the whole idea of the concert. Then she would tell herself that she was doing this for Romania and she would do it with all her might. This was why she had agreed when the pastor's wife had insisted on going with her to purchase her gown—long and white, and modest enough, Esther had insisted on that, but soft and velvety and unlike anything she had ever worn. She had gasped when told the price, and rather reluctantly placed her cherished $200 on the counter. She had saved it all these months for her family in Romania.

"You'll get it all back," Mrs. Cripps had whispered as they had left the department store. "We're anticipating a really large love offering and you can take all expenses out of that. It's for God's glory," Mrs. Cripps assured her. "He has gifted you with a beautiful face, and a wonderful voice, and you must not be careless of these gifts."

When, however, the good woman had wanted to add some touches of makeup Esther had protested. "Please," she pleaded. "I'm not used to it and really don't like it. Besides, do I actually need it?"

Betty Cripps put her hands on her plump hips and surveyed the girl before her. "No, you really don't, my dear, only you will be under the spotlight. But you have got a marvelous complexion. Ah, what it is to be young!"

This was the first time she had really gotten to know the pastor's wife. She was a good-natured, talkative lady, rather forceful at times, and very down-to-earth, a balance, she was fond of saying, to her "heavenly minded husband." She had helped arrange the girl's dark locks on top of her head, said a prayer with her, and sent her on stage. Now, looking at the girl as she stood there, Betty thought she looked like a veritable angel come down to earth to inspire the children of men.

Ron thought so too and gave his mother a sidelong glance as Esther began her first song. He had been surprised that she had seemed eager to come that evening. She couldn't miss hearing his gypsy queen, had been her remark. Now he could see she was utterly confounded. She had imagined the Romanian would be some wild-eyed, countrified girl with boorish manners and outlandish dress. This graceful, ethereal figure was not at all what she had expected.

Esther began with a few Romanian folk songs followed by several English hymns and some contemporary numbers, several of which she sang with Margaret.

"Is that Esther?" whispered Mike Crawford. "She looks almost unearthly." Ron had glanced at his friend from time to time and seen that he was completely carried away by Esther's singing. He was glad he had invited him that evening. He studied Mike's face. It was drawn and white, with dark circles under his eyes.

"It's Esther all right," he whispered back. He studied the young singer intently. Was this the same girl who had joined him for a pizza that first day in her new country? Len had coached her well. She sang with confidence and a measure of poise, and yet it was still the same Esther after all—pure, modest, sincere, and breathtakingly beautiful.

Several seats behind Ron, John Popescu sat entranced. His niece had obviously inherited her mother's voice as well as her beauty. He glanced at his girls beside him and saw they looked very proud of their cousin. They had decided to turn out as a family though Ramona had protested at first. She hadn't wanted to go back to Len's church.

In the intermission, Esther gave a simple, twenty minute account of her life, of the tragic death of her parents, of the courage of her Christian brothers and sisters in the face of tremendous odds. Sobs were heard throughout the audience, and when she began to sing again, she sang of the Christ Who was rich yet for our sakes became poor. There was such a hush in the sanctuary the silence could almost be felt. Esther was spent and the tears poured down her face as she repeated the words, "But He became poor to ransom my soul." Then, gathering all the courage and strength she possessed, she concluded with the stirring song, "Down from His Glory." Her audience knew that the words, "Oh how I love Him," came as a true testimony from a girl who had seen more than her share of suffering and sorrow and kept her faith.

A tousle-headed young man in the back seat bent forward to his companion as the last words faded away and the audience, after a minute's stunned silence, broke again into thunderous applause. "She sure has changed a lot," he whispered.

"Think so?" asked Hugh with a slight smile, for Hugh Gardner it was. He and his grandson, Aaron, had come to spend a few weeks with his aged mother of ninety-two who lived near Terre Haute, and had seen the advertisement for the concert in the local paper. He had been almost sure it was the same Esther he had prayed for every day since he had met her on the plane. And, though indeed more Westernized at least outwardly and with a poise and dignity that utterly amazed him, he immediately recognized the same bright-eyed, innocent girl he had so taken to from the time he took a seat beside her on flight 233 from Paris to Indianapolis.

"They're spoiling her already," Aaron commented in a low voice.

Hugh patted his grandson on the shoulder but only asked quietly, "Did she sing as if she were spoiled?"

"Well, maybe not. I mean she was as sincere as anyone could be but...."

"Yes, I know. I know, my boy. But she has some way to go yet to be really affected by all this praise."

"Maybe," replied Aaron doubtfully. "I guess I'm going by what I'd be like if I were put in her place."

Hugh smiled. "I'm afraid experience is, after all, the best teacher Aaron," he whispered. "Esther will learn many things in the next months. It won't be easy for her and she'll sure need our prayers."

But now Len Atwood was taking the stage once more. "I am sure, ladies and gentlemen," he was saying, "you have all been moved to the depths, as I have been, by this stunning performance, and that you will allow the Lord to loosen your purse strings and give as you have never given before."

And they did. It seemed that everyone was giving. The offering plates where piled high when they were taken into the vestry to be counted.

At last, the concert was over. Everyone it seemed wanted to shake hands with the young singer. Len had escorted her into the vestibule and she was standing with Margaret between the older pastor and his young assistant. As Hugh and Aaron approached them, her tired eyes caught Hugh's keen gaze. She sprang forward and taking his hand forgot about everyone around waiting to get a word with her. Drawing him aside a little, she exclaimed, "Oh Mr. Gardner, how very good to see you! I read and re-read your note and those words mean so very much to me."

"I still pray for you every day," Hugh replied warmly. "And what about the Velvet Curtain?"

Esther smiled. "I've felt like it was smothering me a bit at times, like tonight for example. But I suppose that's only natural."

Hugh waited a moment before replying gently, "Well, Esther, this curtain is very pervasive and is really everywhere here in the West. But if and when it gets too much for you, remember, I'm there in the mountains of Tennessee, ready with a listening ear, any time, day or night."

But here Ron came up and wanted to introduce her to his mother. She only had a moment to whisper "Thank you" to Hugh and he was gone, lost in the crowd.

She turned with a sigh to find Ron's mother waiting to speak to her. "A wonderful performance," the older woman told her. "And my son and nephew evidently think so too," and she glanced from Len to Ron knowingly. "Well done. Keep up the good work," and she disappeared into the crowd.

Esther didn't know how to take Mrs. Atwood. She sighed softly to herself as she leaned against the wall. "You're absolutely worn out. I'll take you home," Ron said gently. "Oh, just a moment, here's someone you know wanting a word with you."

"Well, Esther, I didn't know you were such a star." It was Mike. "I'm sure glad Ron invited me. I thought maybe I would never get my wish—to hear you sing I mean."

Esther looked intently at the tall young man shaking hands with her. He was noticeably thinner than when she had first met him those months ago, and something in his voice brought tears to her dark eyes. "Oh Mike, you don't know how sorry I've been for my attitude that night. I want you to forgive me."

Mike smiled. "That's all in the past. And tonight makes up for everything. Your voice is marvelous. I was truly blessed. And, Esther," his deep voice shook with emotion, "when you've got a moment, pray for your friend and admirer, Mike Crawford, will you? He's sure going to need it in the coming months." He shook her hand heartily and was gone.

"He's having a major operation next week," Ron whispered in her ear. "But come on, let's go; you need to get home."

Esther let herself be led out to the car without protest. Len ran after them. "Esther, guess what," he shouted. "You've taken in at least $1000 from tonight's concert! I'll phone you with the exact figures tomorrow."

"You did wonderfully," he went on and then, as he handed her into Ron's car, he gave her a light kiss on the forehead. "Good night, and may the Lord bless and reward you for your effort for His Kingdom." And he was gone.

"Some brass!" Ron was muttering into the steering wheel. And Esther thought she heard him say, though she was never quite sure if she had heard right, "Mixing religion with flirtation. Just like him, the rascal!"

Ron had insisted on driving her to her concert. It had been a long time since he had taken her anywhere except to school and now as they sped homewards, Esther seemed tongue tied. Ron broke the silence. "You did wonderfully, Esther. I couldn't believe it was the same girl I ate pizza with six months ago."

Esther said nothing. She knew it was meant as a compliment but was not sure she could take it as that. Ron seemed to read her thoughts and changed the subject abruptly. "By the way, the Moscow Symphony Orchestra has come to Indianapolis. Will you go with me on Sunday evening to one of their performances?" He paused, "And let's have the whole day together away from my cousin's prying eyes—first church in the city, then lunch, then maybe the Gardens, and then the Messiah." He glanced at her meaningfully and added, "Can you stand a whole day with me, without Rachel, that is?"

Something in his tone made her drop her eyes. Before she could respond, he went on, "I've something I want to say to you. I wasn't sure if I should, but tonight, sitting watching you sing your heart out, I felt it was time I ought to tell you a little of my story. So do me this one favor, please."

Esther nodded, unable to speak. What was he going to say? What did he mean by "his story"? She was still trying to answer that question when she slipped between the sheets that evening. It had been a long day and a rewarding one too. Just think, $1000! But this change everyone seemed to be talking about—had she really altered that much? Was she so different from the young, diffident Romanian girl with her solid black shoes, threadbare skirt, and gold blouse, sitting on the bench in the October twilight, waiting for her Uncle's limousine to whisk her away to a new home and a new life? No, she told herself. She was no different at heart—only on the outside. And after all, wasn't it the heart that mattered?

Chapter Twenty-Four

Ron's Story

Ron and Esther had decided to go to the Romanian church in the city that Sunday morning, and, of course, had been again invited out for lunch. They had stayed so long that they had gone straight to the concert. It had been all Esther had expected and more.

"You love music, don't you?" Ron commented as he helped her into the car.

"It's in my blood," was the reply. "My parents were both opera singers. That's how they met."

Ron stared in surprise. "So that explains it."

"Explains what?"

"Oh, a lot of things."

Esther looked at him quizzically as he started up the engine. "I don't know quite what you mean. But I know I've inherited their musical ear and I hope, some of their talent. Mother taught me to sing when I was very young and then I had some lessons at school."

"But I thought your father was a poet and a preacher."

"Actually he didn't preach much," the girl explained and she shivered slightly.

"You're cold," remarked Ron, turning on the heater full blast. "But what happened to his career in the opera then?"

"A friend of his, another singer, went to some of the meetings held by the Lord's Army. It's an evangelical movement inside the Orthodox Church. He was very taken with some of the people there and took my dad along with him. It wasn't long before his whole life was transformed. He gave all his talents to God and felt he should give up opera. Mother and he weren't courting then but were casual friends. Actually, she was closer to Uncle John at the time. He really loved Mother." Esther paused. She knew now that unfortunately that love had never fully died. "Then she gave her life to Christ, too, and found that she had more in common with Dad than with his brother. My uncle was devastated and immigrated to America. And, well, you know the rest, or most of it."

Ron was silent a long time. Esther noticed that he was more

self-conscious than normal. Maybe he was only reflecting her own attitude.

"Are you hungry?" he asked suddenly, as he pulled off the interstate.

"Not really," she said truthfully, "but I am thirsty."

"Let's pull in somewhere for a milkshake, and anything else you would like."

"Thanks so much for this evening," she murmured. "You are very kind to me."

"Kind? That's what you think it is, isn't it?" Esther thought she could trace a little bitterness in his tone. "I drive you to college every day and spend all my spare time at school with you out of sheer kindness. How charitable of me and how admirable!"

"Ron!" Esther sounded reproachful. "You're being sarcastic. But that's what you told me at the beginning, you know, and I believed you."

"Well, of course you believed me for I meant what I said. But, look, we can talk better inside," and he stopped the car outside a Dairy Queen and they were soon sitting in a secluded corner, confronted with two large milkshakes.

"Oh Ron," she laughed. "You really are spoiling me; I'll be putting on weight fast at this rate. In fact, I've already gained ten pounds since coming here."

He smiled. "You needed to gain a bit." There was an awkward pause. "I meant what I said shortly after you came to America, and I still want to help you all I can and be your friend. But...."

"There's that but again."

"Yes there's a 'but' all right. You see, I..." he stammered. Esther stared at him. She had never seen the self-composed Ron like this before.

"It's no use," he burst out. "I'll just have to be blunt. After all, what can you expect from me? Do you think I'm made of steel or iron instead of flesh and blood? Here I am, seeing a young, talented, intelligent and extremely attractive girl every day, eating with her, studying with her, driving with her, and trying so hard to pretend as if I were her big brother. Well, I'm not her big brother," and he slammed his fist on the table. "I'm just a guy who thinks she, that is that *you*, are absolutely fabulous in every way and who finds it increasingly hard to act so calm and patronizing all the time. Oh Esther, are you that naïve? Isn't it as plain as the nose on your face that I'm absolutely nuts over you?"

Esther's face was a picture. Ron could not tell at first whether she was shocked, upset, or pleased. Then a deep blush spread over all her features as it fully dawned on her what he had just said. She couldn't believe it! He, Ron Atwood, who was good at everything and who could have any girl he wanted at the turn of a hat, was fond of her, the simple, old-fashioned and very religious girl from Romania?

She pinched herself to make sure it wasn't all some fantastic dream from which she would soon awake. Yes, it was true. There he was, sitting opposite her, nervously playing with his watchband, his face flushed, his eyes fixed on the napkin on his lap, looking for all the world like a guilty child who has just confessed to some misdemeanor. She tried to speak but the words stuck in her throat.

Ron leaned towards her across the table. "Look, I know you are too modest, too naïve, to have ever imagined all this. You're not like any girl I know. But now I'm in your hands. You're independent now, with your own car to drive as you've reminded me at least once." He grinned a little. "And you're quickly getting the hang of college life. Anyway, there're only a few weeks more before the semester ends. You can give me my dismissal if you like. Besides, Len phoned me the day before the concert." He paused as if not knowing how much to tell her.

Esther was all ears but she said nothing. He went on. "He says folks are talking about us and that he overheard you and Margaret Cripps discussing me."

"He only told you half then, or probably he only heard half which was just as well. Actually, we were discussing both of you."

Ron grinned again in spite of his obvious nervousness. "Oh you were, were you? And how did that come about."

"Margaret asked me which of the two Atwood boys was my boyfriend." It was out before she could help it.

"And what did you say?"

Esther avoided his gaze. "Well, I told her neither."

Ron said nothing and she continued slowly, "I told her you and I were simply friends and that you had wanted to help me adjust to life here. As for Len, on my part at least, our being together so much lately was only for the sake of the concert." Esther would not tell him more of the conversation. She had told enough, she figured.

"Well, Len said he had warned you that in his opinion at any rate, I was not a Christian. And that it was not wise for us to be...." Ron could not finish the sentence but he knew Esther understood what he was trying to say. She looked so youthful and innocent, he thought, and so very winsome. He cleared his throat and said gently, "Esther, I've been frank with you. Now it's your turn. I have been feeling that the time would come when we had to be open with each other."

The girl froze. Whatever was coming, she wondered? "Are you and Len getting attached to each other in any way?" His voice was tense.

Esther was relieved that she could answer his question so easily. "No, Ron, not in the slightest. He's really not my type," was her quick response.

He heaved an audible sigh of relief. That was one hurdle over. Then he continued. "Well, if the answer had been yes, that would have been it all over with us. But as it was a decided no, then I need to go on. So what I'm really trying to say is," he paused again, "that I would like to put our friendship on a different basis. I have told you how I feel about you and I want to know if you are getting fond of me too? Just be honest with me. I desperately need to know."

Esther remained silent for such a long time that Ron thought she would never answer. He knew she was inherently shy and felt maybe he had put her on the spot too soon. But he had no alternative. They couldn't go on any longer as they were.

Esther was searching for the right words. She had always assumed that when she was able to cope even tolerably well with life here in the States, Ron Atwood would just simply drop out of the picture. But now she was not sure she wanted that. He had become a part of her life in America. And he had been so much the gentleman, that she had grown to respect and like him very much. So she finally raised her large, speaking eyes to his blue-grey ones and began slowly, her face still suffused with color, "I've been fooling myself a bit, trying to think of you only as a friend and brother but, yes, I'm getting fond of you too, I really am. I mean, I've been spending a lot of time with you too, you know, and I'm not made of stone either."

She had dropped her eyes again and did not see the pleasure and relief that flooded Ron's face, though she did hear his long sigh of relief. "You don't know what that answer means to me, Esther," he said and now he was not trying to mask the tenderness in his tone. "But I need to get two things straightened right away. This question of my being a Christian or not. What do you feel about it?"

Esther appreciated his straightforwardness and replied, "Well,

Ron, it depends on what you feel about Christianity. I mean, are you a believer?"

"A believer?" he echoed. "Well, I certainly believe in God and in His Son."

Esther sounded relieved. "Len says you are not religious at all."

"Len says a lot of things," growled Ron. "What he means is that I've never gone to church regularly except for about a year when I was a senior at high school and only really went to please my girlfriend. And Len senses that I've just no use for his type of Christianity."

Esther met his eyes as he continued, "I don't want to blacken my cousin in your eyes even though I can guess that he has hinted certain things about me." Esther remembered Len's insinuations and said nothing. Ron went on in a low voice, "Well, that brings me to the second point we need to get clear. But it's getting late and I think maybe I need to get you home. We can't have respectable Ramona phoning the police about us." He laughed, and Esther couldn't help but join in as he escorted her back to the car.

Neither of them spoke much during the drive home, but as they turned into the familiar driveway, Ron said softly, "We need to talk a bit more, Esther. I have to be completely open with you. I know I can trust you, and I'd rather it came straight from me than from my cousin."

Esther had a lot to think about as she brushed her hair and prepared for bed that night. What would Ron say to her tomorrow, she wondered?

The next morning, Esther found it hard to concentrate and was glad when her classes were over and she sat with Ron on the faded green bench under a tall pine tree. He had taken her to a nearby park. It was one of those glorious days when spring has made a surprise debut.

"And now for my story," he began, his voice betraying his nervousness. It was obvious to Esther that whatever he was going to tell her was not easy to relate. She listened attentively, reveling in the warm rays of the sun and the stillness of the mid April afternoon.

But Ron was continuing: "I was very popular at high school; I was band leader, star baseball player, top in my class in most subjects, and so I suppose it wasn't surprising that I was also a favorite with the girls." Esther gave him a sidelong glance and he grimaced a little. "I know what you're thinking already. This is a typical success story. But I don't think it will be what you think," he added soberly. "I suppose though, I was your stereotype of a boy growing up in middle-class America.

"My mother divorced when I was fifteen. Maybe I should tell you that Dad was brought up in a Christian home but rebelled when he was in college, met mother, and married against his parents' wishes since they didn't consider her a real Christian. She was brought up Episcopalian but hardly ever attended church. As for Dad, seems like he was the black sheep in his family." He paused and Esther could tell that it hurt him to speak of his father.

"Dad's brother was Len's father," he went on. "He had a conversion experience later in life, became a pastor, and took a church out West about six or seven years ago. Len stayed on here and went to college locally. Our families have never been close. They think we're real heathen," he grinned. "We only went to church at Christmas and Easter. My aunt, Len's mom, was always trying to convert me but with little success. I wasn't attracted to their religion. It seemed superficial to me and Len and I had little in common.

"Then Dad began to drink. He got in with other women and broke Mom's heart." Ron's face clouded. "Of course there were faults on both sides. Always are. But I stuck up for Mom and we got real close after Dad left. I was her pride and joy. She spoiled me, I don't mind saying. In fact, I suppose everyone spoiled me. I was used to getting my own way." He paused with another sidelong glance at his companion who was smiling a little to herself. But she said nothing and motioned for him to go on.

"I had plenty of girlfriends though I wasn't serious with any until Sherri came along. She, I suppose, was my counterpart in some respects—popular with the boys, clever, athletic, very pretty, and also very spoiled, though she was quite religious, which I definitely was not. She was a member of The Living Vine Church in the next town. We gravitated to each other and I started to date seriously for the first time."

"What does 'serious' dating actually mean?" Esther interrupted. "I've never really figured it out."

Ron grinned. "Who really has? But I suppose you might say that dating is taking a girl out somewhere just for the fun of it, and you might date one girl one week and another the next. Serious dating, on the other hand, is sticking to one girl over a period of time with the intention or thought at least that you might end up marrying her."

Esther made no comment. She understood now why folks had talked. Ron guessed what she was thinking. "You are wondering if I have been dating you all these months, right?"

The girl blushed and nodded. "In a sense, I have dated you, though not seriously of course," Ron told her staring up at the pine tree above them. "I mean I've certainly taken you out to lunch many times, and occasionally to church but, and you'll probably be shocked at this, most dating generally implies some kissing and cuddling at the end of the date, and quite often it goes a lot further than that."

Ron was embarrassed but knew he had to come out with it. "But to go on and get this over with once and for all. You need to know what sort of a fellow I really am before you decide if I'm the kind of guy you want to get to know better." He cleared his throat and took the plunge: "Esther, I was no better than my peers. This was the only kind of dating I knew. So when Sherri and I got to know each other better, we became more and more physical until we did what many couples I knew did, we had sex together—more than once, to be honest with you."

Esther looked away. Ron bit his lip nervously. How he hated having to tell Esther all this! But she had to know the worst about him. She couldn't live all her days with her head in the sand.

The girl sensed his embarrassment and raised her eyes to his face, encouraging him to go on. He gulped a little before continuing: "I knew several of my friends had done the same as I had and so I reasoned that it was OK to show my affection in this way as I was really very fond of Sherri, even though I had no idea of what real love was and was certainly not ready to settle down and marry her. I was just a kid and not mature enough to get involved in such a relationship.

"All during this time, Sherri would take me to her church each Sunday. She even had me singing in the choir and joining the youth group. I'd feel real uneasy at times, knowing I was only there for her sake. Well, maybe that's not quite true. I think I also went to salve my conscience a bit. I suppose I figured that it was a 'plus' for me in the eyes of the Almighty. God knows I had plenty of 'minuses' ticked up against me. And I met some real friendly people there who made me feel right at home.

"But one day in May, actually the day we both graduated from high school, a day I will never forget," and his voice trembled a little, "Sherri told me during our celebrations that she was expecting a child. It was due just before Christmas. We were still children ourselves, just turned eighteen, and the news overwhelmed me. Thing was, she seemed pleased about the news and I could see she wanted me to marry her. Of course, my mother was upset and shocked, not so much at what we had done, but that we hadn't been clever enough to take care of the consequences.

"Looking back on it," Ron went on, determined to get it all out before he changed his mind, "I think Sherri had really counted on this happening. She was from a poorer home than I was and wanted to 'step up in the world' as she termed it. My mother wanted her to have an abortion; she wouldn't think of my marrying the girl, but Sherri refused and I wouldn't force her to do something like that. It was her choice, after all. I finally and very reluctantly agreed that we would get married and bring up the child ourselves. Sherri started using Scripture on me. Pity she hadn't done it before," he added bitterly. "I felt trapped, and it maddened me to know that the whole thing didn't seem to bother her much at all, with all her religion. I knew I didn't actually love her, but also knew if I was man at all, I couldn't leave her in the lurch."

Esther stared at him. She couldn't help thinking that this just might be the dark side of freedom her uncle had talked about on her first night in her new country. She couldn't comprehend half of what Ron was telling her. Each sentence seemed to reveal another aspect of Western culture that shocked and stunned her.

Ron reddened a little under her gaze as he went on hurriedly: "So I trusted Sherri and we planned to be married in three months' time just before I began college in the fall. I hoped that, in spite of the mistake we had made, maybe we'd make it after all." He stole a look at the girl opposite him. She was pale, he thought, but she motioned for him to go on.

"It was the beginning of the summer, so I remember thinking it a bit strange when she announced that she had decided to go away to some relative in the south for a few months. I realized later why she did this. She didn't want me to know how far along she was in her pregnancy. So I was not prepared for the shock she gave me just before she was due back when she phoned me from a hospital in Atlanta. She had given birth to a baby boy and declared it was mine. I knew from the timing that it just could not be my child, but no one would believe me.

I was frantic. I knew the girl had played me double, so I visited her home for the first time, unknown to her. She had always tried to keep me from going there. Her sister finally let the cat out of the bag. Evidently Sherri had kept up two boyfriends for months. The other guy was also a church member but for some reason, I had never taken to him. I had noticed he was always very friendly with her. But then, she was that way with everyone so I had no idea she was two-timing me.

"Finally my mother and I insisted that tests were done to prove that the baby was his child. So I was exonerated in a way, that is, in the eyes of my mother and my friends. But in my own eyes I was as guilty as ever. Luck had it that I escaped a life of misery for of course, I broke the engagement and within a few weeks she was married to the other guy. I determined that I would never be taken in like that again and that I'd never get involved seriously with a girl I didn't intend to marry."

Ron had come to the end of his story and leaned back on the bench and closed his eyes. Esther was silent and after some moments, he sat up and bent towards her, "So now you know the worst about me. If you want nothing more to do with me, I can't really blame you but I'd rather it happened now before I get more fond of you," and he leaned back, folded his hands resignedly, like a prisoner awaiting his sentence.

Esther had never realized she was so terribly lonely until that moment, had never been fully aware of the hunger deep inside her for love and protection. Her Aunt Ana had done her best, but she was not a blood relative and had found it hard to show affection to the two young girls in her care. For four whole years, Esther had been her sister's protector and guide but her heart ached for someone to fulfill that same role in her own life. When she had arrived in America, she had basked in her uncle's love, but lately he had been seeking his companionship elsewhere and had little time to spare for his orphan niece. And now this tall, strong, and very capable young man was falling in love with her. She knew enough about him already to guess that this was no mere flirtation or the fancy of a moment. She sensed that his love would prove a rock of Gibraltar, if she would let it, in her frightening new world.

Two lone tears began to trickle down her cheeks as she stole a glance at her companion from under her long eyelashes. He raised his eyes to hers. "Why Esther, you're crying! I've shocked you, frightened you."

Esther gulped. "You certainly did shock me, Ron, but frighten me? No. You could never do that."

Ron's eyes brightened. "That's more than kind of you to say that. I don't feel a bit worthy of your trust." The young man's voice trembled slightly with pent-up emotion. Esther put up a quick prayer for the right words to say. Her heart was pounding. Her mouth was dry. But she began in a low, clear voice, "I'm so glad you told me all this. I want you to know that I don't think any the less of you for what you have said. I...." but she got no further.

The young man sat bolt upright, his eyes shining, and, not knowing what he was doing, he took hold of her hand and held it firmly in his own as if it was his anchor and stay. Then he reddened and dropped it suddenly. "Sorry, I was carried away. Go on Esther, go on."

But Esther could say nothing for what seemed to Ron an eternity. Finally she ventured a look into his eyes. They were searching hers for the answer he so longed to hear. At last she began in a voice so low Ron had to bend forward to catch her words: "This is all so new to me, Ron. Back home, at least the way I was brought up, girls didn't go out 'seriously' as you call it here, until they were pretty much engaged. And I'm not ready for that yet."

Ron nodded understandingly. At least she hadn't cast him off, not yet anyway. "But," she went on, "I'm not in Romania but in America. So I'll have to find out what's right for me to do in my new life. Just give me a day or so, please, and I'll give you a clearer answer. You see, I must ask God about it."

For just a moment, Ron wished there were no God in the picture. It seemed to complicate matters. But then it swept over him that if he wanted this wonderful girl to eventually become his wife, he would have to get used to reckoning with God. So he just said as calmly as he could, "That's fine. Of course you need time. I've overwhelmed you a bit. At least you haven't dumped me on the spot. That's a comfort."

Esther gave him a look that spoke volumes as they both rose from the bench. He wanted to take her in his arms right there and then and ask her to be his wife. But he knew that would spoil everything. It was getting chilly and Esther shivered as a breeze rustled through the trees above them. He reached for her red jacket and put it round her.

"Thanks Ron. You take good care of me."

"Have to," he answered lightly. "If I didn't, you'd get sick on me and that would mean waiting maybe weeks for an answer. Couldn't have that, now, could I?"

Esther smiled up at him. She felt so safe in his presence. And Ron left her that evening, hoping in his heart that her God would not be too hard on the both of them—on an orphan girl who needed someone to take care of her in a scary new world, and on a young man who, for the first time in his life had really and truly found a girl worth finding, a good, beautiful, fascinating, extraordinary, thoughtful, sweet, angelic.... He had still not run out of adjectives when he turned into his driveway a few moments later.

"Come down to earth, Ron Atwood," his mother told him over supper. "You're in a dream. Bewitched it seems like to me."

"Well, Mom, it depends. If angels have it in their power to cast spells over us mortal men, then I'm bewitched all right and hope I stay that way for the rest of my life." And he rose abruptly from his chair, gave her a resounding kiss on the cheek, and vanished to his room where he stayed for the rest of the evening.

Sleep was slow in coming to Esther that night. Her heart was a turmoil of emotions. Ron Atwood falling in love with her! She couldn't believe it. She knelt for a long time by her bed, trying to tell God all about the events of the day, not that He needed telling. He already knew, she figured. But that's what she always did—told Him everything. And then she asked Him what to do.

She was still not sure what His answer would be when she fell asleep about midnight and dreamed that she was back in Romania, that her life was being threatened by her old tormentor, and then Ron appeared out of the blue and whisked her away from danger. As she awoke with the daylight streaming in the window, she thought she had her answer. God had sent Ron to protect her, for who else had she? Uncle John no longer had much time to give her and there was no other man in her life to whom she could turn. And as for Ron's being a Christian, well, he certainly was not an unbeliever and seemed to be more Christian than his pastor-cousin. Anyway, what did being a Christian mean now she was no longer in a country ruled by Communism? Besides, she wasn't going to give her final "yes" for a while to come. She had to get to know him better first. Things were done differently in America and she had to adapt. Hadn't even Hugh Gardner told her that?

So when her chauffeur drove up next morning, it was a blushing and timid girl who greeted him at the door. Ron thought he had never seen her look so lovely as he handed her into the front seat. They had driven some minutes in silence when he pulled into a lay by. Esther looked up at him for the first time.

"It's OK," he reassured her. "I came a few moments early today on purpose. I have to hear my fate before we start classes this morning. I have an exam, too, so be gentle with me, please Esther."

"Oh Ron, you'll be late and it's part of your finals too."

He grinned. "Don't worry. There's plenty of time." He reached for her hand, then hesitated.

"It's all right, Ron," the girl reassured him in as calm a voice as she could muster. "I am willing to be your...." She hung her head and dropped her eyes in confusion.

"My girlfriend?" he stammered. "You really mean it?"

"Yes, as long as we go slowly," was the reply. "I need to know you better before I could be sure that you were someone God wanted me to be with all my life."

Ron nodded. "Of course. But you sure have made my day." He brought her hand to his lips and kissed it almost reverently. "We'll get to know each other in the coming months, that's for sure, and I won't push you in any way. If I do go too fast, you are to let me know right away"

"I will. Just remember that I'm new to all this. And you see, in Romania it was simpler. I mean, a person was either a Christian or not. It was not easy for someone to say they were a Christian and be a hypocrite inside. To confess your faith meant maybe imprisonment, torture, and certainly forfeiting a good career or job. But here anyone can claim to be a Christian—presidents, football players, movie stars—well just about everyone it seems like, so it's confusing to me. All I know for sure is that you do believe in God so are definitely not an unbeliever and that you seem to act like a Christian in many ways though I do wish...." her voice trailed off.

"What do you wish, dear?" he asked gently.

"I wish you really did love my Heavenly Father. I'm not sure you do, and that could be a real problem between us."

"Well, I'm willing for you, my beautiful angel, to teach me how," and he gave her hand another kiss before he released it and started up the engine. "You can be sure that I'll be a willing pupil," he added as he put his foot on the accelerator.

Esther looked wonderingly up at his face. Things had happened so fast she was in a dream but, at present at least, it was a beautifully pleasant dream, one from which she wished she would never need to awake.

Chapter Twenty-Five

Graduation

It was Esther's first graduation service in America. She glanced at Mrs. Atwood who was gazing intently at the podium. Her face was wreathed in smiles and no wonder! Not that she or anyone else was greatly surprised that Ron was graduating magna cum laude and valedictorian of his class. He had beaten Marci by only a fraction of a point. The applause was deafening as the Dean handed him his diploma. Esther clapped along with the rest, proud to be a part of this celebration. The tall, broad-shouldered gentleman to her right stooped and whispered in her ear: "Aren't you proud of him, my dear?"

"Yes, very," the girl whispered back. She had taken to Ron's father from the start. He seemed an older version of his son in appearance, though with a worn, troubled face that showed the wear and tear of life more than most men of forty-six. Esther had felt much more at ease with him than with Ron's mother who, though extremely civil, made her feel as if she posed some threat to her son's happiness or security. Ron told her later that any girl he would pick would be given the same treatment.

"Now if she chooses the girl, that's a different matter," he told Esther with a grimace.

The ceremony over, the graduates congregated on the spacious lawn, talking with faculty and guests. Marci and her classmates had invited Ron to join them for a weekend of celebrations at the beach, but he had said he had other plans.

"Would you have gone if it hadn't been for me?" she had asked him when they were alone.

"I don't think so, Esther," he replied slowly. "Ever since my experience with Sherri, I've shied away from that type of thing. I can guess what partying like that will entail and I don't want anything to do with it."

"Marci will blame me," she told him with a wry smile. "Did you see how she looked at me when we met on the lawn?"

"I sure did and I'm awfully sorry. But you'll have to get used to it, if you aren't already. Someone with your beauty and charm is going to generate a good deal of jealousy from certain quarters."

"I don't think it would matter what I looked like as long as the handsome and popular Ron Atwood had chosen me for his girlfriend," and Esther took his arm as if she had done it all her life. "Where are we going now?"

"Mother's laying out a spread at our house. It'll be a bit awkward with Dad there."

"Maybe I'd better not go," suggested Esther, pulling back.

"You're going all right young lady," he told her, laying his hand possessively on hers. "You're my girlfriend now and I want everyone to know it. And having you there'll make things easier. Dad really likes you. That's obvious."

"I like him too," Esther replied simply. "Look, there's Ramona."

"Ron, your Mom's just invited me to your house for refreshments. Mind if I go with you?" Ramona was breathless. She had had a job to catch them before they left the campus. "Marci brought me but she's staying a while so I need a ride back to Velours."

"Jump right in," Ron told her, helping her into the back seat.

"So she invited you too, Esther?" her cousin asked as she straightened her white mini skirt.

"*I* invited her of course," Ron put in. "Didn't you know that she's my girlfriend now, Ramona?"

Ramona laughed. "So what? You've always got a girl on the go, only you're never serious so Esther had better watch out."

Ron was hurt but tried to laugh it off. "You are giving me my pedigree, Ramona. But I don't think you understand me," and as he spoke, he reached over and took Esther's hand. Ramona stared at him. He had never taken her hand like that. "I'm really serious this time, though how it'll go in the long run between us depends on this young lady. *My* mind's already made up." His voice was firm and his face flushed. Ramona saw that she had to believe him. He was terribly in earnest. "After all," he went on, "I thought you would have guessed by now about me and Esther. I mean, we have spent a lot of time together lately so I thought it was no secret."

Ramona was never long at a loss for words. Gulping a little, she tried to make her voice sound normal as she began, "Maybe I'm real naïve, but Ron, when a guy like you goes around telling girls that he's 'just friends you know,' that he doesn't intend to have any sort of romantic relationship for a long time to come, I really believe him. He's honest, he's decent, so he'll mean what he says. Well, I suppose I should have known that you can't believe any guy these days, not even you." Her voice was just a trifle piteous and went to Esther's heart. She wished she could drop through the floorboards.

Ron looked as if he had been stabbed in the back. At first, anger surged within him. Swinging around, he turned and faced Ramona, grey eyes looking straight into blue. But something in those sky-blue eyes went to his heart. Maybe he had hurt her more than he had thought.

"Look Ramona," he began more gently. "I'm no saint. I've told Esther the story of my life. She knows much more about me than you do, but she still trusts me and she believed me when I told her I was getting very fond of her. You probably don't know how fed up a guy becomes with girls who want him only for what he can give them and are always wanting a lot more than he is prepared to give. Well, for the first time in my life, I found someone who wasn't like that."

The girl in the back seat was silent. Ron noticed that her face was pale under her makeup and she looked in shock. Here was a new Ron Atwood and she didn't know what to do with him.

Ron started up the engine and there was little talking for a long time. Then, hiding the hurt deep inside, Ramona began to chatter about college, the coming party at the beach, and her plans for the summer vacation until they reached the Atwood residence where she talked to anyone and everyone and made herself so agreeable that Ron's mother pronounced her one of the most charming girls she had ever met. But David Atwood's eyes turned to the slim, dark-eyed girl at his son's side, and he was glad for once in his life that the boy's tastes were like his own.

"I'm worried about Ramona," Esther told Ron as he drove her home that evening. "This weekend of partying won't do her any good and I'm afraid...." She paused, not wanting to finish the sentence.

"Listen, let's get one thing clear before we go any further." Ron's voice was firm. "As Ramona herself said, I made it clear from the start that I was not going to get serious or be romantic in any way with her. And yes, I'm worried about her, too, and if anyone should take any blame it should be me, not you. But you don't know your cousin as well as I do. This is not her first weekend of partying and it won't be her last. It's a way of life I got heartily sick of. That's why, when you came into my life you were...." He paused, and then continued slowly and hesitantly as if surprised at his own words, "an answer to prayer, or as I often tell myself an angel sent straight from Heaven to keep Ron Atwood on the straight and narrow."

"An answer to prayer!" repeated Esther to herself as she knelt by her bed that evening. "Oh God, am I really? Can I really be an answer to Ron's prayer?" There was no audible response to her question as she waited silently in the darkness. Her pulse quickened as she thought over the day's events. "He loves me," she whispered into the shadows, "and surely, God, that is your answer to me. He needs me and I need him. I can love both him and You, can't I, for You are LOVE?"

The next morning ushered in a new life for Esther Popescu. School was out for the summer. Ramona was away at Virginia Beach and then would go on with Kelly to spend a month in Florida. Rachel and her mother had left for a vacation in the mountains. Uncle John no longer spent much time at home so Esther would have felt very alone if it had not been for Ron who was never far away—taking her shopping, driving her to church, teaching her to ice skate, or taking her out for a meal. She was still rather reluctant to go to the movies but thought nothing of spending the evening with her boyfriend watching a video in the den. Ron had smiled at what he considered one of his girlfriend's few inconsistencies. But it mattered little. As long as he was with his beautiful girl, he was in the seventh heaven.

There were times when Esther did have some misgivings. She could not believe that she, the poor little Romanian girl was being treated like a queen, but had she a right to receive all this attention from her Prince Charming? Was she leading him on into a relationship she would one day have to break?

Once she confided in Margaret who much to her relief had set her fears at rest. "Don't worry," she had said putting her arms round her. "You're not married yet or even engaged. And I see such a difference in Ron. He's coming to church regularly; and if he isn't a real Christian just yet he soon will be. And besides, it seems like God sent you to each other. He's been such a real friend to you just when you needed it most and you are showing him the Christian way."

Margaret's reasoning made sense to Esther. She had prayed for help and hadn't God sent Ron to her? And besides, she was more than glad that her strong, handsome boyfriend was never far away. She had never experienced such a feeling of belonging since her parents had died.

So it was small wonder that Ron Atwood meant so much to her during those spring and summer months of 1988. When it slipped out that the Romanians always "said it with flowers," he would come to get her on a Saturday night with a rose, or carnation, or even a large bouquet which he would present on bended knee, half in fun and fully in earnest.

Although Ron never pressed her to change her ways, and would now and then remind her of how beautiful she had seemed to him in her gold blouse and black skirt the first day they met, Esther did not want him to suffer because she looked so different from his friends. Pants gradually replaced skirts, and, because he liked it that way, her hair was nearly always loose around her shoulders. Ron soon found out that, like most other girls he knew, Esther was really very fond of pretty clothes, so he more than once insisted on taking her shopping and nearly always paid the bill. And while Esther would still say most emphatically that it was the heart that mattered, she couldn't help but notice to her secret pleasure, that what she wore certainly did make a difference. No one eyed her now like they once did, and Ron's mother, whom she had visited once or twice, had remarked what good clothes sense she had.

Nearly every Sunday morning saw Ron and Esther sitting side by side in Pine Grove Evangelical Church. Both of them, however, were keen to avoid Len who, though he tried to hide it, was evidently displeased with their friendship, and once Esther suggested they try another church, but they agreed that, though far from perfect, Len's church was by far the best around. Occasionally, when Len got too much for them, they took off to the Romanian church in Indianapolis.

At times, Esther found herself wishing that Ron would look more at the preacher and less at her during the sermon. And she had a strong feeling that he tolerated rather than enjoyed the services. Even she found the altar calls hard to take. The pumped up emotion jarred on her. But Pastor Cripps' preaching was generally inspiring and the singing heavenly, and her prayer was that Ron would come to know the Lord more intimately as time wore on. It did worry her that his world was revolving more and more around her. What would happen, she wondered, if, being human, she one day failed him? But the intoxicating pleasure of the present drowned out any worries about the future. And as the weeks slipped by, these fears became less and less. The Velvet Curtain hardly ever seemed to bother her any more, though she kept telling herself she must be on the alert and never forget that it did exist.

When Mary returned from her vacation, every Friday found Esther enjoying her aunt's home cooking, playing a game of Scrabble, and sometimes practicing her music. Mary, she discovered, was an accomplished pianist and Esther had persuaded her to bring the grand piano over to her apartment even though it meant other furniture had to be put into storage. Music had always been therapeutic for Esther, and while she sorely missed the piano, she would play it every Friday. Best of all, she saw it was doing its healing work in her aunt's life. Mary gradually thawed towards her niece and soon found herself looking forward to those Friday evenings together.

One such Friday in early June, Esther found her young cousin studying her intently as she sat at the piano, playing some new pieces she had just learned. It rather disconcerted her, especially when Rachel exclaimed suddenly, "Esther, I haven't heard you play 'Numai Harul' for ages now. You used to play it nearly every week. Have you forgotten it?"

"Why of course I've not forgotten it. How could I?" Esther's tone was indignant. "But I like the challenge of new things sometimes, Rachel."

"So I've noticed," the girl said significantly, and smiled slyly at her cousin as she left the room.

Esther tried to forget Rachel's words and thought she had succeeded, when the next evening she met her cousin just as she was going out with Ron. The girl eyed her from top to toe. Then turning to Ron she said in her sweetest tone, "Why don't you get Esther to enter the State beauty contest. I think she has a good chance to be Miss Indiana, don't you?"

Esther stared at the girl, mouth open. Ron took her hand and squeezed it. "Yep, she sure has, Rachel, but I'm not sure she would like all that went with being a beauty queen and I'm not sure that I would like it either."

Esther smiled her thanks. But Rachel had not finished. "Well, maybe not," she conceded, "at least not yet. But think about it Esther. You'd get an awful lot of publicity that would help Romania, and all those poor orphans over there. Beauty queens contribute an awful lot to charity."

"What on earth is the girl talking about?" Esther muttered as she held up her long skirts and got into Ron's car. It was his birthday and they were going to join his mother at a restaurant in the city.

"Just look in the mirror and you'll know," he said smiling. "You truly look a beauty queen tonight. But all the same, I didn't like her tone. What's she up to?"

"Don't really know," sighed Esther as they set off.

She soon forgot Rachel's words in the whirl of the evening's events. Ron's mother was more than gracious, the food was superb, and Ron in the best of spirits. He had refused to invite anyone else. He wanted the two women in his life to come to know each other better and had even managed to coax Esther to tell at least part of her story. She had omitted some of the saddest parts he noticed. Maybe she had reckoned that a birthday party was not an appropriate place for such family histories.

It was only when she took off the long, pale pink gown Ron had bought especially for the occasion that Esther had time to think. She glanced at the dress as she hung it in the closet. It was down to her ankles with short puffy sleeves and a decent enough neckline. But it had been very costly. Well, she hadn't paid one penny for it, had she? She still had the $1000 for Romania saved up for when she could find a safe way to send it. True, her $200 had evaporated, but she had plenty more to send. And she had needed some cash for herself. But a beauty queen? What had that strange girl meant? And her words the night before, "You don't play 'Numai Harul' any more Esther," rang in her ears. Did Rachel think she would spend her life singing one plaintive song over and over again? Poor Rachel, she needed to pray for her. She had gone into her shell again somewhat but then, she hadn't seen much of her of late. Well, she would take the very next Saturday and give it just to Rachel.

Chapter Twenty-Six

More Surprises

It was a sizzling afternoon in mid June. The pool looked so inviting that Esther and Rachel decided to take their first swim of the season. Esther had scarcely seen her cousin since her graduation from high school a few weeks before. Rachel had been pronounced valedictorian of her class but had shunned all publicity and refused to celebrate. It was all a fuss about nothing, she had told her family and had added with a scowl, "Anyway, we're being hypocrites to act so happy all of a sudden when our family's going to ruination." Esther had wished she could spend more time with her young cousin and was glad when Rachel had suggested a swim that afternoon.

"Glad you don't wear a bikini," the younger girl remarked, as her cousin dipped one toe into the water, "though I'm not so sure your handsome boyfriend will share my opinion."

Esther blushed crimson. "Why, you don't think...?"

"Oh you little innocent! Where have you been all your life? Ron's probably as used to half naked girls as he is to eating ice cream in summer. Ask him. See what he says."

Esther said nothing. The weather had been so cool that the question of swimming hadn't yet arisen.

"I'm probably about the only girl in Velours who doesn't parade around in a bikini, apart from you, that is," continued Rachel, who seemed in an unusually talkative mood. "Oh don't praise me, Esther. It's probably more that I don't want to show off my scraggy figure."

Esther put her other foot into the water. "Well, I've been brought up to think a girl shouldn't tempt a fellow by revealing too much of her body, especially a Christian girl. I suppose, though, I'll be tested now to see whether these ideas are really my own or just my parents'."

"Yep, you sure will," and her cousin gave a short laugh. "With a figure like yours and a boyfriend who has not been brought up to think like you, you'll be tested all right."

Esther didn't like Rachel's tone. "I trust Ron completely," she said sharply.

"Of course you do. Who wouldn't! He's a great guy. But bikinis are a way of life round here, in the summer of course," she added with a short laugh. "But to tell you the truth," Rachel was in earnest now, "even though I don't profess to be one of your sort of Christians, when Ramona and her friends get together, even I get embarrassed!" Rachel adjusted the strap of her green bathing suit. "They might as well go in the nude for all they wear. It's great to enjoy a swim without having to weave in and out of half-naked bodies," she went on, ignoring Esther's shocked expression. "By the way, my sister's coming back tomorrow, you know, and bringing Marci and Kelly with her. And you can be sure there'll be boys galore wherever Ramona is. She's lost pounds of weight, she says, and is as brown as a berry. She'll be eager to show herself off. So this is our last chance for a quiet swim."

Esther stared at her cousin. She had no idea Ramona was returning that weekend though she wasn't really surprised. She had been away from home six whole weeks. "I'd better get the spare room ready in the basement," she told Rachel.

"No need to do that. They can sleep in mine. It has two beds, you know. I'll make myself scarce while they're around."

Esther patted her cousin on the shoulder. "I'll miss you, Rachel. I feel a lot more at home with you than with Ramona's friends."

"Thanks, not that I see much of you these days. That boyfriend of yours totally monopolizes you. By the way, you're not coming to Mom's tonight, are you? It's Friday you know." Rachel's tone was a little plaintive.

"Sorry, Rachel, but I've got to sing in a large church in Indianapolis on Sunday and Len wants me to practice tonight."

"Can't you do it tomorrow, then?"

"Not really." Esther sounded apologetic now. "Ron's taking me to an Amish restaurant that's opened in the country about twenty miles from here. Oh my goodness, it's five thirty already. Ron's coming at seven. If we want a swim we'll have to get going," and she plunged into the water.

Half an hour later the two girls ran laughing and panting back to the house, draped in their beach towels.

"Where's your Dad?" Esther asked, as she slid open the patio doors. "He should have been home from work by now."

Rachel had no time to reply. They could hear John's voice calling from the hallway, "Rachel, Esther, where are you?"

"Here," they told him, as they pulled their towels tighter about them.

"Well, my pretty mermaids," he began as the two girls stood dripping in the kitchen, "you'd better get to the shower before you flood the place out. Anyway you don't need to get me supper. I'm going out again and I'll be away till Sunday."

Two pairs of large, dark eyes were fixed upon him. He shifted uneasily from one foot to the other.

"Business trip again, Dad?" Rachel was the first to find her voice.

"Sort of," John told her, but his shorts and T-shirt didn't look much like business. "Business and pleasure, you could say. I need a bit of relaxation sometimes. Can't work all the time."

"Of course not," his daughter assured him, her eyes narrowing a little. "I know you're a workaholic and need one weekend in three all to yourself and to your business friends."

"Counting now, are you?" John's voice was getting edgy now.

"Of course. I count everything; you know that, Dad."

John was silent as he made for the door. "Well, I'm a bit late so I'll be off. Take care of yourselves. You won't be lonely with Ramona and her crew descending on you tomorrow."

The girls had no chance to reply. As the door shut behind him, Rachel turned in anger to her cousin. "He's got a woman friend, for sure. I just know it. He's never had so many business weekends away before, never, not even when Mom was impossible to live with."

Esther shook her head mournfully as she left the kitchen. She didn't want to believe Rachel, but in her heart, she knew her cousin was probably right. She had been really very worried about her uncle for some weeks now. Rachel's words only confirmed her fears. He would start when the phone rang, look guilty when he had to tell her he wouldn't be home till late that evening, and to top it all, had already spent two or three weekends away from home. She had mentioned her concern to Ron once or twice. He had given her a rather peculiar look but told her not to worry. Her uncle was old enough to take care of himself.

She wished at times she could pray with Ron about her worries—her uncle, her sister and how she was to get her over to the States, her aunt who seemed to be growing sadder each day, and Rachel who was definitely bunkering down once more in her "tunnel home," though she had come out of her shell a bit more that afternoon, Esther had noticed. But gradually as the weeks slipped by, she had become so engrossed with her wonderful boyfriend that her family's troubles seemed to have taken a back seat. Ron told her she had suffered enough in her brief twenty years to last a life time. Now she should relax, enjoy herself in a decent, respectable manner, bask in his attentions, and thank God that He had given her a protector at last. And to the lonely orphan girl, his strong arm, open purse, ready humor, and above all, his growing love, made her feel that at long last she "belonged" to someone. It was, she told herself nearly every day, a wonderful feeling.

But now, as she slipped on a white top and blue slacks, (she still hadn't ventured in public in shorts,) and reached for the hair dryer, her heart felt like lead. Their family was breaking up and she could do nothing to stop it.

She had just brushed out her hair when the doorbell rang. She gave a quick glance in the mirror above her dresser. Esther smiled to herself as she tripped downstairs. There was little fear now that she might disgrace her boyfriend. And that was a comfort.

"Well, beautiful," Ron greeted her as she opened the front door. "You're glowing with health. Been swimming?"

She blushed. "Yes, with Rachel. Only I can't swim very well, you know. I stay out of the deep end."

"I'll teach you, don't worry. I'll have you diving from the high board before the summer is out."

Esther said nothing as she led him into the kitchen and began preparing some supper. "Don't you want that?" he queried. "You don't look too happy about it."

"Ron?" She hesitated, blushing scarlet.

"Yes?"

"Would you expect me to wear a bikini?"

Ron couldn't believe his ears. No girl had ever asked him that before. But then, Esther Popescu wasn't like any girl he had ever known. That was one reason why he had fallen for her. But what could he honestly tell her? He supposed he had expected it, even anticipated once or twice the pleasure of seeing her in one. He thought a moment before replying, "I suppose I've just taken for granted that most young girls take this chance to show off their figure a bit. We guys don't object of course. I mean, why should we?"

Esther stood stock still. At times like this, she realized the gap that still existed between herself and the young man who was fast falling head over heels in love with her. Back home, whenever the youth group had gone for a swim together, and that was very rarely, the girls had seen to it that they were pretty well-clothed. It was an unwritten rule—modesty at all times, even in the water! Here, she thought, she'd have to relent a little, but bikinis?

"So that's what you'd like, I mean for me to wear one?" Esther felt she had to get to the bottom of the question.

Ron took the last bite of pizza before answering, "Look, Esther, to be honest, part of me would love it. I mean, I'm made of flesh and blood. Maybe you haven't realized that yet." He was frustrated and couldn't hide it, but the look in her eyes melted him instantly. He came up and took her hand. "Esther, I'm only too aware how differently you've been brought up. And come to think about it, I wouldn't expect you to wear one, and in a way, wouldn't even want you to. After all, I admit that while bikini clad young mermaids are great to look at, they don't exactly help a guy to keep his thoughts pure. So, set your mind at rest, please."

His tone was pleading. The girl relaxed. This was why she felt so good being with Ron. He was so willing to adapt to her, put up with her old-fashioned ideas. So why shouldn't she adapt a little too? It was only reasonable.

"Listen Esther," he was speaking again. "You can trust me, can't you?"

"Trust you? Oh yes," She looked into his eyes. "It's not a question of trust, Ron. It's...."

"A question of modesty, right? Ron sighed a little, as he took a seat on the bar stool by the window. "Now look, as far as I'm concerned, it's all settled in my mind. You're the only woman in the entire world with whom I want to share my life. Now, if that's settled, can't I enjoy you a bit at times—nothing indecent you know?" He saw her expression and added hastily, "There's no time to talk about it now. We'll have to gulp down a few bites and be off. We'll have more time tomorrow. Remember? We have a special date you know. So be prepared for an extra wonderful evening." Something in his tone made the girl curious. He had mentioned that Saturday evening several times during the last few days. He had something afoot, that was obvious.

"Thanks for the supper," Ron told her fifteen minutes later.

"It wasn't great. We were swimming late. Besides, when Uncle's not home we don't bother so much preparing supper. He's away for another weekend, you know."

Ron gave her a strange look. "He's away, you said?"

"Yes. Come to think of it, this is his third weekend away in the last few months. He never used to gallivant like this. I didn't like to pry, though Rachel did ask him this time if it was a business trip and he said that it was both business and pleasure."

Ron swung round to face her. "My mother said exactly the same thing a few moments ago."

Esther stared in disbelief. "You don't think...?"

Ron said nothing. It was all surmising but the whole thing looked very suspicious. In fact, he had suspected it for some time. "I think Mom's having an affair with your uncle." His words were slow and deliberate. "But wait, is your uncle's divorce through?" he asked as they got into the car.

"Yes. It came about a month ago. Didn't take long as they'd been separate for more than a year."

"Then it's not really an affair, is it? He's free, I suppose, and so is she."

"Free?" Esther repeated, her voice much shriller than usual. "Free? Oh I forgot. This is the land of the free, isn't it?"

"Come, Esther, sarcasm doesn't suit you. I know you're upset. But as I've told you before, we can't let these two spoil our lives. You've had enough troubles to last an eternity. Here we are at Len's. We can talk about it later if you like and you can cry on my shoulder. It would give me a marvelous excuse to kiss away your tears, now wouldn't it?"

Esther smiled in spite of herself. Ron was right, really. She couldn't let all this spoil her life. And maybe it was all "evil surmising" as the Bible called it. Until she knew definitely, she'd better not think any more about it.

The next day was a busy one preparing for Ramona and her guests. Jean bustled about even more than normal. "When are you going to learn to leave all this cleaning business to me?" she told Esther crossly when she caught her changing the sheets in Rachel's room.

"But this is extra, Jean," the girl protested as she shook out a pillow and straightened the dainty floral comforter.

"Nothing I can do in one morning is extra. Don't forget that. Now be off with you. I can't do with you around. You make me nervous."

"Me?" Esther couldn't believe her ears.

"Yes you, Miss Perfect. One day, maybe, you'll realize the effect you have on folks. You're just too good to be true, that's your problem."

That evening, as she watched the countryside spin past, for Ron was driving extra fast it seemed, Esther remembered Jean's words. "Ron, am I really 'Miss Perfect' as Jean called me this morning? She says my problem is that I'm too good to be true and that I intimidate folks."

Ron let out a long, low whistle. "That woman certainly has a unique way of putting things. You certainly seem too good to be true to me, sitting here beside me. But you are rather intimidating at times, you know."

"Me? But I can't be. I mean, I feel so timid and insecure."

"I know you do. But now look at you tonight. Oval face, large dark eyes fringed with long lashes, clear skin, ruby lips, thick glossy hair—all perfect. And then you've the figure of a model. You can wear anything and get away with it, you have a voice like an angel and a character to match, well, most of the time that is." He grinned, remembering the birthday party. "And you seem so good at everything. I think that's what makes Jean scared of you."

"But I'm not good at everything. You know that." Esther's tone was reproachful. "I'm not athletic in the slightest. I can't draw. I'm no mathematician and haven't much clue about science in general. And I'm really very shy which can be quite a handicap sometimes. Anyway, look who is speaking." Esther's tone was teasing now. "You frightened me good and proper that first day I saw you in the kitchen with Ramona, with your immaculate shorts, bronzed skin, and stylish haircut. And I certainly was far from perfect that morning in my gold blouse and worn black skirt."

Ron looked wistful. "Oh I don't know, Esther. You looked awfully good to me. I sometimes wonder where my little Romanian gypsy girl has gone."

"She hasn't changed inside, I promise, Ron," her voice was defensive.

"I hope not. Not for a good while at least." Ron couldn't honestly tell her that she hadn't changed inside. How could he know for sure anyway?

They had a job to find a parking place in the restaurant parking lot and had to wait for half an hour before a table became vacant. But at last they were seated, and a pretty girl in a long blue cotton dress and white pinafore, her thick blonde hair tucked away under her headdress, handed them the menu.

"Maybe I should dress like that," Esther whispered. "The head covering reminds me a bit of Romania. It would make you and everyone else think that I hadn't changed after all. But please, Ron, do explain about the Amish and the Mennonites and the differences between them."

Ron complied as best he could but soon their food arrived and Esther thought she had never tasted such excellent cooking since she had arrived in the States.

"I like the atmosphere here," Ron said as he pushed his plate to one side and sat back in his chair. His eyes roamed round the long room with its low ceilings, its dark oaken beams, polished wooden floor, and imitation candles on each table. "It's otherworldly."

"Like me?" Esther asked with a sly smile.

"Like you were, certainly. Oh blow it! It's so confusing! I wanted to help you adapt, to change, I suppose you could say, into an American version of yourself, and now that you're doing it so admirably, I half wish you were still in your long skirts and gold blouses."

Esther flushed. "So you would have still dated me dressed like that, still taken me everywhere on campus, still introduced me to your very fashionable mother, still taken me to concerts, still showed me off to your friends?"

"I get the point," Ron said with a short laugh. "You don't need to go on. And you're perfectly right. No, I wouldn't have, that is, I simply couldn't have. These Amish girls," and he nodded in the direction of one of the waitresses, "have a fascination about them because they're different, but they certainly wouldn't fit into my world, and you wouldn't have either as you were when you first came. But now you fit in very well indeed, so well that...." He stopped abruptly and reached into his pocket.

The room had emptied and there was no one left except a few couples at the other end of the large dining room. "I've something for you," and he leaned across the table. "Put out your hand and close your eyes." She obeyed, and trembling all over, opened them a few moments later to view the most beautiful diamond ring she had ever seen on her third finger. She gasped, blushed, and raised her large speaking eyes to her companion's face.

"You can't really be surprised, Esther. You would have been blind if you had not realized that I almost worship you. I have taken the liberty to put this ring on your finger. You have the ability to take it off and hand it back to me if," he faltered, "if you feel that I am not the one with whom you could spend your life. I know I am not good enough, not religious enough, not clever enough, not...."

Esther held up her hand. "No more, Ron, please. No more. Yes, I've not been blind. I've known that you were falling in love with me and...."

"And...?" repeated Ron, his heart pounding so loudly he was sure she must hear it.

"And I am almost sure, Ron, that I love you too."

"Almost?" The girl blushed but looked directly into his grey-blue eyes which were searching hers for the unequivocal answer he longed to hear.

"I've never been proposed to before, Ron," Esther dropped her eyes, "so this is all so new to me. You've been so wonderful to me and utterly spoiled me that I want to be sure I'm not just carried away with it all. And," she added, almost as an afterthought, "Of course I need to ask God about it before I say my final 'yes.'"

Ron frowned. He didn't want to have to wait any longer. Then his face relaxed a little. "Of course, Esther. I think I understand. I really hadn't intended to show you the ring here in public, but I couldn't wait any longer and in a way, it seemed an appropriate setting. But we'll continue this in the car. Come, let's go."

Esther was too stunned by the events of the evening to say a word as they cruised homewards. She glanced down at her hand and realized that the ring was still on her finger. She gazed at it in silence. It was a beautiful token of Ron's love for her. She felt at that moment that she didn't deserve either it or him.

The sun was beginning to set as they left the main road and followed signs to a State Park. Minutes later they pulled up by a small lake. They were alone. Everyone seemed to have gone home for the evening. They parked the car and walked towards the water, then stood in silence, hand in hand, gazing across the lake towards the low hills beyond. After a few moments, Esther withdrew her hand and gazed at the ring. The diamond caught the rays of the setting sun as she slowly and reluctantly took it off her finger. "It's so beautiful," she breathed; "every girl's dream. But I can't keep it, not just yet, Ron."

Ron sighed a little. Sometimes he wished she wasn't so very

much the "Miss Perfect" that made the cleaning lady feel so ill at ease. "I'm glad you like it. I had hoped you would take it home with you tonight, but if you can't give me a final answer tonight, I'll just have to wait a bit longer. Only remember, the ring is here, waiting for no one but you. And," he added wistfully, "please, don't keep me waiting too long. I don't think I could stand it. I know you think that we shouldn't have much physical contact before we get engaged. That's what you've told me you know," he added quickly for he saw the surprised look on the girl's face.

"Did I? Well, I suppose that's what I was used to back home. But...."

"Well, but what? Go on," he encouraged.

"Well, it's been hard on me too, you know. I'm not made of stone any more than you are," and she laid her head on his shoulder. "I do love you, Ron Atwood. I know I do, and I'll have to show it sometimes. I'll give you my final answer very, very soon. Till then...?"

But she got no further. She was in his arms. "Till then," he murmured between kisses, "till then you'll have to trust me as you always have. But I've got to show you I love you, at least this once," he told her passionately as he held her close.

"Another car has pulled up," Esther whispered some minutes later, half glad, half sorry for the interruption.

"Maybe it's just as well," Ron muttered as he released her reluctantly. "I promise you I won't do that again till you give me your answer, but after that, I'll do it to my heart's content. So be prepared."

"Give me another few weeks, Ron, that's all I need," she assured him as he helped her tenderly into the car.

Esther could never remember the rest of that ride. She was as one in a dream, almost drunk with happiness. Her lonely, orphaned heart longed to belong to someone and now she felt she truly did. She almost felt that that beautiful ring was still on her finger, that she was still in his arms, that she had given the "yes" he was waiting for.

Although the ring was still in his pocket when he returned home that night, Ron felt as though their engagement was an established fact. He was almost sure that Esther was falling in love with him. That "almost!" How he wished it were not there! But if she did love anyone, it was him, not anyone else, that was certain, and that was a great comfort.

Chapter Twenty-Seven

Ramona Disappears

How would he break the news to his family? This was the predominant thought in John Popescu's mind when he dropped Diane off at her house late that Sunday evening. They had just become engaged. With a ring on her finger, Diane would be sure to tell everyone now. Well, he would break the news gradually, gently, diplomatically. Not tonight, though. He couldn't do it tonight. Tomorrow he'd find a way somehow. He didn't think Ramona would take it too hard, but Rachel and Esther? He shuddered to think how the news might hit them. And Mary? Oh bother Mary, he told himself as he stroked the goatee beard he had grown of late, just to please Diane of course. He supposed his whole life would now consist of pleasing Diane. A demanding woman she certainly was. Then why on earth had he proposed to her last night? Did he love her? He wasn't sure. He was fond of her, in fact, rather infatuated with her. After all, she was extremely good-looking for forty-eight, was wonderful company, and seemed to have plenty of money. And that last factor had influenced him more than he cared to admit even to himself. And she needed him with her many physical ailments. Anyway, he never expected to truly love again, not like he once had.

A long drawn-out sigh escaped him as turned into his driveway. Then why was he getting married again? Why was he lonely, with three girls waiting on him? But down deep, he missed married life. And Diane was lonely too. And she had chronic heart problems which flared up from time to time. She needed someone to take care of her. True, she had a devoted son but one day soon he would fly the nest. It looked like his beautiful niece would be his choice. He had thought it would have been Ramona, but why not Esther? She deserved it still more after all the suffering she had been through. But did she love the young man? How could he tell? Anyway, what was love, true love? He had known it once, or thought he had. Maybe it had all been an illusion. Maybe life was one grand deception. If so, he might as well get the best out of it before it evaporated in his face like a bubble.

Esther heard the car door slam shut and knew her uncle was back, but she couldn't face him just yet. She dreaded what he had to tell her. Ramona had gone out with her friends for the evening and had not yet returned. In fact, Esther hadn't seen her cousin since she had come back from Florida. They had arrived early Sunday morning and had slept long after she had left for church.

Meanwhile Rachel and her mother were having a long chat. They had kept their suspicions secret for weeks but now it had all come out. They were both convinced that John Popescu had a lady friend with whom he was spending weekends now and then, something he never would have considered in his earlier years. But who that lady was neither had any idea. He had kept it a well-guarded secret.

Mary slept poorly that night and woke with a terrible headache. By mid-morning, she felt nauseated and wished she had not signed up for summer school. She had offered to teach English to immigrants, partly for the extra money she could earn, and partly to give herself less time to brood over her personal tragedy. When her class had finished, she made straight for the rest room and found an empty stall. Two of her colleagues entered just after her.

"You'll never guess who took the chalet next to us this weekend!" one was saying. Something in her tone made Mary prick her ears.

"You were at Gatlinburg, right?"

"Yes. And we never expected to bump into our next door neighbors, so to speak."

"Well, Gatlinburg is very popular, you know, Elsa. But come on, who was it? Sounds as if you have a juicy piece of gossip to share with me."

Mary felt sick. She knew that the Spanish teacher, Elsa, loved to find out her colleagues' secrets and spread them all over the school.

"Well, it was the virtuous John Popescu and his lady love," Elsa seemed to be chewing every word with great relish.

Mary froze, dreading what was coming next.

"You don't mean it?" the other woman was saying. "Well, I heard his divorce was through now so I suppose he's free."

"Free," muttered Mary to herself, grinding her teeth. "That's what they call it, is it?" Anger surged within her. But worse was to follow.

"Yes," Elsa went on. "He's a single man now but won't be for long. The woman was flashing an engagement ring around."

Mary's heart nearly stopped beating. She collapsed back onto the toilet seat. She couldn't let the others know she was in there. It would be too humiliating both to them and to her.

"But who was the woman? Did you know her?" was the next question.

"No. But I think she works for him. She's very good-looking—small and petite, short auburn hair, in her late forties probably, real stylish and a bit snobbish, I'd say."

"Well, if what you say is really true, then I sure pity Mary. She's never gotten that man out of her heart. But she'll have to come down to reality. He's out of her life forever. And, let's face, it, she asked for it didn't she?"

"Sure did. Lost pride in herself and went into her cocoon. Never talked unless she had to. Must say though, she's improved a bit lately. She's a great teacher, say that for her, but she obviously wasn't that great a wife. John Popescu doesn't seem a very hard a man to please."

Mary leaned her head on the wall, forgetting for once that it wasn't that clean. She was usually so particular about toilets. "Obviously wasn't that great a wife!" The words stuck into her like a knife. But who was working for John—in her forties? She had heard that Diane Atwood had started to help as receptionist. It had to be her. She thought she was going to faint. The slight ray of hope that had kept her going for months now, was gone. All was darkness. Her efforts had failed. And worst of all, she couldn't stop loving him, even through her anger and despair—it was still there, seemingly unquenchable.

She waited till the women had gone and then stumbled to the wash hand basin. Her hand trembled uncontrollably as she reached for the faucet. Splashing cold water on her face helped a bit. She staggered to the faculty lounge and flopped into a chair. She was glad she had no more classes that day.

Once back in her apartment, Mary collapsed onto the sofa and began to weep uncontrollably. Rachel found her like that some hours later.

"Mom, what on earth's happened?" There was no response.

"Mom, speak to me. It's Dad, isn't it? You've found out something about Dad?" The girl's voice was sharp, urgent. She was trying hard to beat back the waves of despair that threatened to engulf her. Her mother needed her to be strong right now.

Mary nodded but kept her head in her hands. Rachel sat down beside her and waited. After a while, it all came out. Rachel patted her mother's hand and her voice was much softer than normal as she whispered, "Well, at least we know the worst now, Mom. And together we'll make a new life for ourselves."

"New life?" Mary looked up at last.

"Yes, a new life. You must put this behind you. We'll move away somewhere. Life isn't over yet, you know. You've still got me. I'll never leave you Mom, never."

Mary gazed at her daughter tenderly. Here was the rebellious, taciturn Rachel turning comforter. She smiled in spite of herself.

"You know, Rachel, I think I'd like to have Esther pray with me."

Rachel stared at her mother in disbelief. "You can't believe that your mother would want to pray, can you?" Mary's voice was sad. "I never told you that I used to teach Sunday school and Vacation Bible School, did I? Or that your grandmother was a very religious woman? I broke her heart, you know, when I went to college and rebelled against church and against her?"

Rachel's mouth fell open. "No, I never knew that Mom. I can't remember Grandma, you know. She died when I was very young." She did know that her grandmother had been a single mom in the days when single moms were taboo in decent society. But that was all.

"Yes, Rachel. I'm sorry you never got to know her. I really broke her heart and it was such a good heart." Mary let out a sob. "I was a very selfish girl. All I thought of when I went to college was how to look good. No, that's not right—how to look better than all the other girls. I had to be tops in everything. And if I had several boys on a string and a party nearly every weekend, then I was happy, or fancied I was." Mary stared at the beige carpet at her feet.

"Sounds like Ramona;" Rachel's tone made Mary sit up.

"I was worse than Ramona," Mary said firmly, defensive of her elder daughter, "or at least worse than she's been, up to now. I'm afraid she's getting wilder as the months go by. And I'm a lot to blame. It looks as if she doesn't mind about the divorce, but she's hiding her feelings—drowning them in all her partying, her boyfriends, and now by giving herself a new look."

Her daughter nodded as Mary went on: "I loved parties too. I met your Dad at one and fell head over heels in love with him. I was determined to get him and I did. I think I always knew he never loved me like I loved him. But I told myself that would change when we got married."

"Then why did he marry you, Mom?" The question was out before she could stop it. Mary turned beet red and bit her lip.

"I made sure we had to get married," she muttered as she hung her head. "But I sure have paid for it," and she buried her face in her hands once more.

Rachel was silent. She wasn't exactly surprised at what her mother was telling her. It explained a lot of things.

"I'll have to phone Esther," Mary exclaimed a few moments later.

"But wait, Mom. Esther doesn't know that it's Diane Atwood. It'll come as a shock and remember, she's involved with it being Ron's Mom."

"I know," Mary said slowly. "But Esther's a strong Christian. She'll cope somehow. I need someone to pray with me, Rachel, to show me the way back to God."

She rose and took the phone from its cradle. She knew John would be away at work so wasn't surprised when Ramona answered.

"Ramona? Why, welcome home." Mary tried to sound normal. "Had a good trip?"

"Fabulous. I've lost twenty pounds and am as brown as a berry."

"Congratulations." The words seemed forced. She couldn't imagine a slim Ramona. "I need to speak to Esther a moment," she added.

"I'm afraid she's out, Mom."

Mary flopped back in her seat, disappointed. "Is it real important? Can I take a message?" her daughter was asking.

"No. It's all right."

"Probably see you at the weekend if not before. Bye for now Mom," Ramona's voice sounded faraway.

"Bye," Mary echoed mechanically. It was no good. God didn't seem to be working things out for her. For weeks she had fought daily battles against the old bitterness that constantly threatened to control her every thought. But now it was just too much. Esther wasn't there when she needed her. As for God, He seemed an eternity away. No, she'd have to go it alone, just as she had always done.

But John remarrying! It was all a horrid nightmare. She closed her eyes to shut out his face—those eyes that spoke volumes; that smile that had turned many a woman's head. And his voice—low and musical. And the woman? She saw her too, but it was not the auburn-haired Diane who rose before her as she buried her head in her hands. It was the dark-eyed beauty of long ago—the face that had haunted her dreams so many times. And then she knew the truth, felt it deep within her, that her ex-husband did not really love his bride-to-be any more than he had loved her. This Atwood woman would be no happier than she had been, at least she hoped not. She didn't deserve to be.

It was good that Ron and Esther could not see Mary Popescu at that moment—eyes glittering with revenge, an unnatural smile on her thin lips. It would have made it even harder for Esther to accept the news of her uncle's forthcoming marriage. Ron had learned of his mother's engagement the evening before and dreaded telling Esther, for he sensed the moment she had opened the door to him that morning that John had not yet broken the news. Happily, she made a hard task just that bit easier by commenting as they drove down the driveway, "You know Ron, Uncle John is as bad as a teenager. He keeps very late hours. Why, he came in after I did last night."

"I know," said Ron in a way that made the girl start.

"You know? But how?"

"He was at our place when I came home last night."

That was all he said, but it was enough. She grasped immediately all that that one sentence implied. "Oh no, Ron! Oh no!" she wailed in a tone that went straight to Ron's heart.

"Where are you taking me?" queried Esther, as Ron swung the car onto the interstate.

"To the Gardens. Somewhere quiet and solitary. We need freedom to talk or to cry," he added as he saw the anguish in her beautiful features. Soon they were walking, hand in hand, down the avenue of trees, past the flower beds, conscious only of each other and the weight pressing down upon their spirits.

Esther was the first to speak. "Has Uncle John...?" she hesitated, unable to get the words out.

Ron understood what she was trying to say. "Yes. It seems all settled. They are to be married the 17th of August."

The girl turned white as a sheet and might have fallen had not

Ron's strong arm held her. He drew her to a seat and laid her head on his shoulder. "Cry it out," he murmured in her ear. "I'm sorry you're taking it so hard."

Esther sat in stunned silence for some minutes before she stammered, "Oh Ron, Uncle John and your mother of all people!"

"Yes," was the comment, "your Uncle John and my mother!"

Esther had no way of knowing from his tone what his personal feelings were. In a way, she was not as involved personally in this whole affair as Ron was, or poor Aunt Mary, or Rachel and Ramona. At the thought of her aunt's reaction to the news, of the deathblow to all her hopes of reuniting, slim as they had been of late, Esther broke into uncontrolled sobs. Ron let her cry for some time, saying nothing but gently pushing back her glossy black hair which had fallen into her eyes, and stroking her small, delicate hand which lay trembling in his.

Then he spoke. "Esther," his tone was gentle as if talking to a small child, "Esther, let's look on the bright side of things. These two are of age. They've lived their lives. If they can get a bit of happiness out of their union, who are we to grudge them this? And anyway, you and I won't be too involved if, that is, if we set up house on our own soon."

Esther stopped sobbing, but the look she turned on Ron alarmed him. It was questioning, and, yes, almost condemning. "Why Ron," she exploded, "how can you say such things. I wasn't unhappy because of how it would affect me though I did feel badly for my cousins. But I felt most of all how wrong it all is. I mean, Aunt Mary still loves her husband, ex-husband, I should say. And before Christmas, she tried to make it up with him. She called off the divorce but he sued on his own account. I can see why now. He already was thinking of another woman."

Ron stared at her for a moment. So that was why she was so upset. She was thinking of the wrongs and rights of it all. "Well," he answered slowly, "I suppose that in your eyes my mother is wrong too. I mean, she's divorced as well."

Esther bit her lip and then replied, measuring carefully every word she said. "Well, I don't agree with divorce at all. But you told me once that your father had a drinking problem and was impossible to live with and that there were other women involved too, so in a sense that puts her in a different light from Uncle John. Scripturally, he really has no basis for divorce. His wife was never unfaithful. I know she was pretty difficult to live with for a while, but she said she was sorry and would have tried to make a go of it again. But it was just no use; he already had your mother in mind; that's obvious looking at it in retrospect."

Ron ran his hand through his thick blond locks and whistled softly. "I can't follow all your ramifications of Scripture, my dear," he said. "And anyway, I don't think your uncle would consider himself your kind of Christian, so these rules wouldn't apply to him, would they?"

Esther looked at him thoughtfully. No, she concluded, they wouldn't really apply to him.

"I'm feeling very sorry for your Aunt," Ron went on, "but from what Ramona told me she made things pretty hard for John. And now that the first shock is over, I can look at the situation in a saner light. As I said before, what they do doesn't need to affect us very much."

"Maybe not, Ron," Esther replied thoughtfully, "but I've got to speak to Uncle John. I think he has acted disgracefully. Can't you see," she pleaded, taking him by both hands and gazing up at him as if her life depended on his agreeing with her, "that it is so wrong to reject one woman on the grounds of incompatibility and go off with another before the ink is even dry on his divorce papers? And," she added, her eyes blazing, "it's worse than that. I can see now that he's been having an affair with your mother. He's been off on long weekends for months now."

Ron nodded. "Yes, that's pretty obvious now. But don't get too involved, Esther. It'll only bring you more problems. Sure that wasn't wise of either of them, but if they intended to get married then maybe it wasn't so terrible after all."

"Ron Atwood!" Esther had exploded now. "What are you saying? You mean if we get engaged, then it's OK for us to go off like that?"

Not being a hypocrite, Ron could not pretend that he shared her indignation, even to please his beloved Esther. He could not tell her that he had struggled with the dream of such weekends with his beautiful girlfriend. After all, he had made up his mind to be careful until he met the woman he loved. But after that? In his eyes, he would be as good as married, especially once Esther gave her consent to be his wife. Oh sure, he had not suggested such a thing out of respect for the girl he loved. He would never ask her to violate her conscience. Never! He loved her too much for that. But he just couldn't pretend he felt as strongly as she did about it all. So he answered very deliberately, weighing each word, "No, *we* couldn't do it Esther. I wouldn't expect *you* to ever do such a thing. But everyone isn't like *you*, unfortunately. I know your uncle and my mother have acted unwisely and selfishly. But come, if you are going to adapt to American life, you will have to get used to divorce. It's all around us."

Ron knew he had blundered as soon as the words were out of his lips but, like all words spoken, they can never, never be recalled. Esther drew back from him and blurted out indignantly, "Get used to divorce?" She almost shouted the words in his face. "Never, Ron, never. And," her voice steadied but he could never forget the look she gave him, "if you go into a marriage with me feeling that divorce is to be tolerated and is a viable option, who's to say that...."

It was Ron's turn to become annoyed. "So you doubt me, do you? As if I'd ask you to marry me and then turn round and divorce you." He got up from the bench on which they were sitting and started pacing back and forward, kicking the gravel as he did so, and muttering to himself. Esther had never seen him so upset.

She waited until his pacing became less agitated and, rising from her seat, laid her arm gently on his and said softly, "Ron, it wasn't that I doubted you, but it's just that, if we don't go into marriage feeling that it is for life and that divorce is taboo come what may, then it leaves a loophole. Can't you see that?"

Her pleading voice, her dark imploring eyes, her gentle touch, all calmed him instantly. "Sorry, Esther," he said in a low voice. "I lost my cool. Forgive me."

"I got a bit upset myself, Ron," she admitted. "Come, sit down again and let me commit it to God. He has allowed all this to come up and knows how to help us cope with it."

Ron sat down obediently beside her as she poured out her heart to her heavenly Father. It was the first time he had heard her pray openly and it awed him, filled him with admiration for this wonderful girl by his side, and yet, at the same time, strangely enough, it frightened him. She was entering a world to which he had not yet found the key and when Esther finished and said gently, "Now, Ron, it's your turn," he looked positively scared as he whispered, "No, I can't. That is, I don't know how."

"I'll teach you," was her soft reply. But Ron was not yet ready for such tuition. It was OK for Esther to pray, to be a saint, to have her own convictions about things like divorce, but as for him, it was enough to follow her from afar, to bask in her light, to let God love him through her and hope that He might see just a little bit of worthiness in his own heart. After all, he wasn't such a very bad fellow, was he? He mustn't be for his beloved girl to be as fond of him as she was.

Esther sensed his reluctance and did not press him further. But it was a very troubled young lady who drove home that afternoon. They had eaten lunch but both were more silent than usual. It seemed as if their joy had been suddenly darkened by an unexpected shadow, a threatening shadow that came and went when least expected, that haunted their conversation, and dimmed their laughter. But, Ron told himself, this would all pass. He was not going to let all this separate him from this gem of a girl whatever it took.

When Esther entered the door, her uncle was waiting for her. He could see by her expression that Ron had told her the news. He was about to step forward when his niece held up her hand. "Uncle, wait," she protested, "I know all about it and I'm terribly disappointed, terribly." That was all she said but her tone, the look in those eyes of hers, carried him back twenty-five years. His niece whom he really adored was going to reject him just as her mother had done. He couldn't stand it and turned on his heel and left the room.

Esther burst into tears and fled upstairs. When she came down several hours later her uncle had gone out. She supposed Ramona had too. She had only seen her and her two friends for a few moments that morning. Slim and brown, her cousin looked more glamorous that ever, but her gaiety seemed forced and her eyes had lost their brightness, Esther thought. She preferred the plump, jolly Ramona of old.

She had told Ron she wanted an evening to herself, but as the hours dragged by she longed for someone to talk to. There was no piano now in the lounge on which she could give vent to pent-up feelings. She considered phoning her aunt to see how she had taken the news but her reticence kept her back. After all, she didn't know Mary that well yet. So kneeling by her bed she told God about it as she always did and went to bed somewhat comforted.

It was only the following evening that it dawned on Esther that she had not seen Ramona for two days. She knew that the three girls had spent much of their time in the pool since they had come back. But when she went for a solitary swim after lunch, there was no Ramona in sight. By six o'clock she was really worried. She opened Ramona's bedroom door. She was not there. She went downstairs to the basement and called her name. There was no answer.

She had not seen her uncle since the evening before. Finally, as she was showering before bed, she heard his car. She dreaded meeting him, but, putting her personal feelings aside out of deep concern for her cousin, she slipped on her dressing-gown, ran lightly downstairs, and knocked at her uncle's door.

"Yes?" John's voice was unusually gruff.

"Uncle, excuse me, but have you seen Ramona?"

"Ramona?" John looked up unconcerned. "She's probably out with her friends as usual."

"Well, I haven't seen her all day. She didn't come down for breakfast or lunch. And actually, her car wasn't in the driveway when I got up this morning."

"You don't mean she's been out all night?" and John's face flushed in anger.

"Maybe she's at Marci's house, or Kelly's?" Esther suggested.

"Doubt it. And anyway, she should let us know so we wouldn't worry. She's going wild lately."

Esther said nothing and her uncle continued. "Please, phone her friends, will you Esther? There's a good girl."

Esther thought privately that it was his place to phone them but went obediently to the kitchen to look up some numbers. Marci and Kelly had been with Ramona for weeks now. Maybe they had gone off together. She'd try ringing them anyway. They were at home which seemed strange, as they had planned to stay at Ramona's through the weekend of the 4th. They both seemed to be holding back something though they told her straight out they had no idea where her cousin was at that moment. They had said "at that moment," Esther noted. She was almost sure they knew something about Ramona's disappearance.

She was just giving up, when she saw, underlined in the phone book, Norman's number. Norman was Ramona's new friend, an art student with long hair and earrings. She had brought him back with her from Florida much to her father's disgust. He lived in Indianapolis but seemed to be away from home most of the time.

Esther hesitated then took the plunge. Tremblingly she dialed the number. A woman's voice answered curtly, "Yes. Who's there?"

"It's Esther Popescu, Ramona's cousin. Her father's anxious about her as she didn't come home last night and wonders where she is. Have you any idea?"

The woman on the other end gave a rather sinister laugh. Esther shuddered. "I don't know for sure, but I've a good idea where she is," and the woman laughed again.

"Where? Please tell me! Her Dad is worried about her."

"Tell her Dad that his daughter is a grown woman now and it's none of his business where she spends her nights. As to where she is, well, I suspect she's wherever my son is. Tell him that too, will you?" and the receiver went down.

Esther stood in shocked silence. Her uncle came up behind her and put his hand on her shoulder. His niece forgot all about her anger and threw herself into his arms. They stood like that for some time.

"I just don't know why she's done this," John muttered.

"Don't you, uncle?" It had come out before she could help it. She couldn't help but think that Ramona's sudden disappearance had something to do with John's coming marriage. But maybe he hadn't told her yet.

Her uncle was silent as he flopped into his favorite chair by the window. Esther was nervous but she had to know. "Uncle, did you tell Ramona?" she stammered. Esther's tone was so low her uncle had to bend forward to catch her words.

"Tell her what?" His voice was sharp.

"About your engagement."

He bit his lip. "Yes, I told her. It was easy to tell *her*. I knew *she* would understand."

Esther's eyes met his but she said nothing. "Yes," he went on in a lighter tone, "she laughed and congratulated me, gave me a kiss actually. No, Esther, Ramona's not like you. She didn't take it hard and I'm very sure this sudden disappearance of hers has nothing to do with my news. It's one of her whims. Probably that crazy guy with the earrings and a face like Judas has dragged her off with him somewhere."

His niece gave him a searching look but remained silent. "Well it's time you had your beauty sleep, young lady. Off to bed with you."

Esther made no move. "Uncle John," she murmured. "I don't

think you're right about Ramona but then, I don't know her like you do. But one thing I do know," her voice grew firmer as she spoke, "and that is that you're making an awful mistake and those who love you most will suffer most."

John rose stiffly from the chair. His eyes narrowed and his lips tightened as he brushed past his niece and made for the door. "Who made you a judge over me, eh? Thank God everyone doesn't see things like you do, Esther," he spluttered. "I've respected you and your religion and God knows at times I've wished I could be like you." He paused with his hand on the door knob. "But," and his voice seethed with anger, "I thought you would at least try to understand a lonely man who's seeking a little bit of personal happiness after more than twenty years of married misery. But no, it's all right and wrong with you. You've no give in you, no bend, when it comes to things like this."

John turned his back on her abruptly as he slammed the door behind him, leaving Esther standing thunderstruck in the middle of the room. She had never expected this reaction from her beloved uncle. Was he right after all? Was her religion as unattractive as all that because she tried to stick to God's moral law?

Her brain reeled as she climbed into bed a few minutes later. Too weary and sick at heart to kneel and pray, she could only groan, "Oh God, I'm so confused, so unhappy, so disappointed," as she pulled the pink sheet over her. She lay for some time, gazing up at the ceiling. That same smothering sensation she had not felt for some weeks now, threatened to suffocate her. She threw back the sheet. It seemed unbearably hot. Maybe the air-conditioning wasn't working properly. The minutes ticked by and then, as she grew calmer, a Voice seemed to whisper from somewhere deep inside her, "Think of your poor aunt. It's she who is really suffering, and your cousins. They need your prayers." But Esther was too upset to think of anyone but herself, as she flopped back on the pillows. Life had been so wonderful of late. "Why, oh why, did this happen to destroy it all?" she muttered in frustration as she drifted into a troubled sleep.

Chapter Twenty-Eight

An Invitation

It was the first time Esther had ever seen Diane Atwood cry. When she had heard that Esther was upset about the news of her marriage to John Popescu, she had insisted that the girl come over right away and have a good long talk with her.

Esther sat beside Ron on the sofa, tense and apprehensive, listening intently to the distraught woman opposite her tell, between her sobs, of her difficult life with a drunken husband, of the eight years since their divorce when serious heart problems began to show up, of her struggle with her nerves, and then finally of what John's companionship had meant to her. "We probably didn't do right not to let you both know of our friendship," she concluded, trying to suppress her sobs. "Yes, we have had an affair if you want to call it that," Diane's voice grew a little defiant. "But we intended to get married anyway, so what was the harm in that?"

Esther was inwardly shocked at the woman's words but, for Ron's sake, tried hard not to show it. She leaned forward in her chair, her hands gripping her knees: "Mrs. Atwood, please believe me when I say I've nothing personal against you. Nothing at all. It's just that I also see my aunt's side to the whole question. She really wanted to try again with Uncle John and I think they might have made a go of it." Esther was now near tears but she went on bravely: "I know she made it awfully hard for him but for the girls' sake, he could have made one more try at it. And I honestly think he's done wrong to...." She paused, then looking steadily at the woman opposite her went on, "to think of another woman before the ink was dry on his divorce papers. I mean, it has affected Rachel a lot already, this separation and now Ramona seems to have gone off track."

Esther stopped, for Diane was getting angry. Ron winced. He was only too well acquainted with his mother's moods, especially of late; he knew they could change direction like the wind that was just then howling in the trees behind the house, a precursor of the storm that had been forecast for that evening.

"Gone off track has she?" Her voice was shrill. "And you blame it on us? What about your part in the whole thing? Ever stopped to think of that?"

Esther looked inquiringly at Ron whose face was dark as thunder. "Enough of this, Mom. Esther doesn't know what you're talking about."

"Oh doesn't she though?" Diane spluttered. "Doesn't she realize that Ramona was crazy about you and when you turned to her it sent the girl berserk?"

"Mom, that's not true," Ron protested. "I know Ramona. Esther and I were friendly long before she started to act up. Ramona had a crush on me, that's all. Believe me, I know all about it, and even if our friendship has bothered her, I had made it quite clear even before Esther came on the scene that we were friends, nothing more."

Esther had gotten up from her chair and had knelt by the distraught woman's side. She took her hands in hers and stroked them gently. "Mrs. Atwood, please listen. I really feel for you, I do. But can't you see that I also feel for my aunt and cousins and just hate to see another home disrupted when it just might be mended?"

Diane looked at Esther for a moment and gradually her anger faded. How could anyone be angry with such a girl for long? Ron heaved a sigh of relief as he saw his mother's mood change. But Esther had not finished. Clearing her throat she went on, "You see, Mrs. Atwood, I feel marriage is for life. Sometimes, as in your case, divorce may be necessary. But it is a different scenario with Uncle John. And as long as there is no remarriage, then there is always a chance, maybe a faint one, of reuniting, and oh, just think of what that means to the children."

Diane looked at Ron and raised her eyebrows. His father had never remarried though he had been unfaithful several times over the years. Both mother and son knew that David Atwood was trying hard to turn over a new leaf and that he still loved his wife. But he had made so many promises in the past that his family had long since ceased putting their hope in them. Ron, though, had to admit that the Christmas holidays he had spent with him had been the best in years. His dad really did seem different and he had told his mother that.

"Well, Esther," Mrs. Atwood's voice was pleasant but firm, "we both know now how the other thinks about the whole matter. But I have made up my mind. John needs me; I need him. We seem made for one another and I hope in time, we will prove that our union is a success. And I called you over tonight because I can't bear to have you upset with me." She smiled. Esther was still kneeling by her chair. She took her hand and led her over to where her son was sitting, head down, wishing this scene might be over. Putting her arms round them both she whispered, "Let's love each other in spite of our differences. I've always wanted a daughter and now it looks as if, some day soon, I might really have one."

Esther was glad it was ending this way. She lifted a tear-stained face to Diane. "Thank you," she responded. "I'm glad we could talk it out."

"Now let me get you two some refreshments," said Diane brightly, bustling off into the kitchen. Emotionally spent, Esther tried to keep back the tears that would come. Ron put his arm round her. "Come Esther, that's enough about this for the present. Let's think about this Ramona of yours. You know, that Norman fellow isn't much good. Maybe we can do something."

Esther brightened at the prospect of helping her cousin, and that evening was spent in talking over plans. In the end they agreed to wait and see if she came back on the Saturday. "She's of age, Esther, that's the trouble." Diane, always the perfect hostess, served them ice cream and cake and the clock struck ten before they realized it.

"I still feel, Ron," Esther told him as they said goodnight, "that Ramona's doing this to forget the trouble at home. And if only Uncle would think again about all this, it might bring her to her senses."

"It'll take a miracle to change that pair, Esther. They're both set on this. And what can we do?"

"Pray, Ron, pray," she told him as she bade him goodnight.

"Pray?" Ron echoed as he drove home. "I only wish I could. I really do."

That week was a difficult one for everybody. Saturday came and went and still no Ramona. When Esther returned from an evening with Ron, she found her uncle pacing the floor, waiting for word of his truant daughter.

"Let's go to bed," Esther urged, and finally as the clock struck one, he reluctantly agreed. Esther finally drifted into a troubled sleep. She really did love her cousin and hated to see the direction her life was taking. And sometimes, she would blame herself just a little. Maybe if she hadn't come on the scene Ramona and Ron could have really hit it off together. They had seemed to have so much in common. But Ron had been adamant on that score and he knew more about things like that than she did.

Next morning, Ron called for her as usual at nine to take her to church. Her uncle was still sleeping as she crept down the hallway and out the front door. She found Ron looking in amazement at something. She followed his gaze and there, standing beside her little car was Ramona's Toyota Camry.

"She's back!" Esther exclaimed, a world of relief in her voice. "Should I go and see if she's awake? No, she must be exhausted. But Ron, lets come back right after church today. I can't wait to see her."

Ramona finally came downstairs as Esther was getting a bite of lunch for Ron and her uncle. Esther ran towards her and gave her a hug but the girl did not respond. She stood there limply; her beautiful curls had lost their bounce; her face was blotchy, and her eyes glazed.

"Hi everyone," she said as casually as she could. "I'm back. No, I don't want to eat much. Just a drink of something, Esther."

As the day wore on, Ramona became a little more like herself and by evening she was trying hard to make it up to her father who remained cold and aloof. Finally, when they had all watched the news in silence, Ramona perched herself on the arm of his chair as she often did, and began to stroke his thick, wavy hair.

"Upset, aren't you?" she asked, almost playfully. "I know you're waiting for me to apologize."

"Of course, Ramona. You had us all worried to death," was the curt reply.

Ramona drew a long breath. She wanted to play her cards well. "Well, of course I'm sorry for having you all worried about me. But, don't you think, Dad, that you owe us an apology as well?" The words were softly spoken but Esther saw the gleam in her blue eyes. "You're the oldest and should set a good example," she went on. "At least, that's what you've always taught us, right?"

"Me?" John sounded as if he had not heard correctly.

"Yes, Dad, you," the girl replied planting a kiss on her father's forehead as she spoke. "I mean what about those weekends when you just took off and disappeared with your lady friend. Like father like daughter. Right?"

The words were lightly spoken but Esther sensed a wealth of meaning behind them. John was thunderstruck and had no reply ready so Ramona went on, "So, I've just followed your example, that's all. Maybe I took it to an extreme a bit," she conceded, "but then, I'm only 20."

By this time her father had regained his composure somewhat at least. "Well Ramona," he replied as calmly as he could, "I don't think our behavior is the same at all. I intended to get married as you know now. But you...."

"How do you know what I intended to do or not do, Dad?" his daughter retorted, tossing her head. "For all you know, I might be thinking just like you. Maybe we could have a double wedding or a triple!" and she gave a laugh, hard and metallic, as she threw a significant glance at her cousin. She slipped off her father's chair and made for the door. Esther shuddered inwardly. What was happening to their family?

"But Dad," Ramona's hand was on the doorknob as she spoke, "don't you worry. You've a right to happiness. And I'm glad it's Ron's Mom. She's fabulous." Her father relaxed and managed a faint smile. "Just remember that I've the same right, that's all," and she slipped out of the room before John could make further comment.

"I so hate to hear Ramona talk like that," Esther confided to Ron the next day after relating what had happened. "What's happening to our family, Ron?"

"Oh Esther," Ron drew her to him. "If everyone were only more like you, this world would be so different. When will you tell me if you consent to make my world better and brighter?"

Esther dropped her eyes. "Before you go to law school, Ron." She saw his face darken. She had told him a few weeks and now it was two months before he'd get an answer. "I promise I'll decide by then," she went on brightly. "Will that satisfy you?"

"Have to, won't it?" he grumbled. "That gives you two whole months. How I wish it were two days. So much can happen in two months, Esther."

"Yes, Ron, but that's where trust comes in, doesn't it?"

"Trust in you? That's easy."

"No, not in me. In God, Ron," she told him simply.

"In God? Well, you trust your God for me, Esther, and I'll trust you."

"*Your* God," Esther repeated to herself as she made the supper. How she wished he had said "*my* God."

That night, her prayers were not about Ramona, or Gabby, or her uncle, but all about Ron, for if Ron did not know God personally, what would happen to all their love and their beautiful times together? God must answer her prayers. He really must.

Esther would never forget that last week in June as long as she lived. She thought back wistfully to her first days in America when she would sit with her uncle and cousins in the living room on a Sunday evening, playing a game, or watching a video, or just talking. But now? Uncle John was never at home, or hardly ever, and Rachel and her mother had taken off again for a break somewhere. Ramona was away most weekends, but, she told them, she was only staying with Kelly or Marci. Home was so dull these days, she told Esther. She would be glad when college began again. As for Norman, he seemed to have dropped out of her life as suddenly as he had entered.

It was Ron, once more, who came to Esther's rescue. He would encourage her to look on the bright side of things. They must keep focused on their relationship, he told her, and not let anything else mar that. They must keep it what it was—pure, loving, and ongoing. Gradually she became less concerned about her uncle. And Diane Atwood was so loving and kind to Esther that her heart was melted. Maybe she really did deserve someone like John to take care of her; she had suffered so much. As for Aunt Mary, she said a prayer for her every night and promised herself that she would spend more time with her when she came back. Of course, Esther was still against divorce, and would never think of it for herself. But she couldn't interfere with others' lives, could she?

Then, on July 1st, Esther received a very unexpected phone call that gave her little time to think about Ramona, or Rachel, or her Uncle John. A well-known Christian singer had suddenly taken seriously ill and was not able to perform at a concert to be held in a large auditorium in the city center the following Saturday and Sunday evenings. One of the chief organizers of the event was a personal friend of Len Atwood and had asked him if he knew of anyone who could stand in at such short notice. Len had mentioned Esther's name but had suggested he phone her directly.

"I...I'm very flattered, I am sure..." stammered Esther completely overwhelmed by the request, "but I'm not sure I'm good enough or experienced enough."

"Len has highly recommended you, Esther, and you will be well paid for this performance. Hundreds will be present you know. It's a great opportunity not only to witness for the Lord but to make others aware of your ability."

"But I don't know many contemporary songs," she protested. "I've only been over here about nine months."

"I know," was the comment, "and we've considered that. But no one else is available at such sort notice and Len suggested you sing some Romanian numbers. Then you still have over a week and he thinks you could learn a few songs pretty quickly. He's willing to coach you."

Esther was still silent. "Tell you what," the man suggested, "come over tonight, if you can, or tomorrow at the latest, and sing a few for us. If we think you're not suitable, we'll tell you. Len said he would bring you."

Esther remembered her decision never to refuse an opportunity to witness for the Lord and so gave her consent rather reluctantly, though feeling strangely excited at the prospect of singing in front of such a large audience. But Len take her? Len coach her? She did not want that at all.

When Ron heard of her invitation that evening, he stared in unbelief. "Wow, Esther, that's one of the largest concerts held in this area. It is extremely popular. Why even though I wasn't a regular churchgoer I've attended several times. I can't believe they've asked you." He paused. He was pleased, or was he? Did he want his beloved girl to be stared at by hundreds if not thousands of spectators? Did he want her to be coached night and day for a week by his conceited cousin who already had an eye on her, he knew? And more than all that, what would it do to her? Could she take the praise he was almost sure she would receive? What if she became a star overnight? He had been attracted to her because she was different. Would she remain that way if suddenly pushed into the limelight? And yet, what a chance for her! And he would be so proud to see her up there, looking like an angel from Heaven. No, he couldn't, shouldn't stop her, but one thing he would do, he'd stick by her day and night—if Len had to be there, he'd be there too!

This unexpected turn of events threw all their plans for the 4th of July off kilter. Esther was too busy practicing to have time to go to the firework display. "You go with your mother and Uncle John, Ron," she had urged. "Don't miss the celebrations just because of me."

"Seems like you don't know me after all, Esther," he had told her. "Where you go I go, especially when that cousin of mine is anywhere near. And next year, we'll make up for it, you wait and see. We'll celebrate good and proper!"

For only a moment, fear had gripped Esther's heart. Next year? Who could tell what awaited them both next year. Their present happiness was too good to last, wasn't it? Then she brightened. This time last year she had felt so very alone, but now Ron had come into her life and made all the difference, so why worry about next year? And she never forgot his words as she smiled up into his face.

"After all," he whispered tenderly, "there's nothing to celebrate when you're not there. You are my celebration!"

Chapter Twenty-Nine

The Velvet Curtain Again

Marjorie Porteous looked at her watch. Hugh Gardner and his grandson were due any moment. But the program would start before they got there if they didn't hurry. It was quite an event for her old friend to consent to watch anything on TV. He must be very interested in this young Romanian singer to make this effort. Just then, she heard his car on the driveway and a few moments later they were settled in her family room just as the announcer was saying, "Ladies and gentlemen, I want to introduce a very special young lady to our audience tonight—Esther Popescu from Romania."

"So it is Esther," Hugh remarked as he peered at the TV. "You were right after all, Aaron. Well I never," he commented, rubbing his nose as he usually did when something perturbed him. "Who would have thought of it! Nine months in the USA and on her way to stardom!"

The young singer was met with a hearty round of applause. She seemed very self-conscious as she bowed to the audience. It was obvious she wasn't used to this sort of publicity. "Why she's quite a beauty," exclaimed Marjorie. "Are all Romanian girls like that?"

"Not all," Hugh told her smiling. "And certainly not all are like Esther Popescu. But on the whole, they are very beautiful, at least I think so, but then, I was married to one, remember?"

"Why Granddad," Aaron put in, "look, she's wearing that same white dress she wore for the concert in the church, remember?"

"I don't much remember what women wear," muttered Hugh. When Aaron's friend had told him that a young Romanian was standing in for one of the singers that night, Hugh had begged his grandson to go to Marjorie's and watch the concert. But Aaron had told him that he should go too. He knew that his granddad would quiz him about the performance until it made his head ache and he always hated being cross-examined about anything, especially about pretty young girls.

"Oh come, Granddad, I know you don't like TV but for once, come on. Watch your young prodigy. Keep an eye on her. Maybe she'll need your advice or help one day."

"Might not even be Esther, Aaron," he had grumbled. "After all, there's more than one Romanian girl in this part of the world." But he had given in after all, though very reluctantly. But Esther was beginning to sing now. He could tell she was a little nervous and didn't always know how to handle the mike.

"Glad she doesn't swing and sway around like most of them," Hugh said, "and she's certainly dressed modestly, though I'm afraid that can't last long if she becomes a star."

"Maybe she'll beat the system, Granddad." Aaron's voice sounded doubtful. "But fame's a dangerous thing. Not that I know much about it," and he gave a short laugh. "Must say, though, she's got more poise than she had last April."

"Poise? Is that what you call it? Yes, she has. But listen to that applause. It would turn anyone's head."

They both listened as Esther sang song after song, some Romanian, some contemporary. Her voice thrilled her audience as it always did and Aaron made a mental note that it was the first TV show that his grandfather had watched to the end for many a long day. Finally it was over and they were back home once more.

Hugh Gardner flopped into his favorite chair. "Please get me a good cup of English tea, Aaron," he begged. "I'm parched, and only you can make a decent cup in this neck of the woods. Oh, but I'm glad to get home again!" And Hugh lay back on the recliner and breathed a sigh of content. "All this TV viewing is hard on an old man."

Fifteen minutes later, Aaron put down his grandfather's favorite mug on the coffee table beside him. Hugh took long sips of the best English tea sent regularly every year by a faithful sister from across the water.

"Well?" Aaron asked as he took a seat opposite Hugh, kicked off his shoes and crossed his legs.

"Well?" repeated the older man.

"She was quite a hit, wasn't she?"

"Yes. And I suppose we ought to be grateful she's not more spoiled. There's still something unique about her."

"Are you going to watch her tomorrow, Granddad?"

Hugh shrugged his shoulders. "Guess I will," he muttered. "Got a feeling it might be quite different and I'm not sure I can trust you to give an honest report. You're not good at that, you know, especially when it comes to things like this."

Aaron grinned. "You're right there, Granddad. But I still can't quite understand the intense interest you feel in this young woman."

"Of course you don't understand it, my boy," and Hugh gave Aaron a peculiar smile, "but I think, somehow, that one day you will."

The next evening it was different right from the start. When the girl entered the stage there was a gasp from the audience and then a thunderous applause. "Is that Esther?" Aaron found himself exclaiming as he lent forward to get a better view. Yes. It was Esther all right and dressed in an ankle length, gold dress, not quite strapless but almost, which clung to her shapely figure and shimmered in the spotlight. Gold always suited her. Her olive skin glowed and her eyes shone like stars. A yellow rose peeked out of the masses of wavy black hair which hung in waves about her shoulders. But it was not just her dress or her hair that was different. As she began to sing, the audience was electrified. There was no fumbling with the mike now; she seemed in complete control both of herself and of her audience; her body swayed slightly to the rhythm of the contemporary song she was singing. No one could have guessed she had learned it in less than a week.

"Listen to that applause," Aaron commented as Esther concluded with "Amazing Grace." "It's thunderous. She's captivated the crowds tonight. Just look at them."

"And you too," commented Hugh wryly. His grandson had listened spellbound through the whole performance.

Aaron reddened. "Well, she's pretty fabulous, Granddad. I mean her voice is simply superb and the cameras seemed to focus on her face tonight." He stopped. He wasn't going to say anything more in front of Marjorie.

They all watched as the crowds surged round the young singer. Hugh could imagine what might be the results of this weekend's performance—sponsors offering to make her a real hit, companies offering to record her voice, invitations to concerts all over the country. She was well on the way to fame.

Hugh rose from his chair. "Thanks for letting us come, Marjorie," he said as he shook his friend's hand.

"It's been a pleasure to be of some use," the good lady had replied. "But we really need to pray for that young lady, Hugh. Something went wrong between last night and tonight."

"Most would say something went 'right,' not 'wrong,' Marjorie," he replied quietly. "But of course, I agree with you." Neither Aaron nor his granddad said much as they drove home.

That night was a restless one for Hugh Gardner. But by morning, after some hours of laying his burden at the feet of his Master, he fell into a peaceful sleep. And the next day he noted in his diary which he kept regularly: "Watched Esther Popescu sing last night on TV. Stunning performance but too much of the Velvet Curtain visible, to me that is, not to her, I fear. Sometimes wish she was safe within the Iron one again."

Chapter Thirty

Rescuing Gabby

"Congratulations!" Esther wheeled round to see young Connie Frith standing a few yards away. She hadn't seen the girl for some time. They had struck up a friendship of sorts during the past months though they only met at church. Connie, always outspoken, seemed to be keeping tabs on the older girl, watching to see how she walked, talked, dressed, and acted. It was as if, for the impetuous teenager, Esther was too good to be true, too holy to last long in the fast-paced world of the eighties.

Esther had just pulled into the church parking lot. It was the Wednesday evening following her concert performance. "Congratulations!" Connie repeated as Esther closed the car door behind her. "You've made it at last."

"Made what?" queried Esther, who had grown a little apprehensive of Connie's comments.

"Been accepted by our generation, of course, what else? Wow, but you were a hit last Sunday evening! I've scarcely seen anything like it!"

Esther blushed crimson. It seemed everyone was saying the same thing. Phone calls, letters, and offers to record her singing had poured in.

"Well, Connie," Esther answered airily as they entered the church together. "It seems God has opened the door. It's all His doing."

"That snazzy gold dress and two handsome escorts, eh—all His doing?"

Esther usually took the young girl's comments with a pinch of salt but this time they nettled her to the core. Brushing past Connie, she tossed her head haughtily. She wouldn't stoop to answer such taunts. Connie shook her auburn curls at the retreating figure and said in a voice she was sure Esther could hear, "Well, well, who would have thought it? My heroine has crashed from the stars. She's like all of us now. Just like I predicted."

Now thoroughly angry, Esther turned back and was about to confront the girl roundly. It took a great deal to rouse Esther, but once roused, as her sister had told her often, you had better duck for it. But something in Connie's eyes stopped her. Was it pain, disappointment, even anguish? Whatever it was, her anger subsided in a moment. Putting her arm round the younger girl, she whispered softly, "Forgive me Connie. I'm a bit uptight with everything, you know. I'm not used to all this publicity." But Connie pulled away. She would not be pacified, at least not quite so easily.

"I don't want apologies, Esther," she muttered as she turned on her heel. "I just want someone to stand up to things, set a different standard for us to follow—someone Christian, I mean. And I had hopes that it might have been you, in your quiet way. But...."

At this point Len came down the hallway. He surveyed the two girls for a moment. It was obvious Connie was on some hobby-horse of hers again. That was nothing new, but the usually serene Esther seemed extremely perturbed. He soon had her by the arm and was piloting her into the sanctuary. "Don't pay a bit of attention to that girl, Esther. She's a spoiled youngster and probably downright jealous of your success. You were simply...."

"Don't. I can't take any more, Len. I really can't," Esther interrupted, her lip quivering. She dropped his arm and hurried to take her usual seat a few rows from the front.

After the service, everyone crowded around Esther. It seemed as if the whole congregation had seen the concert on TV. How proud they were of her, they told her. It was fantastic! What a glory to God she had been! How she had looked, acted, sang! The pastor, however, was a bit more subdued in his comments. "Great performance, Esther," he said kindly. "You are surely gifted with a wonderful voice but don't let all this publicity go to your head," and he patted her gently on the shoulder. "Give God all the glory. You've got a wonderful career ahead of you if you can retain the humble spirit that has so marked your singing up until now."

Esther half appreciated, half resented his words. "Thank you, Pastor," she mumbled as she made it out into the clear night air. She was thoroughly worn out emotionally, and flopped into bed that night utterly exhausted. "Dear Lord, I'm so tired," she murmured sleepily as she switched off the bedside light, "but bless me and keep me and all I love tonight. Amen."

The next week was a repetition of Wednesday evening. Everywhere she went she heard how good she was. At first it wearied her though it never failed to gratify her vanity. Then she grew used to it, even expected it, so that when Ron never spoke of her performance, though he had highly praised it that Sunday evening, she grew petulant with him. It hurt him at first, but he was only too ready to excuse the girl he adored. She was tired, overwrought, worried about Ramona, about Gabby, about her uncle's wedding. She had a right to be just a bit cross with him at times.

Then one morning, Esther went to the mailbox as usual. Fan mail was beginning to pour in but this morning there were only two letters awaiting her. She paid little attention when she saw that one was postmarked Arkansas. She had received a letter the day before from California from someone who wished to sponsor her as a singer. Ron had joked that she would need to hire a private secretary when he left for law school. He had helped her buy a desk and a filing cabinet so she would be more organized.

She slit open the other envelope first. It was cream-colored and lightly scented. Yes, it was what she expected, only more elaborate than seemed appropriate under the circumstances. The wedding was to take place on August 24th at St. Margaret's Episcopal Church where Diane Atwood attended occasionally. A few weeks ago Esther would have balked at the idea of going but now she told herself as she laid the invitation on the desk, it would be the only Christian thing to do.

As she opened the second envelope, two folded pieces of paper fell out on her lap. She picked up the first and unfolded it. Why, it was Gabby's handwriting! She was both puzzled and alarmed. With bated breath, she began to read:

"Dear Esther,

"You will be surprised to receive this letter but I couldn't miss the opportunity. I've been wanting to get word to you for weeks but didn't know how. I was getting desperate and asked God to let me find some way to reach you. My prayer was answered. Ralph Potter from a Baptist church in Arkansas visited us briefly last week. Of course, he had to stay in a hotel and was closely watched all the time, but I managed to slip him this letter, as I doubt if anything I'm writing is getting to you. Esther, what I say is very urgent. It has seemed that Mr. Potter came to our church just in the nick of time."

Esther's pulse began to quicken and her hand trembled as she read on: "As you will remember, I graduated last month. I know you intended to get me over to you some time this year but as I haven't heard from you at all, I don't know if that is still on or not.

I know it's awkward when you have to depend on Uncle John for everything. But you need to help me get out of this place, and soon. I'm sorry to bother you, Esther, but I have to tell you something.

"A few weeks before I graduated, I was leaving school one afternoon, when I felt I was being followed. I stopped to tie my shoe lace, hoping that whoever was behind would pass me. But he didn't, and when I reached the park he came up beside me and I saw who it was."

Esther paused and her face blanched. She could imagine the scene exactly and guessed what was coming. Dreading the worst, she forced herself to read on: "You can guess who, Esther. You know him only too well. I had half expected to meet up with him before too many months had passed, but was still totally unprepared when it happened. I shook in my shoes as I made myself look up at him. 'It's Gabriella Popescu, right?' he asked.

"I nodded and looked at the ground. 'You're not much like your sister,' he commented. I nodded again, glad for once I wasn't like you—beautiful, I mean. Then he grabbed my arm and muttered hoarsely, 'She's gone to America, hasn't she? Where is she? Give me her address.'

"Of course I knew that by 'she' he meant you. 'I haven't got it here,' I told him, stalling for time. He swore and stamped his foot. Shaking my arm he looked round then muttered in my ear, 'Bring me her address tomorrow, this time, here in the park or else....' He didn't need to say any more. I shuddered and kept my eyes fixed on my shoes but would not reply.

"'Stubborn aren't you? Just like her, only more so, I'd say,' and he gave an awful laugh.

"That laugh did it. I went berserk. I freed myself from his grasp looked right up in his face and shouted, 'No! I won't give the address to you! I won't! If you get it, and I'm sure you will, it won't be from me.' I gave him one of my 'Gabby' looks as you call it and fled. He didn't try to follow, but I knew he was stark, raving mad.

"Of course, as you can guess, this was not the end of it. The next day I made sure I was not alone when I came home from school, but I knew I was being followed again. I couldn't tell my friend Roxana anything about it, of course, so when we came to the traffic lights where we part company, I bolted for home. But he was there before me, waiting in the entrance. You know how dark it is there. I was really frightened especially when he grabbed me again by the arm and looked me up and down over and over again. Then he gave his horrible chuckle: 'Not too bad after all, Gabriella. *You'll* do, if I can't have *her*.' Then he slipped me a note and disappeared into the darkness.

"When I got upstairs, I opened the note. It said, 'I've already gotten her address. But she'll probably ignore any letters I send. You give her my address and phone no. and tell her immediately that she'd better get in touch with me right away. If she isn't in the country by September, tell her that her baby sister will do very well as a substitute. Tell her that. And tell her that, if her sister tries to hop it to America like she did, she'll not find it as easy. And just you remember, both of you, that America isn't that far away any more.'

"I'm mailing you his address and phone no., Esther, but to a wrong address. It'll never get to you but I can tell him I sent it. Why does God allow these Communists to encourage us to be so devious? I'm deceitful enough without any encouragement. But still, it's not really a lie, is it?

"Esther, Aunt Ana says I must get out of here right away. It won't be easy but I have my papers already. If I get money in time, that is by the end of the month, I'm going to Poland with the school on their summer trip, they still have a few vacancies, and the American Embassy in Warsaw there will take care of the rest. I won't mention names here, but you and I both know who can help me do this. I've already mentioned it to her and she's more than willing. She agrees that I might have more trouble than you did at the immigration here in Bucharest. Things are getting worse, and *he* will have the authorities looking out for me this time. They'll use any excuse to detain me if they possibly can. But I need money for that trip and for my fare. I'll need about $800 in all. I'm sorry Esther, but there's no other way out. You know what will happen if I stay. Aunt Anna says she doesn't mind what happens to her. She thinks the worst will be she will lose her job and she can trust God to take care of her. She thinks that Ceaucescu won't last long, that there are signs of change in the air. I sure hope she's right. And I hope *he* doesn't pester you at your end somehow, but I know Uncle will take care of you and you're a lot safer over there than here, that's for sure.

"Please write me immediately via Mr. Potter. His friend leaves for Romania on 24th of July. The school trip begins on August 1st. So you see, I need the money right away. If this fails, then I can't see me getting over to you any time soon and what will happen if I don't leave here, I shudder to think. Please help me. Please.

"Your very loving sister, Gabby."

Esther's hand shook as she refolded the letter and undid the second sheet of paper. It was just affirming what Gabby had said, that he, Ralph Potter, would see that her sister got the money if Esther could send it right away.

Esther looked at her watch. Ron would be over soon to take her to a practice session with Len; Ron always insisted, if he possibly could, on accompanying her to these sessions. It being the summer vacation, he was pretty much his own boss. She had another big concert that weekend in Cincinnati and had a lot of songs to go over before Saturday.

When Ron arrived, he could see immediately that something had happened. Esther said nothing but handed him the two letters. His eyes fell on the wedding invitation. "Is this what has upset you?" he asked taking her hand in his.

"No, Ron. I mean, it did upset me a bit of course, but no, it's not that."

"Are you going to the wedding, then?" Ron couldn't help asking.

"Yes," she replied quietly, "if you are. I mean, it's the only Christian thing to do."

Ron looked at her in amazement. "She wouldn't have given that answer a month ago," he said to himself. "I didn't know I had that much influence on her."

Then she started to shake again. "Read the other letter, please Ron, read it now."

Ron began to read. It wasn't at all what he had imagined. Gabby in trouble? And his beloved Esther! She had never even hinted that she had been in such danger. His eyes blazed as he handed her back the letter.

"That *monster*," he growled. "How dare he threaten you in this way! Tell me all about it Esther, please. I'm here to protect you, you know."

Half an hour later they were sitting together on their favorite park bench by the river. Esther slowly and painfully began to talk about those dreadful weeks and months when she had been hounded by the son of the Party chief in Ploiesti. He had met her during her last year at high school and for a whole year had never left her in peace. He would ogle her in the classroom, follow her home at nights, send her very suggestive notes, and in short, make her life almost unbearable. Only God had protected her, she told a shocked Ron, and once she had made a very narrow escape. The more she avoided him and snubbed him, the more he pursued her. He told her he would have her at any cost. He had seemed to take perverse delight in trying to corrupt a girl who was known to be a Christian. She was also pretty sure it had been he who had gotten his father to offer her that job as interpreter.

"Esther," Ron said after they had read the letter for the third time. "I don't think it would be wise to ask your uncle for the money right now, but I'm not short of cash you know. Gabby's fare won't make much of a hole in my bank account."

"But Ron," Esther exclaimed turning her big eyes full on his face. "I can't ask you for $800 just like that."

"I'd do this for any real friend and you're much more to me than that, you know."

Esther blushed, sighed, and then smiled slightly. "Actually, Ron, I've been thinking. With all the money I'm getting for my singing, I can pay it myself, or just about."

"But it'll cut you short. Anyway, you will need some when that sister of yours arrives."

"That's true. We'll not be staying with my uncle after he marries. We're going to Aunt Mary's and I'll need to give something for our board. OK, Ron, you can pay it for just now."

"For just now?" he echoed. "We'll see about that! After we've got this practice session over, we'll go home and get a check mailed right away. We've no time to lose."

"Oh, I do hope she gets here OK," Esther muttered as they got back into the car. "It's a bit risky what she's doing."

When they returned home, Esther immediately sat down and wrote a letter to Gabby and mailed it that very day with a check made out to R. Potter to be delivered in cash to her sister as soon as possible. The check also included the $1000 she had received for the church in Ploiesti. It was a relief to get the money off her hands. And Aunt Mary, hearing the whole story, assured Esther of a home for Gabby and herself as long as they needed it. "Rachel will sleep with me," she announced, "and you two can share the other bedroom. Cramped quarters, but I guess you're used to that."

Esther heaved a sigh of relief when Ron slipped the envelope in the mailbox outside the post office. "What's worrying me most, Esther, is: are *you* safe even in America?" he asked her as he put his foot on the accelerator.

Esther shrugged. "Who knows, Ron? I'm a lot safer than I was, that's all I can say."

"What is Gabriella like, Esther? Is she like you?" Ron asked suddenly as they sped homewards. He wanted to get her mind on brighter subjects.

Esther had laughed her silvery laugh as she replied, "Oh, not at all, Ron."

"Not as beautiful then?"

Esther hesitated. "Why you've seen a picture of her, Ron. Judge for yourself."

"Going by the photo, she's not a patch on you. But photos are deceptive sometimes," he told her. "What's she really like?"

Esther thought a moment. "Gabby's like the wind, like the sun, like a tornado, like a rainbow. One moment she's laughter; the next she's tears." Esther paused. She was seeing her young sister's face before her as vividly as if she were there in the car beside her. She went on, "She's much lighter in complexion than I am, in fact, much more western looking. I suppose she wouldn't be called beautiful. Her features are a bit irregular, but her personality makes up for it. That's what makes her so attractive. Then she has large green-grey eyes which, when she speaks, literally dance with life, and her smile is the warmest you will ever see. But when she gets upset, you'd better watch out!"

"So she's a real handful at times! Think you can manage her in new surroundings? How will she adapt? And Esther, how will she take to the new 'you'?"

Esther was growing resentful of any allusion to the change that had come over her and she was about to retort rather sharply when the thought struck her forcibly. How would her Gabby take to America and, yes, what would she think of her older sister now? She was so unpredictable; Esther had a feeling that there would be some real storms before the girl would settle down to the American way of life. And how would she react to Ron, she wondered?

"Will there be room for you all in your aunt's house?" Ron asked.

"It will be a squeeze for a while but Aunt Mary is eventually buying another with money she's getting from the divorce settlement."

"Well, maybe by next summer, there'll be plenty of room."

"Maybe," Esther repeated blushing, and then added as an afterthought, "if God wills."

Chapter Thirty-One

Esther's Answer

Esther awoke in a sweat. It had been months since she had had such a nightmare. She guessed the cause. It was that letter she had received the day before. Her beautiful pink bedroom still seemed bristling with danger though she was wide awake and the sun was streaming in the window. All night long, *he* had been pursuing her and it seemed *he* was still there, maybe in the closet, or under the bed, or in the garage. It was the same nightmare she had had many times in the days which had seemed so far away—the days when she had to creep home from school afraid that she had been followed. Now it was all so very vivid once more. Maybe she was not safe even in America. Maybe *he* and his father had their spies even in Velours. Then she laughed at the thought. Impossible!

She remembered how, in her tiny bedroom on the fifth floor of the tall apartment building in Ploiesti, she would have to spend some time on her knees before she had been able to extricate herself from the blanket of fear the nightmare would cast over her. So she knelt down on the soft, pink pile and began to pray. But after a few moments, she sprang to her feet. Why Ron would protect her! She must tell him her fear. Sure, God was her greatest Protector, she knew that, but didn't He use humans to answer prayer sometimes?

"I'll be right over, Esther," Ron's calm voice was reassuring her some minutes later. And he was. With him close beside her, she felt the fear lift.

"You know, darling," he whispered, "this may be a sign from God that you need me to protect you always. Married good and proper, that *monster* wouldn't dare touch you."

"I've been thinking just that, Ron."

She did not need to say any more. She was in his arms. He had a right to hold her. She was his, now.

"Just one question," Esther asked pulling away from him a little. "Are engagements binding here in the West? I mean, is it almost the same as being married?"

Ron bit his lip. Why did she have to ask that? Then he understood. "No, Esther. I know you've told me that in Romania it is, but here, no, it isn't quite like that, though I think we take an engagement far too lightly here. I know some friends who seem to run in and out of them as they would a fast food bar. But of course it isn't the same as marriage. You know that. I wish it were, though," he added as he kissed her passionately.

"Oh Ron, you're so understanding! You know I'll take it seriously. And it does seem that God is showing that I need this very badly, need *you* badly, that is." Esther longed to feel that ring on her finger and to know she had the right of Ron's protection for she still felt very unsafe. She held out her hand, trembling as she did so.

Ron slipped on thc beautiful ring and whispered, "Now you're mine and no one or nothing is going to take you away from me."

"I certainly hope not," Esther murmured, as she felt his arms around her. "I need you very much."

"And I need you too, my angel. But when shall the great day be?" He looked into her eyes, waiting for an answer.

"I'll leave that up to you. Do you want to wait till you graduate from law school, or until I finish at ISU?"

"There's no way I can wait that long especially...." He paused.

"Especially?"

His face flushed as he answered hurriedly, "Especially since I love you so passionately. It makes waiting almost impossible especially...."

"There you go again," Esther told him laughing. "Especially what, Ron?"

"I'll explain another time, Esther. Not today. Don't worry, it's nothing terrible only rather private. I promise I'll tell you some day. Now, how about us getting married next summer? You'll have another year of school behind you before you have to change colleges." He saw the surprised expression on Esther's face and added with a smile, "Of course you'll have to change colleges. It'll be too far to commute from Nashville and I'll be an established law student there by that time. Of course, you know that our house will be free as Mom's moving in with your uncle."

Esther nodded. "We'll only be together at the weekends for the time being," he went on, "but that's probably just as well." There was a long silence. "So," he continued, "when we're married, we'll just need a rented place in Nashville where we can stay during the week. Oh my Esther," and he drew her closer, "a year seems an eternity. But at least I can hold you now, kiss you, make you feel you and I belong together."

The minutes ticked by. Neither wanted to move. The lonely girl had found her haven at last. No longer need she face life's storms alone. No longer need she dread what the future might have in store for her.

"I can't believe this is happening to me," she murmured blissfully.

"Nor I," Ron whispered, stroking her hair. "I. . . ." he stopped abruptly. Ramona had entered the room and was standing staring at them, a strange expression on her face.

Esther turned scarlet. She had forgotten that her cousin usually made her appearance about this time of morning. She tried to pull away from Ron but he held her hand firmly in his.

"Well, Ramona," he said in as normal a voice as he could muster, "won't you congratulate us?"

Ramona glanced at the sparkling gem on Esther's finger. For one brief moment her face revealed her inner feelings. Then it passed, and with wonderful self-control she gave them both a kiss saying, "Why of course. I wish you both all the best." But this was all she could muster. Turning on her heel, she was gone.

"Poor Ramona," Esther sighed, "I think she's still fond of you."

"She's jealous, that's for sure, but I think it's more of your ring than of my love."

Esther was silent. He was probably right but still, Ramona's face haunted her at times. She really did love her cousin but they had so little in common. And what about her own love for Ron? Did she love him for what he truly was or for what he could give her, for what he could be to her? Did she even know who and what he truly was? Ron broke into her reverie.

"Esther, I'm afraid it won't be possible to have a family celebration with all this going on between your uncle and my mom. But at least you and I can celebrate, and first, I want us to get an engagement photograph taken. And, please, put on that gold dress you wore when you were such a hit at the concert in Indianapolis."

Esther gasped in astonishment. "But you never said a lot about that evening, Ron. I didn't know if you approved or not."

He gave a short laugh. "Approved? Well, it was a shock at first; I wasn't used to seeing you dressed like that. And I didn't like the idea of you being stared at by so many fans. But now I've gotten used to the new Esther and I rather like her, especially now that I can take her in my arms and feel that she belongs just to me." He drew out his wallet from his pocket and held it out to her. There, staring back at her, was a photo of herself taken that memorable evening.

It all came back to her in a flash. She had been so embarrassed when the organizers of the concert had kindly yet firmly told her she needed to liven up a bit if she were to be a real success—make more of her gorgeous figure, smile a lot more, use a little makeup, wear a more eye-catching dress. She remembered how she had gasped when they had put a shimmering, golden gown into her hands and told her to try it on.

At first she had protested. Ron had turned his head away, not wanting to influence her, but Len had reminded her of the tremendous influence she could be on the teenagers who would listen to her songs, if she were willing to appear just a little less angelic and saintly.

Esther recalled how she had still hesitated. She had remembered that fleeting sensation of an imprisoning something choking her, and although no one threatened, or cajoled, yet she had a distinct sense that if she did not comply, then this would probably be her last performance. Her whole future was at stake. She had thought of Gabby, of her friends in Romania, of what she could do for them with some cash in her pocket. She remembered, too, seeing a picture of her friend Margaret Cripps at her engagement party, in a dress not unlike the garment she was holding in her hand. Here in America, it seemed like freedom reigned even in a Christian girl's choice of a wardrobe. She was no longer in Romania with its iron-clad rules. She had liberty in Christ, hadn't she? And whatever would give Him glory and enable her to reach thousands with her singing, was legitimate, wasn't it?

The next thing she knew, she had been ushered into a small dressing-room. She remembered slipping the dress over her head and walking over to the full length mirror in the corner. She had gasped at the image that stared back at her. The gown seemed to highlight every curve and shimmered in the light of the florescent bulb above, accentuating her dark hair and bronzed skin. She hadn't realized the straps of the gown were so flimsy, or the neckline quite so plunging. She wasn't used to revealing so much bare flesh to hundreds of spectators. What would her father have thought had he been alive? Could he see her now, she wondered?

Just then, a young woman about her own age knocked at the door and peeked in. She had gazed at Esther in admiration. "You're simply gorgeous, Esther," she had told her. "But here, let me do up your hair, touch you up a little!"

Fifteen minutes later she had taken another look in the mirror. Her hair had been piled in soft layers on top of her head, exposing her bare neck and shoulders. Turning round slowly and eyeing herself from top to toe, she had felt chills going up and down her spine. She was sensational and she knew it. Surely God hadn't created her that beautiful just to hide it all under a bushel? Would it hurt, just this once, to parade her charms just a little as long as, in the long run, she gave all the glory to God? Taking a long breath, she had turned from the mirror and slowly exited the dressing-room.

She hadn't needed to see their expressions to know that she had stunned everyone present. Now, as she stared over Ron's shoulder at the photo, she relived those delicious moments when that huge auditorium had erupted in applause.

"Well?" he asked.

"I don't look an angel, that's for sure, unless," she added wryly, "there are glamorous angels in Heaven. But maybe I just reveal what I really had inside me all the time. I've often been told I should have been a model even when I camouflaged everything in my long skirts and high-necked blouses."

"Exactly, and though, like I told you before, I still sometimes have nostalgia for that old gold blouse and black skirt, I don't think that was the real you. So go up and change and this time, wear the dress just for me."

Esther slipped upstairs and took out the shimmering gown. She stifled a few qualms of conscience as she slipped it on, piled up her hair and applied a little makeup to her fine features. After all, this was a picture to last a lifetime.

Ron took one look as she waltzed into the room half an hour later. A few seconds later and she was enfolded in his arms. "You're simply unbelievable Esther," he murmured softly, "absolutely unbelievable. Come on, let's dance together."

"But I can't dance, Ron."

"I'll teach you some day. But not just now. Let's be off to the photographers."

It seemed to both Ron and Esther as they dined out that evening that the phantom that had flitted between them ever since John

Popescu had announced that he was getting married had disappeared at last. And when he was finally alone in his room that night, Ron Atwood found himself on his knees for the first time in years. After all, he felt it was only right to thank God for such a gift as his beloved Esther. And so began a nightly ritual. "I wonder if God won't hear me for her sake," he would sometimes mutter to himself, when he felt as if his prayers got no higher than the ceiling.

Uncle John and his fiancée took the news of their engagement in their stride. They had expected it for some time and were too occupied with their own coming marriage to give it much thought. Esther hardly saw Ramona, though when she did, she was pleasant enough. Aunt Mary, the girl noticed, seemed particularly glad. Rachel alone remained glum. And one day she told her mother that she was pretty sure that Ron Atwood was just not the right man for her wonderful cousin.

"Oh you'd think that of any fellow who asked for Esther's hand," and Mary laughed.

"It's not just that, Mom," Rachel added. "Ron hasn't got a clue when it comes to all this about God. Esther makes excuses for him, but he's not on her wave length. Either she'll have to change or they'll have trouble."

"Well, you have certainly thought it out," said her Mother, amazed at her younger daughter's perception. "But couldn't Ron become like Esther? Isn't that an alternative?"

"Of course it is," assented Rachel, "but I'm afraid that once he gets his prize, he won't want anything else. And really, Esther isn't that strong in some things. I think he'd be the one to change her though he wouldn't mean to. And I'd hate that. In fact," and she lowered her voice as if her cousin might overhear her, "I'm afraid he has already changed her a bit."

Mary was silent. She knew Rachel was right. Her niece never seemed to have time to visit now on a Friday evening. There was no hymn singing at the piano, no games of Scrabble. But in spite of the fact that Ron was Diane Atwood's son, she had a soft spot for the young man who always treated her with the utmost courtesy and kindness.

"Well," she conceded, "she has changed, Rachel. I admit that. But I don't think you can blame it on Ron as much as on her new popularity. What girl wouldn't be affected? After all, she's human like the rest of us."

"Yes, Mom, but she began to change before she started all this singing," and Rachel gave a significant thrust of her chin as she always did when she was making a point she was very sure of. "What worries me most," she went on, "is that Esther doesn't talk as much about God as she did, and, well, she's just more like everyone else."

"I still don't think it's all the poor boy's doing," Mary commented. "For a celebrity the girl's still pretty humble and approachable. But Rachel," and her mother looked at her daughter closely, "is that your only reason for not being happy about Esther and Ron?"

Her daughter flushed scarlet and darted out of the room. "My poor girl," Mary muttered softly, "things don't seem to go right for her. What will happen to her in life, God only knows!" She stopped. Yes, God knew; that was a comfort. Mary Popescu had thought a lot about God lately—two troubled daughters to worry about, her husband forsaking her for another woman, financial problems—who else could she turn to except God? One of these days, she figured, she would, like the Prodigal Son, make her way back to the Father, one day very soon.

Chapter Thirty-Two

John and Mary

"Esther?" It was Rachel's voice. "Can I speak to you a moment?"

Esther sighed. As usual, she had spent too long dressing for her concert and now she was late.

"Sorry, Rachel, not right now. I've got to be off to Cincinnati immediately. Ron's waiting in the car. I'll phone you back tomorrow? Right?"

"Have to be," Rachel grumbled. "I don't suppose you're going to *the* wedding, are you?"

"Actually, I am," Esther told her. "But look, I really have to go. Talk to you tomorrow. Bye."

"Why are you looking so black, Rachel?" her mother asked her as the girl hung up the receiver. "I take it Esther can't speak just now?"

"It's not that Mom, though, yes, she's off to another of those old concerts of hers. They're the ruination of her."

"Of Esther?" her mother exclaimed. "What are you saying? Give the girl a break. She's not had much joy in her life, you know. She deserves any that comes to her."

"But you haven't heard all, Mom," Rachel said, flopping disconsolately into a chair. "She's actually going to *the* wedding."

Mary said nothing for a few moments. Her daughter's words had stabbed her, yet why should she be surprised? What else could she expect when John's new wife would one day become the girl's mother-in-law? "Well, she's engaged to Ron, isn't she?" she commented, trying to sound calm. "So it's only to be expected that she should go, isn't it?"

"It isn't normal at all, not for the Esther I used to know," countered Rachel. "Mom, she's changing so fast. How can we stop her?"

Mary looked thoughtful. "I don't think we can, Rachel. We could pray, though God knows I'm not much good at that sort of thing."

"Me neither," said her daughter sarcastically. It was time to change the subject. "Mom, what's Dad going to do after they marry? Is he going to sell the house? I mean, you still haven't received anything from the divorce settlement, have you?"

"No," replied Mary slowly, "I haven't. You see, when I dropped the divorce and your Dad took it up, he had to get a different lawyer. I had used our family lawyer and he wouldn't take on Dad. Said it would be very awkward. I found out later that John didn't really start the divorce proceedings till nearly Easter so it's only been settled a very short time. And there have been some complications over the house. Actually, I have to see him and my lawyer on Monday. He'll either have to sell up the business or give me the house as I'm due half of all his assets."

"Well, Diane's got a house. What's the problem?"

"It's not as simple as that," and her mother let out a long sigh. "She owns her house jointly with Ron and wants to leave it to him when he marries, so they'd rather live in a place they felt was all their own. And, of course, your dad doesn't want to have to sell."

"So what are you going to do, Mom?"

Mary stared out of the window. Just what was she going to do? That was the all-consuming question.

"Does Dad owe much on the house?" Rachel asked.

"Yes, quite a bit. Even if he lets me have it, I don't think I could meet the payments."

"You both are in a bind, aren't you? This is the price of divorce, I suppose," and the girl's eyes narrowed as she spoke.

"Well, Rachel, I'm to blame partly for our having bought such an expensive house. I bugged him for years for things. I didn't have his love so I wanted his money. I was always craving something 'bigger and better.' And I suppose, to substitute for the love he couldn't seem to find for me, he gave me anything I wanted, anything to fill the vacuum in my life. But it didn't work."

"Wonder what Dad's bride-to-be thinks of all this."

"Haven't a clue. I may know on Monday. But I do want to speak to Esther before then."

"Why, Mom?"

"Because I want her advice. I've a feeling I ought to do something but I'm not quite sure what, and I need to know before Monday. Rachel, I really think I need to get to know Esther's God." Mary spoke rather hesitantly. It was a difficult admission to make, especially to her daughter, but the urgency of making her peace with her Maker had been growing on her for weeks now.

"She won't have time before Monday to speak with you, Mom," Rachel warned her. "You wait and see."

"No? But I think she'll make time when she knows what it's about."

Rachel said nothing but went upstairs in a bad mood. She had so counted on Esther to back them at this time and now she was actually going to that wedding. What was coming over her? It wasn't all Ron. Something seemed to be surrounding her cousin and smothering that something very special that had made her so unique.

Mary didn't bother her niece until the next afternoon. She reckoned Esther would be back home from church by that time and would have had her lunch. Ramona answered the phone. She was usually in on a Sunday, sleeping off the effects of one of her parties. Mary longed to do something for her daughter but didn't know how. She felt at least partly responsible for much of the tragedy unfolding right within her family.

Ramona wasn't keen to talk. She sounded out of sorts as she always did these days. Mary saw very little of her, but each time they did meet, the haggard, weary, and even hopeless expression on her daughter's once beautiful face, made her heart ache with a pain that scarcely ever went away. She longed to put the bounce back into those lifeless golden curls, and to call back, somehow, that fresh sky blue tint into the languid and often glazed eyes that seemed to stare right past her. Mary suspected, though she never breathed her fears to anyone and even hardly dared admit it to herself, that Ramona was probably taking some form of narcotics.

Holding the receiver in one hand, Mary put the other to her aching forehead. The voice at the other end of the line conjured up so many memories of a happy, carefree child, whose beauty would arrest even the girl at the checkout in the supermarket, or the attendant at their local gas station. She and John had been so very proud of their blue-eyed darling. And now? Trying hard to beat back the waves of remorse which suddenly swept over her, Mary asked in as normal a voice as she could muster, "Is Esther there, Ramona?"

"No, she's gone with Ron to see his Dad in Louisville," Ramona replied in a dull monotone. "Won't be back till late tonight."

As Mary hung up, two large teardrops plopped onto her hand. Wearily she leaned back in the chair. Ever since she had heard of John's plans to remarry, a knot had been building up deep inside her. She remembered that afternoon, shortly after Ramona's return from her week in Florida, when they had all met in John's living room. It had been horrible. Rachel had flown off the handle, Esther had cried herself nearly sick, and Ramona had immediately taken her car and spent the next few days away from home. As for her ex-husband, he had tried to remain cool and collected through it all, but Mary recalled vividly the hurt, even angry expression on his face when he had discovered that none of the girls wanted to live with him after he married.

She had tried for the family's sake not to show her suffering, but now it seemed she could take no more. Esther had been her one hope. She might have shown her how to pray. Then she stopped. The prodigal needed no one to show him the way back to the Father. And she had been just like him. She had spiritually gone into a far country and spent all, and, as a consequence, had completely broken her mother's heart. As for her father, she had no idea who he was and probably never would know. Now, although it was too late to make it right with her family, it suddenly dawned upon Mary that she could be reconciled to her heavenly Father. Like that young man in Luke 15, she would get up from the far country and make her way Home. She couldn't pray pretty prayers any more, but she certainly felt His presence as she knelt down in the kitchen long after Rachel had gone upstairs. She knew that her girls needed her to have an anchor outside herself.

"I'm coming to You, Father," she stammered. "I've sinned against You, but please forgive me and take me back into Your heart and Home."

It wasn't immediately that she felt the assurance that she was back in His arms again, but late that night as she lay thinking, wondering, and praying, she knew He had come to meet her; she was safe in her Father's House once more!

Monday at eleven found Mary facing her ex-husband across the polished, mahogany table in the law offices of McNealy and Sons. Her attorney cleared his throat and straightened his tie as he turned to John who sat, silent and tense, waiting for the lawyer to speak.

"Your ex-wife wants me to inform you, Mr. Popescu," Ralph McNealy began, "that she withdraws her right to immediately receive one half of your assets." His tone was matter-of-fact, but his words had an electrifying effect on the man sitting opposite him. "Please note the word 'immediately,'" he went on in the same vein. "Mrs. Popescu has, of course, not withdrawn her financial claims upon you as your former wife, but she demands nothing for two years. At the end of that period, you will meet together again with myself and with your lawyer, and we will work out a payment settlement which will extend over the succeeding years. How and when she will receive her portion of the settlement can be determined at that time. I have asked her that any reasons she may wish to give for this extremely generous action of hers be given to you privately as I am not concerned with the 'why's' and 'wherefore's,' only with her final decision. So please sign here if you are in agreement."

John grabbed the pen as a drowning man grabs the rescuer's rope. Then he stopped just as it touched the paper. "Wait," he said; "I need to make one thing clear to Mary first, and that will probably best be done privately. If she's still of the same mind after talking to me, I'll sign the paper before leaving your office."

The lawyer nodded his agreement and rose to leave. "Take your time. This is important business," he told them as he left the room.

The door closed behind him leaving John and Mary Popescu alone together for the first time in months. There was a long, awkward silence. John toyed with the pen in his hand. Mary nervously played with her watchstrap. John was the first to speak:

"Needless to say, Mary, I'm very taken aback by this new development. I need, however, to make one thing clear." He laid down his pen as he spoke and lowered his eyes. How he wished it were all over. "Do you realize that this action of yours is only making my future marriage more certain?"

His words cut Mary like a knife. She was about to resort to her old sarcasm but she bit her lip. "I realize that, John," was her quiet reply.

"Then why on earth have you done this? You won't be able to buy a house now, will you?" His tone rose as he lifted his eyes to her face for the first time that morning. She had changed a great deal in the last few months, he noticed. She was more like the woman he used to swirl around the dance floor those twenty-three years ago. It seemed, for a brief moment, that she was back in his arms again. She had been wonderful company and he had been the envy of all his friends. But that almost irresistible physical attraction he had felt for the beautiful Mary Grant had not been enough to fill his heart or life or see him over the rough patches that come to all marriages. He suddenly dropped his gaze. He had no time for such thoughts now.

"John," Mary was speaking now, "as you know only too well, I didn't have your love so I wanted your money. And you seemed willing to give me all I asked for. So it's only fair that I do this, isn't it? No," she added flushing as she saw his eyes narrowing, "this is not to try to make you relent. But fair's fair and besides," what she was going to say was very hard but it had to be said, "I can't undo the years, but I've been doing a lot of thinking and I've decided I need God in my life, badly. Yesterday, I asked His forgiveness for my years of rebellion against Him and He has forgiven me." She paused. "And I want your forgiveness too."

John stared at her in amazement. This woman he had come to almost despise had had the courage to do what he could not do. "Forgive you?" he stammered. "Of course I forgive you. That's all in the past now. We've got to get on with our lives, haven't we?"

"Yes, that's exactly what I'm trying to do in the best way I know how." Mary's voice trembled as she went on: "I can't pretend that I really wanted to do this today. I still get very angry with you at times but I can't allow bitterness and revenge to ruin my life any longer. I know that what I'm doing brings me peace. And as for buying a house right away, no, that's impossible at the moment, but the place I've got is comfortable enough for the time being. Besides," she added blinking back the tears, "I'm not sure where I really want to settle just yet. Depends on what the girls do in the coming months, I suppose."

John Popescu was very uneasy. Her words disturbed him. He could deal with the old, taciturn, selfish, nagging Mary, but this woman sitting across from him, her blue eyes fixed on his, and two large teardrops trickling down her pale cheeks—he couldn't deal with this woman. She was too much for him. She might conquer him yet. If he hesitated now, he wouldn't have the courage to go ahead with his marriage.

Mary guessed what he was thinking. A faint hope rose within her. She still loved this man. Her eyes met his. "She's really beautiful," John thought. "After all, will Diane Atwood satisfy me any more than Mary could? And there are the girls to consider. It would be so good to be a united family once more." For a split second, both felt that current between them that had been missing for years.

John's fingers relaxed their grip on the pen. Should he give it another try? But then, visions of the ring on Diane's finger, the gnawing conviction he would be in a hole financially if he didn't go through with this marriage, the thought of publicly breaking his engagement—all were more than he could handle. It was too late. He had gone too far already. If only this woman opposite him had decided to change her life a few years ago, it would probably have been a different story. But now she had made her bed and she'd have to lie in it.

Mary saw John's expression harden. Her heart sank as his fingers closed round the pen. A few seconds later it was done. John got up to leave. "Thanks," was all he said, as he brushed past her and out into the warm summer morning.

Some moments later, Mary's lawyer found her staring out the window and into the street beyond, still as a statue and nearly as white. She didn't seem to hear him enter the room. "God bless you, Mrs. Popescu," he said, putting aside his lawyer's tone and manner for a brief moment. "You are a very brave woman." He held out his hand. "Remember, you know my number any time you want advice."

Mary mumbled her thanks as she rose to leave. Ralph McNeally watched her as she exited the office and made her way to her car. "That man's a fool to throw away a woman like that," he muttered to himself. "But then, most men are fools nowadays when it comes to the women." Ralph could speak from experience. Married twice, he knew all about divorce and its consequences.

Mary hurried back home, her heart bursting with a mixture of emotions. She had not made her decision in order to bribe her husband back into her arms. She wouldn't have stooped to that, and of course, those tactics would never have worked. But now the last shred of hope had gone. The man she still loved was determined to go his way, regardless of the hurt he was causing his loved ones. Anger surged within her. She had been generous and what had he done in return? Why, oh why, did she still love John? It was all so unfair. Life had cheated her. God had forsaken her. She had done what was right, but nothing good had come of it.

Two hours dragged by. Engulfed in self pity, Mary could not pray. She knew she was fast sliding back into the woman who had walked out on her husband, deprived her children of the warmth of love when they most needed it, and broken her mother's heart. Fear gripped her. She could bear to lose John. She had faced that for months now. But God? She could not, would not let *Him* go. Yet He wouldn't stay in a heart filled with bitterness. She knew that.

Her recent decision had not been some sort of bargain with the Almighty. It had simply been unconditional obedience to the Voice of her new Master. And hadn't He done so much more for her? His obedience had taken Him to the cross. Could hers take her anywhere else?

When Rachel came in for supper that evening, she was amazed to find her mother humming to herself as she washed the lettuce and cut up the tomatoes.

"Good news, Mom?" she asked, helping herself to a drink of juice from the refrigerator.

Mary dried her hands. She came over to her daughter and drew her into her arms. "Maybe not the kind of news you want to hear," she whispered in her ear, "but I feel at peace, completely at peace at last." Then she told Rachel all that had happened in a low, tremulous voice.

The girl pulled away from her and almost shouted, "You're a fool Mom. You've made it easy for Dad, so easy. And what for? So you could get peace of some sort? And what about me? About Ramona?" Rachel's voice was bitter and her words cut into her mother like a knife.

"For goodness' sake, Rachel," Mary began angrily, "can't you stop being so selfish and see that...." She stopped suddenly and fled from the room. She clenched her fists as she threw herself on her knees by her bed. This was not the way to deal with Rachel. She knew the girl would eventually see that she had been right, but it would take time and a lot of real consistent Christian living in front of her. But for just now it was hard to take. She wanted at least one human being to understand her, to tell her she had done right.

Mary wept her heart out that night, regardless of the minutes ticking by on the clock by her bed. She was only conscious that she was no longer a solitary, bitter woman with dried up affections and wasted emotions. She had found Someone at last Who delighted to pour out His love in such torrents upon her that she could do little else but weep in relief and in quiet, unremitting joy.

Her tears made a large, damp patch on the floral comforter, but Mary didn't care any more how much she cried. "Oh God," she began, "I'm new to all this. I can't understand what's happening to me. All I know is that I've done Your will and feel Your healing touch on my life. Please do the same for my family. Please heal my girls. They're hurting badly. Please help them to find Your forgiveness and peace as I have done. Their wounds are deep and are still bleeding, but Your Word says that You came to heal the brokenhearted. That's us dear Lord—the Popescu family—me, Rachel, Ramona, Esther, John—that's us!"

As the sun set behind the steeple of St. Jude's, just a block from her apartment, and the shadows lengthened in her little bedroom, Mary finally straightened her aching back and cramped legs. Her face was radiant. She felt full of love for Rachel downstairs, bitter and oh so unhappy, for Ramona, trying in vain to forget her sorrow, for Esther, smothered by her new life and all it was bringing, and for John, poor John. She was aware that he, too, knew the way to God but was not taking it. It was too costly. Something told her that it would eventually cost him far more to go on in his own way so she prayed for him, and yes, even for Diane Atwood, though that was a lot harder. Rising from her knees, she told God honestly that it would take some time to really love that woman, but some day she felt she would, she really would.

Chapter Thirty-Three

Enter Gabby

Rachel and Esther scanned the passengers as one by one they made their way through the automatic doors, luggage piled high on their buggies. Esther remembered when she had come through those same doors, travel-stained but eager-eyed, frantically searching the waiting crowd for a welcoming smile reserved just for her, and a placard with her name printed in bold, black letters.

Ron had wanted to come with the girls, but Esther had thought it wiser to introduce him later. She had even hidden the ring in her pocket; she didn't want that to be the first thing that caught her sister's quick eye.

"What does she look like?" Rachel queried.

"A little taller than I am but thinner, at least, thinner than I am now," and Esther grinned. She had gained about twenty pounds over the past ten months, but it suited her, though she would never admit it. "Look, there she is; over there. She hasn't seen us yet."

Rachel followed the direction of her cousin's pointed finger. There, pushing a cart on which was perched one shabby brown suitcase, was a young girl about her own age, with a mop of very unruly light brown hair, dressed in well-worn blue jeans and a pale pink T shirt. The sleeves of a green, corduroy jacket that had seen better days were tied around her slim waist. Her eyes darted from face to face as she stood still for a moment, searching the waiting crowd for the face she knew so well. Finally, with a shout that startled those standing nearby, she gave the cart a huge shove and ran up to where the girls were waiting.

"Estera!" she cried, abandoning the buggy and throwing herself at her sister with a vigor that nearly knocked the older girl off her feet.

"Gabby!" was all Esther could get out. Her voice choked as she stroked the disheveled brown head pressed against her cheek. The younger girl was also crying.

Rachel also sniffed and wiped her eyes. "Welcome to the USA," she told her cousin, as she held out a bouquet of yellow and white roses.

"Yes, Gabby, this is your cousin Rachel," said Esther, remembering her manners. "And Rachel; this is my very own sister, Gabriella Maria Popescu."

"Hi," said Rachel awkwardly. Gabby had buried her nose in the flowers and was inhaling their perfume. She lifted her eyes and fixed them on her new-found cousin for a moment or two. Esther held her breath. Her sister had the habit of sizing up a newcomer in the twinkling of an eye and showing her like or dislike very decidedly. Then she breathed a sigh of relief. The two cousins were smiling and shaking hands. It seemed that Gabby sensed a kindred spirit in the dark, sallow-skinned girl in front of her, who looked much more Romanian than she did.

Gabby didn't appear to be as stunned as she had been those ten months ago, Esther thought, as they made their way to the car. The lights everywhere fascinated her sister as they drove home to Velours. From a world of darkness she had, in a brief twenty-four hours been propelled into an illuminated world of extraordinary color.

It was only when they were alone together that the weary traveler showed her fatigue. She flopped down exhausted on the bed her uncle and Jean had brought into Esther's room for her. It would only be for a few weeks, Esther explained. After the wedding they would both go to their aunt's.

Esther was relieved that, so far, Gabby had made no comment about any change she might have observed in her and hoped that the transformation everyone talked about might only be in their imagination. If Gabby hadn't mentioned it, it mustn't be very obvious, for she was as open as a book. Perhaps Esther had forgotten that she had deliberately tied her hair back in the old way and dressed in very ordinary clothes that evening. And then, there had been no mention so far of Ron or of her role as a budding Christian singer.

"How was the journey? I mean, did everything go smoothly in Poland?" the older girl asked anxiously as she slipped into her pajamas.

"Yes, it did." Gabby was glad to be able to speak in Romanian once more. "But if it hadn't been for Alina Topov, the biology teacher at school, it would have been nearly impossible to get here."

"Alina? Yes, I remember her," Esther said dreamily. She could visualize the short, chubby woman of about forty-five whose brother was a pastor; for years she had run a tight rope between the Evangelicals and the Communists with amazing dexterity. Now, it seems, she had dared to come to Gabby's rescue. Once in Poland, Alina had helped the girl contact the American Embassy just in case of trouble at the airport, though all the papers had been intact. She had even gone with Gabby to buy a ticket to the States. She had taken a risk in doing this, but had whispered as she waved the young girl off at the airport in Warsaw that she wanted to do at least one thing for God to make up for all her compromises.

Esther listened intently as Gabby told of those last weeks in Romania. "Did you see *him* again?" she asked somewhat fearfully.

Gabby looked at her sister. She really didn't want to speak about it but she couldn't avoid it now. "Yes," she admitted reluctantly, "he waylaid me coming home from school and asked if I had sent you his address. I said yes, for I had, only you'll never get it." She gave a short laugh and went on: "He warned me again that you'd better contact him before September or else, and he never finished his sentence. But let's not talk about that any more. I'm here with you at last, Estera, and that's what matters."

Gabby gave a long yawn as she fished out her heavy cotton nightdress from her suitcase. "Oh Gabby, that's far too warm for weather like this," her sister remonstrated.

"It's all I've got."

"Well, there're plenty in the dresser over there. See?"

Gabby's eyes widened as she opened a drawer. "What an assortment!" she exclaimed. "Let's see, which shall I choose—this dainty pink nightdress with frills all over? Oh no, that's too grand for a peasant girl like me. These blue pajamas with the teddy-bears all over them? Yes, they'll suit me just fine."

Gabby turned and caught her sister's reflection in the mirror opposite. "Oh but you're more beautiful than ever, Esther," she exclaimed as she gave her sister a long, goodnight kiss and then climbed in between the soft pale blue sheets. "What have they done to you here?"

Esther said nothing. There was time enough to explain. For one night she would enjoy Gabby's love and trust. That was enough to go to sleep on.

The next morning Gabby was up at daybreak and had begun to unpack. She tried to work as noiselessly as possible, aware that the form in the bed by the window had not yet stirred. As she tiptoed towards the closet she did not see Esther open her eyes. Pushing back the sliding doors, she started back in astonishment and whistled softly to herself. Why, here were enough clothes to fit out at least a dozen girls back home! Thinking her sister still asleep, she reached for the golden gown which immediately caught her eye; she stole a fleeting glance at the bed by the window, then took it from its hanger and slipped it on with smothered expressions of amazement and amusement, as she paraded in front of the full length mirror.

Conscious of eyes upon her, she started, blushed, and then waltzing round the room exclaimed, "Oh, if Aunt Ana could only see me now, Estera, in this long, slinky outfit. What do I look like?"

In spite of her initial annoyance at the young girl's nerve in putting on her clothes without permission, Esther smiled indulgently. "Like a fish out of water," she replied thoughtlessly. She bit her lip as soon as the words were out. They sounded so patronizing; Esther remembered that if Gabby hated anything it was when she put on her big sister air with her.

Gabby knew the older girl was right, of course. She was only too aware that the dress did not go well with her short, bobbed hair, girlish face, and angular figure. She had always felt inferior to her beautiful sister, not believing those who told her that in five or ten years' time she would also be considered an extremely attractive young woman. She did not realize that her very striking personality, sparkling eyes, radiant smile, and fair, clear skin, went a long way to make up for features that were somewhat irregular, or a form that had not yet quite filled out. To her, Esther had always seemed the perfection of beauty, culture, talent, and saintliness. But this dress did not seem like her sister in the least.

So when she had heard Esther's rather thoughtless reply, she wheeled round and faced her, eyes blazing. "Once upon a time you, too, would have looked like a fish out of water in this," and she held the skirt of the offending garment away from her in disgust.

Esther cringed. "Gabby, I hardly ever wear that dress," she began.

"But you have worn it, at least once?"

"Yes. I was asked to sing at a very large concert in the center of the city some weeks ago and they, well, they sort of made me wear that the second night."

"How could anyone make you wear *that,* especially in America?" Gabby's words cut like a knife. "Now back home I could imagine that happening, but here? I thought we were in the land of the free?"

Esther had swung her legs out of bed and sat facing her sister. "Oh come, Gabby, I don't mean that anyone forced me at gunpoint or threatened imprisonment if I didn't wear it, but it was hinted that if I wanted to continue to perform I would have loosen up a bit and be more stylish."

"Well, you certainly loosened up all right," muttered Gabby, hanging the offending article back in the closet and getting out the long white gown Esther had also worn that weekend.

"Now that's something I could picture you in," and the girl nodded in approval. "But what clothes you have! I suppose they're also for your performances. But not all these pant suits and jeans and tops! Now who on earth persuaded you to wear trousers? No one could in Romania! And look at your shoes! Let's see: one, two, three. . . . There are fourteen pairs at least not counting your boots. And handbags—one for every two pair of shoes to be exact. Wow! You certainly have done well for yourself in nine or ten months!"

Esther did not appreciate her sister's tone and told her so. But Gabby once started, was very hard to stop. "But you can't have bought all those beautiful clothes just for performances, Esther. And wherever did you get the money from to buy them? Maybe there's a prince charming somewhere who's come for his little Romanian Cinderella? Oh, I forgot, republics don't produce princes. But you're turning as red as a beet! You *have* got someone!"

It had to come out sometime, thought Esther. "Yes, I have," she admitted holding out her hand. She had put on her ring as soon as Gabby was asleep but had kept it hidden while they had been talking.

Gabby's eyes sparkled. Taking Esther's hand in hers, she examined the diamond carefully. "How gorgeous!" she exclaimed excitedly. She leaned over and gave her sister a resounding smack on the cheek. "So you didn't wait for your next of kin to give her OK before you put on the ring?" Gabby spoke half in fun and half in earnest.

"No, Gabby, I didn't, but I still want your approval. Ron is taking you and me out for a meal tonight. You'll be able to give your verdict then."

"And if I disapprove, you'll break it off? But you can't. Once engaged you're as good as married."

"Not in America," Esther told her. "But anyway, I'm sure you'll like him. You couldn't help but like him."

"Oh couldn't I though?" retorted the girl as she slipped on her shoes. "But my opinion won't count much one way or another. Anyway, I'm dying to see your prince." Gabby clapped her hands in anticipation. "Is he tall, dark, and handsome? He must have something about him to do what no Romanian boy has ever succeeded in doing—winning the fair lady's hand."

Esther pressed her hand to her forehead and sighed. Something about Gabby's chatter annoyed her. The younger girl's face fell. "Not used to me, yet, are you, Estera? Well, I'll leave you in peace and quiet," and she ran out the door, slamming it behind her. Esther sighed again. First morning in America, and her stormy sister had already disturbed the peace!

Gabby seemed restless all day. First she explored every nook and cranny of the backyard. Like Esther, she loved the wide expanse of lawn and trees. She only saw her uncle for a few moments before he went off to work. "She's not a patch on her sister," John thought as he got in the car, "but she looks like a sharp little thing and has a smile just like Andrei's."

Gabby ate a huge breakfast. She had to sample nearly everything in the fridge—orange juice, grapefruit, sausage, egg, bacon. And then to top it all, she wanted to try out the cereals—Raisin Bran, Cornflakes, and Rice Crispies.

She leaned back and patted her stomach as she drained her second cup of strong coffee. "That's a breakfast for a king, Estera. No wonder you've gained weight though I must say you don't seem to eat that much."

"No, I'm on a low fat diet," her sister told her. "I won't get into my dresses if I go on like I am and I certainly can't afford to buy new ones all the time."

Gabby raised her eyebrows but said nothing as she set out to explore. "What large TV's!" she called back to Esther from the living-room. "I can't wait to try out all those videos and cassettes—nearly all the classics are here. I can't think why on earth you bothered with boys when you had all this to keep you occupied."

Esther put away the last dirty plate in the dishwasher and followed her sister into the den. She smiled in spite of herself. "Please don't put boys in the plural Gabby. That's not accurate. There's only Ron in my life and he's not exactly a boy. But as for all this," and the diamond ring sparkled as she waved her dainty hand in the direction of the TV, "the novelty of all these things will wear off in time; you wait and see."

"In time," agreed Gabby, but added as she caught sight of her uncle's library, "maybe in ten years when I've listened to all the tapes, seen all the videos, gotten fed up with all the TV shows, and maybe met my very own Prince Charming." She grabbed a book as she spoke and buried herself in the recliner.

"Wait, you can put your feet up like this," and Esther showed her how to push the lever. Gabby leaned back and let out a long sigh. "What bliss! No wonder it's spoiled you silly."

Esther frowned and bit her lip. "You haven't finished unpacking," she reminded her as she left the room. Gabby groaned and then shouted after her sister's retreating figure, "I'll be up in half an hour when I've scanned this one book, I promise."

Esther was glad Rachel was there to keep her sister occupied. Her cousin hadn't appeared yet but would be down soon. She was exhausted and Gabby had wakened her so early with all her antics she had not had her usual beauty sleep. Her constant evening performances had turned her into a night bird. She felt annoyed with her sister's remarks on her clothes and annoyed with herself for feeling annoyed.

She was relieved when her aunt arrived later that morning to take the girls out shopping. They had stopped at McDonald's for lunch. Gabby had consumed two Big Macs and a large milk shake, Rachel had announced with a grin when they had come home late that afternoon. Esther had given her sister some money to spend and wondered if her first shopping spree would be anything like hers. She was not surprised when the girl returned with only three pairs of jeans and some tops and sweaters. "I can wear your clothes for Sundays," she had announced.

Esther frowned. "They don't fit you well or suit you. You should get your own. I gave you enough money."

"I'm eating so much I'll soon fit into your clothes," her sister said mischievously, then her face changed as she added, "Besides, I'm not going to spend all that on clothes when Aunt Ana is nearly starving back home." Gabby's voice was firm and there was a glint in her green-grey eyes. "You've got enough for both of us, and more."

Esther was about to reply when Rachel spoke up. "I can't understand all you two are saying when you speak in Romanian like that but I can guess. And, Esther, can't you remember what you were like ten months ago? You would spend hardly anything for the very same reason."

Something in Rachel's tone made Esther bite her lip. Yes, she did remember all too well. But she had moderated, she reasoned. She had been far too extreme, and Gabby was too. As for Aunt Ana, she would want them both to be happy and enjoy themselves. So she only smiled rather patronizingly at her cousin and buried herself in a book.

Gabby decided to take a dip in the pool before supper. She was an excellent swimmer, and it was only when Rachel warned her that she would be burned to cinders if she stayed in the hot sun any longer, that she could be persuaded to leave the pool.

That evening Ron arrived and was introduced to a scarlet faced Gabriella Maria Popescu. The sun had caught her fair skin and Esther had forgotten to warn her to wear some sun screen. Ron couldn't help staring as the girl came down the steps to meet him. She had raided the closet on the sly but decided that only the Romanian gold blouse and garage sale black skirt would really suit her. "It's Esther," Ron told himself, "and yet it isn't." How he wished the girl had not worn those very same clothes. It gave him a nostalgic feeling that wouldn't go away.

"You veree handsome," Gabby pronounced in her broken English. "You and my seester, veree good pair."

Ron grinned and thanked her for the compliment but he felt a bit uneasy under her steady scrutiny. He reddened but met her gaze and held it. It was her turn to blush and lower her eyes.

Gabby said little that evening. But she could understand most of what was said as could be seen by the change of mood on her expressive face. Ron studied it during the meal. She was a fascinating child, for child he considered her. She appeared very immature beside her older sister. No, she was not nearly as beautiful, not yet at any rate, but it seemed as if life were brimming up inside the girl, overflowing to those around. Once she could talk fluently, they would have some wonderful discussions, he predicted, and arguments, too, he reckoned.

Gabby did more than justice to the three course meal. Esther noticed that she didn't seem to react as she had done to the waste of food all around her. Was her sister more insensitive than she had been?

It was over her second dish of ice cream that Gabby popped the question Esther had been half expecting all evening: "Ron, you Chreestian?" she asked suddenly.

Ron looked startled; her words seemed to hit him like a bullet. Esther had asked that same question, but much more gently and diplomatically. Of course, the girl's limited English made everything seem abrupt, he was aware of that, but there seemed such a wealth of hidden purpose behind those three words that it threw him completely off balance.

"Why yes, Gabby, I think so," he stammered. "I mean, I believe in God; I go to church."

"But you Chreestian like Estera?"

Ron breathed easier. "No, of course not," he replied without hesitation. "After all, who is a 'Chreestian' like Estera? But I hope with her help to be one some day."

Gabby shook her head and replied, "But some day ees not today, Ron." Her knife and fork clattered to the table as she held both hands parallel to each other. "See, you thees hand, Estera that hand," pointing in turn to both hands. "Now eef you married," and she intertwined both thumbs together as she spoke, "and you together always, and you down heer," she lowered the left hand, "and Estera up heer," and she raised the right hand, "then what ees happening?" and she peered at both her companions intently.

As the question was directed to Ron, he answered quietly, "I drag her down, or she lifts me up?"

"Depends who more strong what happens, Ron." And she sat back, folding her arms as if to say, "And that settles it."

The illustration had been so simple and yet so forceful that no one spoke for a while. Then it was Ron's turn to act as questioner. "What about you, Gabby, are you a Christian?"

For just a moment the girl was caught off guard. She had not been expecting Ron to turn questioner. But she collected herself in an instant.

"No, Ron, I not Chreestian." It was spoken simply, and directly.

Esther turned abruptly to her sister. "Come on, Gabby, that's not true," she remonstrated. "You are a Christian."

"No, Estera. I not Chreestian. I not explain in Eenglish."

"Go ahead and speak in Romanian," suggested Ron. "Esther will interpret."

"Estera," the girl began in her native tongue, "tell Ron that maybe I might be called an American Christian but I am definitely not a Romanian one."

Esther interpreted for Ron. He chuckled in spite of his nervousness. They had embarked on a touchy subject, one he always tried to avoid for he felt that it was the only thing that could divide him from his sweetheart.

"I saw Father die," Gabby's voice was low and sad. Ron saw tears in her eyes as she went on: "He gave his whole life for God's work and what happened? We lost a father when we most needed him, and mother too, for that matter. But Father's death was because he was a Christian, a Romanian one," she added significantly. "How can I be his type of Christian when I'm not prepared to die young for my faith? Maybe some day I will be ready. Then I'll prove that I am a real Christian. Now you, Estera, I know you *were* ready. That's why I don't want you to become an American Christian."

Ron stared at the girl as Esther translated her words for him. She was so direct. But seemingly oblivious of the effect she was having, Gabby continued earnestly: "Now, Estera, tell Ron I like him very much." Ron inclined his head to show his thanks for this kind statement. "But," and her keen eyes darted from Ron to Esther as she spoke in English once more, "if you marree heem, you be an American Chreestian." Then, seeing the consternation on her sister's face, she added cheerfully, "But that ees no problem Estera. You already an American Chreestian, I theenk. But you know, if you so deeferent in ten months, what you be in ten years?"

Ron could see by Esther's face that she was very upset. "Now look here, young lady," he exploded, "you stay out of our affairs. Here you are, not even twenty-four hours in our country and you're preaching at both of us. How can you know what an American Christian really is? Wait till you've been here a while before you give your verdict."

Gabby turned a very innocent face towards Ron and said very meekly, "You right, Ron. I only heer very leetle. I wait one week, then I tell you if I right or not."

"One week," spluttered Ron, now thoroughly roused. "You need years before you can judge a culture correctly, or a religion."

Gabby said nothing more, but the evening had already been spoiled as far as Ron was concerned and he sensed Esther felt the same. Rising, he suggested it was time to go home. The sisters said little to each other that night, but the older girl did a lot of thinking. One day, and Gabby had put the fat into the fire. What would she do tomorrow, and the next day, and the next?

Saturday morning, Gabby was up bright and early as usual. When Jean rang the doorbell at eight, it was she who answered it.

"And who are you, young lady?" Jean asked, peering at the tousle-headed figure in the shabby grey dressing-gown.

"Me Estera's seester. And you?"

"Me cleaning lady," Jean replied, mimicking the girl with amazing success.

Gabby stared in surprise then her face broke into one of her most captivating smiles. "You very funny lady," she exclaimed.

"And you are not a bit like your sister!" was Jean's comment as she laid down her bag on the kitchen table.

"No?" Gabby's voice sounded pitiful.

"Don't worry. I wouldn't want you to be like her."

"Not like Estera?"

"No. One of her is enough in the house. Oh, she's wonderful I'm sure, but too perfect. Scares the daylights out of me."

Gabby had no idea what that last statement meant but knew it was not flattering to Esther. And she couldn't help but agree with this strange little woman that her sister was, at times, too unbearably perfect.

After lunch, as they got ready for the concert in Louisville, Gabby told her that the cleaning lady was a real dear. The older girl could not believe her ears. "She and I don't hit it off, Gabby."

"I know. She as much as said so. But do you know, she's got an invalid husband and a grown son who's got the mentality of a five year old? That's enough to make anyone a bit sharp at times."

Esther nearly let the dress she was holding drop to the floor. She shook her head in amazement. "Wow, you've learned more from Jean in one morning than I've gotten out of her in nine or ten months! How do you do it?"

"I don't do anything," Gabby said with a slight smile. "I'm just me and somehow people like to talk to me—tell me all their troubles. Maybe it's because I've had so many of my own. But then you have too, even more than I've had, so it can't be that."

Esther said nothing for there was no time left for further conversation. But she couldn't help asking herself as she slipped on the new blue dress she had bought the previous week, what did her gangly, over-talkative, sometimes annoyingly blunt little sister have that she didn't that made folks open up to her like they did?

Half an hour later, Esther was introducing Gabby to Len who usually accompanied her to her concerts as he was by now her accepted accompanist. Ron and she, now more sure of their relationship with each other, had learned to at least tolerate the flamboyant youth pastor, if not really like him. They had hoped the younger girl would have been too tired to think of going that evening, but Gabby was game for anything. Esther feared how she and Len would get on. If she had had reserves about him, what would her sister's attitude be?

But to her great surprise, Gabby was all sugar. She asked Len questions in her quaint English all the way to the concert, or nearly all the way—innocent questions they seemed to Len—all about religious life in America. He soon took the bait and boasted of all the music he had composed, of all the concerts he had played at; he told her the titles of the best religious contemporary hits and what Esther was learning to sing. And on and on it went. Before they had reached their destination, Gabby had acquired a much better idea of at least one brand of American Christianity than many have in a lifetime. Ron and Esther were in the front, but overheard most of the conversation. They soon gathered the young girl's clever game and groaned inwardly, exchanging significant glances from time to time.

At the concert, Ron kept a close eye on the young girl by his side. His father had also come to hear Esther and had eyes for no one else. Gabby's gaze, too, was riveted on the stage. Ron saw the wonder in her eyes when her sister began to sing. Admiration, amazement, fear, and maybe just a little jealousy, were all evident on her expressive face. Not quite as alluring in her blue dress as she had been in her gold one, Esther was perhaps more truly beautiful. And she was learning how to modulate her voice until she seemed to have a pulse on every emotion which vibrated in those listening. Len had arranged for her to have voice lessons once a week though Ron didn't think she needed them. But Esther knew she had room for improvement and had agreed. She was thinking of majoring in music when she went back to college, though sometimes she even debated if she really would go back to school as she could quite easily make singing a full-time career. But Ron had told her that she badly needed a degree. If her voice failed for some reason or other in the future, she would have nothing to fall back on. If the truth were known, his real reason was that he did not want Esther to perform without his being close by and if he were stuck in law school for another three years, that would not be possible.

Gabby was unusually quiet all the way home. Of course, she was trying to cope with culture shock and all that went with it, but it was her own sister that puzzled her the most. It really did seem that Esther was enjoying life to the full. She was more outgoing, more vivacious, more humorous than she had been in the old days. It was obvious that Ron idolized her, her fans adored her, and her uncle spoiled her. She was growing more beautiful every day or so it seemed to those who loved her best. And her fame as a singer was spreading.

Who really was this beautiful woman who had captivated her audience that evening, the young girl asked herself as she stared out into the darkness? Sometimes she imagined that they were both back in Romania, walking hand in hand through the park, sharing their secrets, their hopes, and their troubles. But that night when the light had been switched off and the only sound was the ticking of the clock and the chirping of the crickets in the garden below, it seemed that the sleeping form in the bed next to her was a stranger, and when she would try to stretch out and touch her beautiful sister, she would melt into thin air, laughing tauntingly as she did so as if saying, "Why, Gabby, you can't catch me now. I'm in another world from you—a wonderful world. Some day, maybe you'll discover this new freedom too."

Chapter Thirty-Four

Gabby Speaks Her Mind

That Sunday, Gabby had gone with Ron and her sister to Pine Grove Evangelical Church and then to lunch afterwards at a nearby restaurant. She had refused to comment on the service and had been much quieter than usual. But she had done justice to the elegant buffet and seemed to enjoy every bite.

Back in their room that afternoon, the girls were relaxing on their beds, each with her favorite book.

"I'm so full, Esther," Gabby had remarked stretching full length and patting her abdomen.

"Well, that's your own fault, Gabby," her sister sounded just a little reproachful. "You didn't need to get all those refills, you know."

"Didn't I? But it was all paid for."

"Yes it was. And you were more than welcome. But I just don't quite understand." Esther hesitated not wanting to hurt her sister unnecessarily.

"What don't you understand?"

"Well, you seemed so careful about not spending money on clothes when Aunt Ana is nearly starving back home, yet you didn't bat an eye at all the waste in that restaurant today. I remember my first experience in a buffet. I was nearly sick and had to go outside."

Esther had tried not to sound self-righteous but it was no good. Gabby sprung up into a sitting position, eyes blazing and was beginning to retort angrily when she bit her lip, slid back down in the bed and muttered, "It's no use explaining. You won't understand."

"Try me." Esther's voice was encouraging. She half regretted that she had begun the subject in the first place.

"Well," Gabby sat up again, "it seems a bit useless making myself sick over what I can't help but what I can help—why that's different."

"Meaning?"

"Meaning that when Ron's paid for my lunch, I might as well make the most of it. Moaning and groaning about extravagance won't put more money for my Romanian friends back in my pocket. But if denying myself an extra dress or jacket will give me a few dollars to put by for them, well, that's different."

Esther was silent. She was relieved to discover that her sister was not as insensitive as she had imagined but annoyed that her reasoning somehow made her feel very uncomfortable.

"Well, Gabby, I don't think denying yourself a dress or jacket is really much denial after all. Clothes don't mean much to you, but books now, or. . . ."

"Stop it. I get the message." Gabby reddened and turned her face to the wall. "I suppose only time will tell how all this luxurious living will affect me," and she turned to her book once more. Esther closed her eyes. She seemed to be always arguing with her sister these days. It hadn't been like that at home in Romania. They had always gotten on so well together even though they were very different.

In the following days, Rachel and her newfound cousin became close friends. Gabby's quaint English never failed to bring a smile to her rather sullen features. "I don't understand how you can read English so fast when you have difficulty speaking it, Gabby," she commented one day when her cousin had been reading solidly for several hours in her favorite seat by the window.

"Oh Rachel, you know eet more eesy to reed than talk," Gabby replied, reddening.

"That's true," agreed Rachel laughing, "but there's more than the normal gap between your reading and speaking ability. But then you're not normal in any way Gabby."

Rachel could not have paid the girl a truer compliment. She grinned and then buried herself once more in her book. Rachel shook her head as she went into the kitchen to make supper. Gabby would wear her eyes out in no time reading as she did. But it was better than watching TV. It rather wearied her when her cousin flipped from channel to channel making comments to herself in Romanian as she did so. Rachel was not a TV lover and it bothered her to see Gabby's fascination with the "box." More than once she had literally dragged her away from the screen. "It's not good for your eyes," Rachel would tell her cousin, "or for your morals either," she added once.

Gabby flared up instantly, "Then why you have eet in house?" she asked defiantly.

"*I* don't have it," Rachel told her. "If it were up to *me*, I'd put it in the dumpster tomorrow."

Gabby looked at her, wide-eyed, and said nothing, but after that she did modify her TV viewing considerably. There were so many other things to grab her attention. She was fascinated with garage sales and brought home a bag full of trinkets that made her sister groan. "It's clothes you need, Gabby, not all that junk."

"It's not junk. I'm going to give them as presents to all my friends in Ploiesti. Why, Estera, they're so pretty. Look at that picture frame, and that little figurine. And these flowers look like real," and she waved an artistic looking bouquet of artificial roses in the older girl's face. "And besides, I only gave four dollars for everything."

Esther sighed. She was so grateful that her sister had Rachel as her constant companion. It was she who taught Gabby to play Scrabble, who discovered she was an amateur artist, and above all, who found out they had one passion in common—they both adored poetry. Rachel would read to Gabby from one of her poetry books and then wait in amused silence as her cousin tried frantically to translate each stanza into Romanian verse. Rachel often marveled at her comprehension of English when her progress in speaking it seemed so unusually slow.

And while the two cousins were daily getting to know each other better, Esther was always busy—practicing her songs, writing to her fans, sometimes singing a solo in some church in the area on a Sunday, sometimes performing at a concert. And, of course, there were constant dinner dates with Ron whenever she was free. Life was hectic but she liked it that way. It gave little time for any disquieting thoughts that Gabby's coming had brought. She tried not to show her hurt when it became obvious that her sister seemed to prefer an evening with Rachel rather than accompanying her to one of her concerts.

Ramona came on the scene about a week after Gabby's arrival. She had been away once more with her friend Kelly to the beach. She was civil enough to her younger cousin, but paid little attention to her. She was secretly glad she was not a beauty like her sister. Sometimes she could hardly stand seeing that flashing ring on Esther's hand or the look of adoration on Ron's face. She knew in the bottom of her heart that he could never have loved her like that and it made her sad as well as jealous.

Gabby wondered how Esther could have ever thought her cousin pretty but the Ramona she was seeing was a far cry from the Ramona of ten months previous. She was dieting drastically and was nearly as slim as Esther now. But her new figure did not suit her, as Rachel had told her one day. She was no longer the good-natured, shapely girl who had met Esther when she had first arrived in America. To be more in fashion, she had frizzed her flyaway curls which, her family thought, did not suit her in the least. And though her father rejoiced that Norman was no longer in the picture, he was not sure he liked his replacement much better. He had never dreamed that Claude Iliescu would ever succeed with his daughter, but his persistence over the years had at last seemed to be finally paying off. For several weeks now, Claude had taken Ramona out each weekend.

Esther shook her head privately and thought her cousin had gone mad, but Mary Popescu knew better. She sensed that the persistent young Romanian, who could certainly not boast of a handsome face or cultured air, was giving the girl what she was needing most—love, for it was obvious that he simply adored Ramona and had done so for some years. To everyone's amazement it seemed as the days wore on, that the girl was gradually gaining back some of her bloom. What no one but her few close friends knew was that Claude had insisted on her getting off the drugs she had been taking ever since her week in Florida with Norman. He had, in a sense, been her lifesaver. She was only too aware of all she owed her new boyfriend. He was quick to capitalize on Ramona's gratitude and soon it was obvious to everyone that the girl who had spurned his attentions for so long was now becoming very dependent on the gawky youth with the strange, glittering eyes and bold smile.

It seemed that only Ramona saw some good in Claude. Gabby took to him no more than her sister had done. Even Jean, who hardly knew him, had formed a negative opinion of the young man. "He's not good enough for Ramona," she confided in Gabby as they watched the two drive off together. It was Gabby's second Saturday in America and she had just made Jean a mid-morning cup of tea. "Ever since your sister grabbed Ron for herself, Ramona's not been the same," she added, draining her cup and placing it in the sink.

"My seester grabbed Ron?" Gabby repeated. "I don't theenk so. That's not what Estera said."

"Of course not. She wouldn't admit to that. And I don't mean she literally grabbed him. But there're other ways of getting hold of young men, Gabby. Maybe you're too naïve to know about all that yet. Oh I don't mean Esther did anything terrible. She's too saintly for that. But she acted so vulnerable, you know. And that together with her face and figure did the trick. But I can't stay chattering to you all day. I've got to clean your uncle's bedroom," and she stalked off, dust mop in hand, leaving a rather disconsolate girl behind her. Not many minutes later, Gabby heard a loud cry and ran upstairs to find Jean standing in the hallway, face ashen, wringing her hands and exclaiming, "I've done it now. What will Mr. John say? He'll think I did it on purpose."

"What will I think you did on purpose, Jean?" asked John, running up the stairs.

Jean said nothing but led the way into the bedroom. Gabby followed with Esther close at her heels. Pointing to a pile of shattered glass on the floor by the dresser, Jean muttered, "I was dusting as usual, but the cloth caught that picture of the lady on your dresser and broke it."

For a brief moment, John revealed the dismay he felt inside. There, lying by itself on the dresser, was the picture of a very beautiful woman whose large, soulful eyes stared up at him. It seemed that she was bidding him a final farewell. Only Esther guessed what might be flitting through his mind at that moment.

"It's OK, Jean. Accidents will happen," John told the distraught woman, as he took the picture in his hands.

"Why, that's mother," Gabby exclaimed as she caught sight of the beloved face. John smiled grimly.

"Yes, that's your mother, all right. And that's your father," and he pointed to a much smaller likeness of his brother on top of the bookcase by the window. "Actually, I've been meaning to ask you girls," he turned to his nieces as he spoke. "Do you have a large picture of your mom? If not, maybe you'd like this?"

His hand trembled as he held out the picture. Esther realized the emotion that lay behind his words. "Yes, Uncle, we'd love it. I've several small photos of her but not a large one like that. It got destroyed in the earthquake."

"Then take it. I'm glad it'll find a good home. So you see, Jean, you've really done the girls a service by breaking that picture," John said, turning to the little woman who was still too upset to speak. She had prided herself that she had hardly ever broken anything in all her years as cleaning lady. Her face brightened; she was relieved that the incident had ended so happily.

"But why did you say I might think you did it on purpose, Jean?" John wanted to know as the girls closed their bedroom door behind them. Jean dropped her eyes as she muttered, "Well, I once made a comment about that picture to Esther that you wouldn't have liked and I thought she might have told you."

"Esther's not a tell-tale," John told her sharply. He resented the woman's attitude to his favorite niece. "But let's not talk any more about this. Like I said, it's turned out all for the best."

"What was all that about, Esther?" Gabby asked, as her sister placed the picture on their dresser and they stared at it lovingly together.

Esther put her arms around her and whispered softly, "Uncle was in love with our mother, Gabby, but she preferred Dad. He was heart-broken and has never fully gotten over it. In fact, I think it caused some real problems in his first marriage."

The girl's eyes widened. "In love with Mother? Oh Esther, how tragic. And now he's marrying again. Does he love Mrs. Atwood really and truly?"

"I don't know, dear. I surely hope so."

"And is that why Uncle's so very fond of you—because you look like *her?*"

"Maybe," she muttered, brushing a tear from her eyes. There was silence for a few moments and then Esther announced in a matter-of-fact tone, "We'll have to get some glass for this soon, or the dust will ruin it, Gabby,"

"Yes, Esther," replied her sister as she left the room. She wanted to be private for a while for she had a lot to think about. Some minutes later found her wandering in the back yard, lost in a world of her own. John caught a glimpse of the lone figure from his bedroom window and thought how much the girl reminded him of his brother. His eyes roamed from the miniature on the book case to the empty spot on the dressing table. The picture was gone now for good. It was just as well. If ever he were to have a successful marriage, he had to put Sylvia Popescu out of his heart and mind forever.

None of his family had any idea of the turmoil John had gone through that week after he had met Mary at the lawyer's office. He had manfully faced Diane about the true state of his finances—how much he owed on the house and the sizable loan he had taken out to start up his business. He should have told her long before, Diane had told him sharply. This had begun their first, serious quarrel, and no one, not even Ron, knew how near they had come to breaking up. It soon became obvious that his fiancée had thought him much wealthier than he really was. But when he had placed the document Mary had drawn up into her hands, she had been pacified. There would be no need to sell the business or leave his beautiful house, he had assured her, at least not for a few years, and by that time they would have found a solution.

"That woman must still love him an awful lot," Diane had commented to herself, as she thought over Mary's recent magnanimous action. Sometimes she doubted if John loved her any more than he had loved his first wife. But she didn't really care. He had taken good care of his family and he would take good care of her too. And when she gazed into his handsome face and felt his strong arm around her, she realized how necessary he had become to her and knew she could never give him up. She hardly ever saw her son now; another love was filling his heart and mind. Sometimes she felt extremely jealous of the young woman who had wormed her way into the hearts of both the men in her life. Couldn't she be content with just one?

Now, as John watched Gabby pace the lawn, he realized in full what his coming marriage would mean. He would lose his nieces' company and would no longer be able to be their protector in the way he had envisioned. But Mary would watch over them, he knew that. And he had not as yet become really attached to Gabby. But Esther? How he would miss that girl! But what would become of her? She would marry Ron, of course, but would she? Would this God she professed to love so much cause her, like her mother before her, to break another's heart—maybe for life?

That noon, as they ate their ciorba together, John's eye caught the calendar hanging above the counter. "Next week's your big concert, Esther?" he asked, as he reached for another piece of bread. All those years in America had not lessened his appreciation for fresh bread. He refused to buy it from the supermarket, having discovered one little bakery in town whose baked goods satisfied even his fastidious tastes.

"Yes, Uncle, but I'm real nervous about this concert," his niece told him as she took his dish for a refill.

"You, nervous? But you're an old hand at it now, aren't you?"

"This time will be different. It's a sort of competition and I'll not be singing as many Christian songs as I usually do."

"Oh, you'll be fine. You'll outshine everyone else as you always do."

Esther blushed but said nothing. "Isn't that right Gabby?" her uncle asked, turning to his young niece.

"Of course, Uncle."

"I take it you're going with your sister?"

"No Uncle." Gabby's tone was firm.

"No? I am surprised. Not going to give moral support?"

Gabby dropped her eyes and two large teardrops rolled down her thin face. "Crying?" John asked playfully. Esther gave him a warning look, but it was too late. Gabby had had enough. Jumping from her stool, she almost ran from the kitchen.

"I just can't understand your sister, Esther," John remarked, shaking his head.

"She doesn't like all my performing, Uncle." Esther's voice was sad.

"Jealous?"

"Maybe a little."

"Give her time; she'll come round. She has to get used to the new you."

Esther frowned. "I'm not that different really. At least, not inside."

"Sure are outside, my dear, very different!"

"Improved?" Esther couldn't help but ask.

"Depends what you mean. If you mean that you could now go in for the Miss World competition, yes, you're much improved. Couldn't have done that in your old black skirt and shoes that I first saw you in that evening that now seems so very long ago." John's gaze was wistful and it made Esther uncomfortable. Men! They were a real conundrum, she thought, as she cleared away the dishes and went upstairs. She opened the bedroom door and stopped. There, full length on her bed, was Gabby, sobbing her heart out.

Esther went over and laid a comforting hand on the girl's shoulder. Gabby pushed it away and sprang up, eyes blazing, and faced her sister. "I don't want your sympathy, Esther, I want your love. I want the old you back."

Esther's dark eyes flashed fire as she stepped back a pace. "Oh you do, do you? Then you'd better realize once and for all that the old Esther Popescu could never have brought you over here. She had no money, no influence, no friends. Just think about that for a moment, before you start condemning me."

"I'd rather be back with you in Ploiesti than here," sobbed Gabby, collapsing on the bed once more. "Esther," her voice was mournful now and stabbed her sister like a knife, "you don't know how miserable I really am. I hardly see you, and when I do, you're in a different world from me completely. I can't reach you or touch you. And worst of all, I don't feel you love me like you used to."

Esther sat down on the bed beside the distraught girl. She had neglected her sister. She would do better, spend more time with her. Ron would understand. "I'm sorry, Gabby, very. I'll promise to do better in the coming days."

"Do better?" Gabby's voice was sarcastic. "With this big concert coming on, then the wedding, I'm sure you'll do better!" She paused, then changing her tone and grabbing her sister's hand she said imploringly, "Oh please don't go to that wedding, Esther. Think of Aunt Mary."

Esther gazed at her sister for a moment then shook her head. "I can't back out now, Gabby. Aunt Mary doesn't seem to mind that much, and after all Uncle's done for me, it's the least I can do."

"Esther Popescu," and Gabby looked her sister straight in the eyes, "all this fame, this fan mail, this money pouring in, it's ruining you. You're becoming proud and unbearable. And Ron's making you into a glamour girl who thinks more of clothes than of her sister," and Gabby let out a pitiful wail.

Esther's patience was running thin. "I'll listen when you talk about my danger of being too popular, Gabby. I know that's a real problem. But when you bring Ron into it, that's another story. Ron didn't influence me to go to the wedding. He didn't even ask me to go. And he never ever encouraged me to get into this concert business. I decided myself, so there!"

Gabby dropped her eyes, took a gulp, and began, "I don't think you and Ron will be really happy, Esther. He's not the kind of Christian you are, or I should say, you were. I just can't...."

"Stop it, will you," Esther was nearly shouting. "I've had enough. Stop being selfish, Gabby Popescu. Or at least allow for a little selfishness in me, now and then. I'm tired of being held up as the perfect saint. Well, I'm not. You complain about me being too perfect, but when you discover I'm not, then you turn on me. Can't you understand that I was terribly lonely at times when I came here first. Then I got really frightened when you wrote that letter. I realized that I needed a protector. I prayed and God sent Ron just in time. He's an answer to my prayer. And he says I'm an answer to his. Time will prove it. You wait and see!" and she fled the room, not wanting her sister to witness her distress.

Knowing that her uncle had gone out, Esther retreated to the den and collapsed onto the sofa. She felt wretched. She could not allow herself to believe that all Gabby had said was true. She would not believe it. She had asked God to guide her and He had. He had led her to Ron; He had helped her to earn her own money. She had been able to rescue her sister from danger. She stared out the window and watched the fleecy clouds chase each other across the deep blue sky. Why, oh why had Gabby to come and spoil it all?

Ron was away for a few days. He would be back in time for the big concert in Chicago. The thought of Ron and the concert made her feel better. She couldn't do anything suddenly. She couldn't just change everything overnight. And anyway, what on earth should she change? She liked life as she was living it. But maybe she *was* neglecting the others just a little. She would try to be more thoughtful.

Rachel had invited Gabby to spend the afternoon and evening with her and it was late when she made her way to bed. Esther, for once, had taken an early night. The next morning, Gabby woke to find a smiling sister, up much earlier than usual and reading her Bible.

"I'm sorry I've been thoughtless," Esther said, putting her arm round her. Her sister shrugged her shoulders and jumped up. She didn't want to talk about it. She sensed Esther was trying hard to be her old self but it was no good. Esther had changed for good. She'd just have to accept things as they were and make the best of them.

Chapter Thirty-Five

The Two Sides of Esther Popescu

"Margaret?"

"Yes, Dad."

"I want a word with you before you go. You'll be with Esther and Ron a lot this weekend. Maybe you ought to know that I had a phone call from Len last night. He's very worried about your young friend."

Margaret Cripps was getting ready for her trip to Chicago. Esther had asked her to accompany them as Gabby had refused to go. She was to sing to recorded music so Len wouldn't be needed this time.

Margaret put her overnight bag on the bed and followed her father into the living room. "You said Len's worried about Esther?"

"Yes."

"Why, Dad?"

Keith Cripps cleared his throat. He didn't really know how to begin. He loved peace and sensed that his daughter might not like what he was going to say. "Well, he feels that the girl's making a mistake to marry his cousin."

Margaret gave a short laugh. "Of course he'd think that. He'd marry her himself tomorrow."

Her father frowned. He didn't like such aspersions cast on his youth pastor. "Watch what you say, Margaret. I don't think Len's letting any personal feelings get in here. He travels a lot with them, remember, and has come to know Esther pretty well; he feels that she will be unequally yoked if she marries Ron Atwood."

Margaret toyed nervously with her engagement ring. "I know Esther has thought over this a lot, Dad. But she told me Ron had repented for his past life, not that he was as bad as some, but he's not been brought up like she has."

"Repented? That's good." Pastor Cripps' face relaxed a little. Then he frowned again; "But it depends what you mean by repentance. Is he born-again, that's the question?"

Margaret stood up. "Oh Dad, I'm no theologian as you know.

And I'm a bit more liberal than you are in some of my views as you also know. But to me, Ron's a better Christian than his cousin."

She had let it out now and waited apprehensively for her father's reaction. His face was grave as he replied, "Well, you may be right in a way. I mean, he may act more the real gentleman and all that. But if he hasn't really committed his life to Christ then in the final analysis, he won't make it to Heaven, and Len will. Our acceptance with God is based on our faith in Christ alone, you know that."

His daughter shook her head. "All I can say is that it would seem very unfair if Len got into Heaven and his cousin shut out, and God's never unfair, is He?"

"No, Margaret, but His ways are past our ways and may look that way sometimes."

Margaret did not reply. She felt very frustrated at times with her father's orthodoxy. She had become extremely fond of Esther and had been so glad that her friend had found someone to give her a bit of happiness after her life of suffering. Not that she hadn't had a few qualms herself about the whole affair, especially when Esther had recently asked a rather personal question. She could recall the whole conversation very vividly.

"Margaret," her friend had begun, "I want your input on something. It's personal and a bit embarrassing. But you're my closest girlfriend, so here goes." The girl had cleared her throat nervously and gone on, "You're engaged yourself and so have a lot more experience than I do with this sort of thing."

Margaret had smiled at that but motioned for her to continue. "Apart from sex before marriage which I know should never be under any circumstances, what is permissible between a young man and woman who are intending to get married?"

The question had somewhat shocked Margaret at first, not expecting it from the reserved and old-fashioned Esther. But she had gulped a little and then replied, "Well, you're right that premarital sex is totally taboo for Christians. Apart from that, well, all I can say is that I'm glad my fiancé and I aren't together much. We couldn't take it."

Her friend had looked at her for a moment. "So it's a question of how close a couple can get without overstepping God's moral law, right?"

Margaret had hesitated before replying, "I think that's about it,

Esther. Each couple is different and it should be talked out between them. But if they both think alike on the subject, then it makes it a lot easier."

Margaret remembered the expression on her friend's face and it had troubled her—frustration, despair, what had it been? She hadn't quite known, but whatever it was it had disturbed her. Something deep inside told her that maybe Len had a right to be a bit worried. But she wasn't going to admit that to her father, not yet at any rate.

She saw he was waiting for some response so she went up to him and threw her arms round his neck, "Oh Dad, you're such a dear. I trust your judgment far more than Len's. It's more unbiased. As for my own, I'm a bit confused just now, but I'll keep an eye open this weekend in Chicago and really pray about it. If I feel that there is a danger, then I'll be glad to speak to Esther though I think it might come better from you."

Her father seemed satisfied. "God has a perfect time for everything, Margaret, and who knows, if we pray, maybe He'll do things His own way, without our interference."

His daughter was to think about these words many times in the weeks that followed, but for the time being she was too busy packing for the weekend to give more thought to such serious matters. And during the trip that followed, she couldn't help but notice Ron's adoring glances and Esther's radiant smile; she decided to throw all misgivings to the wind. God wouldn't want something so beautiful to be spoiled, would He?

Esther was a great hit that Saturday evening and no one was very surprised when it was announced that the young singer from Romania had been judged the best of all the singers in her category. As well as a cash prize of $1000, her success meant that her name would be blazoned all over the States.

It was very late before she left the auditorium. Fans were there wanting autographs; several well-dressed gentlemen offered to sponsor her; Esther was overwhelmed but gave no promises. She was already being sponsored by a Christian businessman, but here was the opportunity for wider fame in the secular world.

They were to spend the weekend in Chicago, so the next day they went to church with Margaret and her fiancé, Robert, who was attending seminary in the city. The afternoon was their own and, worn out from her performance the evening before, Esther slept for hours. But soon it was time to attend the banquet held in honor of the prize-winners. Margaret had not been invited so took the opportunity to spend more time with her Robert.

When a toast was suggested for all those who had won prizes the previous evening, Ron gave a sidelong glance at the girl by his side. He had never seen her drink wine and presumed she never touched alcohol. He saw her toy with her wine glass for a few moments before raising it to her lips.

"I'm a bit surprised you drink alcohol," he whispered in her ear.

"Are you?" she smiled back. She looked lovely in that scarlet dress, Ron thought. "Most of my friends back in Romania take a little on special occasions," she told him, as she joined in the toast.

The rest of the evening, the wine flowed in abundance. Esther and Ron had a few glasses, but some of the young men took much more than that. Esther didn't like the way several of them ogled her from time to time, and she noticed that Ron didn't like it either. She wasn't used to such gatherings and was glad when it was all over. She realized more clearly why her parents had grown to dislike any form of strong drink even though it was certainly not taboo in the church where her aunt attended, as long as it was kept in moderation. She could recall vividly the arguments her father had had with some of his closest Christian friends on the subject and wondered what he would have thought of her that evening.

It was just after nine when they got back to the motel. They knew that Margaret wouldn't be back till late. She had gone to a church some distance away. It was a very sultry evening and they were tired and hot, so Ron suggested they go for a late night dip in the pool. Esther went to her room to change. She had thought perhaps they might have a chance for a swim that weekend so had come prepared. She gazed at her swim suit, lying in one corner of her suitcase. Esther had become accustomed to appearing in her bathing suit in front of her fiancé, though it had taken some getting used to. But she had never ventured wearing the bikini Ramona had given her and dared her to wear. Now she dived into another corner of the case and fished it out. Maybe it had been Ron's comment the week before as they had been swimming together, "You sure would look fabulous in a bikini, Esther," that had made her stick it in at the last moment.

Now she hesitated. She so wanted to please Ron. He had been so good to her and of course, she was curious to see what she really would look like in a bikini. Even Margaret wore one, so what harm was there in it? In America, do as the Americans do, she told herself.

A few minutes later she eyed herself in the bathroom mirror. It certainly wasn't the most substantial of bikinis but she had to admit that, bronzed and shapely as she was, she certainly looked eye-catching in it. For just this once, she felt like throwing her inhibitions to the wind. She grabbed a towel and ran downstairs to the pool. Slipping up behind him, she put her hands round Ron's neck and laid her head on his shoulder. As he swung round and faced her, his mouth dropped open in astonishment. He couldn't believe his eyes, neither could some of the other men present, or so it seemed, from the stares the girl was receiving. She thought she could hear a low whistle coming from not far away. Esther was plainly the center of attention. She stood there blushing.

"Well?" she asked mischievously.

For answer, Ron swooped her in his arms and made for the pool. A minute later she was laughing and spluttering in the water.

"I'll pay you back for that, Ron Atwood," she retorted, when she could get her breath. And she did. Was this his angelic little Romanian or some enticing mermaid, he wondered, as they dried themselves half an hour later.

"Oh but you're so beautiful, Esther," he murmured, as he put his arm around her, "so very beautiful."

The girl made no response except to reach up and give him a long kiss. She felt strangely elated that night. Her conversation with Margaret came back to her. "Anything's OK," she thought, "as long as we don't let it get out of control." But when Ron suddenly grabbed her hand, and started pulling her in the direction of his motel room, she began to shake violently. Part of her desperately wanted to go with him. Would it really be that wrong? Her passion was getting the better of her, she knew that; she had never felt like she did that evening. She glanced up into Ron's face and that did it.

They had reached room no. 56 when they heard a voice calling them from the terrace below: "Esther! Ron! We came back early. Come down, can't you? I want you both to get to know Robert a bit better. It's still not that late."

Esther clutched the iron railings and let go Ron's hand. She thought she could hear him swear softly to himself, something he had never done before in her presence. He motioned for her to answer her friends. He was totally unable to speak. So she leaned over the balcony and answered as normally as she could, "OK Margaret, we've been swimming. Just wait a few moments and we'll be down."

"Why did she have to come back early!" Ron grumbled, as he put his key in the lock. Esther said nothing as she disappeared into her own room to change.

Margaret acted as usual that evening, so Esther guessed that she had no inkling of what had happened. She thought of pouring out her pent-up emotions to her friend as they prepared for bed but something held her back.

The next day as they drove home to Velours, both Esther and Ron spoke little for some time. Margaret had wanted more time with Robert so had stayed on a few more days in Chicago; this meant that they were alone once more. Esther was the first to speak. "I won't wear that bikini again till we're married," she said in a low voice.

"That's bad news." Ron kept his eyes on the road ahead as he spoke.

Esther blushed scarlet. She hadn't been prepared for that answer. "But it wasn't right of me, Ron. I want you to forgive me," she told him pitifully.

Ron looked at her in amazement. "Forgive? What's there to forgive? You were wonderful last night. You got rid of some of your inhibitions for a change and it was like Heaven. I was hoping it just might be a foretaste of pleasures to come."

The girl by his side was silent. "Of course, I'm glad for your sake that Margaret came along just at that time," he went on. Then he stopped in amazement. Esther was crying softly to herself.

Ron frowned. Somehow, her crying bothered him. "What on earth's wrong, Esther? We had a fabulous weekend, so what's there to cry about?"

His voice was harsher than usual. Esther blinked back the tears. "But, I mean...." Esther stammered. She was embarrassed and annoyed that Ron wasn't making it easy for her to get out what had troubled her all night. "When you grabbed me by the hand last night and nearly dragged me upstairs, you didn't intend to...?"

The young man gripped the steering wheel tightly as he replied. "Intend to what? And I could ask you the same question. Putting on a bikini, is one thing. All the girls I know do it. But sidling up to me and kissing and embracing me like you did when you had so little clothes on is quite another. Oh, come on Esther. We were both completely carried away with our passions and you know it. And to tell you the truth, I very much doubt if I, at least, could have stopped myself before it was too late."

Esther shuddered and edged away from him. "Don't treat me as if I were a moral leper," he growled. "I'm a man, remember, as I've told you before, and you're a woman, and an alluring one at that! Anyway, it wasn't all on one side, you know. I've never seen you act like that, and it nearly drove me crazy."

"I suppose I did start it all." Her voice was low, restrained.

"So what if you did. Oh come on, Esther," Ron spoke more sharply than usual, "let's not fool ourselves. It was a perfectly predictable situation, at least, from my point of view it was: a glass or two of wine; a beautiful, almost naked girl in my arms who turns all her charms up full blast; a night-time swim, and both of us in love; so, come on now, be honest, what does it all equal?"

"But it would have been so wrong, Ron."

"No," he nearly shouted, "I don't think it would. And don't look so shocked. Are you telling me it was wrong for us to feel passionately for each other? Aren't we in love?"

"Yes, but love and passion aren't one and the same thing, are they?"

"Pretty much."

Esther frowned. "But Ron, love goes deeper than passion, doesn't it?"

Ron thought a moment. "Suppose you're right. You can have passion without love but not love without some passion at any rate. I felt passion enough for Sherri but not real love. But for you, I feel both, only they're so entwined into one that I can't extricate one from the other."

"Exactly. I feel the same way." Esther was glad she could agree with him on that at least. "And listen, Ron, I'm not saying that it was wrong for us to feel that way, but we nearly let it get out of hand."

"Out of hand? What did God make us of—stone? You know very well that He didn't. He made us a man and a woman, made us for each other, didn't He? And we're going to get married, aren't we? Isn't that what the ring on your finger is all about? I didn't buy it just so you could flash it around and make Ramona green with envy, now did I?" He paused. Esther had rarely seen him as agitated before. He grabbed her hand and squeezed it so hard it almost made her cry out.

"What really makes marriage, Esther?" he asked, tension rising in his voice; "a pastor's blessing? a marriage certificate? a white dress? or union one with the other in body, soul, and spirit?"

"But marriage has to have a total commitment one to the other, doesn't it, witnessed by others, and blessed by God?"

"I don't think I could be any more committed to you than I am, Esther." His voice trembled. "But maybe you don't feel the same way. Is that the problem?"

"Ron!" her voice was reproachful now. "You know better than that. But I mean, this commitment has to be hallowed, blessed, and witnessed by others, doesn't it?"

"Is that in your Bible?"

Esther hesitated. There was no text that said exactly that. "Well, it does say that a man has to leave father and mother and cleave to his wife."

"I'm ready to do that tomorrow."

The girl sighed. He really was proving quite impossible, this usually easy-going young man of hers. "But you haven't done it yet, Ron. We haven't made that public commitment. In the eyes of the law, we won't be married until there is a certificate and a ceremony. And God tells us to obey the laws of the land. Anyway, the Bible teaches clearly that the union you talk about should consummate the marriage, come after our vows, not before. We should enter our marriage relationship pure." She had said those last words without thinking what effect they might have on the young man by her side.

He groaned. "Pure? Well, you know I'm not that, Esther. But look, I do know what you're trying to get at and I really respect you as well as love you. Let's make it legal then right away so that our passion for each other can be what you would call legitimate." He reached for her hand. It was trembling in his. "Look darling," his voice was very tender now, "I know how you feel and I'm very glad for your sake that we didn't enter room no. 56. But you did tempt me, really, Esther. It seemed I had discovered another side to the girl I loved and it was awfully tantalizing." He paused as he saw her expression. "You were sending out signals that you wanted me."

"I was?" Esther sounded surprised, even shocked.

Ron laughed. "Of course you were, and I think you must know that. You're surely not that naïve!"

Esther blushed crimson and was silent for a moment. Then she gave her companion a sly look from under her long lashes. "So I go back to my long skirts and blouses. No swimming together? No kissing? No hugging?"

"Are you serious?"

"Then what's the solution?"

"We'll just have to be apart more till we're married."

"No, Ron, no!" Esther wailed.

"You can't have your cake and eat it too." She looked up at him. He was deadly serious.

"Look," he added in a lighter tone. "I'm going away for some interviews in Nashville. Won't be back till the night before Mom's wedding. So let's both think about this. There's bound to be a solution."

Ron tossed and turned in bed that evening, trying in vain to get at least a few hours' sleep. That weekend had revealed that Esther Popescu had two sides. He needed time to think, to weigh up this new Esther that was emerging, an Esther that he himself had helped create. And he just couldn't forget the conversation he had overheard that evening of the concert. Just before it had ended, the man sitting behind him had commented to his companion, "That girl can adapt to anything. She's both a bewitching gypsy—sensual, alluring—and at the same time a beautiful angel. With that combination, she'll rock Hollywood with no trouble, maybe not right away, but in a few years' time. If she can acquire a little more sensuality and still retain at least some purity, she'll become one of the greatest hits ever."

But then another voice, a woman's, had replied, and Ron had tried to block out that voice all that evening, "Yes, I agree. I've always said that the mixture of sensuality and spirituality is irresistible. And that girl sure has both, and they're not put on either. But my guess is that her sensuality will win out in the end. If you give it an inch it takes a mile. And she'll be no exception. She'll break many a man's heart in the next few years—probably go through three marriages at least before she reaches fifty."

"What, that girl?" the first voice had exclaimed incredulously. "Never! She's too pure for that."

"No one can keep pure long in show biz, Dave," the woman had replied. "She'll be ruined in a year."

"Let's hope she stays out of it then," was the rejoinder. "God knows we need to retain some purity in this world."

When Ron had relayed as much as he could remember of this conversation to Esther, she had raised her eyebrows. "I'm not that good, Ron," she had said. "No danger of me being a Hollywood star."

"But that's not the point," Ron had protested. "If you ever got an offer like that, would you accept it?"

The girl had blushed scarlet as she replied, "I don't think I could, Ron. And anyway, would you want me to?"

"No, I wouldn't. Like the woman implied, I don't think our marriage would survive if you did."

Esther had been silent a moment before replying, "Well anyway, the question really is, do you want me to accept one of the offers I got last night? Not from Hollywood of course, but not from a Christian company either."

"I would think that a question between you and your God," Ron had replied softly.

Esther had looked at him for a moment before answering slowly, "Yes, of course it is, but maybe Pastor Cripps can give me advice."

"Maybe," had been the doubtful reply.

Now as the clock in the hallway struck three, Ron knew that something had to change between them. But one thing he was sure of, he wouldn't let her go. She was the only girl he could ever love, come what may. Whatever price he had to pay to get her would be worth it, short of being an utter hypocrite. He would never stoop to that, not even for the sake of the lovely Romanian, or would he? Hadn't he been one already without realizing it? And who would change who after they married? He visualized Gabby sitting opposite them in the restaurant. "Depends who strongest," she had said in her broken accent.

He sat bolt upright in bed. "I am," he had shouted into the darkness. "I am. I need to be. I'm her tower, her strength. And I'll never lead her astray, never."

"Won't you?" a voice whispered back from within his own soul. "And what were you doing last night then if not leading her astray?"

"But she led me into it," he argued. "I only followed my heart. That's not wrong, is it?" His breath came short and fast. Clenching his fist beneath the bedclothes, he muttered: "I'll never give her up. I can't give her up. I'll die before I give her up. I can't live without her!"

Ron slumped back on the pillow. Emotionally spent, he turned over to face the wall. Could it be possible that he was becoming God's rival for Esther's love? He shuddered. If he was, he would probably lose in the long run. How could any mortal win under those circumstances? But then, couldn't they both share the girl with each other. Yes, that was the solution. He closed his eyes and smiled. He'd share his Esther with the Almighty and then, in return, surely God wouldn't mind sharing one little girl with him, would He?

Chapter Thirty-Six

A Chat over Lunch

Esther was surprised to see a light in the living room when she got back late that Monday evening. She found Gabby sitting curled up in the recliner, waiting for her.

"I saw you on TV, Esther," her sister told her as she made a cup of tea.

"And?"

"You were unbelievable, but...."

"Yes, but what?"

"Well," Gabby said slowly as she set Esther's cup on the kitchen table, "you seem to be exiting my world. Soon I won't even have a sister."

Esther tossed her head as she often did these days. "Nonsense, child! I'll take you with me wherever I go."

Gabby gave her a long look. "That's what I don't want. I can't be your satellite forever, you know."

Esther gave a short, nervous laugh. "As if you could be anyone's satellite for long, Gabby."

Gabby bit her lip and then blurted out, "Oh Esther, do you have to go to the wedding on Saturday?"

Her sister stood up straight, eyes blazing. "Yes, I do, Gabby. I have to go. It's the only Christian thing to do. Come on, you know I don't approve of what they've done."

"Then why go?" burst out Gabby. "I know it hurts Aunt Mary awfully. But it's hurting you still more."

"Me?"

"Yes you. Next thing, you'll have the morals as well as the looks of one of those stars on TV."

"Much you trust me, Gabby," spluttered Esther, stalking out of the room.

"Well, looking at you on TV the other night, you weren't far off."

But Esther had gone. Her head was splitting and she was

downright angry with her impudent sister. At that moment she wished Gabby were back in Ploiesti. She was spoiling everything for her. Everything!

All that week, Esther was out of sorts. Uncle John was too occupied with his wedding on the Saturday to take much notice of his nieces though he had seen Esther on TV and congratulated her heartily on her success. In fact, mail was pouring in. But Esther was tired and cross. Gabby's unnatural silence troubled her. She missed Ron terribly and felt life without him would be unbearable.

On Wednesday she had gone to the midweek service at church and stayed behind to talk to Pastor Cripps. Gabby had stayed at home as usual. She had refused to go to church for several weeks now. The pastor seemed unusually reserved in his comments. He had seen her performance, of course, and was glad she had managed to sing a few Christian numbers, but he did remind her she was treading on dangerous ground. God had gifted her tremendously. She must be very careful what she did with those talents and use them only for His glory.

Esther was secretly mortified by his words. Something in his manner convicted her. She had thought of asking his advice about going to the wedding but it was too late, she thought. Even if he advised her against it, she couldn't back out now. The pastor had told her he wanted to speak to both Ron and herself as soon as they could find a suitable time to get together. Esther wondered if Margaret had been talking to him but doubted it. Margaret would have spoken to her first, she thought.

Thursday morning Esther awoke feeling very restless. She had never been more confused in all her life. That weekend in Chicago had unnerved her. Her ideas of right and wrong were no longer clear. She wondered if it was the Velvet Curtain again. By noon, she had made up her mind to have a good heart-to-heart talk with her Aunt Mary. She knew that her aunt had made her peace with God and seemed a new person, from the little she had seen of her.

"Of course I'll talk with you, Esther," her aunt told her. "Come for a light lunch with me. Let's meet at Wendy's. It's close by. Rachel's home, and I think you want a private talk, right?"

"Yes Aunt, I do. See you in half an hour."

By the time Mary had arrived at Wendy's, Esther had already placed her order. The dark circles round the girl's eyes immediately caught the older woman's attention, as she seated herself opposite her niece at a table in a far corner of the restaurant. It wasn't long before Esther opened the conversation.

"I may as well not beat around the bush, Aunt. I need your advice."

"Mine?" Mary smiled. "Such as it is, I'll be glad to give it, if I can. Depends, of course, if it's in my line or not."

"Oh yes, I think it's in your line, especially since you've become a Christian."

"So you've heard? Oh, Esther, it's been such a wonderful month for me. Everything's new."

Esther patted her aunt's hand. "I'm so glad. I've prayed for this for a long time. But I really need to talk to you, to an older woman who's had experience in life and yet who sees things from a Christian perspective. I've talked to Margaret some and she's wonderful, but young like me. And there's no one else. Oh, there is Mrs. Cripps, but I don't know her very well. So you see, I've no one but you."

"I'm so glad you feel free to come to me," Mary told her. "Now, just pretend, if you can, that I'm your mother; I'm sure you know that I'll treat your confidences as I'd treat Rachel's or Ramona's."

And so Esther told her everything, not only about the events of the past weekend but all that had preceded it. An hour passed and she was still talking. Mary knew she had to let it all out. At last, it seemed that she had finished. There was a long silence and then the older woman leaned over the table and took her niece's hand. "Esther, you're really unsure of your engagement to Ron, aren't you?"

The girl flushed. "Not really, Aunt. He's seemed such an answer to prayer. I can't think God would have me give him up."

"Then what is troubling you?"

"Well, I feel so ashamed of the other night. I wonder what would have happened if Margaret hadn't appeared just then." She dropped her eyes as she spoke.

"I think you were playing with fire, Esther." Mary's tone was gentle but firm.

"What do you mean?" Esther still kept her eyes fixed on the remains of her hamburger.

"Well, first of all, you both had drunk some wine." Esther didn't like the way her aunt was speaking now.

"Was that so very wrong?" she asked, frowning just a little.

Mary weighed her words carefully. "I suppose I am just a bit surprised that someone as strict as you in other things would indulge yourself in this."

"I wasn't indulging at all," the girl protested heatedly. "I only had two glasses. We do the same in Romania from time to time. Over there, it's not considered wrong for Christians to drink just a little as it seems to be here." Visions of her father rose before her. "At least most of my friends think that way," she added hastily.

"What I was just trying to say, Esther," her aunt's voice was low and soothing, "was that I know from quite a bit of experience that wine loosens the inhibitions and heightens the passions, so that may explain at least some of what followed in the motel. Then," she continued, brushing the crumbs from her lap as she spoke, "you deliberately put on a bikini, and played up to him when you were almost in the nude—a thing you had never done before."

"I did have something on, Aunt Mary." Esther was on the defensive now. "A bikini isn't considered almost in the nude, you know. Nearly everyone wears them, even church people."

Mary gave her niece a searching glance. "I may be old-fashioned, but I can't see why nudity is considered wrong everywhere except at the beach or in the pool where men have plenty of leisure time to stare at women to their heart's content."

"You don't need to go on about it, Aunt," Esther protested. "I get the message."

Mary gave a wry smile. "You must think it's not in character for me to turn preacher all of a sudden, but I'm just trying to show you that after weeks and even months of your pent-up emotions—doing what you did was like setting a match to a tinderbox."

"So you don't agree with Margaret that as long as the final boundary isn't crossed, everything else is between the couple? I mean...."

"I know what you mean, Esther. No, I don't really agree with her. I think that what happened that evening proves it."

"Proves what?"

"That sometimes when passions are really roused it's hard to even know how near you are to that final boundary as you call it, and before you realize it, you've both passed the point of no return."

"But Aunt, I knew it would have been wrong and I'm almost sure...." Esther couldn't finish her sentence.

"Esther," Mary's voice was very serious now, "I think it's time we older folks were more open about our own mistakes and sins.

You see, I wasn't a Christian when your uncle and I were dating. I became pregnant with Ramona before we married. I thought that might be the only way to get him to marry me." Mary's voice trembled. "I'm very ashamed of what I did though I know it has all been forgiven, but I can never undo what was done, never." Mary turned her head away to hide the tears.

"Thanks for being open with me, Aunt. But surely you're not hinting that we shouldn't show any affection to each other? After all, we are engaged." Esther's tone was a little peevish. Her aunt wasn't quite handling the situation as she had thought she would.

Her aunt looked deep into her niece's beautiful eyes. "I really think you know what I'm getting at, Esther. Too much physical intimacy is unhealthy before marriage. I've not always thought that way but I do now. And I think the secret lies in both man and woman feeling the same way about all of this. If each knows that there are barriers that should not be passed before marriage, then that makes things a whole lot easier."

Esther toyed with her watch strap. Mary saw she was very uneasy. She leaned forward again and asked softly, "That's the problem, isn't it?"

Esther nodded, tears filling her eyes. Mary came round to the bench where she was sitting and put her arms round her and said in a low voice, "Then, Esther, you need to be very careful that your married life doesn't begin on that basis."

Esther started. "What do you mean?"

"I think the Bible asks how two people can walk together if they are not agreed, doesn't it?"

Esther rose. "Then you're saying I should give him up?"

"I'm saying that you should think over these things carefully and talk them out with him, Esther. I know he's a wonderful young man, but if there's already a gap between you, that gap will not lessen after you're married."

"It's only on the one level, Aunt. We've so much in common apart from that."

"But it's on the most important level of all, Esther. Surely you can't think that knowing God can be relegated to the back burner, can you?"

"But I'm sure Ron does know Him, maybe not like I do. But then I've been privileged, you know, and he wants me to teach him the way, he really does."

Mary bit her lip. She gathered up the two trays and made for the trash bin without saying a word.

"Are you angry, Aunt Mary?"

"Angry, Esther? No. Just very concerned. But I'm learning slowly that prayer is the best way to see problems solved, not merely talking."

Esther rose. "Thanks for listening to me. I really appreciate it. I know Gabby's worried about me; I think the pastor is too and you also have your questions about all this. That's obvious. I can't go past what you all think. And yet...."

"It's really what God thinks that's most important, Esther. But you look tired, worn out emotionally. We've talked enough for one day. You know my phone number. I'll be available day or night."

"Just like I haven't been," muttered the girl, picking up her handbag.

Mary squeezed her hand. "That's in the past, Esther. Listen dear, remember that God doesn't condemn you for your feeling for Ron. You're human. But He must have first place in your life. Never forget that."

Esther nodded as she walked over to her car. "Just one more thing." Mary had come up behind her. "I've found that God likes it best when we listen to His whispers. But sometimes He finds He has to shout to get our attention. And oh, Esther," the girl noticed that there were tears in her aunt's eyes, "please don't wait till He has to shout. I did, and look what happened!"

Esther was about to speak, but her aunt had gone. "Please don't wait till He has to shout," rang in her ears as she drove homewards. To say that she felt better after her talk with her aunt would not be telling the whole truth. In a way, she had been relieved by opening her heart to someone, but Mary hadn't said the things she had hoped to hear. Anyway, she just couldn't give Ron Atwood up. She had no strength to do so and she had gone too far to back out now. She had committed herself to him in so many ways. Then there was the wedding in two days' time. Her aunt hadn't even discussed the wedding. She just couldn't refuse to go now. Maybe she'd take ill. That'd be a good excuse for not going.

Esther's head was splitting when she opened the front door and flopped into the nearest chair. She thought it was just the result of her emotions but when an hour later she began to chill, she searched for the thermometer she knew her uncle kept in the medicine cabinet and stuck it under her tongue. Three minutes later she couldn't believe her eyes. 102 degrees! No wonder her head was aching, but plenty of liquid and several Tylenol brought her fever down somewhat.

Gabby had arranged to spend the night with her cousin so Esther went to bed early and managed to snatch at least a few hours' peaceful sleep. The next morning she felt a little better, and kept dosing herself all day. But when Gabby returned that afternoon, she found a very sick sister lying listlessly on the bed, face flushed, eyes glazed.

"You're burning up, Esther," Gabby exclaimed, feeling her hand.

"Take my temp. Gabby. I haven't taken it for hours," Esther murmured.

Her sister obeyed promptly and gasped in dismay. "103 degrees! Uncle's out, but maybe we should take you to emergency."

"There's no one to take me right now. Wait a bit, Gabby. It's maybe the flu. I'll just have to stick it out."

"You can't go to the wedding tomorrow," her sister exclaimed trying hard to keep the gladness out of her voice.

"I'll go if I can, Gabby. See, I've put out my clothes for tomorrow."

Gabby was silent. Her sister sure could be stubborn when she wanted to. But when eight o'clock came Esther's fever was as high as ever. "I'd better tell Ron, Esther. He ought to be warned that you won't be going tomorrow. It's only fair."

Esther groaned but agreed. Gabby tried to dial his number but he was out. She kept trying for two hours but to no avail. She then rang her aunt but there was no response there either. Then she remembered that Mary and Rachel had gone away for the weekend to a friend's. They wanted to be out of town when the wedding was going on.

Gabby would never forget that night. It seemed interminable. She thought that she had never seen Esther look so ill.

"I'll be OK, Gabby," Esther assured her in a tone so tender it made Gabby's heart ache. She wanted the old Esther back again but not at this price. Sitting down on the edge of the bed she caught sight of the tan handbag her sister had given her. As she placed it on her lap, her mind drifted back to their life together in Romania and she was scarcely conscious that, all the while, her hands were feeling through the pocketbook. It seemed that Esther had emptied it out, except for one folded up piece of paper which was tucked away in one of the zip pockets. Gabby unfolded it hardly knowing what she was doing. She thought later that she never should have been reading Esther's private notes. At the time, however, it seemed pretty insignificant. Esther had told her of her meeting with the strange little man on the plane, so the name Hugh Gardner seemed to ring a bell. But the words "Velvet Curtain" caught her eye. Whatever did he mean? She would have to ask Esther when she got better. So, putting the note back where she had found it, she closed the purse softly and slipped out of the room.

Gabby tried phoning Ron once more at eleven but there was still no reply. She had better get to bed, she thought. Maybe her sister would have improved by morning. That night, as she listened to Esther tossing and turning she wondered why she had come to this strange land in the first place. But those nightmare walks in the park, and then the harrowing moment when she thought she might have been turned back at the immigration, all reminded her that she now had no home but America. She had burned her bridges behind her and was here beside her sister, for better or for worse.

Chapter Thirty-Seven

Farewell to Mike

Ron breathed a sigh of relief as he saw the lights of Velours ahead. It had not been a good week for him. He had done well at his interviews, but something, he told himself, had gone wrong during his weekend in Chicago. He had gotten a brief glimpse of the earthy side of Esther Popescu. It had made him feel that they were at last on the same level—that she was no longer some super-saint who beckoned him on to impossible heights of morality and sanctity. And yet, strangely enough, it had frightened him to realize the influence he seemed to wield over the girl. In time, what would his influence finally do to her? Gabby's words at the restaurant haunted him. Maybe she had been right after all.

He turned into his driveway. It was still only nine o'clock. He had time to contact Esther and make sure all was set for the wedding the next day. Just as he went to pick up the receiver to dial her number, the phone rang, and an unfamiliar voice asked, "Is that Mr. Ron Atwood?"

"Yes."

"I'm Nurse Cromwell at the City Hospital and I'm phoning on behalf of Mike Crawford; he's asking for you. He is in room no. 514."

"Sorry, but I've just gotten back from a trip. Can you tell him I'll be there tomorrow afternoon?"

There was silence on the other end and when she spoke, the nurse's voice was low but firm: "Mr. Atwood, if you wish to see your friend alive, you will come immediately."

Ron was stunned. He knew Mike was in the hospital in the city and had intended to visit him after the wedding was over, but he had no idea he was as near the end as that.

"Tell him I'll be over within the hour," he answered as he hung up.

He tried to phone Esther before he went but the line was busy. Forty minutes later, he was at his friend's bedside. Mike was awake but very weak. Ron could not believe the change that had come over him in four or five weeks. One look, and he knew that his old school buddy was dying.

"Thanks for coming, Ron," Mike whispered, as Ron pulled up a chair by his bed. "They tell me I've not got long."

"I know," was all Ron could answer. He wasn't used to visiting someone as sick as Mike. Yet as he gazed on the familiar features of his friend, he noticed a peace and serenity that he had not seen there before, the same expression he had seen on Esther's face when he had first met her those ten months ago.

"I tried to contact you earlier in the week but you were away." Ron had to bend over the bed in order to catch Mike's words. "I want to tell you something. Last week, before I was rushed here, I phoned Pastor Cripps at the church." Ron's eyes widened. Mike had never been religious as far back as he could remember. They had been buddies at high school and had done everything together, from baseball to double dating. But the sick man was continuing: "Ever since I heard Esther sing 'Amazing Grace,' I've been searching for that grace. I wanted to make my peace with Him. And I have." His eyes closed but a beautiful smile lit up his wan features.

Ron sat watching him. He lay so still that it seemed he was sleeping, but after a few moments his eyes opened and he reached out for Ron's hand. "Oh Ron," he murmured, "what I've missed in life! You were always a much better guy than I, so I don't know if you need to find God, too, or not. But if you do, please don't give up till you find Him." Two large tears trickled down his ashen cheeks as he spoke.

Ron did not know what to say. A thousand emotions seemed to surge through him. Just then, he heard footsteps in the corridor and the next moment a young woman entered the room.

"Sarah!" Ron exclaimed. It was Mike's older sister whom he had not seen in years. She was too emotional to speak. She shook Ron's hand in silence, beating back the tears, then leaned over the bed to give her brother a kiss. "Mom and Dad are coming any moment," she whispered.

Ron rose to go but Mike was still holding his hand. "Just one more thing Ron," he muttered weakly. "Pull out that drawer and take that envelope lying in the right hand corner. It's addressed to Esther. Give it to her after I'm...." He paused and closed his eyes. His face took on such pallor that Ron glanced at Sarah. She nodded and rang the bell for the nurse. Just then, an older couple came into the room, out of breath, anguish written all over their features. Ron excused himself. This was family time for Mike on what might well be his last evening on earth.

Sleep came slowly to Ron Atwood that night. Mike's words, "I don't know if you need to find God, too, or not. But if you do, oh Ron, don't give up till you find Him," haunted him.

"No, Mike," he whispered into the darkness, "I don't think I have found Him. But I don't know how, I really don't, except that I hope Esther will show me the way."

Chapter Thirty-Eight

Lifting the Curtain

"Ready, Ron?" queried Diane Atwood as she put the finishing touches to her hair. "Oh bother the phone! Who can be ringing us today of all days?"

Ron picked up the receiver. "Ramona? Yes? What?" His mother saw his face blanch and her heart sank. It was bad news of some sort, that was evident. "No, can't be! Really?" His face was even whiter now. "I'll try and run over for a moment. Be there right away."

Brushing past his mother and grabbing the car keys, Ron headed for the door. "Sorry Mom, but Esther's got a raging fever. She can't come today of course. No one seems to know what's wrong exactly, but she's very ill. I'm popping over for a few moments." Then seeing his mother's worried expression, he assured her, "Don't worry, I'll make it in time to the church."

A few moments later, Ron found Ramona's report all too true. Esther was delirious and scarcely recognized him. Her fever had begun on Thursday evening, Gabby told him. She had been dosing herself with all sorts of medication so that she would be able to go to the wedding. Sure enough, there lay her outfit on the chair, a long pink gown, with shoes and handbag to match. Ron's eyes scanned the room. He noticed piles of letters on her desk, from fans he supposed, and on the dresser stood their engagement photograph. The beautiful girl in the picture smiled up at him, radiant with health and happiness.

"What shall we do, Ron?" asked Ramona, her voice breaking into his reverie.

"I'm supposed to be at the wedding in ten minutes. I'm one of their witnesses, worse luck," he added. "But I think we need to get her to the Emergency room. If she's been like this for hours and nothing seems to bring down the fever, then it must be something serious. I'll call 911 immediately. You and Gabby had better go with Esther. And someone needs to phone your mother and sister. Oh, but they're out of town, aren't they?"

Ramona nodded. "I'll certainly not stay for the reception," Ron went on as he made for the door. "My mother will be disappointed but surely she'll understand that Esther's life is worth a hundred such weddings." Then he paused. "Oh, I forgot, Ramona. You were going too, weren't you?"

The girl nodded again and was about to speak when a voice behind them interrupted: "I'll go with Gabby." Ron turned round and there was Jean, standing in the doorway. She had entered without them noticing. "John will be upset if none of his family is there."

Ron looked at Ramona. It was true. John would want someone to represent his family. And he felt instinctively that the cleaning lady might have had more experience with sick people than Ramona.

"I'm glad to go with Gabby to the hospital," Ramona faltered, "but maybe...."

"I'm going, and that's that." Jean's voice was firm.

"Will Estera die?" blurted out Gabby, her eyes widening in fear.

"I don't think it's that bad," Ron said, trying hard to believe his own words. "It might be nothing serious after all, but a high fever like this is not to be taken lightly. I am sure that with appropriate treatment, everything will be all right very soon," and he stooped and gave Esther a quick kiss before slipping downstairs to dial the rescue squad. He gave clear instructions how to find the house, and told them to be quick; then he jumped in the car and raced down the driveway.

How he got through the ceremony Ron would never know. He didn't get a chance to tell John about his niece till it was over, but when he whispered in the bridegroom's ear how sick Esther was, the older man's face blanched. "We'll cut the reception short," he whispered. "I'll be over as soon as I possibly can." Ron nodded as he bolted for his car.

In the hospital, he found Jean and Gabby in the waiting room. In the corridor, several perplexed doctors were shaking their heads in frustration. "We don't know what's exactly wrong with your fiancée," they told Ron. "She's very ill, and we'll have to get that temperature down first of all and then run some tests. Her fever is dangerously high."

Ron would never forget that day. It seemed interminable. It was early evening before Ramona and her father made it to the hospital. John took one look at his niece and turned to Ron. "I can't go out of town with the girl as ill as that. After all, I'm responsible for her really. She's like a daughter to me." He was trying to beat back the tears. "I'll wait till Monday at least and see how things are then. I've got to get back to your Mom, though. She'll be wondering what's happening."

Everyone else, including Jean, had insisted on staying all day. But after they had had a bite to eat in the cafeteria, Ron told the others to go. They could relieve him in the coming days, but he wasn't leaving the hospital that night. Gabby at first refused to go home, but Jean managed to persuade her to see the wisdom in getting some rest. She would be needed later on, she told her, and couldn't let herself get worn out too soon.

At about nine that evening, Ron got a chance to talk to a grave-faced young doctor who told him that Esther had contracted rheumatic fever. They would begin treating her immediately but the danger was that her heart could be affected for life. She would have to stay in the hospital at least one week if not two and then a long period of recuperation and complete rest and quiet would be needed, somewhere in the country preferably, maybe in the mountains or by the sea. Ron grimaced. There were only ten days before he had to leave for law school, but at least he could spend them with the girl who had become such a part of his life.

He would never forget that night. Esther was in intensive care, so he was only allowed ten minutes at a time with her every few hours or so. He tried to get a few winks of sleep in between, but to little avail. His heart was too heavy. When he was allowed in to see the patient, he found her delirious. He would hold her burning hand, mutter soothing words, or moisten her parched lips. In her delirium, she would cry out repeatedly. "Take it away. Take it away. It's the curtain. It's smothering me. Oh please, will someone take it away?"

And all Ron could do was bend over her and whisper softly but reassuringly, "Of course, darling, I'll take it away. See, it's not there now. It's gone."

The next morning, Gabby turned up bright and early. She was tearful but brave when she heard the doctor's verdict. Day after day found Ron at the hospital. John had postponed his honeymoon and insisted on relieving the others from time to time. Ron's mom even showed up on the Sunday evening. After all, she had reasoned, Esther was now not only her son's fiancée but her niece through marriage.

And of course, Gabby, Rachel, and Aunt Mary were never far away. They had returned home late Sunday evening and had been at the hospital early the next morning. Ramona came daily, and so did Jean who surprised everyone but Gabby by her sudden devotion to the girl who had previously seemed a thorn in her flesh.

There had been visitors from the church, too: Margaret and her parents, Len and young Connie Frith, and several others. Pastor Cripps had put his hands on the sick girl's head and prayed fervently for her. His tender-hearted wife and daughter had tears in their eyes as they left the hospital. They had not been prepared to see Esther so very ill. That Wednesday evening, the congregation at Pine Grove Evangelical Church joined together in special prayer for her. Cards and flowers began to pour in, not only from church members but also from some of Esther's fans. Several announcements had been made in the Christian press and on a few local radio stations that the beautiful singer from Romania was seriously ill and had had to cancel all her engagements. The nurses made feeble jokes to Ron about his fiancée's popularity but no one felt much like laughing.

After three days, Esther was still in intensive care. "Something is aggravating the fever," the doctor told Ron. "She keeps mentioning a curtain. Any ideas what the problem could be?"

Ron shook his head. But a nagging thought dogged him after that. He guessed that she would have been troubled after that weekend in Chicago. Had *that* anything to do with it? More importantly, had *he* anything to do with it?

"Gabby," he said over lunch in the hospital cafeteria, "the doctor says something is bothering your sister, aggravating her illness, preventing the medicine from taking the effect it should. She keeps talking about a curtain. Any ideas?"

"About curtain? I no idea. No, wait." A sudden thought struck her and she reached down for her handbag tucked tightly between her legs. Fishing out the folded note from Hugh Gardner, she handed it to Ron. "Read that," she told him as she leaned back in her chair and watched his expression as his eyes scanned the page. His brow furrowed when he reached the last few sentences: "If ever you feel that the Velvet Curtain is getting too much for you, get in touch with me. I'm available, day or night. I have had some experience with it in my lifetime and have helped not a few young folks to be extricated from its entanglements."

"So it's that fellow who's put this curtain idea into her head. Whatever he means, I've no idea. Well, there's his phone number so here goes. I might as well discover what it's all about."

Ron made his way to the nearest phone which was on the first floor and dialed Hugh's number, heart thumping as he did so, but the friendly voice at the other end of the line somewhat reassured him. This man didn't sound very much like a fanatic.

"Ron Atwood, Esther's friend?" Hugh queried. "Well, and what can I do for you? Is Esther OK?" His voice sounded worried.

"Actually no," Ron replied. "She's very ill with a high fever—rheumatic fever, the doctors say. But she isn't responding to treatment like she should, and they think something's on her mind and that if we can get to the bottom of it she could begin to improve. You see," Ron paused for breath, "she keeps talking about a curtain and asks me to lift it from her. I asked her sister Gabby who's recently arrived here in the States, if she knew what Esther was talking about and she said she had found a note of yours in a purse Esther had given her. So now I'm hoping that you can explain about this curtain. Esther's life may depend upon it."

There was a long silence at the other end. Hugh gathered that Ron and Esther had become very close. And since seeing her on the TV he also knew she was a very popular young lady. Yes, the Velvet Curtain had closed in all right, he was almost sure of that.

Hugh prayed for guidance. Just what should he actually say to this young man? After all, how much could he understand of Velvet Curtains? Then there was her sister. Maybe her coming had something to do with it all. He cleared his throat. "Ron," he asked, "can you put Gabriella on the phone to me, please? I need to ask her a question or two before I can explain anything intelligently to you."

"Certainly, I'll go get her if you'll hang on a minute, but I should warn you that she speaks in broken English. You may have a hard job to understand her over the phone."

"I'll handle that," was Hugh's reply. He sensed Ron's reluctance but knew he just had to speak to Esther's sister.

"And, if you don't mind, Ron," Hugh spoke kindly but firmly, "it will be better if she speaks to me privately. This is a very important matter and I think the young girl would be freer to speak out her mind if she were alone."

Ron was too polite to show his annoyance, but he didn't trust what Gabby would say to Esther's mysterious friend. He found Gabby standing not far away, staring into space, her grey-green eyes filled with tears. "Speak your best and clearest English, please, for your sister's sake," he told her as he handed her the receiver. He felt angry at this girl for coming into his life and spoiling his happiness. Esther would probably have been OK if things had gone on as they were.

Gabby was nervous as she introduced herself and did her best to answer Hugh's questions honestly. But it wasn't easy. She had had no problem in spluttering out her feelings to Esther, but here was a complete stranger probing into their personal lives. Despite Ron's advice, her English was even more broken than usual, and Hugh was finding it very hard indeed to get the gist of what she was trying to say. It was obvious they were getting nowhere fast.

There was a long pause when neither spoke. Then Hugh began to speak in Romanian, not fluently it was true, but very understandably and amazingly correct. Gabby's eyes opened wide until she remembered hearing that he had been married to a Romanian.

"Listen, Gabby," Hugh's voice was insistent, even stern, "your sister's recovery is at stake, maybe even her life. Please just answer a few questions as clearly as you can. Did you speak to Esther about her friendship with Ron?"

"Her engagement you mean?" Gabby couldn't help but splutter. "Well, yes, about two weeks ago."

Hugh's voice was gentler as he asked, "And what was her reaction?"

"She was angry at first, then terribly upset. And then she went and spoke to Aunt Mary. I don't know what went on between them, but Esther came home quite troubled. Mr. Gardner, do you think I caused Esther to get sick? But wouldn't you have been worried if you had been me? I mean, she's just not the same sister I knew in Romania." Gabby was growing defensive now.

"I'm not blaming you, Gabby. I just want to understand what is bothering Esther. Now, is your aunt there? Could I speak to her please?"

It took a few moments to find Mary. Ron frowned as he saw her take up the receiver. He stared unseeingly down the long corridor, heedless of the nurses scurrying too and fro. A vision of white-clad, angelic Esther rose before him, her large, solemn eyes gazing at him reproachfully. She was oh so beautiful, but, and he laughed bitterly to himself, it seemed that angel girls like her were not for him, tainted as he was by earth-living. He was too weighed down with his humanity to climb to celestial heights to woo them.

"Excuse me, but Esther's calling for you, Mr. Atwood." The angelic vision had suddenly turned into a white-robed nurse, standing at his elbow and waiting patiently for him to come back to reality.

"How is she?"

"Worse if anything," was the grave reply. "You'd better come right away."

It was true. Esther was worse. "Please, Ron, please lift the curtain. Please." Her eyes were wild as she reached out her hands to him. What could he say or do? Just then he felt a hand on his shoulder.

"Ron, Mr. Gardner wants to speak to you. I'll stay with Esther for a few moments."

It was Esther's aunt. Ron heaved a sigh of relief. He didn't want to talk to Hugh, but at a time like this, he felt utterly helpless in the presence of the sick girl. As he hurried out of the room he thought he heard Mary say softly, her voice low and comforting, "Dear Lord Jesus, please, please touch my dear niece. Take away the fever. Calm her and help her to feel Your Presence." He heard no more. What was wrong with him? He couldn't pray like that.

"Hugh needs to speak to you, Ron," it was Gabby, urging him to hurry.

"I know, I know," he replied rather irritably. He noticed Gabby's compassionate expression and resented it. He didn't need pity from her of all people.

"Ron," Hugh began slowly, "please, try not to get too upset for Esther's sake, when I tell you that I think her illness may have something to do with you. Gabby admits she told her sister how distressed she was over the change she saw in her and that she was concerned about her engagement to you. Then when Esther talked to her aunt about everything, she found that she was also troubled. All this happened about two weeks ago. Now, I understand this is very hard for you to hear, but please let me just try to explain a few things and then I'll be through. And remember, it is for her sake, Ron."

Ron was fuming. Everything was going wrong, everything! Yet he knew he had to keep his cool at all costs, so, summoning all the will power he could muster, he stared down at the receiver in his hand and said nothing. Hugh marveled at his self control. "I think I see the problem, Ron, but of course, I could be wrong. I think Esther was beginning to realize through her aunt's words and Gabby's attitude, that there was a big change taking place inside her—I'm not referring to a cultural one, that was only to be expected, but a spiritual one. I mean, she was faced with the possibility," Hugh's words were very deliberate now, "that her friendship for you was supplanting her love for God."

"What on earth are you trying to say?" Ron was almost shouting into the receiver. Gabby couldn't help over-hearing these words and groaned inwardly. She had set the cat among the pigeons. But Ron hadn't finished. He went on, trying in vain to keep calm, "I've respected her religion; I've taken her to church and I've even tried to pray, tried to speak to God. So, Mr. Gardner, how can you blame me?"

"I'm not trying to blame you, Ron," Hugh said compassionately. "I'm trying to unravel this mystery of Esther's illness. But can't you see that there is an area of her life that you can't enter? God meant everything to her, Ron, please understand that. Now...."

"You don't have to go on, Mr. Gardner," Ron said bitterly. "I know all about Esther's love for God. And I admit she has changed a bit lately. But maybe Gabby and Mary forgot to tell you that she's become a star overnight. Are you taking that into your reckoning? She pretty nearly has the world at her feet, or soon will. Now if that doesn't change a girl, what does? So how come everyone's worried about my influence on her? Why don't they worry about her fan mail, about her appearances on TV and all the rave reviews in the papers, about all the praise she gets wherever she goes? And why don't they blame my cousin Len for some of it. He got her started in all this; I sure didn't." Ron paused, out of breath. "I wasn't at all happy about it, especially at first."

Hugh had not seen Esther's performance the week before but his grandson had relayed every detail to him, so he said slowly: "Yes, I think that's gone to her head a bit. But the doctors say something is hindering her recovery. I think something more personal is bothering her. To a Romanian, an engagement is almost like a marriage contract, and to break it would be almost unthinkable. And yet...." Hugh paused. How he wished this were all over. "And yet, Esther may have come to the conclusion that she has to choose between you and God and that may be almost killing her."

Hugh thought he could hear a smothered sob at the other end of the line but he wasn't sure. "And it's no use me explaining all about the curtain," the older man was continuing. "It involves far more than Esther's relationship with you. And it affects all of us from time to time. But I think you and you only are the one who can lift it from her just now. I mean, Ron, you can release her from her engagement and give her back to her God."

There was such a long silence that Hugh thought for a moment that the young man had hung up on him. But then he heard Ron's voice, very subdued and very low saying, "Thank you, Mr. Gardner. I know you're trying to help. But I need time."

"Unfortunately, there isn't time," was the reply. Hugh's words rang in his ears as he brushed past Gabby in the hall and out into the open air. He felt like collapsing. Had it come to this? He had been afraid of something like this ever since he had started to love Esther. But he had to think. Had to have time. But there was no time, Hugh Gardner had just told him so. The doctors had said the same thing. Her fever was not abating as it should. In fact, he ought to be back in there with her at that very moment. To save her life he'd have to do something immediately. But, if she did get better, what would he do? Go back to her? That would be a hypocrite. Then become like her? Impossible! Mike had urged him too, but it was no use. He couldn't seem to do it. He was in a different world and had tried to adapt to Esther's, but it had been fake. Gabby had seen right through him. Maybe one day he would find her God, share her world and her faith. But meanwhile he might lose her to someone else—he couldn't bear the thought.

Just then, he saw Gabby standing at the entrance, beckoning to him. A few moments later, he entered the little room where the young woman he almost idolized lay, her aunt kneeling by her beside, her cool hand on the girl's burning brow.

"Ron, lift the curtain please," she was muttering.

His voice choked as three times he attempted to speak but no words would come. Esther tried to sit up but flopped back on the pillows, her large dark eyes staring wildly at him, "Ron, Ron, please, lift back the curtain. The velvet one. Only you can do it. Please." She sat up again and gripped his hand.

Mary slipped away unnoticed. She sensed the sick girl had reached a crisis. Only Ron needed to be in there now.

Taking Esther's thin, white hand in his, he began tremulously: "Esther darling, I will lift the curtain if I possibly can." He broke down. How could he say what he knew had to be said. He just couldn't do it. Maybe she'd get better without that being necessary.

The girl gripped his hand so tightly that he winced. "The curtain, Ron. It's the curtain. You have to lift it, now, right now." Her eyes became even wilder as she raised herself in the bed.

Ron sensed it was then or never. He leaned towards her till his face nearly touched hers. "Esther, darling, I release you." His words were uneven, almost incoherent. Maybe she couldn't make them out. Yet it seemed that her grip on his hand lessened just the slightest. "I give you back to God. Go, get well; go back to your own world." The words came easier now as his tears splashed down on the bedclothes. "Darling, I am lifting the curtain. There, see? It's not smothering you any more."

It was only too true. Esther had let go his hand as she sank back in her bed exhausted but with a look of peace upon her features that Ron had not seen for days. A few moments later, she had fallen into a deep sleep.

That evening, the doctor had wonderful news for them. Esther had turned the corner. The fever had broken. She would be out of intensive care in a day or so. Ron turned away, his whole frame shaking with sobs.

Gabby came up to him when the doctor had gone and put her hand on his. "Ron, you veree, veree brave man." The girl leaned forward; Ron could feel her tears as she kissed him lightly on the cheek. All his pent-up anger against the girl melted in an instant. "Please get some sleep," she continued. "She be better now. I stay with Estera till tomorrow."

Ron took her advice. He was glad he could return home and weep his heart out. He had no God to turn to, no God he really knew, that is, though he tried to pray on and off all that night.

Meanwhile, Esther was doing well and the next day she was sitting up and taking a little nourishment. That evening, she was out of intensive care. "Where's Ron?" she asked anxiously.

"He stayed with you for days, dear, and is exhausted," her aunt told her. She had spent as much time as possible in the hospital feeling partially to blame for her niece's illness. She had asked herself over and over again if she had been wise to be as open as she had been with her niece. But deep in her heart she felt a peace and was able to pray: "Thy will be done."

"Knowing you had turned the corner we begged Ron to go and get some rest," she told Esther gently as she patted her thin hand. "He'll be here shortly. In fact, here he is now," she added, getting up from her seat. A smile lit up the girl's wan face as the young man, looking very unlike his usual, spruce self, entered the room.

He went up to her and kissed her on the forehead. "Wonderful to see you so much better, Esther dear," he whispered as he took a seat at her side. In the brief conversation that followed, it was obvious that she remembered nothing of what had happened during her delirium.

The following day, Ron had to be off to Nashville to start law school. At least, he reasoned, Esther was out of danger and her aunt would see that she was well cared for until he returned that weekend. As for the future, he could not face it just yet though face it he must and soon, for both their sakes. And though he was very careful to keep his thoughts to himself, Esther couldn't help noticing that his farewell kiss was more restrained and fell asleep that evening wondering about it.

After a few more days, the patient returned home to her aunt's apartment to convalesce. Ramona had agreed it would be better that way. She had visited the hospital several times and was very worried about her cousin. She really did love Esther in spite of the waves of jealousy which sometimes had completely overcome her. But she had other things, too, to occupy her thoughts. Her father had gone off at last on his honeymoon and would be returning in ten days with his new bride. Could she stay on with them? She didn't think so. She would move in temporarily with her friend Kelly who lived in an apartment in Terre Haute. At the present, there was no room at her mother's for her with her two cousins there, and Esther would need nursing for a long while to come, the doctors had said; they had given express instructions that she must not return to college that semester and, if at all possible, she should spend some months recuperating by the sea or in the mountains. Ramona had considered moving in with her mother if Esther and Gabby did go away for a few months, but had finally decided it wouldn't be wise. She had calmed down a lot in the last few weeks, but her friends weren't exactly Mary's type, or Rachel's either for that matter.

During the next few days, Esther began to recollect more of what had happened. With her returning strength came the same nagging question which had so troubled her ever since the Chicago trip. She learned how she had asked in her delirium for Ron to lift the curtain from her but so far, Gabby had not told her of the phone call to Hugh and Ron's subsequent action, so Esther was unaware to whom and to what she owed her recovery and in a sense, her life.

The more she thought about her dilemma, however, the more agitated she became, until after only two days at home, she began with a fever once more. When Ron returned that Friday evening, Gabby met him in the hallway and warned him that her sister was ill again. She laid her hand on his arm and whispered, "Estera not know what you did when she veree ill, Ron, and she very worried again. She not speek much to me but I theenk she realize what might be problem and why she so ill. She not know what to do and so she veree sick again." This was a long speech for Gabby so she paused before adding quietly, "For second time, Ron, it up to you." And with that the girl opened the door and gave Ron a gentle shove into the room, then tiptoed softly away.

Ron stood gazing down at the sick girl, tossing and turning in a fitful sleep. He could see immediately that she was worse again. He would have to tell her what had happened that awful afternoon. Sitting down beside her and gritting himself, he laid his hand gently on hers and said softly, "Esther, Esther!" She was awake in an instant and a glad smile flitted across her flushed face, but only for a moment. In its place was that shadow that had first come between them those several months before.

"Esther, darling, you are worse again. Why is it?" His tender tone made Esther weep silently. She turned her head to the wall, her whole frame heaving with sobs. Ron knew her weak body could not stand such emotion for long so he began, "Maybe if you know what happened when you were ill, it might help. Maybe if I repeated what I said to you in your delirium and what seemed to calm you instantly, it might do the trick again."

"What did you say, Ron?" the sick girl asked weakly. "No one has told me anything about it."

"I'm sure they haven't," was the somewhat grim reply. "But when you were very ill, so ill that," his voice broke, "so ill that they thought you might not recover, I went in and found you raving about a curtain, a velvet one."

Esther opened her eyes wide and muttered, "They told me I talked about a curtain."

"Yes. You kept asking me to lift it. And this particular day, you sat up in bed, stared wildly at me, and said it was I who could lift it. Well, I had answered you before without really knowing what I was saying, but this time, when I bent over you and murmured, 'Yes, I'll lift it darling,' I had some inkling of what was bothering you."

"You did?" Esther was more than surprised.

"Yes, dear. Everyone was so worried about you that I asked Gabby if she had any idea what was troubling you. She handed me the note Hugh Gardner wrote you, so we phoned him. I don't know all they said to each other but when he spoke to me later he...." Ron stopped. He could not go on. Esther was listening intently, chest heaving. He had to get on with it or he would do more harm than good.

"I can't go into everything now, Esther, but Hugh tried to explain how you and I are in two separate worlds and how you probably feel you are losing something precious." He couldn't go on but put his head down on the bedcovers and wept softly. Esther wept too as Ron continued: "So I knew I had no time to waste. It was literally life or death with you so I went in and when you asked me to lift the curtain I said, and meant it, 'I do lift it darling. I release you.' And, Esther," he could hardly get the words out now, "I say again what I said a week or more ago: I do lift the curtain, whatever it is, and I do give you back to God."

He buried his head once more in the blankets so that Esther could not see his tears, for they kept on falling, try as he would to stop them. There was such a silence in the room Ron could almost hear his heartbeat. After a while he stole a glance at the sick girl. Although she was still weeping quietly and her eyes looked so tender Ron couldn't stand to look into them, there was a look of perfect peace on her wasted features, still beautiful even in sickness.

She stretched out her small white hand, and patted his bronzed one. "Oh Ron, you saved my life. You are still saving it. Thank you, oh thank you!" Then she added, "I'm awfully weak, Ron; I can't talk any more now. We'll have to discuss this later, but God bless you for what you have done and reward you and...."

But Ron had left the room. He could not stand it any longer. Mixed emotions surged within him relentlessly—unfeigned pleasure that he had once more brought healing and relief to his beloved girl but a deep hurt that she had been undoubtedly relieved by his release of her. He didn't want any of God's rewards for what he had done. What he wanted and only that was to have his beautiful Esther back in his arms again, smiling up in his face.

"God means more to her than I do," he muttered as he slammed shut the car door. "Oh well, if that's what she wants let her have it." But later, alone in his own room, his mood swung again. Of course she would chose God. What had he to give her compared with that spirituality that had so marked her and attracted him in the first place?

Meanwhile both her cousins and her aunt were nonplussed. What touch had Ron Atwood that seemed to bring instant relief? Gabby debated whether she should tell them but decided it was not her place to do so. She marveled at Ron's strength, but what his reaction would be eventually she shuddered to think. Maybe he would turn against God for good; maybe he would blame her for it all; maybe he would marry some worthless no-good on the rebound. It was all a big "maybe." As for Esther, she would probably suffer internally for weeks, maybe months, but with the quiet resignation of a saint. Maybe she would never marry. Maybe Ron would eventually find her faith and they would be reunited. But Gabby suspected that her sister had not been deeply in love, not the kind of love she was capable of, at least. She could only hope and pray that they'd both get over it eventually. Yes, Gabriella Maria Popescu did pray from time to time in a spasmodic sort of way. Not like Esther of course. But then, who on earth was like her wonderful, beautiful sister?

Chapter Thirty-Nine

Their Last Ride Together

"Is that Mr. Hugh Gardner's residence?" It was the voice Hugh had been expecting to hear for several days now.

"Esther! Why my dear, how are you?"

"I've been very ill, Mr. Gardner, very. I'm some better now, but the doctor says it will be weeks, maybe even months, before I'm back to normal. He also says I need to recuperate in the mountains or by the seaside. And I wondered if you knew of a place near you in Tennessee where I could come with my sister for a few months."

"I'm so glad you phoned, Esther. I knew you were ill and have been praying for you," Hugh told her. "I am very sorry you have been through such a dark valley. But let's see, yes, there is a lady down the road who takes in guests."

"My sister Gabby will be with me; she has been here nearly two months now. She came three or four weeks before I took ill."

"Good timing, I should say. There'll be room for her as well. When would you want to come and how will you get here? Shall I come to fetch you?"

"No, thanks a lot though. Either Aunt Mary or Ron Atwood will drive me. It's not been decided which yet. And the sooner I come the better, the doctor says. And Mr. Gardner," Esther continued a little tremulously, "you said if ever the Velvet Curtain got too much for me, I could look to you for help. Well, it has nearly smothered me."

The girl was sobbing almost uncontrollably. Just then, Gabby took up the conversation: "Excuse me, but my sister is still very weak," she explained. "Please give me directions and arrange a time, Mr. Gardner?"

The Saturday following was arranged upon, the directions given, and all was settled. The question was, should Ron take Esther and Gabby or not? Esther had not really had a good long talk with him and with Gabby in the car, she could not really open up even though her sister knew, or so it seemed, almost everything about her. Then she had an idea.

"Gabby dear, would you mind if Ron took me alone on Saturday? It probably will be our last ride together."

"Like Browning said," put in Gabby with a significant lift of her eyebrows.

Esther stared at her. Her sister surprised her daily by her knowledge of the English poets. Her own knowledge was very scanty compared with Gabby's. "I need to be alone with Ron," she went on with great difficulty, "even though it will be awfully painful. And Aunt Mary can take you the following day. I know she won't mind."

John had just returned from his honeymoon and Ramona was helping his new wife settle in, but they both found time to make a brief visit the Friday before Esther was to leave Velours. Her uncle didn't stay long. He felt awkward being in Mary's apartment again, but he planted a loving kiss on his niece's pale cheek and told her to get better quickly for all their sakes. He'd miss her terribly, he said, and Esther believed him. His niece little realized how he often felt guilty at pushing ahead with his marriage just when the girl had needed him so badly. He worried that her harum-scarum sister would not prove an adequate nurse in the coming weeks. He had heard of the broken engagement and his heart ached for both the young folks. He only hoped Ron would get over his heartbreak quicker than he had.

His wife, however, had heaved a sigh of relief when she heard the news. "Somehow, I never was too happy about Esther," she told her son, as he helped her move another of her trunks into the hired van one sunny Saturday morning.

Ron's face was like thunder as he replied, "No, I know you weren't. But don't think that now I'll be free to marry any girl you think is suitable. If I can't have Esther, I'll end up a sour old bachelor."

"It's not that I had anything personal against the girl," his mother told him, ignoring his last statement. "She's very wonderful in many ways, but I never felt she was the girl for you, Ron."

"Well, if she isn't the one, then no one is," her son told her, as he got into the driver's seat.

His mother said nothing but she worried a great deal about him. He had grown morose of late and spent a lot of time alone in his room. His appetite, too, had fallen off and he was losing weight. One good thing was that he'd be kept very busy at law school. He'd soon forget his Romanian gypsy girl, or would he? Knowing Ron, she wasn't quite sure.

But Ron was certainly not morose when he drove up to Mary's apartment early that memorable Saturday morning. He felt a terrible pain in his heart as he thought of the parting that lay just ahead, but he wasn't going to make it harder for the girl he loved by being glum and sullen in front of her.

Esther was still very weak and needed his strong arm to help her into the car. He had placed cushions and rugs on the seat and arranged everything with a tender care that tore her to pieces. For the first half of the long journey, they said little and when they did speak, it was merely about Ron's first few weeks at law school, or Gabby's plans for college, or where they should stop for lunch.

It was only when they were well into Kentucky that Esther turned to her companion and with a great gulp began, "Thank you so very much for saving my life, Ron."

Ron gripped the steering wheel tighter and looked straight ahead as he replied, "I had little alternative, Esther. Circumstances pressed me into it. And really, you should thank your sister or this Hugh Gardner of yours." He spoke a little bitterly. "And maybe if it hadn't been for your relapse those few days later, I wouldn't have kept my word. But when for the second time in a week you revived when I said I released you and gave you back to God, I had to stick by it and I do, even now, though it is so very painful."

Esther longed to comfort him but feared it would only make their final separation harder. "Ron," she began falteringly, "I can imagine what courage it took that day to do what you did. I still can't thank you enough."

Ron's face clouded. He really didn't want her thanks. He wanted *her*. He let out a long sigh as he swung the car into a lay-by where they could get a wonderful view. The mountains stretched as far as the eye could see, tier upon tier of them. It was breathtaking.

"Would you like to sit a little on that bench? The air might do you good," he suggested. So, supported by his strong arm, Esther staggered to the nearby seat. She was still so weak she could scarcely walk.

"Esther," Ron began when he had made her as comfortable as he could, "what are your plans for the next months?"

"I'm staying in the mountains till I get better. That's all I really know for sure, Ron."

"And when you return to Velours, I'm not supposed to see you?"

"I don't think I will return, at least, not to stay. I think it's best not to, Ron, for both our sakes. I couldn't be so close. Oh I know you'll be away a lot at school, but you'll be back often. And there's your mother and Uncle John. No, I have made up my mind to find a home somewhere else, maybe with Great Aunt Lucy."

"What are you going to do about school?"

"I don't know. Gabby wants to go with Rachel who's transferring to UT in Knoxville in January. I could transfer there too, though I don't feel like going anywhere just now."

"I should think you don't," Ron said tenderly. "But the big questions is, shall we meet again in a year and then see how we feel about the future?"

Esther turned her face away. What should she say? Should she give this young man at her side hope or not? "Ron, you know you have a brilliant future ahead of you," she began.

"And so do you, even more brilliant."

She flushed and dropped her eyes as she answered very slowly, "I'm not sure about that any more. I think I'll give all that up and become a missionary."

He stared at her in dismay. "What? Are you serious? You mean you'll stop singing altogether?"

"I don't know, Ron. I see how wrong I've been and how proud. I just feel my place is back in Romania or somewhere needy like that. I may go to Bible College for a few years. This is just a thought. I've mentioned it to no one but you."

Ron bit his tongue. This was her natural reaction to all that had gone on, probably, but if these plans materialized, it would seal his doom all right.

"But," Esther added, wanting to cheer him up a bit, "as you suggested, we could meet in a year's time and review the situation."

Ron brightened. "OK then. A year from today—the 7th September, 1989. That's a date!" he added with a wry smile. Then his face darkened. "Wait a bit. Maybe it's not such a good idea after all. I mean," his voice trembled, "unless one of us changes drastically we're just going to face another parting. And I couldn't stand that."

Esther looked out over the mountains, her eyes filling with tears. "I suppose you're right, Ron. But if one of us changes, then that would make things different, wouldn't it?"

"Little hope of either of us changing in any way that would bring us close again," Ron muttered, his face clouding. "We're both in a bind, Esther. There seems no way out except our going our separate ways."

"We can hear about each other from Uncle John," Esther suggested weakly.

"So we can. He's my stepfather now," and he grimaced a little. "Meanwhile, get better, try to forget about me, and throw yourself into your Christian life. I think, though, you're going to find out that you can't go back to what you were. Life moves on, you know."

Esther stared at him and shook her head. She must recapture her old trust and faith. And to do that she must relinquish all her ambitions and her vanity too. Then she gulped as she reached into her pocketbook slung round her shoulder.

"One thing more, Ron." Esther paled as she spoke. This was going to be very hard to do but she reached into her bag and took out the precious ring which she had not worn since she had been ill. "Take it. I've no right to wear it any more."

Ron winced as he took the ring and put it safe in his inner pocket. "It will burn a hole right through to my heart if I don't get rid of it soon," he thought, but he only said very quietly but firmly, "This ring is yours and yours alone Esther. If you never wear it again, no one else ever will."

There was a long silence. Then Ron took her hand in his. "Esther," he muttered, overcome by emotion, "I'm going to take you in my arms one last time without even asking your permission. Let it be your reward to me for, as you put it a few moments ago, saving your life. For I do love you, only you, and I just can't bear to part with you."

He looked mournfully into her eyes, then took her frail form in his strong arms and kissed her tenderly. "There," he said, sitting her down on the bench, "that will be my parting kiss. We will be in public after this. Oh it's so very hard, Esther. But," and he pulled himself together as he saw she was shaking with sobs, "what a brute I am to think of my own suffering when you're still so weak and frail! But I must ask you one question. I just must. If I were to share your faith, do you really, truly, honestly, love me enough to marry me?"

Esther found herself quailing underneath his keen gaze which plumbed her own soul even deeper than she had done herself. "Ron," she began rather hesitatingly, "I've never felt for anyone as I feel for you. I'm terribly fond of you, but I'm still so young, you know, and so new to life here, and you've been so wonderful—charming, handsome, kind, and spoiling me at every turn of the road. Yet I feel that I really do love you, for *who* you are not just *what* you have given to me, and," her voice grew firmer, "if you shared my faith in God, I *know* I would become your wife."

Ron looked at her intently. She was being as honest as she knew how, but something told him that just maybe Esther's love for him was not as deep as his for her. As far as he was concerned, he didn't think he could ever consider another woman as long as he lived, but he very much feared that, given time, she would meet someone else, a true Christian as she would call it, who would be her soul mate in every way.

The rest of the journey was passed in near silence. It had been arranged that Esther would go straight to Marjorie Porteous' house where she found such a warm welcome awaiting her that she was completely overwhelmed.

"There, honey," said the motherly soul, "there's your bed. I've got it all ready for you." While Marjorie was helping the sick girl settle in, Ron had gone up to Hugh's where he was to spend the night. He told Esther he would look in the next morning before going back to Nashville for another week at law school.

Neither Hugh nor Ron ever told Esther what had transpired between them that September evening, but it was a very chastened looking young man who bade her goodbye the next morning. In a sense, they had already said their real farewells so there was not much more to say.

"Well, I'm off now, Esther;" Ron tried to sound casual. "Get better soon, and take care of yourself, please. And oh I nearly forgot," he reached into his pocket. "Here's a letter Mike left for you before he died."

He held out an envelope marked, "For Esther" written in a shaky hand.

Esther took it and laid it on the table. "Drive safely, Ron," the girl told him, her voice trembling, "and every success in your studies."

He turned away, but it was too much. How could he leave the one and only girl he had ever truly loved like this? Marjorie had discretely withdrawn to another room so they were alone. He took her hand and pressed it to his lips. "Remember, darling," his voice was choked now, "my heart is yours for always. You've made me a better man while I've dragged you down from...."

"Don't, please don't, Ron. I can't take it. I want to thank you for all...."

"Now it's my turn to say 'don't.'" Ron turned away and blinked back the tears. "It's all happened as it should. I never was good enough for you, my angel, never! We were born into two separate worlds. You tried to enter mine but it did you no good; as for me, I just can't seem to enter yours. Maybe one day...."

He felt her tears on his hand for he was still holding hers as he spoke. Resisting an overwhelming urge to have one more kiss, he dropped it abruptly and turned towards the door.

"Good-bye, Esther," he called as he exited the room. "Remember me sometimes, won't you, in your prayers. I sure need them." He closed the door softly behind him and he was gone.

He saw her at the window as he turned to look back just that once more. So frail, so slight, and yet so lovely, he thought, as he got into the car. The Velvet Curtain whatever it was had been removed. Her life had been saved maybe in more ways than one. But who would really look after her now? Why, oh why, did religion have to play such a part in this girl's life? Why had that sister of hers come on the scene just when she did? Oh, there were a thousand "why's" clamoring to be answered. And he had no answer, that was the problem.

As he sped along the interstate, he thought of Hugh Gardner and the advice he had given him the night before, most of which he was not yet ready to follow. All he felt capable of doing was to throw himself into his studies, graduate with honor, and maybe do some good in the world with the money he was sure to make—maybe open an orphanage in Romania and call it "Estera's House." He smiled grimly at the thought. As for ever putting that ring on her finger once more, he shook his head sorrowfully. She was a world apart from him, as he had just reminded her, and even if he did meet God some day, she would probably be a missionary by that time in some faraway land, married to some noble, saintly fellow. But though she might never wear it again, he would keep it close to his heart, for always.

Meanwhile Esther was reading Mike's letter. It seemed that her singing had done some good at any rate. A smile lit up her wan features as she read of how he had found, at last, God's amazing grace.

"And now, Esther," he concluded, "good-bye. I'll see you in Heaven one day. And remember, it was the simple, modest, white-robed little singer who pointed me to Christ, not the glamorous, popular star who nearly blew men's minds away with her beauty.

"Don't let America spoil you Esther. And remember, you won't help Ron by going his way. You won't help him by trying to enter his world. You may just have to lose him to find him. But the finding will be worth all the losing, so hang in there, and see God work."

Esther put down the letter and took a chair by the window where she could see the river winding its way through the bottom of the garden and the stately maple swaying in the light September wind just outside the bay window. It would change its green dress in a few weeks for a gorgeous red one. God had surely made His world beautiful. Why, oh why, had sin ever entered it, and sorrow, and heartache?

She laid her head back on the cushion. She felt so weak and helpless and alone. She had escaped, at least for the present, but she had lost Ron, maybe forever, in the process.

Mike's words, "You may just have to lose him to find him," came back to her just then. "I sure have lost him," she told herself, "but I just don't know about the finding."

A curtain, she hoped it wasn't the velvet one, seemed to hide the future from her weary eyes. But even if it were the Velvet Curtain again, this God of miracles had delivered her once and He would do it again, wouldn't He?

Chapter Forty

The Curtain Falls

Aaron Gardner had just returned for his mid-term break at grad school to find that his incorrigible grandfather had invited a bevy of young women to supper. The guests were due in half an hour.

"I wanted to spend a quiet evening with my beloved Granddad," he grumbled, "not to be bombarded by five women, all speaking at once probably, giggling and tittering at everything I say or you say for that matter."

Hugh knew him better than to take him seriously. He had observed that in spite of his awkward ways with girls, nothing pleased his grandson better than to be in the company of the fair sex, especially if they had a quick mind and vivacious personality.

"You haven't even asked who my guests are," remarked Hugh, his eyes twinkling.

"Don't really want to know," returned Aaron, still feeling out of sorts. It had been a difficult half semester so far, and he was wrestling with questions that baffled even his keen mind. Now he wanted a few days of peace and quiet in his beloved hills and his grandfather had spoiled it all.

"OK then, it will be a surprise," Hugh had told him. And it was. When Mary Popescu's car drove up the long driveway, Aaron became curious. Gabby got out first, pulling Rachel and Connie Frith after her. Connie had promised Esther when she left Velours that she would pay her a visit and had come to the mountains with Mary and Rachel the previous evening.

"Look," Gabby shouted, oblivious that anyone was watching, "this is my favorite view in all the world."

"Better than the one from Dad's old cabin in the Alps back home?" another voice had asked from inside the car. Aaron had heard that voice before, but where? Then he remembered—at Indianapolis airport, almost exactly one year before. But Gabby had come up to him and was stretching out her hand.

"You are Mr. Hugh's grandson, Aaron? He talks a lot about you. I'm Esther's sister, Gabriella Maria Popescu."

"And I am Aaron Philpot Gardner," returned Aaron.

"I hope your grandfather tell you that we all come to your house tonight."

"He intimated that we would be privileged to entertain five ladies for supper but he did not tell me who they were to be. Won't you introduce me to your friends, Gabriella?"

"Call me Gabby," she said. "Gabriella is for Sundays. Gabby is for every day."

Aaron laughed, and he had a very hearty laugh indeed. Soon they all joined in and before they reached the patio steps, he had shaken hands with everyone, Esther included, who he noticed, was a mere shadow of the girl who had captivated her audience some months before. Looking as if the wind would blow her away, she let herself be led up the steps by Rachel and placed in the recliner on the porch which she always occupied in her visits to "the old man of Tiny Gap."

In no time at all, the meal was ready. Marjorie was there, and acted as hostess. Hugh was in his element. Aaron served the drinks and cleared away the dishes, dropping a pile of plates in the process, much to the amusement of the girls. But he laughed at himself, picked up the broken pieces, made a profuse apology to his grandfather, and then proceeded to get into an argument with Gabby as to whether English was superior in every respect to Romanian. When it was evident that Esther was tiring fast, Connie led her friend back to the recliner in the patio and perching on the arm of her chair, she began to smooth Esther's dark locks which, she noticed sadly, had lost some of their luster.

"Esther," she began. "I want to tell you while we're alone, that I'm sorry for the way I talked to you at times. From the very beginning, you were my heroine, though I showed it in strange ways. But I really came to think that you were just like all of us until...." she paused to give her friend a warm hug, "until you had the courage to escape the rat race."

"I didn't have the courage to escape, Connie. If it had been up to me, I'd never have done it. God made my escape possible by using others to help me. And Mr. Hugh has another word for what you just called 'the rat race.' He calls it the Velvet Curtain, don't you, Mr. Hugh?" for the old gentleman had approached their corner and overheard the last few sentences. "Tell Connie about it, please, and about the way of escape. She has struggled with it like I have."

"Who hasn't?" was Hugh's comment as he sat on a chair opposite the girls. "But I think your young friend here, if she isn't too tired, can tell you herself about her experiences with the two curtains."

"Two?" Connie queried, looking puzzled.

"Yes," Esther put in, "there certainly are at least two." She leaned back in her chair, and a dreamy look came into her eyes as she began to tell about her life in Romania and how, through God's providences, she had fled in the nick of time from the Iron Curtain and then of her second more recent escape from the Velvet Curtain.

Connie was fascinated. "I suppose prayer is our main protection from this Curtain, Mr. Hugh, but how can we be on our knees all the time?" queried the girl, tossing her auburn curls as she always did when somewhat nonplussed.

"Prayer is really dependence upon our Father for everything, Connie," Hugh answered thoughtfully.

"That was my trouble," admitted Esther. "I became so self-confident I got awfully proud; Connie; you know that," she added blushing.

"Who wouldn't with your talents and looks!" exclaimed Connie.

"Well, my talents seem to be my ruin," she declared mournfully. She paused, as she noticed Hugh shaking his head gravely at this, though he made no comment. "As for my looks," she went on, "I'm not sure about them either any more." There was a slight sob in her voice which went straight to Connie's sympathetic heart.

She bent down and whispered softly, "Esther, you're more beautiful to me now than you were when you were 'Esther Popescu, the star singer from Romania.' You were too perfect in those days. Now, I know you're human."

"She sure is," put in Gabby coming up just then. "But Mr. Hugh, I very sorry to interrupt, but can we have a game of Scrabble? Scrabble will help me stop argue with your irascible grandson."

"Bravo, Gabby," said Hugh. "Your vocabulary is improving at a tremendous speed."

"Did you ever hear her speak in her broken English?" asked Rachel mischievously.

"I no speak Eenglish that way now," laughed Gabby. "I learn better."

"Yes, you've improved tremendously, Gabby, in such a short time. Whatever happened?" Hugh asked curiously.

Gabby's face sobered instantly. "Well, Mr. Hugh, it began in the hospital when I tried to talk to you on the phone and you not understand. Then you spoke Romanian."

"Romanian?" Connie sounded surprised.

"Yes, my wife was Romanian," Hugh told her. His eyes took on that same dreamy, wistful look that Esther had noticed in the plane those many months before.

"You must miss her very much," she whispered.

"Miss her? I miss her every single day, Esther, which may be surprising when I tell you that we were married only ten years. She has been gone now thirty-five years."

The girls stared at him. "And you never think to marry again?" Gabby asked.

"Not seriously, Gabby," Hugh replied, "though I get awfully lonely at times. But go on with your story, Gabby."

Gabby's face flushed. "Well, after I speak to you that day, I ask myself what happen if you not speak Romanian."

"But you couldn't help it if you didn't know English well," Connie put in comfortingly.

"But I really did, Connie. Don't be surprised. Mom teach me English just like she teach Esther, but I never speak it. I only want to speak Romanian. Later, all my friends know me that I was very nationalistic. Esther knows that is true."

"She sure was a stubborn one," her sister agreed, "and had a real prejudice against anything Western. But I always suspected she knew more than she let on. For a start, she read English pretty fluently."

"Yes, Rachel see that too and wonder," Gabby said with a laugh. "But when you very ill, Esther," Gabby turned to her sister, her voice very gentle now, "I decide to learn fast to speak English well. You are not there, so I talk more. I am very surprised when I find I speak better than I think."

"She even surprised me," put in Esther.

"She's full of surprises, this sister of yours," Hugh said with a grin. "But if some of you are going to have a game, you had better begin soon."

While some played Scrabble, and some chatted with their host, Mary spent the time in the library, browsing among her host's collection of rare books which was the envy of book dealers for miles around.

Two hours later, the game was finished. Rachel, to Gabby's great delight, finally beat Aaron by just three points. The young man looked at the quiet, sad-looking girl with new respect.

"You're very good, Rachel," he commented as they put away the board.

"Because I beat you?" Rachel asked a little sarcastically.

Aaron reddened, gave a short laugh, then changed the subject. But Rachel would not be drawn into any conversation. She never felt at home with boys and had marveled how Gabby could act as if she had known this strange young man all her life. She longed to be in the quiet and seclusion of her little bedroom at Marjorie's house. How she loved it in the mountains. She wanted to stay here always.

Just then, Hugh entered the kitchen where they had been playing and caught the girl's wistful expression. He hadn't gotten a chance as yet to speak to Esther's cousin.

"I hear you beat my grandson. Congratulations! That takes some doing!" he said, patting her on the shoulder. "And I would like to get to know you better. Staying long at Tiny Gap?"

"No," Rachel told him. "We're just here for mid-term break. We go back the day after tomorrow."

"Well then, how about coming to see me tomorrow with that young cousin of yours? She tells me you like poetry. I've written quite a bit. Like to see it?"

"Yes, Mr. Gardner," was all the reply Hugh could get.

"Then take a stroll up here tomorrow afternoon."

Rachel smiled her thanks. "That man cares about me," she thought to herself as she bade him good-bye.

Mary Popescu had watched Hugh all evening. He radiated hope and stability, something she greatly needed in her life. And now, while the others were getting on their coats, she seized the opportunity for a few words with him.

"Thank you, Mr. Gardner, for all you have done for my niece."

"It has been my privilege, Mrs. Popescu."

"Please call me Mary," she pleaded. "You remind me of my grandfather very much."

"I don't suppose he's still living?"

"Oh no. He's been in Heaven for fifteen years now." Her face clouded. "He died without our being reconciled."

Hugh saw the tears were not far from her eyes. "Well, I'm sure he is rejoicing with the angels right now," he told her, his face lit up with one of his wonderful smiles. "I heard that you had come back Home to the Father, Mary."

"Yes. And it is thanks to Esther in many ways that I did. She's discouraged, poor child, and feels she has been a failure as a Christian but she'll never know what she meant to me right when I needed it."

"And now it's she who needs you," Hugh said softly, as his eyes fell on Esther as she was slowly making her way to the door on her sister's arm. "It's going to be very tough for her for some time to come. She's confused right now and I'm afraid could take a real reaction to all that has gone on."

"She already has, Mr. Gardner." Mary looked worried. "She can't stand to look at her fan mail and tears up a lot of the letters. The man who sponsored her singing says he'll wait till after Christmas before he presses her for an answer as to what she intends to do, but she's quite determined that she'll never sing on a stage again in all her life."

"She's only twenty. Remember some of your reactions at twenty?" Mary winced. She'd rather not remember some of them at least.

"Leave your niece in God's hands," Hugh went on gently. "We adults tend to interfere in young folk's lives prematurely. It doesn't really help them."

"But they so often have to learn the hard way." Mary's voice was very sad. She was thinking of her own youth and of Ramona.

"But you don't help a chicken to hatch by breaking the shell, do you?" Hugh asked, his eyes searching hers.

Mary smiled a little. "I get your message. I'm a good shell breaker, I'm afraid."

"Most of us are," he replied thoughtfully. "Well, the others are waiting for you, so we'll have to continue this conversation at a later date."

A few moments later, a car laden with tired but happy girls chugged down the driveway. "Still grumbling about all the female company?" Hugh asked, as he put his arm on Aaron's shoulder.

"Could have been worse," his grandson conceded, watching the receding car with dreamy eyes. Then he burst into the laugh that always cheered the old man's heart.

"No, I thoroughly enjoyed myself, Granddad. That Gabby's like no one else, except like myself, maybe, poor girl," and he wrinkled his nose. "What a handful she is, and not a bit like her sister."

"No, especially not tonight," commented Hugh. "Esther was very quiet and Gabby extremely talkative."

"What a change in a few months!" Aaron was still thinking of Esther. "She's a mere shadow of her former self."

"But her shadow has more substance than that former self, my boy," said the older man very seriously.

"You talk in enigmas Granddad, though I daresay you're right. But she scares me. She's too perfect. I seem clumsy in front of her. See how I dropped that pile of plates at supper?"

"So you've never dropped plates before?"

Aaron gave another of his infectious laughs. "You know better than that. But I reached my record tonight. All Esther's fault."

"But what about Gabby and the other girls? Didn't they intimidate you too?"

"Gabby? Goodness no, Granddad. I mean, who would she intimidate?"

"You'd be surprised," Hugh said knowingly. "But enough of girls. Let's kneel down and thank our Father for Esther's narrow escape from what might have been a life of sadness and regrets, and let's remember Ron, too, brokenhearted and alone. He needs to feel the Father's love so badly just now."

So, kneeling on the patio, with the crickets chirping on the verandah and the owls hooting in the darkness, Hugh Gardner poured out his heart to the One he loved best of all.

"And Father," he concluded, "keep all these dear young ones from evil. Thank you that Esther is still among us. May she and her sister and their friends, and my grandson here, be kept from the ensnaring folds of the Velvet Curtain. Deliver them in Your own way and time, each one, and, dear Lord, please show yourself to Ron and ease his heartache. May he soon discover that only Your love can truly fill the vacuum in his life. We ask it all for Jesus' sake. Amen."

About the Author

Trudy Harvey Tait was born in Glasgow, Scotland to Edwin and Lillian Harvey, who had come to Britain from America in the 1930's. The Harveys had a dual position as directors of a missionary training school and editors of a magazine, *The Message of Victory*. Educated in Scotland as a child, Trudy married Barry Tait in 1972. They have one son.

Trudy moved to the United States in 1981. She and her husband now reside in the Appalachian mountains of Eastern Tennessee where they continue the publishing work her parents began. Most of the books are compilations, a result of decades of research while editing *The Message of Victory*.

At nineteen Trudy went to Africa to fill in for two missionaries who needed a furlough. More recently, she has traveled extensively in Eastern Europe, and speaks French, Romanian and Russian fluently. She has a B.A. in English and Bible from Milligan College (TN).

This is Trudy's first novel. She has also written a poetry book entitled "Reflections" and has co-authored several books with her mother, Lillian Harvey.

If you are interested in writing to Trudy or seeing the line of books she and her family have produced, write to:

Harvey Christian Publishers Inc.
3107 Hwy 321, Hampton, TN 37658

Email: Trudy@harveycp.com

Or visit us online at:
http://www.harveycp.com